STONE BOUND
Book One of
CHAOS AND RETRIBUTION
by
Eric T Knight

The sequel to
IMMORTALITY AND CHAOS
(epic fantasy series)
Wreckers Gate: Book One
Landsend Plateau: Book Two
Guardians Watch: Book Three
Hunger's Reach: Book Four
Oblivion's Grasp: Book Five

ALSO BY ERIC T KNIGHT

Ace Lone Wolf and the Lost Temple of Totec
Ace Lone Wolf and the One-Eyed Mule Skinner
Ace Lone Wolf and the Black Pearl Treasure
(LONE WOLF HOWLS SERIES – ACTION/ADVENTURE/COMEDY)

WATCHING THE END OF THE WORLD
(ACTION THRILLER)
**All books available on
Amazon.com**

Follow my blog or sign up to my email list at:
ericTknight.com

STONE BOUND
Book One of
Chaos and Retribution
by
Eric T Knight

ISBN-13: 978-1548069766
ISBN-10: 1548069760

Cover by:
Deranged Doctor Design

For Stormy,
Who was so instrumental in getting me
to pick up the pen once again. Thank you.

Prologue: Fen

The man stumbled unseeing down the cobblestone street. The pains were worse today, the worst they'd ever been. Every step was agony. His bones were on fire. His joints felt like they were full of glass. His greatest fear was not that he would die—he'd long since accepted the inevitability of that—but that he would not be able to make it home. If he was going to die today, he wanted only to see his wife and son one last time.

The buildings on this street were built of stone, four or more stories tall and jammed tightly together. This late in the day the street was completely in the shade. Horse-drawn carts moved down the middle of the street. Along the edges hurried people on foot, none of them paying any attention to the man. To the casual observer he was merely another drunk, and drunks were not uncommon in this part of the city.

A new wave of pain hit the man and he staggered, bumping into a woman who was carrying a large basket filled with loaves of bread. "Watch where you're going!" she snapped at him.

Falling, the man instinctively put out his hand to catch himself. When his hand made contact with the wall of one of the buildings there was a cracking sound and the stone split suddenly. The concussion knocked the man back and he fell down.

The woman looked from the crack in the wall to the man and her eyes widened. She gripped the basket tighter and hurried away. Other passersby noticed him for the first time, and began veering around the man, careful to stay out of his reach. It had been years since the red plague last struck the city of Samkara, but people remembered it readily enough. The sweating, wild-eyed man lying on the ground could be infected with it.

The man crawled to the side of the street. He looked at his hand, where he'd touched the wall. The skin was slate-gray and when he tried to flex his fingers they were stiff and he could barely curl them.

The changes were accelerating.

He had to get home.

Careful to avoid touching the wall with his bare skin, he climbed to his feet. Heedless of those around him, he began half-running, half-staggering down the street. People cursed at him as he bumped into them and when he cut across the street to turn down a smaller one he was almost hit by a wagon drawn by a team of horses, the driver snapping his whip near his face.

The smaller street had less traffic and the man made it all the way to his building without running into anyone else. This street was poorer than the one he'd left, narrow and lined with wooden tenements. Gone were the cobblestones, replaced by rutted dirt and garbage.

The man tried to open the door of the building he lived in with his right hand, the one he'd touched the stone wall with, but he couldn't get his fingers to move at all now and he had to give up and use the other hand. He stumbled through the door, not bothering to close it behind him. He dragged himself up two flights of stairs, every step fresh agony.

He reached the door of his home, made it through, and collapsed on the floor.

His wife gave a little cry, dropped her sewing, and hurried to him. Taking his arm, she helped him to his feet and over to the room's sole bed.

Sitting on the floor by the iron cook stove was a small boy, only a few years old, playing with some broken pieces of colored tile. He stared up at his parents with wide eyes, old enough to know something was wrong, but too young to understand what it was.

Not that his parents understood it either. In the months since the strange pains started, they'd gone to every healer and priest they could afford, trying to find out what was wrong, and none of them had any answers.

"I knew you shouldn't have tried to go to work," she told him, gently stroking his forehead.

"It's…it's happening faster," he gasped and held up his right hand.

Her breath caught in her throat as she stared at his hand. She touched it gingerly. "How did it happen?"

"I touched a stone wall. The stone split." A spasm of pain hit him and he winced. When it had passed he looked up at her and what she saw in his eyes made her gasp.

"Your eyes," she said. "They're red, like a fire burns in them."

"What's happening to me?" he moaned, closing his eyes.

She hesitated only a moment before wrapping him in her arms and holding him close.

"I'm losing the feeling in my arm," he said. He pushed his sleeve up and she saw that his forearm was streaked with gray. Even more unusual—she bent closer to get a better look—there seemed to be chips of stone embedded in his flesh.

He went rigid suddenly and his head arched back. His mouth stretched open, so wide that his jaw popped. For a long moment he froze like this, more a statue than a man, then he began spasming. Shivers ran up and down his limbs. His eyes rolled back in his head and spittle drained from his mouth.

He began thrashing violently. She tried to hold him still but the seizure was too strong for her. He bucked and she was thrown off the bed onto the floor. She got back up and went to him, but there was nothing she could do.

Then the building began to shudder, as if it were caught in an earthquake. She pitched sideways and almost fell down. A small crack appeared in the ceiling and plaster dust sifted down. The little boy wailed and crawled over to his mother, wrapping his little arms around her leg.

After a minute, his seizure ended and a few seconds later the earthquake stopped as well. She looked at her husband and what she saw made her scream.

He was lying on his back, unmoving, his eyes wide and staring. His eyes glowed like lava. His skin had turned completely gray. All of his hair had fallen out.

At first she was sure he was dead and she stood there, one hand over her mouth, frozen by fear and grief. Then, slowly, his head turned. Gray flakes chipped and broke off his neck as he did so. The molten eyes fixed on her.

"*Please...*" His voice grated like stone sliding over stone. More flakes broke off around his mouth and fell to the blanket he lay on.

Her paralysis broke and she hurried to him. Her hands hovered over him for a moment as she wrestled with her fear, but love won out and she placed them on his cheeks. His face was cold and lifeless.

"Oh, my love," she moaned.

"Hold Fen up," he said in his broken voice. "I want to see him…one more time."

Tears pouring down her cheeks, she lifted the small boy and set him next to his father on the bed. Fen showed no fear, only curiosity as he leaned forward and touched his father's face.

His father tried to touch him but his arm froze in place halfway. A last tremor shook him.

The fire in his eyes faded and went out.

Prologue: Aislin

Netra was in her cottage, bundling herbs for drying, when she heard the cries of alarm. At first she thought someone had been injured, perhaps one of the workers in the quarry in the hills outside the village where she lived. If that was the case, they would be coming to her, carrying the wounded man to the village's healer. In her mind she was already preparing, mentally reviewing her inventory of bandages, needles, catgut and so on.

But a minute later she realized she was wrong. This was no injury. There would be no bleeding patient hustled into her cottage by concerned friends. The cries of alarm were not drawing closer, but they were spreading.

Perplexed, she put down the herbs, crossed the room, and opened the door. It was only an hour or so after dawn and the sun had not yet broken through the thick clouds that had rolled in from the sea overnight. A brisk wind whipped her simple, cotton dress about her ankles and tugged at her long braid. In the air she could feel the rain that would likely come later in the day.

Her cottage stood on the outskirts of a small village. It was a quiet place, far removed from the excitement and activity of Qarath, the nearest city. A place where the most that ever happened was an occasional injury and the usual ailments that people suffered from. Which made it perfect for Netra. After all that she'd already been through in her life, the last thing she wanted was more excitement.

Her cottage was on the landward side of a small hill, where it got partial protection from the winds that blew in off the sea, so when she looked down into the village, all she saw at first was people milling around, talking and exclaiming loudly to each other. Then she realized that all of them were turned toward the sea, and a number were pointing.

She hesitated, wondering if she should bring her bag filled with healing herbs, ointments and salves with her, then decided not to. It didn't sound like anyone was hurt, and she could always send someone running to fetch it if she needed it.

She headed down the path toward the village and as it wound around the hillside, she saw for the first time what had everyone so excited.

Just offshore was an island.

An island where there had never been one before.

Besides the impossibility of an island simply appearing out of nowhere, there was something clearly unusual about this island. It had a yellowish hue to it and the plants that grew from its surface were of a variety and vibrancy of colors not seen anywhere on land.

Netra stopped, struck by the appearance of this thing she'd thought never to see again.

For this thing that appeared to be an island wasn't. It was a living creature, though not in any normal sense.

She began hurrying down the hill. Her heart was filled with foreboding as she went. The appearance of ki'Loren, and the Lementh'kal who lived within it, could not but bode ill. Something bad was happening or was about to happen and they were here to seek her out.

She didn't want to know why the Lementh'kal had come. She wanted to go back into her cottage, close the door, and bury herself in her work. She'd been through enough in her life. She'd earned the right to peace and tranquility.

But at the same time she knew that she could not avoid this. Whatever it was, it would have to be faced head on.

By the time she got down the hill, every villager was standing on the beach, staring up in awe at the island, which towered several hundred feet in the air. For the adults, it was not the first time they had seen the floating island. The other time they had seen it was during the war, when it had saved their lives. Which did not mean they were happy to see it now. Questions were asked and more than one accusing look was thrown Netra's way as she passed through their midst. They did not know what, exactly, their healer's role had been during the war, and Netra never talked about it, but they knew she had played an instrumental part in it. If ki'Loren was showing up again, it must have something to do with her.

Netra did not reply to their questions. She made her way to the edge of the surf and stood there waiting.

The island was only a dozen yards offshore when an opening appeared in its side about halfway up. A figure appeared in the opening. It appeared to be male, though it was difficult to be sure. He was about the height of a human, but built much more slightly. He was hairless, his skin yellow. His eyes were very large and set somewhat on the sides of his head. He carried no weapons and wore only a thin shift made of some kind of shimmery, almost translucent material.

The villagers went very quiet and took several steps back. Some still carried the implements of their trade—spades, pitchforks, hammers, brooms—and they held these up as if to fend off this strange invader.

The figure saw Netra and his wide, lipless mouth stretched in something approximating a smile. But it wasn't really a smile, more like something he'd seen humans do and was trying to copy. The nervous villagers took another step back.

He waved. "Hi, Netra!" He started down the side of the island but didn't make it very far before he tripped. He bounced and rolled clear down the side and then plopped into the water.

Netra sighed. She'd seen all this before.

He thrashed around in the water for a minute before emerging, spluttering and dripping.

"Hello, Ya'Shi," she said.

"You remember me!" he exclaimed. Up close she could see the white spots and streaks mixed in with the natural yellow coloring of his skin, signs of his advanced age. She didn't know exactly how old he was, only that his age was counted in centuries. Even amongst a people who lived very long lives, Ya'Shi was unusual.

"As if I could forget you," she said. She saw movement in the opening as a new figure emerged and made its way down the side of ki'Loren and she smiled. She remembered Jenett fondly. Jenett was carrying a bundle wrapped in cloth and unlike Ya'Shi she didn't stumble. Rather, she moved with the same eerie, almost supernatural fluidity and grace that marked her people.

Ya'Shi turned, following her gaze. "Oh, that's Jenett," he said offhandedly. "You probably don't remember her. She wasn't nearly as important as me in our last adventure."

"That's what it was to you?" Netra asked. "An adventure? Because it felt like the end of the world to me."

7

"When you're young, like you are, *everything* seems like the end of the world, I suppose," he said. His voice was strange, missing normal human inflections that lend words so much of their meaning, yet somehow he managed to convey an exaggerated condescension.

"Especially the actual end of the world," she replied.

Ya'Shi flicked a grain of sand off his arm. "There was never any actual danger."

Netra gave up trying to argue with him and crossed her arms. "What brings you here, Ya'Shi? Is there a purpose or is this just more of your old foolishness?"

"What's that you say?" he asked, cupping his hand around where his ear would have been, had he actually had one. He peered at her, blinking in confusion. "Who are you again? You seem familiar, but I can't quite place you." The transformation was astonishing. Almost instantly he'd become old and bent, with barely the strength to stand, his mind nearly gone.

Netra sighed again. Being around Ya'Shi was tiring. He flitted through moods rapidly, went from clowning to serious in the blink of an eye, constantly blending profundities with sheer foolishness. Being around him meant being always off-balance, never quite knowing where things were going next.

"I really don't feel like playing your games today. Can you tell me why you're here? I have things to do."

Ya'Shi began nodding as she spoke. "Oh, yes. Things. *Very important* things, I'm sure." He rubbed his hands together briskly and all his feigned age and weariness disappeared. "We must get to business. Vital events are afoot. Huge, cataclysmic, earth-shaking events. We mustn't waste a moment. If ever there was a time that called for great haste—"

"Just tell me already!" Netra snapped. She thought of Shorn then, how angry Ya'Shi had always made him, and wished her old friend were there with her.

Ya'Shi blinked at her, his eyelids sliding up from underneath his eyes, then back down. Quite slowly. "Why, it's the end of the world, of course. I wouldn't waste your time otherwise."

Netra waited for him to continue, to give her more details, but he stood there staring at her, his head cocked slightly to one side. "Well? Aren't you going to tell me any more?"

He frowned. "About what?"

Netra bit off the angry words she wanted to shout at him. "This is why Shorn always wanted to choke you," she said.

He shook his head. "No. Shorn and I understood each other. We were very close. Anyway, here's Jenett. She has something for you."

Jenett was emerging from the water. She looked much like Ya'Shi but was more slightly built and her yellow skin was tinged with green streaks here and there, a sign of her youth. She smiled when she approached Netra—showing the bristles that lined the inside of her mouth instead of teeth—and on her the smile looked more natural, more inviting than Ya'Shi's.

"It is very much my pleasure to see you again, Netra." Her voice was soft, whispering past the ear like a gentle breeze. "Though I wish it were under happier circumstances."

The bundle she was carrying moved, drawing Netra's eye.

"Hurry, hurry! Give it to her!" Ya'Shi was bouncing from one foot to another like an excited child. He clapped his hands together. "I can't wait to see what she thinks of our gift!"

"He hasn't changed," Netra said to Jenett.

"He is Ya'Shi," Jenett replied. "The currents that move him are inscrutable to the rest of us."

"Or maybe he's just crazy."

Jenett frowned. "I understand what you mean by the word, but it has no real meaning among my people. The Lementh'kal are the People of the Way, and it is not for us to judge where someone's way takes them."

She stepped closer to Netra and pulled back the cloth from one end of the bundle.

Netra thought she wouldn't be surprised at anything the Lementh'kal gave her, but she was wrong.

"A *baby*?"

Tiny hands, pink cheeks, and wide, green eyes that stared up at her.

Neta swallowed and tried again. "A baby? You brought me a baby?"

Ya'Shi held up one finger. "Not just any baby. A *special* baby."

"Why…why…?" Netra couldn't seem to get the words out.

"There's no need to thank us."

"It's a human baby," Netra said.

"Yes and no," Ya'Shi said. "There is more to her. Listen."

Netra stilled the question she'd been about to ask and listened. Not with her ears, but with her inner senses, inside where LifeSong could be heard.

"You're right," she breathed. "Mixed in with LifeSong, I can hear the Sea as well." She looked at the two of them, then back at the baby. "How is this possible?"

"When a mommy and a daddy love each other very much…" Ya'Shi trailed off. "Sorry. It wasn't like that at all. But how it happened isn't what's important."

All his silliness disappeared and his tone grew serious. "A storm is coming. A terrible storm. Nothing you or I, or any of us, can do will stop it." He set his fingers on the baby's forehead.

"But she might. She and two others."

Jenett held out the baby and Netra took her. The green eyes had stayed fixed on her the entire time. They were the green of the deep sea and there were flecks of white in there like whitecaps on a windy day.

"One from each of the spheres, Stone, Sea and Sky," Ya'Shi continued. "Only the three of them, working together, have any chance in what is to come."

"I'm sorry," Jenett said. "Truly I am. You of all people know what a burden it can be, saving the world."

"But that's why you're the right person to raise her," Ya'Shi said. "Well, enough idle chat. We must be going so you can get back to your important things." He took hold of Jenett's arm and began to guide her back into the surf.

"Wait!" Netra called after them. "What's going to happen? Where are these other children?"

"One is to the north," Ya'Shi said over his shoulder. "Another is across the sea. Don't look for them. When the time is right they will be drawn together."

"You have to tell me more than that," Netra pleaded.

"Goodbye!" Ya'Shi called, still holding onto Jenett and propelling her firmly in front of him. "Good luck!"

They walked through the surf, then up the side of ki'Loren. They passed through the opening, it closed behind them, and the floating island began to move away.

Leaving Netra with a baby.

Prologue: Karliss

The wind was crazy the day the baby was born. It shrieked around the hide yurt where the expectant mother lay, attended by Spotted Elk Clan's midwife and two other women. It scratched and clawed like a wild thing trying to get in, tearing at the flap, trying to get under the edge of the yurt and send it flying across the high steppes where the Sertithian people lived their nomadic lives.

But the Sertithians were familiar with the ways of the wind and the yurt was strongly constructed and tightly staked down so it stayed intact and in place, though the hide it was made of thrummed and vibrated steadily.

"It will be over soon," the midwife said, as one of the other women bathed the expectant mother's forehead with a damp cloth. "One more long push should do it." The yurt was lit by a pair of oil-burning clay lamps. There were two small wicker baskets containing clothes and another filled with tools and sewing implements. A sheathed sword leaned against the wall of the yurt, along with an unstrung bow and a quiver of arrows.

"For months this child has fought and kicked, as though he could not bear his captivity another moment. Now the time comes and he won't budge. Will he always be this difficult?" The expectant mother spoke in a light tone, but her face was pale with pain. The furs she lay on were wet with her sweat. She was a young woman and this was her second child but she had been half a day trying to deliver the child already.

"Just breathe, Munkhe," the midwife said. "It will all be over soon."

"The *tlacti* told me it would be a son," Munkhe said. The *tlacti* was the clan's shaman. "He said the wind told him so." The other women already knew this. Such things became common knowledge quickly in such a tightly-knit community. They also knew she spoke to take her mind off the pain.

"If Ihbarha said it will be a boy, then it will be a boy," the midwife replied calmly.

Munkhe grimaced as another contraction came on. She gritted her teeth and pushed.

12

"I can see the top of his head," the midwife said. As if to punctuate her words a fresh gust of wind shook the yurt.

"The wind is also anxious for your child to be born," the fourth woman in the yurt said. Henta was elderly, with a severe expression and a downturned mouth that said she rarely smiled. "Perhaps this means he will be touched by it."

"Pray to the four winds it is so," Munkhe said through gritted teeth. She wasn't sure she wanted her son to be the next *tlacti*, but Ihbarha was old. It was past time for a wind-touched child to be born to the Spotted Elk Clan.

"One more push and it will all be over," the midwife said.

Munkhe's back arched as she gave another, mighty push. A cry came from her as the pain increased but she did not let up and a few moments later the baby slid forth into the world.

At that same instant a new shriek arose from the wind as it buffeted the yurt. The wooden pins holding the door flap of the yurt closed snapped under the strain and the flap blew open.

The wind raced into the yurt like a wild animal, whining in its eagerness. It seemed to focus on the child, whirling around it with such strength that for a moment the midwife feared it would be snatched from her and she clutched it tightly to her breast. The other women cried out and Henta made a sign against evil.

Then, as fast as it appeared, the wind was gone. The women stared at each other, shaken and confused.

"Never have I seen such a thing," Henta said.

"My baby!" Munkhe cried, struggling to sit up and see. "How is my baby?"

The midwife brushed the baby's mouth and nose clear. "He is healthy."

"It's a boy?" Munkhe asked.

But the midwife didn't answer right away. She was looking at the baby, a strange expression on her face.

The other women bent close. "Most peculiar," Henta said.

"What's wrong with him?" Munkhe said, fighting against the furs which seemed determined to wrap around her. "Is something wrong with him?"

"It's nothing," the midwife said soothingly. "Help her sit up," she told the others, and when they had done so she handed Munkhe her child.

"Oh," Munkhe said. "I see."

The baby's eyes were wide open, which was unusual by itself. But even more startling was the color of those eyes. They were the blue of a summer sky and blue eyes were extremely rare amongst the Sertithians.

Not only were the baby boy's eyes wide open, but he had a huge smile on his face. He looked like he was laughing at some secret jest.

"I think it is time to fetch the *tlacti*," the midwife said, and the younger of the two women bustled out of the yurt to summon him.

"So long as he is healthy. That is all that matters," Munkhe said stoutly. The midwife and Henta nodded their agreement, but neither of them spoke. Munkhe looked from them to her baby and clutched him close, murmuring to him.

When the *tlacti* arrived he swept into the yurt without a word or look for any of them. The furs Ihbarha was dressed in were old and ratty. He had a piece of felt wrapped around his head like a turban. On each cheek was tattooed an arcane symbol. His white hair was long and twisted into twin braids, into which were tied a number of small bones, colorful stones, and clay discs. Around his neck, on a leather thong, hung his *krysala*, the relic he used to summon and control the spirits in the wind.

He went straight to the baby and took him from Munkhe's arms, who gave him up without complaint. He held the baby up and closed his eyes. He stayed that way for a minute, then lowered the child and pressed his ear to the baby's chest. He listened for another minute, then raised his head.

"He's touched by the wind, isn't he?" Henta said. She tried to keep the unhappiness out of her voice but didn't quite succeed.

The old shaman shook his head. He looked down at the tiny infant, his creased and weathered face betraying his awe and surprise.

"The wind has not marked him. The wind has made its home *inside* him."

Part 1

Chapter 1: Fen

Fen and his mother were heading home when the pounding started.

Fen's mother froze, listening. It was a heavy, dull pounding, something Fen felt in his chest as much as heard with his ears. It seemed to reverberate in the ground under his feet and pulse from the walls of the stone buildings around them. The pounding was rhythmic, like the heartbeat of some vast beast deep underground.

Boom. Boom. Boom.

"They made it to the gates," Fen's mother said. Looking up, Fen saw her put her hand over her mouth as if to keep from crying out.

She reached for his hand. "We have to go."

"I don't need to hold your hand," Fen grumbled, pulling his hand away. "I'm not a little boy. I can walk on my own."

Fen's mother didn't argue with him, just grabbed his wrist in a death grip and started walking as fast as she could, so fast that he had to practically run to keep from falling down. He stole a look at her face as they walked and saw that her lips were compressed into a white line.

She was afraid. More afraid than he'd ever seen her. That got through to him more than the pounding did, made his heart pick up and beat faster. Was the pounding the battering ram he'd heard people speak of? he wondered. Did it mean the invaders were about to break into the city? He looked over his shoulder, down the cobblestone street, afraid he would see enemy soldiers right then, weapons drawn, chasing after them.

Except for other citizens of the city of Samkara, all of them hurrying like they were, the street was empty. And Fen was smart enough to know the enemy wouldn't come from that direction anyway. They'd come from the direction of the city gates, the same direction he and his mother were hurrying.

Fen and his mother lived near the main gates of the city. He could see them from the roof of the building. He'd been up there several times since the siege started, because from there he could also see the enemy soldiers, spread all over the hills and farms

15

outside the city, thousands and thousands of them. They'd been there for weeks now, attacking the walls every day.

At first it was exciting, and he stole up onto the roof whenever he could to watch. It seemed like some kind of great game, a holiday that never ended. In the first few days people laughed about it, and talked about how there was nothing to fear, how the walls would never fall to the Maradi.

But then the great stones started falling out of the sky. They were as big as the wagons the farmers used to bring their crops into the city. Wherever they struck they caused terrible damage. Fen's mother cleaned taverns for a living, and one morning he and his mother went to one of them only to find it gone, nothing left but a pile of rubble. It was like Hentu, god of storms, reached down out of the sky and smashed it with his giant fist.

The catapults threw more than stones. They also flung balls of flaming pitch. Whole sections of the city—usually the poorer parts, where the buildings were made of wood—had already burned. Smoke was always in the air now.

Once the siege started in earnest it stopped being exciting and started to become frightening. The laughter stopped and was replaced by tight lips and fear. Fen saw fights in the streets, some of them bloody. He heard his mother crying during the night.

A few days ago Fen had seen his mother talking with a neighbor woman, an old woman named Elace. He heard Elace telling his mother that when she was a little girl the city she'd lived in was conquered and sacked. He didn't know what "sacked" meant, and before he could find out, his mother saw him and sent him back inside their apartment. Later, when he asked her about it she shook her head and refused to tell him.

Now he wondered if Samkara was about to be sacked.

The sun had gone down a few minutes earlier and the street was getting darker by the minute. Fen wasn't sure where, exactly, their home was, but he knew it was still at least several blocks away. The pounding of the ram was getting louder with every step. Everyone else on the street seemed to be going the opposite way, away from the sound.

All at once there was a terrible cracking sound. His mother came to an abrupt stop—everyone on the street did—and stared off into the distance. More cracking sounds and then the crash of something heavy falling to the ground.

Hard after that sound came a loud and terrible cheer, then the ringing of steel on steel.

Screams of pain and death echoed down the street.

"It's too late," his mother whispered. Her face had gone ashen. She looked down at Fen. "We can't make it home. We have to find somewhere to hide."

Now Fen was glad she was holding his hand. Now he wished she would pick him up and carry him. More than anything he wanted his mother's arms around him. He wanted her to hold him close and tell him everything was going to be okay.

Except that he had a terrible feeling nothing would ever be okay again.

His mother was still carrying the basket of food they'd just bought at the market, but now she dropped it and looked around desperately. Somehow that made Fen even more afraid. His mother never, ever wasted food, even if it was starting to mold. The coins she earned were too precious, too hard to come by, to waste food.

Around them people were running. A man carrying a chicken under his arm crashed into Fen's mother so hard he nearly knocked her down. He cursed her and ran off down the street.

"We'll go to Victory Square," she said suddenly. "Marki will take us in." Marki was one of his mother's friends. She had a daughter only a little older than Fen.

She took off running, pulling Fen behind her. They ran down one street and cut through a market. A few of the vendors were trying to pack up their goods, but most were fleeing. Several of the carts had been overturned and the two of them ran through spilled turnips, potatoes and other vegetables. Leaving the market, they turned onto a smaller street that was less crowded. They were both breathing hard by the time they made it to Victory Square, which was almost empty.

It was a small square, with only two streets leading into it. The buildings surrounding the square were all three or four stories tall and built together. In the center of the square was a statue of some forgotten general holding up a sword. The statue was mostly covered by bird droppings.

Fen's mother led them to a door in one of the buildings fronting the square. It was a thick wooden door with no window. She grabbed the handle and pulled.

It was locked.

She stepped back, craning her neck to look at the upper stories. "Marki! Marki! Let us in!"

Fen saw a face appear at one of the windows—he couldn't see if it was Marki or not—but the person pulled the shutters closed without saying anything. The rest were already closed.

Fen's mother began banging on the door, yelling Marki's name over and over. But no footsteps sounded from the other side. Desperately, Fen's mother went to the next door and tried it. It was also locked. She tried several more doors and every one of them was locked. There were no windows on the bottom floor of any of the buildings, and so they had no way in.

Fen's mother turned to him and grabbed his shoulders, pulling him close to look into his eyes. "We'll have to find another place. That's all. We just have to find somewhere to get off the street. It's okay. Trust me, it's okay." Tears were running down her face and she seemed to be trying to will him to believe her.

Fen knew she didn't believe her own words. More than ever he wanted her to pick him up. His legs were shaking so badly he could barely stand. He realized he was crying too, the tears blurring his vision.

There was a sudden clatter of armor and harsh men's voices. Fen turned, saw soldiers streaming into the square.

It was too late.

Chapter 2

The soldiers pouring into the square showed a white star on their shields and surcoats and at first Fen was relieved. These were Samkaran soldiers. They were going to be safe.

But then behind them he saw a mass of soldiers wearing the emblem of Maradi, a charging bull. The Maradis killed a few of the Samkaran soldiers in the rear and the rest turned, raising shields and weapons, trying to make a stand.

"We have to go, Fen!" his mother cried. "Run!"

She grabbed his hand and they ran for the other exit from the square. But they had gone only a few steps when soldiers appeared there too.

Maradi soldiers.

Fen and his mother skidded to a halt. His mother's head swiveled side to side, looking for an escape.

But there was none.

Whirling, she dragged Fen back to the first doorway she'd tried and began kicking and pounding on it, screaming, "Let us in! Let us in!" over and over.

Fen stood pressed close to his mother, watching wide-eyed as the slaughter commenced.

For it was a slaughter. There was no other word for it. The Samkaran soldiers were outnumbered two-to-one and the Maradi wore better armor, had better weapons.

The Samkarans clustered in a tight knot around the statue and fought with the desperate ferocity of doomed men, hacking and stabbing wildly at the enemy. Fen's eyes were drawn to one of the Samkaran soldiers, a tall, thick-shouldered man wearing plate armor and wielding a huge, two-handed sword. He fought like a madman, screaming curses at his enemies, cutting down men with every swing. Blood poured from a dozen wounds, but none of them seemed to slow him down.

Despite his terror, Fen couldn't take his eyes off him. There was something about the man, something fascinating. He was a force of nature, like a storm. For a time it seemed he might single-handedly stem the tide and Fen found himself clenching his fists, willing the man to victory.

Then a new wave of Maradi poured in. They swept up and over the remaining Samkarans, burying them. The big man screamed with impotent rage and broke free of the wave, once, twice. Then he went down a third time and disappeared.

Fen's mother had given up banging on the door and was edging along the stone wall, pulling Fen along with her. Maybe in the chaos they could escape unnoticed. They might still survive this nightmarish scene.

They made it to the corner of the square when one of the Maradi soldiers spotted them.

"Hey!" he yelled, and ran at them, a bloody short sword in his hand.

Fen's mother screamed and tried to run, dragging Fen behind her in her panic. It wasn't that far to the exit. If they could just reach it, maybe they could get away, maybe they could find somewhere to hide.

But Fen tripped and went down. With a cry, his mother turned back to snatch him up. She jerked him to his feet, but before they could run again, the soldier caught them.

He grabbed hold of her wrist with his free hand, and with his other, the one holding the sword, he backhanded Fen, knocking him sprawling.

"What do we have here?" he snarled. He was wearing leather armor and a boiled leather cap. There was blood on his face and his features were twisted in a bestial snarl. "Looks like I found myself a sweet."

He jerked Fen's mother closer, grabbed her dress and tore it partway off. Fen watched in horror, wishing there was something, anything he could do.

What happened next seemed like it was in slow motion.

Fen's mother reached into the pocket of her torn dress, retrieving the short-bladed kitchen knife she always carried when they went out into the streets. Fen had seen her use it to drive off a thief once, cutting the man's hand so he howled and ran off, cursing her.

The soldier didn't see it. He was staring at her breasts, his mouth partway open.

She stabbed him in the forearm, the little blade sinking in all the way to the hilt.

The soldier yelled and jerked his arm back. "You stabbed me!" he yelled. He seemed to be having trouble believing it.

Fen's mother took advantage of the opportunity and reached for Fen—

The soldier swung the bloody short sword. The blade inscribed a short, wicked arc. Fen tried to cry out, to do something, anything, but it was already too late and he was too slow.

The blade caught Fen's mother in the side, cutting deep. She collapsed in a spray of blood and Fen screamed. Something inside him snapped, something that would never mend, never heal, and he threw himself at the soldier in a frenzy.

The soldier put his foot on her corpse and jerked the blade free. As he straightened up, Fen hit him, his fists swinging, howling like a wild animal.

The soldier threw him off, hard enough that Fen slammed into the stone wall of the building behind him. The wind was knocked out of him by the impact and he fell to his knees.

He straightened up in time to see the soldier looming over him.

"Miserable little rat," the soldier said.

He swung his sword. As if from far away Fen watched the blade descend, noted the drops of blood—his mother's blood—flying from it.

The sword hit him in the chest, there was a burst of pain, and everything went dark.

Chapter 3

Fen opened his eyes. He sat up, blinking. Smoke filled the air and at first he had no idea where he was or what had happened. Confused, he looked on a scene from a nightmare, bodies piled in heaps, blood splashed everywhere, all of it lit by the lurid glow of a city burning in the background.

Then it all came crashing back on him. He turned and saw his mother lying nearby. Her eyes were open, unseeing. Blood soaked the cobblestones around her. An animal sound came from him and he crawled over to her. He grabbed her shoulder and turned her on her back. Her head lolled lifelessly.

Weeping uncontrollably, Fen grabbed her and held her close. "You're not dead, Mama. You're not dead." He kept saying it over and over, as if repetition might make it come true.

How long he stayed that way he didn't know. He lost track of time. His life was horror and grief. He wanted to be dead too. He wanted to be with his mother.

At length a new thought penetrated his brain. He pushed it away, but it kept coming back.

Why am I still alive?

He pulled away from his mother and sat up. In the flickering light from the fires, he could see that his tunic was slit open across his chest. He pulled the slit open and looked at his skin. There was blood smeared everywhere, but none of it was his. There was no wound, only a faint, reddish line to mark where the sword had struck him.

What happened?

There was a sound and movement in the center of the square. Fen stared as one of the piles of bodies moved. Part of him yelled that he should get up, that he should run and hide before it was too late. But he stayed there, watching in horrified fascination.

The pile of bodies shifted again, and a man's gauntleted hand covered in blood emerged. The bodies moved some more and the rest of the arm came free, along with the head and shoulders.

It was the big soldier. He made it slowly to his feet. For a moment he stood there, swaying. He was spattered everywhere with blood. His armor was badly scored and dented. Reaching up, he took off his helmet, let it fall to the ground. Underneath, he was bald, hairless except for the long mustache that curled down past his jaw.

Slowly he turned, surveying the destruction around him. Other than he and Fen, there was no one else alive in the little square. His gaze lifted to the city beyond. Screams of pain echoed in the distance. Flames leapt into the sky. Huge clouds of smoke billowed skyward.

He raised his fists and tilted his head back, screaming rage and sorrow and defiance at the night sky.

"Blood!" he screamed. "Blood and death! Ten times what you have done to us this night, I will return to you, Marad! Ten times! This I vow, this I swear my life to!"

As he said this, Fen saw something strange, something he would wonder about for years.

A shadow appeared behind the bald soldier, growing thicker and darker with each passing second. Soon it was as tall as he was, like a rip in the night. A thin edge of dark purple crackled along the edge of it.

Pale, emaciated hands reached out of the shadow. The hands settled on top of the bald soldier's head. Strangely, the bald soldier didn't seem to notice, but simply stood there with his head bowed, his chest rising and falling with each breath.

What looked like black smoke, tinged slightly with purple, flowed out of the fingertips of the pale hands. The smoke entered through the eyes, nose and mouth of the bald soldier.

The hands withdrew and disappeared into the shadow, which faded and was gone, as if it had never been there.

Fen rubbed his eyes, wondering if he'd just imagined it all. Had he? The soldier seemed unchanged, and he hadn't noticed anything.

The bald soldier bent over and dug around in the pile of bodies. A moment later he found what he was looking for and pulled his sword free of the mass. He wiped it on one of the bodies and made his way out of the pile.

As he was leaving the square, his eyes fell on Fen, huddled there, staring up at him. He paused, his gaze going to the body of

Fen's mother, lying sprawled beside him. New rage flickered in his eyes.

"Come," he said to Fen, holding out his mailed hand.

"She's my mother," Fen said, turning his head and looking at her. The sight sent fresh stabs of pain through him.

"Not anymore," the soldier said grimly.

"I can't leave her."

"There's nothing to leave, lad. Only the past." He pointed out into the city with his sword. "Out there is the future. Come with me and we'll make the bastards pay for this. We'll make every one of them pay."

With one last glance at his mother, Fen rose and walked over to the man.

"I'm Fen," he said.

The man set his hand on Fen's shoulder for a moment. "Barik." Fen looked at his hand. There was so much blood that the gauntlet was completely red. The other hand was the same.

Barik pointed at the body of a fallen soldier. "Take a weapon, Fen, and follow me."

Fen started to pick up the soldier's sword, but realized it was too big for him. In a sheath at the soldier's side was a dagger. He tugged it free and held it up for Barik to see. The blade was longer than his forearm.

"That'll do," Barik said.

They passed out into the city then, from a smaller nightmare into a larger one. Fires burned everywhere. Bodies lay sprawled in the streets. Doors had been kicked in, whole families dragged out, the men and boys killed, the women and girls raped, then killed. Shops had been looted. Smashed dishes and glassware were strewn over the ground.

Here and there wandered survivors, staring around them with dull, dead eyes and blank faces. Some lay curled up on the ground in the fetal position, crying and moaning to themselves.

They were making their way down one wide street when an elderly woman lurched out of the shadows of an alley and threw herself at Barik.

"Where were you?" she screamed, clawing and spitting at him. "Where were you? How could you let this happen?"

Barik said nothing, nor did he try to defend himself. He simply stood there and let her wear herself out, until at last she sagged back, weeping bitterly, her energy spent. But Fen saw the grim, angry look settling deeper into Barik's features as the woman raged, and he knew that Barik was storing this all away, fuel for the fires of his vengeance on their enemies.

Fen clung to that look. His world was threatening to spin out of control, but that look of doom and promise on Barik's face gave him something to hang onto. It gave him something to reach for, shining darkly in a future that otherwise held nothing.

The night was old, dawn only a couple hours away, which meant that the Maradi army had had hours to slake its thirst for violence and looting. It seemed that the Maradi army had withdrawn from the city for they came upon no enemy soldiers, no living ones anyway. To Fen it was as if a tornado had blown through the city, leaving a path of destruction and death and disappearing just as quickly.

They did find Samkaran soldiers, though, in ones and twos throughout the city. Every soldier they met took one look at the fell figure of Barik, stained with blood and death, and fell in behind him. As Barik and Fen moved through the city, more and more of them joined until when Fen looked over his shoulder, he could no longer tell how many there were.

It was nearing dawn, light just showing in the east, when Barik and Fen came upon the first living Maradi soldiers they'd seen all night.

There were a couple dozen of them. They'd dragged a long table out into the street and covered it with food—haunches of beef, smoked hams, olives, loaves of bread and wheels of cheese— and bottles of wine and liquor. They were sitting at the table, drinking and stuffing themselves, telling wild stories of the battle and laughing.

They had no chance.

As soon as Barik saw them, he launched himself at them. He made no sound, no war cry or battle yell, just ran at them with his sword upraised. Behind him poured the rest of his makeshift army.

One of the enemy soldiers looked up blearily right before they got there. His eyes widened and he started to stand. Other heads turned.

The Samkaran soldiers smashed into them, all the ache and self-hatred and fear of the night pouring out at once. Barik's first swing nearly cut a man in half as he turned and tried to raise one arm. He was thrown back into the table, knocking it over, spilling food and drink everywhere.

His next swing took off the head of the man next to him. Then the rest of the Samkaran soldiers got there. They hacked at the enemy soldiers grimly, savagely.

By the time Fen got there, the brief battle was over. Every Maradi was down, their blood draining out into a city that had seen far too much of it already. Then he saw one of them off to the side, trying to crawl away.

With a cry of hatred he ran at the wounded soldier and jumped on his back. Once, twice, he stabbed with the dagger, but the man's armor deflected both blows. The man rolled onto his side and shoved Fen away.

Fen scrambled back to his feet and charged again. Again the armor defeated him, but by then Barik was there and he killed the man with one blow from the gore-stained sword. With the blade of his weapon he pointed to the joints in the man's armor.

"Aim here, and here. That's where your blade will find its way in."

Fen stabbed into one of the joints, felt the blade sink into yielding flesh. He looked up at Barik to see if he'd done it right. When he did, he saw something in Barik's eyes, something he could cling to: Approval.

For a boy who couldn't remember his own father, who'd lost the only family he had in the world just a few hours before, it was everything.

More than anything, he wanted to see that look again.

Chapter 4

By the time the sun came up, Fen was so tired he could hardly think straight. His eyes felt filled with sand. His limbs were made of wood. He dropped the dagger more than once as it slipped from his numb fingers.

Barik looked at him. "Get some rest."

Fen looked around. He'd never been in this part of the city. He didn't recognize anything; he didn't know anyone. "Where?"

There were a lot of people in the street with them, soldiers and citizens alike. Barik turned to one of the women. "Find the boy a spot to curl up." She nodded and reached for Fen's hand.

"I don't want to leave you," Fen said, rubbing his eyes. "I'm not tired."

"You'll find me." To the woman Barik said, "Right?"

She nodded again. "Yes, my lord."

She led Fen away, her grip tight on his arm. Even through his weariness Fen was struck by the way she'd addressed Barik. He was old enough to know that soldiers were not addressed as "lord." Yet she had done so and no one had reacted as if it was unusual.

What had changed?

Everything, he realized. Everything had changed.

A fresh wave of grief poured over him then, so thick and strong he was choking on it. He couldn't breathe. Strangled sounds came from him and tears poured down his face.

The woman looked down on him. She was somewhere in her middle years, no longer young, but not quite old either. Her brown dress was rough homespun, the cloth tied around her hair frayed.

"We've all lost this night," she said. "No one's untouched." She pulled him in and gave him a rough hug. He clung tightly to her until she pushed him away.

"That's enough," she told him, her voice firm, yet not cold. "The dead are gone. We're not. Time to carry on."

She led him to a rough building, two stories of brick and wood. It had escaped the fires, but not the looters. The door had been smashed in. A body was lying before the front stoop. She stepped over it without looking at it and took him upstairs, pointed out a rough straw mat and gave him a thin blanket.

Fen lay down and was almost immediately asleep.

When he awakened the sun was shining through the open window. He sat up and rubbed his eyes. For one blessed moment he was in his own home and any moment now his mother would be calling his name, telling him to get up, that it was time to help her with her cleaning jobs.

The moment passed all too fast and the choking feeling descended on him once again. He was at the bottom of a deep well, the light lost far above him, forever out of reach.

"Push it away, boy."

He turned his head and saw the same woman, bent over a tiny fireplace.

"There's living to be done," she said. She straightened and brought him a bowl of food.

Suddenly ravenous, Fen gobbled the food down, scooping it into his mouth with his fingers. When he was done he held out the bowl for more, but she shook her head.

"There's naught left in the house. Time to go."

He followed her to the door. On the way he noticed something on the floor and he picked it up. It was a crude doll, made of corn husks and clothed in scraps of cloth. There was blood on it. He looked around and saw that there were traces of blood on the floor. She'd cleaned, but she hadn't gotten it all.

The woman turned back around to see why he'd stopped. He held the doll up to her. She took it and he saw her face twist, her eyes squeeze shut. For just a moment she stood like that, then she opened her eyes and took a deep breath. She put the doll in her pocket.

"There's no time for that," she said. "Come. Let's find him."

It wasn't hard to find Barik. The woman asked two men she found who were loading bodies into a cart. They pointed.

They trudged up the street and after a time she asked again, this time an old woman who was sweeping up broken crockery. She pointed without a word.

Everywhere they went there were people in the streets, and nearly every one of them was working. Dead were being gathered into wagons, some pulled by horses or oxen, others by groups of men. Twice they came on lines of sweating men fighting those fires that still burned, buckets of water passing from hand to hand. Even the children helped, piling broken dishes, picking up the pieces they could manage.

At length they came upon Barik. Around him was a knot of soldiers and citizens. He was giving orders.

"You four. I want you working on picking up the dead. Find a cart. Haul them out Reacher's Gate and into the big field there. You men, find shovels. Go out there and help with the pit. We have to get the dead buried before they spread disease."

He turned to another group. "There are still fires burning down in the Fisherman's District. Find buckets and go help."

The people, one and all, took his orders and hurried off. None questioned him. None hesitated.

"He gets it," the woman said. "There's work to be done. We owe it to the living, not the dead." Fen saw her hand reach into her pocket and touch the doll there, but he didn't say anything.

She led him over to Barik, patted Fen once on the shoulder, then left with a group of women who'd been sent on another task. Fen did not look after her. He stared up at Barik.

Barik seemed as strong and unbreakable as ever. Sweat ran down his bald pate, but there was no glassiness of fatigue in his eyes. For the first time Fen saw something in him, something he was to notice many times in the years to come. Barik seemed to burn with an inner fire and in a flash of insight Fen realized that this was where his unyielding strength came from.

Barik had shed his armor at some point, though he still wore his sword, and Fen could see his rank for the first time, emblazoned on his surcoat. Fen had always been fascinated by the soldiers and had memorized their ranks at a young age. Barik wore the symbol of a captain.

Fen looked around. Amongst the soldiers gathered around, receiving orders, he saw one showing the rank of a major. Yet the man accepted Barik's orders as readily as the privates and sergeants around him. Clearly the world had changed in some fundamental way.

When everyone had been given a task Barik looked down, as if noticing Fen for the first time. "Are you ready now?" he asked.

Fen had no idea what he was referring to, but he knew he was ready. He had to be ready. There was so much to be done. He nodded.

"Come with me. It's time to go to the castle."

Fen had to hurry to keep up with Barik's long strides. He hadn't gone far before he developed a stitch in his side, but he bit his lip and ignored it. He couldn't bear the thought of being left behind. He would endure whatever it took. He had nothing else.

Samkara sat on a series of low hills that wrapped around a large bay. The sea lay to the west. At the top of the tallest hill were the high walls, towers and turrets of the castle. Fen had never even been near it, it being so far from the area of the main gate, where he had grown up.

Man and boy followed the streets up and up. Periodically, Barik paused to give orders and people leapt to obey. They seemed to need someone to tell them what to do. Eventually they emerged onto a broad boulevard that led directly into the castle itself. Fen could see that the gates of the castle had also been broken, the heavy timbers lying in pieces on the ground. A score of soldiers stood in the opening, guarding it.

Barik strode up to them and stopped a few paces away. His fierce gaze moved over them and it seemed to Fen that they shifted uneasily. They were castle guard, their uniforms fancier than the plain one Barik wore. A few of the men wore blood-stained bandages.

"There are fires to be put out," Barik said. "The dead to be buried. Work to be done. Why are you standing about here?"

Before they could answer, a man pushed through their ranks and walked up to Barik. "They are here on my orders. They stand guard."

Fen could see from his uniform, heavy with gold braid, and the fine quality of his sword, that he was a high-ranking officer indeed. Maybe even the general in charge of the castle guard.

"And what do they guard?" Barik said. He sounded impatient and Fen had a feeling that he would not tolerate this for long. Fen put his hand on the hilt of the dagger, stuck in his belt. If it came to a fight, he meant to do his part.

The general seemed shocked by Barik's question. He had deep set eyes and a red face that grew redder. "The royal family, of course."

"They still live?"

The general hesitated, and Fen knew the answer before he said it. "Sadly, no."

"Then they do not need guarding. Everyone—" Barik leaned closer to the general. "*Everyone* is needed in the rebuilding of the city."

The general began to splutter. "Who are you, you impudent dog, to come up here and presume to order *me*—"

He got no further.

Barik's sword seemed to leap into his hand. The general fell back, yanking at his own sword, but it was too late. Barik's sword flashed and a line of blood appeared across his throat. He fell to his knees, clutching his throat, choking sounds coming from him.

Barik wiped his sword on the dying man's back, then stepped over him. He sheathed the sword and began pointing at men.

"You six, find every wagon or carriage the castle has to offer. Hitch them and begin gathering the dead. Take any help from amongst the survivors in the castle that you need. That means anyone living, whether they be a serving boy or a lord."

The men barely hesitated long enough to salute, a salute that Barik did not bother to return. They turned and hurried through the broken gates into the castle. Barik began giving orders to the others.

Fen watched, and he began to learn. During the night, when he tried to stab the wounded enemy soldier, Barik had taught him the first lesson in fighting. Now he learned from him a different lesson. He saw how, when the world changed and the old powers fell apart, people looked for a new power, one they could cling to. The man who was strong and decisive could be that power.

Man and boy crossed the castle grounds heading toward the palace. The castle had not escaped the destruction visited on the rest of the city. If anything, it was worse here. For some reason that surprised Fen. He realized he had expected it to be different. The nobility lived in such a vastly different world. He had never imagined that they could be touched by events like the lower classes. He had imagined that there was around them a bubble of sorts, protecting them from the troubles and pains suffered by the rest of humanity.

But he was wrong. They bled and died just like everyone else.

Bodies littered the expansive lawns surrounding the palace. He saw ladies in rich dresses sprawled on the perfectly manicured lawns, their fancy gowns torn, flies crawling on their dead faces.

Before the palace was a wide, circular drive, where the nobility rode up in their carriages for their audience with the king, or to appear at his latest feast or ball. In the center of the drive was a huge fountain, a sculpture of leaping fishes in the middle and a pool of water that a hundred people could have bathed in at once.

Floating in the pool, face down, was a man wearing rich clothing, threads of gold woven into his cloak. Beside the fountain was the body of an older woman, her gray hair still done up in a towering pile on top of her head. One of her hands had been chopped off. The hand lay to the side, the expensive rings that had adorned its fingers gone.

Barik and Fen walked through the remains of the great palace doors and into the grand entrance hall beyond, their footsteps echoing on the marble floor. The room was vast, the ceiling high overhead. Massive, ornately-carved columns reached to the roof. On either side of the room broad staircases curved elegantly up to the next floor. Friezes decorated the walls and statues stood on pedestals. It was wealth and splendor beyond anything Fen had ever imagined.

Blood spattered all of it. Lying sprawled on floor and on the stairs were the bodies of servants, guards, and at least one nobleman. Thick, heavy purple drapes that had once closed off alcoves leading to other rooms had been torn down and trampled. Someone had drawn crudely on one wall with blood.

An elderly man limped up to them. He wore a ruffled yellow shirt with the white star of Samkara stitched to his breast and there was a red sash over one shoulder. He had a large, purple bruise on one side of his face and his white gloves were spotted with blood.

"I am Chamberlain Ketrick and you cannot be here," he told Barik. "The royal palace is off-limits to all who are not..."

He broke off as Barik continued on, ignoring him. He hurried to catch up.

"Have you lost your mind? This is no place for a common soldier," he snapped.

"Gather everyone who survived," Barik told him. "Begin dragging the dead outside. A pit is being dug outside Reacher's Gate. The dead will be buried there. All of them." He prodded a body lying by his foot. The man was portly and wearing clothes made of the finest silk, his boots of polished calf leather. There was a gaping wound in the side of his head. "Start with this one."

"That is Lord Nilson," the old chamberlain quavered. "He is the scion of the Tenysean family. He must be laid out in state for a proper funeral."

"I don't care who, or what, he was. He will be buried with the rest."

The old chamberlain seemed to have trouble grasping what had just been said. "You cannot mean to bury the nobility with the servants?"

"I *mean* to bury everyone in the quickest, most efficient way possible."

"Surely you've gone mad," the old man said. He stamped his foot. "It won't be done! I will not see Lord Nilson dragged out in a pile to lie with a peasant boy."

Barik turned his intense gaze on him. "You will either help, or I will kill you and your body will join his in the pit along with everyone else's."

The old man stared at him for a moment longer, then he turned and limped away, muttering as he went.

"Those who cannot adjust will die," Barik told Fen. "The same mistakes will not be made again."

They made their way through the palace, stepping over bodies. As they went, servants began to come forth out of hiding. All seemed eager to carry out the orders Barik gave them, leaping to their tasks as if he were their king.

Was he now? Fen wondered. Was Barik their king? Could it happen? Could a common soldier rise to the highest position? It was something he had never considered before.

They came to the throne room. The king was still sitting on his throne. Or at least most of him was. His head lay on the floor nearby. There was no sign of his crown. Barik led Fen up the steps of the dais, stopping beside the throne.

"He tried to buy peace with Marad. He thought his coin would placate them. He lived in here, shut off from the real world, listening to those who only told him what he wanted to hear. Those he listened to never warned him that the funds he had diverted from the military, the funds he spent instead on ever more extravagant parties and toys, would one day cost us all. Look on him, Fen. See the price of weakness, the price of excess." He gestured at the opulent throne room, with the gold-inlaid bas-relief on the walls, the thick tapestries, the colored glass in the windows. "None of this means anything against cold steel. Only vigilance and strength counts. Everything else is a waste."

Fen listened. He learned.

And as he did so, his new world began to take shape around him.

Chapter 5

Fen followed Barik out the gates of the castle a few hours later and discovered that several thousand people had gathered while they were inside. Barik came to a stop. The people stared at him. They were people from all walks of life, old women, young women holding babies, children, soldiers, prosperous merchants, beggars. There were even a few of the nobility. The people were hollow-eyed with grief and exhaustion. They were covered in soot and blood. They didn't speak. They didn't fidget. They simply stood there and stared at Barik and Barik stared back.

"This isn't the end," Barik said finally. "Samkara will rebuild. *We* will rebuild. It won't be easy. It will take hard work and commitment. It will take sacrifice. But we *will* rebuild." He clenched his fists. "We will learn from the mistakes of the past and we will be stronger this time. We will make our enemies *pay*. For every Samkaran who fell here, ten Maradi will fall." He held his fist over his head. There was still dried blood on it. "I am the red fist of vengeance and that is my promise to you."

There was no cheering when he was finished. They were too far gone for that. They stared at him while his words sank in.

The words echoed around inside Fen's head. It seemed to him that Barik offered more than vengeance. He offered redemption. He offered a future beyond the smoke and ash of the day. He knew then that he would follow this man anywhere, do anything for him.

Without realizing it, he sank to his knees.

As if that was the signal they were waiting for, others began to go to their knees as well. Only a handful at first, then more and more of them. The nobility were the last still standing, but even they could not withstand what was happening around them and all of them knelt as well.

From his knees, Fen looked up at Barik, who nodded at him, then looked back out over his people. For they *were* his people now, Fen could see that.

"Get up," Barik told them. "There is work to be done."

He and Fen passed through them then, and they shuffled aside to make a lane for him.

As they walked through the mass of people, Fen saw many with tears in their eyes. Some made as if to reach for Barik, but they pulled their hands back before touching him.

They made their way back through the city, Barik again giving orders to those they came across, putting them to work rebuilding. They came to the great wall that encircled the city and climbed the many steps to the top. Barik strode over to the battlements and stared out over the Maradi army. Fen stood on his tiptoes to peer through the crenellations.

He saw that the Maradi were packing up and leaving. Already the road leading east, toward Marad, was filled with marching soldiers, wagons, horses. Behind them they left the debris of their camp, broken weapons, bits of armor, dented helms, torn tents and garbage. Dead horses lay here and there. Some of the land they had camped on was farmland, and the crops had been stomped into pulp. Every tree and bush had been cut down and burned. Fire pits were everywhere, many still smoldering. Those farm houses and barns which had not been commandeered by the enemy officers for use as housing had been burned. There were mounds showing where the Maradi had buried their dead.

Also left behind were the siege engines, the catapults which had rained stones onto the city for days, but also two siege towers, and several trebuchets and mangonels. One of the siege towers had burned. The other stood up against the wall, bodies visible inside it. Just outside the shattered main gates was the huge battering ram that had been used to break them.

"Why are they leaving?" Fen asked.

"They're not interested in occupation, only conquest and plunder."

They stood there for a long time, while Barik stared intently at the withdrawing forces. Fen fidgeted. He was hungry and it had been hours since he'd had anything to drink. But he didn't want to say anything. He didn't want to complain. He was afraid that if he did, Barik would send him away and above all else he didn't want that to happen. He had nowhere else to go.

"It is important to know your enemy," Barik said at last. "If you want to defeat him, knowledge is as good as steel. Sometimes better."

Fen wanted to ask what he could learn from watching the enemy leave, but thought better of it. Tired of standing on tiptoe to see, he backed away. He turned and looked over the city. Smoke was only rising in a few places now. People were visible in the streets, putting out the remaining fires, cleaning up.

He looked up at Barik, remembering what he saw, the shadow that opened behind him, the clawed hands and writhing black shapes. That didn't really happen, did it? It couldn't have. He must have imagined it.

He opened the cut in his tunic and looked down at his bare chest. The only sign of the attack was a thin, reddish mark.

Did that happen either? he wondered. How was he still alive?

Suddenly it was as if the world tilted around him. He felt dizzy, disoriented. It couldn't be real. It couldn't be. He wanted to run back to Victory Square right then and look for his mother. Maybe she wasn't there. Maybe she was at home, wondering where he was.

He was heading for the stairs when Barik's hand fell on his shoulder and stopped him.

"Let go," Fen cried, trying to twist away. "I have to go find my mother. She's worried about me."

Barik shook his head. "You can't go back. You can only go forward. You understand?"

"I don't want to understand!" Fen yelled at him, sudden anger rising up and spilling over. "I want to go back! I want to find my mother!"

Barik shook him roughly. "She's gone, boy. She's never coming back. The sooner you accept that the better."

Fen stared up at him for a long moment. He felt the tears start in his eyes and he turned away, not wanting to let Barik see them.

Chapter 6

It was late afternoon and the last dregs of the invading army was disappearing into the east by the time Barik stepped back. Fen's tears had long since dried up and he was sitting with his back against the battlements. He looked up at Barik, ashamed of his weakness, afraid of what he would see in the grim bald man's eyes.

But he saw nothing there, or at least nothing which pertained to him. Barik appeared lost in his own thoughts.

Fen trotted behind him as he climbed down off the wall and headed back through the city toward the castle. He was determined that his tears would never happen again, for he knew that if they did Barik would cast him aside and he could not bear that.

There was no guard on the ruined castle gates this time when they approached. They were all inside, loading bodies into wagons for the long ride down the hill. There was almost no talking, everyone focused on the work. When they saw that Barik was once again among them, they all stopped. A murmur ran through them, three words repeated over and over.

"The Red Fist. The Red Fist."

They stood straight and saluted, putting fists to hearts, and this time Barik returned the salute. Man and boy entered the palace. Servants scurried everywhere, mopping up blood, carrying away debris. Chamberlain Ketrick limped up. He bowed.

"Food has been prepared for you...Fist." He hesitated, as if checking to see if Barik would correct the impromptu title. When Barik said nothing, he continued. "If you will allow me, I will show you to the dining hall."

Barik motioned for him to lead on. They followed him down hallways and around corners. The servants they encountered all knuckled their foreheads and lowered their faces as their new liege lord passed.

Ketrick led them through carved, gold-painted double doors—now marred by blood and holes where spears or swords had struck—and into a large room with a long table in the middle, surrounded by scores of high-backed chairs. There was a many-paned window at the far end of the room that looked off over the

38

burned-out farms east of the city. A massive chandelier hung over the table and a servant was hurriedly lighting the oil lamps on it, using a long pole with a burning wick on the end.

"Go," Barik told the servant. "A simple candle on the table will suffice. There is work to be done and I won't have you waste your time on that."

The servant hurried away. Ketrick led Barik to the head of the table and after he sat down said, "Your food will be out shortly." Then he stood there, looking at Fen, unsure. Fen, standing off to the side, looked at the floor.

"Bring food for the boy too," Barik ordered. The chamberlain bowed and passed through a curtained doorway in the corner of the room. Barik motioned to the chair to his right and Fen sat down.

A moment later a servant hurried in carrying a large goblet and a decanter. "Would…the Fist like some wine?" he asked.

"Water," Barik said, and the servant went away.

When they were done eating, Barik sat there in silence, lost in thought. After some minutes had passed, Fen gathered his courage, sat up as straight as he could, pulled his shoulders back and said, "I want to be a soldier."

The Fist turned his intense gaze on the boy, studying him. It was hard to sit still under that look. Fen wanted to wilt. He wanted to take back what he'd said. But he forced himself to stay quiet and still.

"Why?" Barik asked at last.

Fen had spent a lot of time that afternoon thinking about this and he knew his answer without hesitation. "I want to defend the weak. I want to protect the women and children, to make sure that this never happens again." As he said the words, he saw again his mother falling to the enemy's blade. He couldn't help her, but maybe he could help someone else's mother.

Barik nodded as if Fen had affirmed something for him. The nod made Fen sit up even straighter.

"Samkara will need all the soldiers she can get," Barik said. "Our army is depleted."

Barik went back to his thoughts. After a few more minutes had passed, Fen ventured a question. "When do I start?"

"You are young—"

"I'm thirteen." Fen realized he had just interrupted Barik and he clamped his mouth shut, surprised at himself.

But Barik didn't seem to notice. He was studying Fen. He seemed to be looking for something. "All in good time, boy."

The chamberlain reentered the dining hall.

"Find the boy a place to sleep."

The chamberlain bowed. "Of course, Fist." He hesitated, but when there were no further orders he motioned to Fen to follow him and they left the room. Once the doors were closed he looked Fen over, noticing the poor state of his clothes, the crude shoes he wore, his roughly-shorn hair.

He looked around and saw a servant boy crossing the hall. "Come here." The boy approached cautiously. He was carrying a bucket of water and a mop. "Find him somewhere to sleep," he told the boy, then walked off.

The boy stared at him. He was about Fen's age, a little bit shorter, with a shock of unruly blond hair and bright, curious eyes. "Who are you?" he asked.

"I'm Fen."

The boy looked at the dining hall doors. "You were just in there eating with the Fist. You must be *someone*."

Fen wasn't quite sure how to respond to that. Finally he said, "I'm going to be a soldier."

The boy's eyes widened. "You are?" Fen nodded. "I want to be a soldier too." He looked down at the bucket and the mop. "I hate mopping."

Fen noticed that the water was stained red. The boy's hands were stained red as well.

"Is there a lot of blood?"

"Not as much as there was. C'mon. Let me throw this out and then we'll find you somewhere to sleep."

Fen followed the boy down the hall to a door which opened onto a narrow, low-ceilinged corridor. They followed that for a while, went through some other doors, then came to a room with an open window. The boy dumped the bucket out the window onto some bushes growing outside, then dropped bucket and mop on the floor and turned back to Fen.

"I'm Cowley. I've lived in the palace since I can remember. I really hate this place. It always needs cleaning."

Fen didn't say anything, remembering how he used to help his mother clean the taverns. Was it really only yesterday that they'd last done that? It already felt a lifetime ago, so much had happened.

"Can I see your dagger?" Cowley asked, interrupting his thoughts.

Fen had almost forgotten about it being there. He pulled it out of his belt and handed it to Cowley. "Be careful. It's not a toy."

Cowley ran his finger along the edge and shivered. "Have you killed anyone with it?"

"No."

"When you're a soldier you will. You'll kill lots of people. Can you ask the Fist if I can be a soldier too? Anything is better than this."

"If I get a chance." Fen wasn't sure if he would. Would that anger Barik? He didn't see why it would. Barik said they needed all the soldiers they could get. Presumably that included servant boys too.

Cowley led him out into a wide hallway with tapestries on the walls and a thick rug running down the center. He went to a door and opened it. "How about here?"

Fen peeked inside. The room was dim, but there was enough light for him to see a heavy wardrobe, a table with a mirror hanging over it, and a huge bed with a canopy and lots of pillows. It looked like the sort of room a princess would sleep in. He wondered if it actually was the princess' room and if she was lying in the pit outside Reacher's Gate with all the other dead bodies. The thought made him shiver.

"I'm not sleeping in here."

"Why not?"

"I'm only…you know. I'm not a prince or anything."

"You were eating with the Fist. He's our new king."

"Still…" He could imagine the old chamberlain finding him asleep in there. He might get kicked out of the palace and never get to see Barik again.

"You sure? The king and his whole family are dead. The nobles who were staying in the palace are dead too. I don't think anyone would care."

"Where do you sleep?"

"In a rat hole."

"Is there room for one more?"

Cowley shrugged and led him through the palace once again. By then Fen was completely lost. The place was huge. The fancy rooms blended into one another. He didn't really like it either. It was too big and he was too small.

They went through a narrow doorway that led into another narrow hallway. "These are servants' hallways," Cowley said. "They're all over the place. The nobility don't like seeing dirty servants underfoot." The way he said it made it clear he didn't think much of the nobility.

They passed a side corridor that smelled of food. "The kitchen is down here. There's a tall man in there with a sour face and a narrow, pointy beard. He's the head cook. Watch out for him. He'll hit you with anything he's got in his hand. Whacked me over the ear once with a rolling pin when I was stealing a pastry." Cowley grinned. "It was still worth it."

They took some stairs down into the basement. Hallways led in two directions, curtained doorways lining both of them. "We sleep down here. It's cold in the winter, but not too bad I guess. There's barracks, where the royal guard sleeps, on the far side of the castle grounds. Do you think we'll get to sleep there once we're soldiers?"

"I don't know. I guess so."

Cowley started down the hall. "There's an empty room at the end. It used to belong to Dimply, but he fell down the well last winter and drowned. I think some of his stuff is still in there."

The room was tiny, about long enough for an adult to lie down in. The bed was a straw mat in the back. There was a stub of candle on an empty wooden box that was turned on its side. Inside the box were a few rough wood carvings and a single, thin blanket. Cowley picked up the blanket and sniffed it.

"Not too bad," he said. "Whatever fleas Dimply left behind should be dead by now. If you think you're going to be cold I could try to scrounge you another one."

"No," Fen said. "I think it will be okay." He stood in the tiny room, feeling more lost than he ever had in his life, as Cowley started to leave.

Cowley stopped in the doorway and turned back. "Try not to take it too hard, okay? It'll get better."

Fen nodded, not trusting himself to speak. He didn't want to cry again.

"And we're going to be friends, right? So there's that."

Fen managed to swallow the lump in his throat and croak out "Yeah" then Cowley left and he was all alone.

Chapter 7

Fen awakened the next morning and at first he didn't know where he was. He heard muffled voices and someone laughed. He sat up. The only light in the tiny room came from a flickering candle down the hall, its light shining under the ragged curtain that closed off the alcove. Then he remembered that he was in the servants' quarters in the palace, that he really only knew two people in the world anymore and he didn't know where either of them were right then.

He put on his shoes and left the alcove. He was cold and thirsty. Two middle-aged women were standing in the hallway, talking. They looked at him.

"Who are you?" one asked him. She had a large mole on her cheek.

"It's the boy what came in with the Fist," the other one said. She had a faded red cloth tied over her hair.

"Oh. I heard about him."

They both stared at him. "What are you doing down here?" the one with the mole asked.

"I was sleeping. Cowley brought me last night."

"That Cowley," the one with the red scarf snorted. "That boy is nothing but trouble."

"You better hope Heris doesn't catch you sleeping this late," the one with the mole said. "He whips servant boys that shirk their work."

"I don't know if I'm a servant or not," Fen said. He felt confused and more than a little afraid. Was Barik going to abandon him? He wondered if he could find his way back to his home. Maybe old Elace, their neighbor, was still alive. Maybe she would take him in.

"If you're down here, you're a servant," the one with the mole said. "This belongs to us."

"Where is Barik?" Fen asked. "Do you know? Is he still here?"

"Who's Barik?"

"I mean the Fist."

"He left ages ago. There's work to be done, you know."

Suddenly afraid, Fen squeezed past them and ran up the stairs. One called after him but he ignored her. Once on the ground floor he could see by the strong sunlight pouring in through the windows that it was midmorning. He'd badly overslept. What would Barik say?

It took some time, but he managed to find the front door of the palace and he hurried out onto the broad steps. Barik was nowhere in sight, only servants and guardsmen busily cleaning up. He had no idea where to search for the man. He could be anywhere. What should he do? He paced the steps, thinking. Then it hit him.

There was work to be done.

On the steps was a pile of broken tiles and some splintered pieces of wood that looked like they used to be a door. He picked up as many as he could carry and went down the steps. A wagon was sitting in the wide driveway, two horses hitched to it. The back was piled with debris. He threw what he was carrying in there and went back for more.

He worked as hard as he could all day, not stopping for food, drinking water out of the big fountain in the middle of the driveway, which fortunately someone had already taken the dead body out of. He cut himself several times and got lots of splinters, but he didn't let it slow him. All he could think was that if he did enough, worked hard enough, maybe Barik wouldn't be angry with him and maybe he wouldn't send him away.

It was after sunset and he was struggling to drag a large piece of a broken statue down the steps when he looked up and saw Barik come walking across the lawns toward the palace. He wasn't wearing armor or weapons today, not even a soldier's uniform. Instead he wore a simple tunic and breeches like a common laborer. His face was smudged with soot and there was more on his clothes.

Fen went back to struggling with the broken statue. He had it almost to the wagon when Barik got there. He looked up at the man.

"I've been working hard."

"I can see that." Barik bent and lifted the piece easily into the wagon. When he turned for the palace once again, Fen followed nervously, hoping Barik wouldn't send him away.

"I overslept," Fen said when they got to the main doors, which were already in the process of being repaired. "It won't happen again."

Barik grunted. Fen didn't know what to make of that, but at least Barik didn't seem mad. He stuck close to the man as he strode through the palace.

Someone must have passed the word to Ketrick that the Fist was coming because the old chamberlain intercepted them in one of the halls. "Will you be taking dinner now, Fist?"

"Yes."

Ketrick looked down at Fen, tagging along, and Fen thought his lip curled slightly. "And the boy, sire?"

"He eats with me."

"Very good, sire. If you will follow me."

"I know the way to the dining hall," Barik said.

"Of course, sire." Ketrick stepped aside and bowed as Barik strode by without looking at him.

Fen hurried to keep up with Barik. His relief that he wasn't being sent away was immense. It was like he'd been holding his breath all day. He looked down at his hands, dirty and scratched from the day's work like Barik's were. The work had helped, keeping his grief and fear pushed back to a manageable distance.

The food—a roast of some kind in gravy with sliced potatoes and carrots—arrived shortly after they reached the table and suddenly Fen realized he was starving. The servant, a woman in a simple brown dress with the white star of Samkara on the breast, kept eyeing the Fist nervously while she spooned the food into large bowls, but the Fist ignored her, lost in his own thoughts.

The servant hurried away and Fen stared hungrily at his food. He wanted to dive right in, but Barik wasn't eating his food yet so he waited. It was pure torture, the smell of the meat and potatoes wafting up to him. He was actually shaking.

Barik came out of his reverie and looked at Fen. "What are you waiting for, boy? You must be hungry."

Fen fairly attacked his food. Its warmth and comfort flowed into every inch of him and for the first time in two days he felt somewhat better.

Barik didn't seem to notice his food as he ate, his brows drawn together in thought. When he was done eating the two of them sat there for a time in silence in the light of a single candle. Darkness had come on by then and the candle lit only their end of the table with its dim, flickering light. The rest of the room hovered between darkness and shadow.

At length Fen mustered his courage and said something he'd been thinking about all day while he was working. "I don't want to wait. I want to learn how to be a soldier now."

Barik blinked and looked at him like he'd forgotten Fen was there. Fen tried to be brave and meet his gaze, but after a few moments it was too much and he had to break away and look down at his plate, wondering if he'd made a mistake in speaking up.

Barik crossed his thick arms over his chest. "You're not strong enough to hold a blade."

Fen took a deep breath. "I moved that piece of statue by myself." He swallowed, remembering his promise to Cowley. "I'm not the only one, either. There's other boys who want to be soldiers too."

"Others?" That seemed to surprise Barik and he uncrossed his arms and leaned forward. "How many?"

"Only one I know of so far," Fen admitted. "But I think he's not the only one."

Barik stared off across the room, drumming his fingers on the table as he thought. "You might be onto something." He raised his hand and a servant who had been waiting in the shadows stepped forward.

"Fetch me General Arkannen."

The servant hesitated.

"What?" Barik's irritation was evident and the servant wilted.

"I...I don't know who General Arkannen is or where to find him."

"Then find Chamberlain Ketrick and tell him. The General should be on the castle grounds somewhere."

The servant bowed and hurried away. Barik looked at Fen. "Are you sure about this? It won't be easy."

"I'm sure."

Barik sat back in his chair and when he spoke again he was talking to himself rather than to Fen. "If Samkara is going to fulfill the plans I have for her, we're going to need to do some things differently. We need better-trained soldiers, for one. The conscripts were next to useless against the Maradi, but the regular soldiers weren't much better. The Maradi far outstripped us in discipline and skill." He paused to pick a piece of food out of his teeth and turned his intense gaze back on Fen.

"But if we start training you young, by the time you're men, you'll be a formidable fighting force. The next time we face the Maradi on the battlefield they won't find us so easy to push around." He nodded approvingly at Fen. "This is a good idea, Fen." Fen swelled with pride. "You've something going on in that head of yours. Keep it up and you'll go far."

"I will do anything I can to help Samkara," Fen said.

"That's the sort of attitude we need. Under the old king we Samkarans forgot that. We spent too much time thinking about ourselves and not our nation. That made us weak, for a people out only for themselves are easily conquered." He gave Fen a sharp, searching look.

"Once you join your new squad you'll move out of the palace and live in the barracks with them. But I'm going to keep an eye on you and now and then I'm going to call you in and ask for a report. I expect you to keep your eyes and ears open. Listen and learn everything you can. Keep using that head of yours. When I call you in I want to hear what you think. I want to know whatever ideas you have. Being amongst the soldiers, you'll have a view that I can't get, stuck here in the palace. I want you to share that with me. Can you do that?"

"Yes, Fist."

"Good. There's something in you, Fen. I can see it. Don't let me down."

"I won't."

A few minutes later the door opened and General Arkannen entered. He was a thin man in his sixties, with a large, prominent nose and a haughty demeanor. His uniform was spotless and looked freshly pressed, his boots shiny, the medals on his chest prominently displayed. His hair was combed back and oiled. He marched over to the table and saluted.

Barik looked him up and down. Fen could see the lines of irritation in the Fist's face as he did so. "In the future, General, when I summon you I expect you to come immediately. Don't waste time putting on a clean uniform and combing your hair."

The general's face tightened and it looked to Fen like he wanted to make an angry retort, but instead he simply said, "Yes, Fist."

"You're going to register a new squad on the rolls."

The general frowned. "Fist, if I may?" When Barik nodded, he continued, "We suffered heavy losses, as you know. Every squad, every platoon, every company, every regiment is undermanned. Wouldn't it be better to put new recruits into one of the existing squads?"

"Normally, you'd be right, but this squad is something different. This squad will consist entirely of boys."

Arkannen's eyes widened. "Boys, sir?"

"Boys grow up into men, don't they?"

"They do. But why? Wouldn't men be better? I can have recruiters combing the countryside tomorrow."

"Send your recruiters out into the city. I want boys around his age." Barik nodded at Fen. "Preferably boys orphaned by the war."

"I still don't understand."

"How many soldiers do we have, General?"

General Arkannen hesitated. "We lost a lot of men, sir."

"How many?"

"Eight hundred and ninety-two who are healthy. Several hundred more who are wounded."

"Do you think we can conquer Marad with eight hundred and ninety-two men, General?"

Arkannen shook his head.

"So it's safe to say that it will be a few years before we are strong enough to strike back at our enemies. Time enough for boys to grow into men."

"But wouldn't—"

"You have your orders, General. That is all."

Some red had crept up the General's neck but he swallowed what he'd been about to say, saluted, and left the hall.

Barik turned to Fen when he was gone. "Impressions?"

"Sir?" Fen asked, confused.

"You were watching, weren't you? Listening?" Fen nodded. "What did you see? I want to know what you saw and I don't want you to hold back."

Fen considered this, searching his memory. Something occurred to him. "I noticed that the general looked…" He searched for the word. "Untouched. Not even a scratch or a bruise. Hardly any of the soldiers look like that. Most have at least one injury."

"And from that what do you conclude?"

Fen hesitated.

"Come, Fen. Speak up," Barik said peremptorily.

"He didn't fight."

"My thoughts exactly. It's my belief that the general passed most of the sack of the city safely in hiding. What else?"

Fen thought some more. "He was very clean." He looked down at himself, his clothes and hands stained by the day's work. "I don't think he's helping with the work."

Barik smiled. "I agree. Anything else?"

Fen took a deep breath and decided to take the plunge, to share one more thing he'd noticed. "I don't think he likes you." Fen paused. That wasn't exactly what he'd meant to say. "I don't think he respects you."

One of Barik's eyebrows rose. "You noticed that too, did you? You're more perceptive than I thought, Fen." He stood and began to pace back and forth, his hands clasped behind him. "The general is part of the rot in this nation that we need to rid ourselves of. He didn't earn his rank by leading men. It was given to him, just like those medals he so proudly wears. The same is true of nearly all the officers. Oh, there are a few good men and others who can probably be salvaged, but most of them will have to go. They'll need to be replaced by real officers, men who know the business of war and have earned their positions. Officers who will lead their men into battle rather than hiding safely in the rear. Officers like you will someday be, Fen."

Fen clutched at his words. They were a promise for the future. They were the foundation he would build on. "I won't let you down, Fist."

Barik put his hand on his shoulder. "I know you won't, Fen. You're the face of our future, you and others like you. With ten thousand like you I'll conquer this whole damned island."

⚔ ⚔ ⚔

Fen left the dining hall with his thoughts in a whirl, staggered by what had just happened. It was all so much to take in.

50

Cowley was waiting for him in the hall and he practically sprang at him. "Did you ask him? What did he say?"

Fen gave him a smile. "He said yes."

Cowley whooped. He began to jump around, waving an imaginary sword. "Goodbye, mops!" he yelled. He stopped in mid-swing and turned to Fen. "When do we start?"

"I don't know."

"Will we get uniforms?"

"I don't know."

"Swords?" Fen shrugged. Cowley grinned and punched him in the arm. "You don't know much of anything, do you?"

"I know that if I work hard I'll be an officer someday. Probably," Fen amended.

"No you won't. You can't be an officer unless your father is a lord." Cowley looked him up and down. "Looking at those clothes, I'd say he isn't."

"The Fist says the army's going to be different from now on."

Cowley snorted. "Nothing's ever different. Not really."

"Now it's you who doesn't know anything."

"Let's go celebrate the good news. I know some girls," Cowley said with a sly look.

"I think I want to go lie down. I'm tired from working all day and I don't want to oversleep again tomorrow."

"It's plain to me that you don't know anything about having fun," Cowley said, putting his arm around his shoulders and leading him away. "Lucky for you that you have me to help you with that."

Chapter 8

A few days later Fen was awakened by someone pulling back the curtain of his alcove and leaning over him. "Are you Fen?"

He sat up, rubbing his eyes. The man was holding a lantern and he couldn't see who he was, only that he was wearing a uniform. "Yes."

"If you still want to be a soldier, follow me."

Fen scrambled up off the mat and quickly put on his shoes. By then the soldier was halfway down the hall and he had to run to catch up with him. "Where's your friend?" the man asked without looking back. "I was told you have a friend who wants to sign up too."

"I'll get him." Fen ran down a side hall to the alcove Cowley slept in. "Get up, Cowley."

Cowley rolled over and groaned. "What do you want? I'm sleeping."

"We're going to start training today. To be soldiers."

"Really? Today?" Cowley got up, put on his shoes and ran after Fen.

The soldier led them out a side door of the palace, across the lawns and into an area of the castle grounds where Fen had never been before. There were a number of low, wooden buildings. Soldiers were stirring, emerging from some of the buildings yawning and stretching. The sun was approaching the horizon.

They followed him to an open area up against the back wall of the castle. There were a number of wooden racks filled with weapons—swords, spears, pikes, maces and halberds. A half dozen other boys were already there, looking lost. "Wait here," the soldier said, and walked off.

The boys looked at each other. Fen could see they were all nervous, though some hid it better than others. One boy in particular, a chubby kid with sandy hair and red cheeks, looked like he was about to cry. One boy, older and bigger than the rest, with dark hair and a sullen expression, stood off by himself, leaning up against one of the weapon racks, ignoring the others.

There were also two boys who were clearly brothers, they looked so much alike. They were both painfully thin and black-haired. Their eyes darted here and there, as if expecting to be attacked at any moment.

Rounding out their little group was a gap-toothed boy who was smiling uneasily, and one boy who was considerably shorter than everyone else.

A soldier emerged from one of the buildings and walked toward them.

"Line up!" he barked.

The boys assembled into a ragged line facing him. He paced back and forth slowly, looking them over. He was a short, wiry little man, his hair iron gray and cut severely short. His nose was flat like it had been broken a lot of times and Fen could see a scar that ran up his forearm and disappeared into his shirt sleeve. He wore knee-high boots and a leather jerkin over a short-sleeved cotton shirt. A long dagger hung at his hip. The badge sewn to his jerkin marked him as a sergeant.

"I've never trained children before," he said at last.

"I'm not a child," the biggest boy said. The others looked at him in surprise. He looked like he was probably fifteen.

The sergeant walked over to him and looked him up and down. "So what are you then?"

"I'm a man."

"Really?" The sergeant's tone was neutral. There was no mockery there. "We'll see, I suppose." He swung to look at the rest of them. "Any other men here?"

The boys exchanged looks, unsure what to make of this. Was it a trap? None of them spoke. Fen tried to appear invisible.

"I'm Sergeant Flint," the man said. "I've been in this army since long before any of you pups were born. I'll be straight with you. I'm not happy about training children. I figure there's lots of things my time would be better spent on.

"But I'm a soldier. And when I'm given orders, I follow them. Right now my orders are to turn a bunch of barely-weaned kids into soldiers. No matter how long it takes. I aim to do just that." He hitched up his trousers and paced down the line again. "Any of you have an argument with that?"

No reply.

"There is one other thing, before we begin. I have been told that I am allowed to rid myself of any who cannot make the grade. Do you know what this means?"

Again, no one answered. To Fen's surprise, Sergeant Flint turned to him.

"What's your name?"

"Fen, sir," he croaked.

"What do I mean by this, Fen?"

"That…if we don't do good enough, we're out of the squad. I think."

A faint smile curled Flint's lip. "There you go thinking, Fen. That's a bad habit in a soldier."

"Yes, sir."

"Fen is correct. If you can't handle what I have in store for you, you will be gone. If you cannot keep up, you will fall and we will leave you. I'm not your mama and it is not my job to baby you. I'm going to be hard on you. I'm going to push you until you drop, then I'll push you some more. There will be many times when you hate me. There will be many times when you want to quit."

He studied each of them in turn, as if he was looking for something. Most of the boys looked down when he was looking at them, but Fen forced himself to meet the man's gaze. To his surprise he saw no harshness in the sergeant's eyes. What he saw instead was a challenge. And he knew that if he answered that challenge, he would find more inside himself than he'd ever known was there.

"I promise you one thing," Flint said, his voice somewhat softer. "If you do what I tell you to the best of your ability and you never quit, I *will* make soldiers out of you. I will make you into the best damn squad in this whole army. That is my promise to you."

"When do we get swords?" the oldest boy asked. He was standing with his hands jammed in his pockets, scowling.

"What's your name?"

"Strout."

"Strout, why do you want a sword so badly?"

The boy blinked, surprised by the question.

"Answer the question, Strout. Say what's on your mind."

"The truth?"

"It is the only thing I ever want from any of you."

"I want to kill the bastards who killed my parents."

Flint let his gaze run across the rest of them. "Anyone else here feel the same way?"

Other hands went up, including Fen's. Cowley's didn't.

Flint nodded. "I know how you feel. I lost people too. But I'll tell you something right now, something you may not want to hear, but it's the truth, which is the only thing I'll ever give you. You'll never get your chance. You'll never find the ones that did this to you. If revenge is your purpose for being here, then best you walk away right now, because revenge isn't enough. It won't keep you going when things get tough, but it might just get you killed in battle. Emotions make you lose your head, and when you lose your head you forget your training and make mistakes. Fatal mistakes."

He was staring at Strout while he talked and when he finished what he had to say he continued staring at him, waiting to see how the boy would react.

"Is that supposed to make a difference?" Strout said. "What you said?"

"Not now. Maybe someday. Maybe to some of you."

"So no sword today."

"Not today."

Strout's jaw was tight and his fists were bunched. Fen had the feeling he was very close to walking out.

"You're staying?" Flint asked him after a moment.

Strout shrugged. "For now."

The sun was rising and it was getting warmer. "We'll start with pushups. Drop to the ground and begin," Flint said, and began counting them off.

What followed was torture. They did pushups until none of them could get off the ground anymore, then it was time for sit ups. Fen did them until his stomach burned and he thought he was going to throw up. Then, mindful of what the Fist had said about working hard and becoming an officer, he forced himself to do a few more. A half dozen other exercises followed until they began to blur together. There was so much sweat running into Fen's eyes that most of the time he couldn't see much of anything, but when he wiped at the sweat it didn't seem to make any difference so after a while he gave it up and focused on simply trying to survive each exercise.

Finally Flint said, "Take a water break."

The boys staggered to a wooden bucket sitting on a stool at the edge of the practice yard. The smallest boy got there first and he was just holding the ladle up to his mouth when Strout snatched it from him and pushed him aside.

The small boy fell down but he got right back up, put his head down and charged Strout. Strout dropped the ladle and the two boys went down, fists flying. The small boy fought hard but he was no match for Strout's size and strength and soon the bigger boy was sitting on his chest punching him.

Fen glanced at the sergeant, expecting him to do something, but Flint was over by one of the barracks, talking to a soldier, and didn't seem to notice. Fen looked around and saw that no one else was doing anything and without thinking he acted.

He grabbed Strout's hand the next time he drew it back to punch the small boy. "That's enough. You won. Can't you see that?"

"Butt out," Strout snapped.

But Cowley stepped up too. "He's right. Give the kid a break. What are you trying to prove?"

Strout jerked his hand away from Fen and gave him a shove as he stood up. "Don't touch me. Don't ever touch me." He went to the water bucket. The chubby boy was drinking and when Strout glared at him he handed the ladle over wordlessly.

The small boy climbed to his feet. His lip was split and bleeding and there was dirt in his hair. "I don't need you to fight my battles," he snarled. "I can take care of myself."

He stomped off and Cowley turned to Fen. "He seemed pretty grateful, don't you think?"

"I couldn't let Strout beat him up," Fen said.

"And now you made two new friends."

"You're a lot of help."

Cowley grinned. "I try."

After the water break, Flint lined them up for another set of exercises but Strout just stood there with his arms crossed.

"Does this mean you're quitting?" Flint asked.

"I'm not quitting," Strout said belligerently. "But I'm done with these stupid exercises. I don't need them. I'm strong enough already, stronger than these kids."

"Let me make sure I'm clear on this," Flint replied. "You don't think you need to do any more exercises because you're already strong enough. You don't see the point. Is that it?"

"Give me a sword and let me start practicing with it."

"You want to go straight to training with a sword? Okay, then." Flint nodded toward a rack filled with swords. "Go get a sword." Strout looked at him suspiciously and Flint added, "I mean it. Go get a sword."

Still looking like he was expecting a trap, Strout walked over to the rack.

"Get one for me too," Flint called after him. "We'll spar."

The swords were ugly things, blunted, dull and badly notched, obviously only used for practice. Still, they were weapons and they could injure a person and all the boys watched raptly, wondering what was going to happen. Was Flint going to beat Strout for disobeying him? And why hadn't Flint at least yelled at him? Wasn't yelling what sergeants did?

"Here," Flint said, "hold it like this." He adjusted Strout's grip. "Put your feet like this, with your weight balanced." His voice was utterly calm, betraying not a hint of anger or even irritation.

He stepped back and faced the boy. "Are you ready?"

Strout's eyes darted around and it looked to Fen like he was regretting his decision but it was too late to back down now. "I'm ready."

"Attack me."

Strout gave a halfhearted swipe with his sword, still looking unsure. Flint easily sidestepped it.

"Not like that. A real attack. Put everything you've got into it."

This time Strout swung a little harder. Flint blocked the blow.

"Better, but still weak. Come on, lad. I thought you said you were strong."

Strout's jaw set and this time he came at Flint in earnest, putting his shoulders into the blows, aiming for Flint's head. Flint blocked the first attack and easily dodged the others, his feet moving constantly. Fen noticed how easy he made it look, how natural.

After about a minute Strout pulled up. He was breathing hard now and the tip of his sword was wavering.

"Your sword's getting a little heavier now, isn't it?" Flint said. "It's not so easy swinging a piece of steel around."

"I'm not tired," Strout insisted.

"Good. Let's keep going. Attack me again. If you can hit me even once I'll let you out of the rest of the day's exercises."

Strout bit his lip and threw himself at Flint, swinging as hard as he could. He didn't even last a minute this time before he had to stop. His mouth was open and he was panting.

"Come on, don't give up now," Flint said.

"I need to catch my breath, hold on," Strout gasped.

"There's no time. Come on, lad. I'm the man who killed your parents. You have me right where you want me. Finish me off. Get your revenge." As he said this, he smacked Strout on the shoulder with the flat of his blade, hard enough that it had to hurt.

Strout muttered a curse and charged him, swinging his blade wildly. As before, Flint easily evaded or parried every attack. And every time Strout began to fade, Flint taunted him some more, insulting him, whacking him with his sword.

Finally, Strout dropped his sword and stood with his hands on his knees, gasping for air. Flint came up to him and jabbed him in the chest with his sword. Strout didn't even respond.

"And...you're dead." Flint wasn't even breathing hard. There was no sweat on his face. "Still think you're strong enough?" Strout glared at him without replying.

Flint turned to the rest of them. "There's a lot more to strength than muscles. There's endurance. Battles can last all day. If you get too tired to fight you don't get to simply leave and take a break. No, if you get too tired, you die. It's as simple as that." He turned back to Strout. "*That's* why you're doing all these exercises. I'm trying to keep you alive."

He picked up Strout's sword and returned both weapons to the rack. He looked at the sky.

"Time for chow. The mess hall's that way. Be back here in half a bell."

⚞ ⚞ ⚞

There were only a dozen or so soldiers in the mess hall and they all turned to look when the boys entered. The mess hall had a dirt floor and a dozen tables with benches. At the back, behind a long table, was the cook, standing over a big pot.

"It's true, then," one of the soldiers said, a young man who still had a bandage wrapped around his head. "They're training children now."

"They're quaking in Marad right now," the one sitting next to him said. A number of the soldiers laughed.

"If you boys are looking for your mama's teats the stable's two buildings over," a man with a bushy mustache said. The laughter was even louder now.

A sergeant, his beard thick and shot with gray, made a show of counting them out loud. "That's eight of them. That means none of them quit yet." He elbowed the soldier next to him. "Time to pay up, Ely."

Ely had his arm in a sling and small, deep set eyes. He handed over a copper coin and glared at the chubby boy. "What's your name, fat boy?"

The boy's cheeks reddened and he looked to the other boys for help. Then he looked back at Ely. "It's Luk...Lukas."

"Well, Lukas, you just cost me a copper. What do you have to say about that?"

Lukas looked like he wanted to run away. His eyes darted around the room. "I'm sorry," he said finally in a low voice.

Ely got up and walked over to him. He was a heavy set man and up close Fen could see that his eyes were badly bloodshot. He poked Lukas in the chest. "You better not go and quit this afternoon, you hear? Your time to quit was this morning. That's what I had in the pool."

Lukas stared up at him, quaking visibly.

"Lay off the boy, Ely," the sergeant said then. "It won't do any good to scare him to death now, will it?"

Ely swung back to look at the sergeant. "What are they doing here anyway, Tempus?" he asked sullenly. "They're nothing but children. Are we wet nurses now?"

Tempus shrugged. "You got a question, take it up with the Fist. From what I heard the orders came down from him. You ain't the only one bent about it. Word is Arkannen is beside himself."

"Arkannen's a twit," Ely grunted. "But in this case I agree with him. They've got no place here. Let them come back when they're old enough to grow hair."

"In case you haven't noticed, we're a little short-handed right now," the sergeant said.

"But *children*?"

"Try to think past your next bottle, Ely. Think long term. Children grow up." He spun the coin he'd won on the table. "You want to try and get your money back, bet on whether the fat one will make it to the end of the day?"

"I want a piece of that," one of the other soldiers chimed in, and was echoed by two more.

"I'll be happy to take your money, then," the sergeant replied. "But there's a long afternoon ahead of these lads and I'll be wanting some longer odds this time."

Fen, standing behind Lukas, was watching the boy while they said this. He saw how Lukas flinched, as if the words were stones.

"C'mon, let's eat," he said, pushing Lukas forward. Strout and the two black-haired brothers had already made their way up to where the cook waited to serve them.

"Use it," he said softly to Lukas when they were past Ely. "Let it make you mad. Prove them wrong." Lukas nodded, but he kept his face lowered.

"Don't listen to him, Lukas," Cowley added. "I know Ely and he's nothing but a drunk. He hates everyone."

The cook, a large, square man with a patchy beard and his left arm missing at the elbow, welcomed the boys when they picked up their bowls.

"Cheer up, boys. It'll get easier, you know. In no time this will all seem like nothing."

"Sure it will," Cowley said, rubbing his arm. "Unless my arms fall off first."

The cook laughed and ladled some stew into their bowls. "You're young yet. You'll bounce back."

The next in line to get food was the boy with the gap-toothed smile. He was staring at the cook's missing arm. Noticing his look, the cook said, "Quite the trophy, isn't it?"

The boy looked uneasy. "How did it happen?"

"Cut myself shaving one day," the cook said. "That's why I don't shave no more."

"Really?" the boy said, then frowned. "That's not what happened, is it?"

"No, but it's better than the real story," the cook said, filling his bowl. "Which has a lot of screaming and bleeding in it." He looked down at the missing arm. "You wouldn't think it, but all these years later and I can still feel it sometimes."

The boys got their food and sat down. Strout sat at a table by himself, his back to the rest of them. The black-haired brothers sat at a table in the corner, away from the others. The other five boys all sat together.

"My name's Cowley. I'm only telling you that so you know what name to put on my grave when I die this afternoon."

"I'm Gage," the gap-toothed boy said. "I've never been so tired in my life. I don't know that I can make it through the rest of the day."

"It ain't botherin' me at all," the small boy said, in between shoveling bites of food into his mouth.

"Sure it's not," Cowley said. "You got a name?"

The boy gave him a suspicious look. "Who wants to know?"

"Uh, Cowley, remember? I said my name like a minute ago," Cowley said sarcastically. "You have some problem with people knowing your name or what?"

The small boy mumbled something but it was lost in the next mouthful of food.

"Maybe more words and less food next time," Cowley said.

"It's Noah," the small boy said belligerently.

"Now, see, that didn't hurt so much, did it? There's no reason we can't all be friendly here. Looks like we'll be spending a lot of time together."

"I don't need friends," Noah said with a baleful look.

"Can you believe this kid?" Cowley said to Fen. "Next time I say we let Strout beat him up."

Noah flipped him a rude gesture and Cowley laughed but he broke off quickly. "Ouch, that hurts. I can't believe it hurts to laugh. What have I gotten myself into?"

"How are you doing, Lukas?" Fen asked the chubby kid. He was bent over his bowl and hadn't looked up since they sat down.

"I'm okay," he said in a small voice.

"You're not still upset about what those soldiers said, are you?" Cowley said. "What do they know?"

"Cowley's right," Fen said. "You made it through the morning. You can make it till the end of the day."

Lukas rubbed his eyes but didn't reply.

"Why do you care? He ain't nothing but a baby," Noah said disdainfully.

"You get beat up a lot, don't you, Noah?" Cowley said.

"You wanna try me?" the small boy said.

Cowley shook his head but didn't reply.

While he ate, Fen looked over at the black-haired brothers. They had their heads close together and it looked like the taller one was saying something to the shorter one. Then it was like they felt Fen looking at them because the taller one broke off what he was saying and both boys looked up and stared at Fen. The look in their eyes was hollow and empty of emotion and Fen looked away, suddenly uneasy.

Cowley noticed. "Strout's an ass and Noah here clearly has some kind of disorder, but those two make me nervous. There's something wrong with them I tell you."

"I wonder what their story is, what happened to them to make them like that," Fen replied.

Noah glanced over his shoulder at them, then went back to his food. "They're ferals," he said. "Nothing but wild animals."

"What do you mean by that?" Fen asked, but Noah got up and took his bowl up for another serving and didn't answer.

"Steer clear of them. That's my advice," Cowley said.

Chapter 9

The afternoon was more of the same. By the end of the day Fen thought he was going to die. He'd never imagined he could be so tired. His arms and legs felt like they were made of wood. He wanted to cry, but even that felt like too much effort. Finally, as the sun was about to go down, Flint called a halt. He told them to line up, then walked down the line looking them over.

"I'll be honest with you boys," he said. "I thought at least half of you would quit today. I deliberately pushed you, wanting to see how many of you stuck it out. And all of you did. I'm impressed, I tell you. The fact that you made it to this point means you can do this." He pointed at one of the low wooden buildings. "That's your barracks. It's your home from now on. Get some chow and a good night's sleep. Tomorrow comes early."

The boys stumbled off the practice yard and headed for the mess hall. "I blame you for this," Cowley said to Fen. "You're the one who filled my head with notions of being a soldier. I'd hit you but I can't lift my arms."

"I may need somebody to feed me," Gage said. "I can't lift my arms either."

Fen recognized some of the soldiers in the mess hall from lunch time. Money changed hands as gambling debts were paid. Sergeant Tempus saw him watching and gave him a wink. Somehow that made Fen feel better. Not much better, but a little bit.

The food probably wasn't all that good, but it tasted wonderful to Fen and he ate three helpings. By the end of the third one his stomach hurt.

When the meal was over the boys made their way to the barracks. It was a narrow, wooden building with a dozen cots arranged in two rows and not much else. There was only the single door and no windows. A wood-burning stove for heat in the winter. On each cot was a thin blanket and at the foot of each cot was a wooden chest for personal items.

Lukas staggered to the first cot and collapsed on it. Strout was on him immediately.

"That's my cot. Get off."

"I got here first," Lukas protested.

Strout grabbed his ankles and dragged him off the cot onto the floor. Lukas wailed but didn't resist. He lay on the floor, whimpering. Strout kicked him in the side. "Go do that somewhere else. I want to sleep."

Lukas rolled over onto his knees and crawled to the next cot.

"Not there. Get further away from me," Strout said harshly.

"What's your problem, Strout?" Cowley asked. "Why don't you leave him alone?"

Strout glared at Cowley. "I don't want to hear him crying during the night."

"Are you always this way? Or are you just having a bad day?"

"You better watch what you say to me or you'll be sorry."

"I already am," Cowley said. He gave Fen a look and rolled his eyes. Strout threw himself down on his cot and lay there with his hands behind his head, staring up at the ceiling.

The boys spread out and chose their cots. Cowley and Fen took cots next to each other. The dark-haired brothers took the two cots at the far end of the room. Gage took the cot across the aisle from Strout and simply lay down with all his clothes on, not even bothering to remove his shoes.

Lukas lay down heavily on the cot across the aisle from Fen. Fen could hear him crying, though he was trying to hide it. Fen wanted nothing but to lie there and go to sleep but his heart went out to Lukas and he went over and sat on the empty cot next to him. "C'mon," he said softly. "Don't cry. Tomorrow will be better. You'll see."

"I can't help it," Lukas sniffled. "I want to go home. I miss my parents."

"I told you I didn't want to hear you crying!" Strout yelled. "This is no place for babies. Stop it or get the hell out of here!"

Lukas sat up, tears running down his cheeks. "I don't have anywhere else to go!" he yelled back. "My parents are dead and they burned my home."

Strout sat up. "And that makes you special? You're not the only one who lost your family. But you don't see the rest of us crying about it, do you?"

"I hate you!" Lukas yelled at him.

Strout shrugged. "So what? You think I care what you think about me? You think I care what any of you think about me?"

"I'm going to say no," Cowley said.

Strout pointed at him. "Keep it up, funny guy. See if you don't get a fist in your face." He looked around at the rest of them. "I'm here for one reason and one reason only, to kill those who did this. You stay out of my way and I'll have no problem with you. Otherwise, I'll drive you out of this squad. I promise you that."

When no one replied, he flopped back down on his cot and went back to staring at the ceiling.

"This has been a lot of fun," Cowley said to Fen. "I can't wait to see what tomorrow brings."

"It'll get better."

"It can't get much worse, can it?"

Fen lay down and closed his eyes. He wanted nothing more than to fall asleep, even though it was barely after sunset, but for some reason he couldn't fall asleep right away. One by one the others fell asleep but he lay there for a long time, thinking about what Lukas had said, about having nowhere to go. It got him thinking about his mother. The days since her death had passed in a kind of blur. He'd been like a leaf caught up in a flood, tossed this way and that, with no time for thought or feeling.

Now, lying there in the darkness with the snores of the other boys around him, he suddenly felt very lost and alone. The pain that he'd been running from caught up to him. He had to bite down on his fist to keep from crying out. He missed his mother so badly. He remembered how she would stroke his cheek after he went to bed and tell him how proud she was of her big boy. A few months back that had started to bother him and he'd told her to quit. He was almost grown up and he didn't need stuff like that anymore. He remembered the sad look she got when he said that, but she'd agreed to stop.

Right then he would have given anything if she was there to do it one last time.

Chapter 10

It was still early the next morning when Flint came in, carrying a lantern.

"Everybody up!" he yelled. "Time for the real training to start."

"It's still dark," Cowley protested, pulling his blanket over his head. "It's not day yet."

"It's day all right. A new day and we have a lot to do." He hung the lantern on a hook and turned back to the door. "Since you're all as green as baby calves and still dreaming of your mamas, I'll take it easy on you this morning. You have five whole minutes to be lined up outside."

"What if we don't make it?" Gage asked.

"It's like I said yesterday. You can quit any time. No one is forcing you to be here."

"I hate that man," Cowley groaned after Flint had left. "I really do."

Fen wasn't sure he'd be able to get up. When he tried to lift his legs they didn't move. They hurt though, bad enough that it felt like he'd torn something. His arms hurt too, along with every muscle in his stomach and back, as he discovered when he tried to roll onto his side.

"Is it supposed to hurt this much?" he asked no one in particular.

Strout stood and stretched. "Don't be such a baby. They're called sore muscles. You get them from working. Something you've probably never done in your life."

"I have too. I helped my mother clean taverns."

"You call that work?" Strout snorted. "Try helping your father blacksmith all day. This is easy." But he winced when he bent over to put his boots on and Fen knew he was hurting more than he let on.

Fen gave up trying to sit up and simply rolled onto the floor, managing to get his arms up just enough to keep from smacking his head. He pushed himself into a sitting position, every muscle crying out.

At that moment he was glad he hadn't undressed before bed. Putting his shoes on was hard enough. He couldn't imagine how hard it would be to put his arms over his head and pull his shirt on. The way they felt now, he might never be able to raise his arms again.

His shoes on, he bent over—gritting his teeth against the pain—and poked Cowley. "Come on, Cowley. Time to get up."

"I don't want to. I changed my mind about being a soldier. I realized I *like* mopping floors and you know why?"

"It's easy?"

"Exactly."

"What about the girls? Are you giving up on them too?" Cowley had said more than once how much girls loved a man in uniform and how many hearts he planned on breaking once he had his.

One eye opened and fixed on him. "That was cruel, Fen. Even for you."

"So you're getting up?"

Cowley groaned and swung his legs off the side of the bed. "I'm getting up. But I'm doing it under protest."

Fen turned and saw that Lukas hadn't moved at all. He went over to his cot and shook him. "Come on, Lukas."

"I can't," came the muffled reply. Lukas had his blanket pulled over his head.

"Leave him alone," Strout barked. "Let him stay there. He's too weak for this. He's still a baby."

Lukas sat up and pushed the blanket away. "I'm not too weak!" he yelled.

"Are too. Too weak. Too fat."

"I am *not!*" Lukas lurched up from the bed, his pudgy hands clenched into fists. "You take that back!"

"Too fat. Too weak. Too scared." Strout said it like a chant.

Lukas charged at him, fists flying. The bigger boy punched him once and then threw him down, where Lukas lay on his side, moaning.

"Why don't you leave him alone?" Fen said.

"Why don't you mind your own business?" Strout replied. "He's a weakling and I don't want any weaklings in my squad." He stalked out the door.

Fen crouched down beside Lukas. "You're running out of time," Fen said.

"I'm *not* too weak," Lukas mumbled. "I hate him."

"Then prove him wrong," Fen said. "That's the best way to get back at him."

Lukas opened his eyes and looked at Fen. Then, wearily, he dragged himself to his feet.

The boys stumbled out into the predawn, rubbing their eyes and yawning. There was barely enough light to see by, the sunrise streaking the sky in the east.

"So who's ready for a nice run down to the docks and back?" Flint said with a big smile.

"Don't we get breakfast first?" Noah asked. From how small he was, Fen didn't think he could be more than eleven. Twelve at the most.

"You'll break your fast after the run. Unless you fall too far behind." Flint grinned wickedly. "In which case you'll miss it."

A chorus of groans and muttered curses greeted these words. It all made Flint's smile broader.

"Cheer up, lads. I have a present for each of you." There was a large canvas bag on the ground by his feet and he reached into it and pulled something out and held it up. The boys peered at it, trying to see what it was.

"Hmm, this is the big one." Flint tossed it to Strout, then pulled out another. This one he tossed to Fen.

It was cold and heavy. "Chain mail?" Fen said.

"The very same. Like real soldiers wear." Flint continued tossing them out.

That improved their moods considerably. They chattered to each other as they pulled their new mail shirts on. The mail was old and rusty and had clearly been patched many times, but it was still mail. Fen fingered a spot on his that had been patched. It was right over his chest. He wondered if the last man who'd worn this had died from the wound.

"Do you like them?" Flint asked. He chuckled. "We'll see if you still feel the same in an hour. Let's move out."

They followed him, running across the castle grounds, out the shattered gates, and down the broad boulevard on the other side.

They hadn't gone very far before the meaning of Flint's cryptic words became clear.

The thing about chain mail, Fen realized, is that it's made of metal. And metal is heavy.

So heavy.

Before they were halfway to the docks he hated his mail shirt and he knew the rest of them felt the same. It was like having a lead weight tied to him, dragging him down.

They staggered up to the docks. The sun was rising by then. Most of the fishermen had already set out in their small boats. The larger boats, trading vessels with triangular sails, their long oars shipped, were being loaded with crates and barrels of goods, bound for either Narom to the south, or Seavale to the north.

"A fine morning!" Flint called out to some of the sailors as he slowed and came to a halt.

"What's with the flock of ducklings following you?" one of them called back.

"They're the Fist's new elite troops!"

"Then we're doomed," another sailor said. "They're naught but children."

"Aye, but children become men. And when these are grown…" Flint cast his eye over them. They were bent over, hands on knees, wheezing and panting. "They'll be something. Won't you, lads?"

He waved to the sailors. "Well, we're off now. The lads are getting restless. Have to keep moving or they get bored."

The boys staggered after him, each of them knowing, and dreading, that the hardest part of the run, the uphill part, was yet to come.

They weren't even halfway back to the castle when Fen heard a cry and a thud behind him. He turned and saw that Lukas had fallen and was lying in the street. He jogged back to him.

"Get up, Lukas." He would have bent down to offer him a hand but he was afraid if he did he would fall down too, and he wasn't sure he could get back up. He was unbelievably tired and the thought that the day was only beginning made him want to cry. Cry and lie down beside Lukas in the street.

"I can't," Lukas wailed. "I can't go another step. I'm done for."

Flint called a halt and came jogging back. "Go wait with the rest, Fen," he said. "I'll handle this."

Flint looked down at Lukas. "You did better than I thought, Lukas. It's no shame to quit now."

"You're not...you're not going to yell at me?" the chubby boy said, sitting up and wiping tears from his face.

"Of course not. You did the best you could. It's not your fault it's too much for you, is it?"

"No," Lukas sniffled.

"But mail shirts cost dear. I'll need that one you're wearing back from you before I go."

Lukas looked up at him. "I have to give it back?"

"What else?" Flint held out his hand. "Give it over now, so we can get on with our run."

Lukas looked doubtful. He turned and looked up at the castle, sitting on the hill. "Maybe I can go a little further."

"You sure?"

Lukas staggered to his feet and took a deep breath. "No. But I'm going to try."

⚜ ⚜ ⚜

Somehow Fen made it up the hill to the castle. Surprisingly, the one who made it there first was Noah, even though his mail shirt was so big on him it hung down to his knees. The small boy ran angrily, muttering to himself the whole time. It was as if he was possessed by his own demons and he was determined to beat them. Maybe he was, Fen thought.

Flint stopped them outside the mess hall.

"What are we waiting for?" Strout complained.

"We're waiting for Lukas." Lukas hadn't yet come into sight.

"Why do we have to wait for him?"

"You're a squad. You eat together. You sleep together. You do everything together or not at all."

Strout looked unhappy at that, but he didn't say anything more.

After a few minutes Lukas came stumbling up. His face was red and he was sweating profusely.

"Now you can go eat," Flint said. "Be in the practice yard in fifteen minutes."

Fen patted Lukas on the shoulder as he staggered by. "Good job, Lukas. I knew you could do it."

Actually, he'd had serious doubts that Lukas could, but it seemed like the boy could use some cheering up. Lukas didn't reply, but the look he gave Fen was grateful.

╬   ╬   ╬

Late in the day, Flint had them stand in a circle.

"Look at those around you," he said. "Tell me what you see."

The boys looked at each other, confused by where he was going with this.

Flint answered his own question. "You see strangers, don't you? Random people you got stuck in a squad with. People you have nothing in common with. Right?"

A few of the boys nodded hesitantly.

"Wrong. There's one thing you all have in common. You're all orphans. You've got nothing. No family. No home. Nothing."

The words were harsh and the boys flinched under them, except for the dark-haired brothers, both of whom were staring at the ground, their faces expressionless.

"But orphans isn't all you are. You're something more. Look at each other again. Go on, look. You too, Wallice and Eben," he said, speaking to the two brothers. Fen didn't think he'd yet heard either one speak a word.

The boys exchanged quick, awkward glances, uncomfortable with what was happening. The brothers barely glanced up, their eyes flicking over the others too fast to make contact, and then back to the ground.

"What did you see?" Flint asked.

"Where's this going, sergeant?" Strout asked. "Why do we have to do this?"

Flint ignored him and continued. "What did you *see?*"

Finally, Fen spoke up. "I saw my squad mates."

"That's better. Still not there, but better. It'll take you some time still, but I'll tell you what you're eventually going to see when you look at the others around you.

"You're going to see your brothers."

Strout scoffed. Flint glanced at him, but let it slide. The others all looked skeptical too.

"Boys, this is your new family. In time they'll be closer than any family you've ever had, because you'll go through things together that you never went through with your old family. You'll

71

sweat together, bleed together. You'll fight each other, of course. But it won't mean anything because you're brothers. You don't believe me now, but trust me, it will come. Now go get some chow. I'll see you tomorrow."

The boys headed for the mess hall. Cowley walked beside Fen.

"What did you think of that?" Fen asked him.

Before Cowley could reply, Strout spoke up. "It's a steaming pile of horse shit. You're not my brothers. I never had a brother before and I don't have one now. Old Flint has gone soft in the head is all."

"If you were my brother I'd have already strangled you in your sleep," Noah said.

"You'd try. But your hands are so small you probably couldn't get them around my throat. I'd probably sleep through the whole thing."

Fen grabbed hold of Noah's shoulder before he could go after Strout again. "He's just trying to wind you up. Don't let him get to you."

"I'm too tired and hungry to care about what Flint said," Gage said. "I just want to eat and sit down for a little while."

╬ ╬ ╬

After eating, Fen and Cowley sat down on a bench outside the barracks. It wasn't quite dark yet. Fen was tired, but he didn't want to go to bed. He was afraid he would have trouble sleeping again, thinking about his mother.

"What are you thinking about?" Cowley asked.

Fen answered without thinking. "My mother." Then he wished he hadn't said it. He didn't want Cowley to tease him.

But instead Cowley surprised him by putting his arm around Fen's shoulders. "I'm sorry."

Fen swallowed hard and tried to get a hold of himself. "That's why I want to be a soldier. I want to be strong. I want to know how to fight. I want to defend Samkara, so that no other children have to see their mothers die."

Now he was sure he'd said too much. Cowley would make fun of him, tell him he was being sappy.

Once again Cowley surprised him. "You're going to be a great soldier," Cowley said. "I can tell that about you. There's something about you, a kind of strength I guess."

72

Fen wasn't sure he'd heard him right. "You really think so?"

"I said it didn't I?"

"Why do you want to be a soldier?"

Cowley gave him a crooked grin. "I already told you. I hate mopping floors. And the girls. Don't forget the girls. I like them even more than I hate mopping floors."

"But there has to be more to it than that. Did you…was your mother killed too? When the Maradi sacked the city?"

"Nope."

"Your mother's still alive?"

Cowley shrugged. "I don't know. She might be."

"How could you not know?"

"Because I've never met her. At least not that I can remember."

"What about your father?"

"Never met him either."

"You've been an orphan your whole life?"

"I guess so."

"Who took care of you? There must be someone…"

"Sure. Sort of. Old Willem has always been nice to me. I guess you could say he's sort of like a grandfather to me. And Aven, one of the cooks, she always puts aside little treats for me."

"And they…were they killed by the Maradi?"

"Nope. None of the palace servants were. Old lady Ella died, but I think it was her heart. She was older than the moon anyway."

"Really? But the Maradi killed so many. How did you all escape?"

"We're servants, that's how. Servants are invisible. No one sees us unless they need someone to blame for something. When the Maradi broke into the palace we were already hiding in our quarters. They didn't even come down onto our level."

"Why not?"

"Why would they? To steal some rags? Servants don't own anything. If *you* were plundering a city, would you bother searching the servants' quarters?"

"I would never plunder a city."

"You sure about that? Even if everybody else was?"

"I want to be a soldier to protect people. I would never harm innocent people."

"What if they were Maradi?"

"I will fight their soldiers. But not the people. Not the women and children."

Cowley laughed. "The funny thing is Fen, I actually believe you."

Chapter 11

Days passed and the training got harder and harder. But so did the boys. Fen no longer felt like he was going to die at the end of every day. He noticed muscles in his arms that had never been there before. It felt good, getting stronger, realizing that he was actually getting somewhere. He still hurt all the time, but he could look ahead to a point where that would change.

One afternoon, after a light meal and a short break, they got a surprise. Flint was waiting for them in the practice yard, a pile of sheathed swords and sword belts beside him.

"Buckle these on," he said, handing the weapons out to the boys. Once they were all buckled on, he said, "Draw your weapons."

Fen's sword wasn't much to look at, coarse, blunted iron with a metal grip and a badly-notched edge. But it was a sword, a real sword, and right then it looked beautiful to him. Most of the other boys were looking at their swords the same way, except for Strout.

"My father made swords," he said, "and he would have melted a thing like this down before he let it leave his shop."

"It's a poor excuse for a blade, it's true," Flint agreed. "But good enough for the practice yard, and good enough until you lads learn how to properly care for a sword. And how to use one."

Strout didn't reply, but his look stayed sour.

Then Flint began to teach them the ways of the sword. He showed them how to parry and how to thrust, making them repeat the simple actions scores of times, until Fen's arm ached and it was hard to hold the sword up. Flint moved among them while they practiced, adjusting grips, critiquing their movements.

"It's a sword, not a club," he said to Eben, the younger of the two silent brothers. "If you swing like that you'll over balance and end up helpless, like a turtle on its back. You boys stop and watch this." He drew his sword. "Eben, take a swing at me. Don't hold back."

Eben's face screwed up and he brought his sword back behind his head, wound up, and swung as hard as he could at Flint, grunting as he did so.

Flint eased back, letting the sword fly harmlessly by him, then, before Eben had a chance to recover, he stepped in and pressed the tip of his sword against Eben's chest.

"And...you're dead. Just like that."

He turned to the rest of them. "The big problem with what he just did is balance. He lost his and couldn't recover it. You boys think swordplay is all about flashing blades, but it's not." He pointed at his feet. "It starts here, with footwork. It moves up into the hips and the shoulders. If you want to be good with a sword, you must remember that. Move your feet and keep them under you. Keep the balance on the balls of your feet and your hips loose. You must be ready to move instantly in any direction and maintain your balance at all times."

He sheathed his sword. "Pair up, and let's have some sparring."

Fen turned to Cowley, but Flint stopped him. "I want you sparring against Strout."

"But he's a lot bigger than me," Fen protested. Strout was a head taller and a lot wider in the shoulders.

"You think you'll never face anyone bigger than you on the battlefield?" Flint said. "He's bigger, but you're quicker. Use that quickness, boy. Move your feet."

Fen dodged Strout's first thrust without too much trouble, swiping at it clumsily with his own sword as he did so. Strout followed that up with a backhand slash. Fen just managed to get his sword in front of it, but Strout's blow had enough force that the blades smacked into his leg hard enough to hurt.

Fen tried his own attack, lunging and jabbing at Strout's stomach. Strout swatted his jab aside and slashed at him again. This time Fen couldn't react in time. His own jab had carried him too far forward and he was off balance. Strout's blade hit him in the shoulder, causing him to yelp. Strout smiled and raised his blade in mock salute.

"Use your feet," Flint said. "Keep moving."

Around them the other boys were sparring, but Fen had no attention to spare for them. Especially not when Strout renewed his attack. The larger boy came in fast and hard, raining blows down on Fen. Fen blocked two of them and dodged another but then came the one he couldn't do anything about.

Strout's blade whistled through the air and struck Fen hard over his left ear. Lights flashed behind his eyes. He fell to the ground and lost his sword.

As if from a distance, Fen heard Flint yell, "Careful! You're not supposed to kill each other!"

Fen blinked, trying to clear his vision. His ears were ringing. Dimly he could see Strout staring at him, his eyes wide.

Flint was still berating the larger boy. "What are you thinking? You could turn the boy simple with a blow like that."

He crouched down in front of Fen and examined the side of his head. "I don't believe it," he said.

"What?" Fen asked. His tongue felt thick in his mouth. He tried to get up but Flint held him down.

"How come you're not bleeding? A blow like that, you should be bleeding like a stuck pig."

"He didn't hit me that hard."

"I saw it happen and he did hit you that hard. Even a dull blade should have opened your skull like a melon. Is your head made out of stone or what?"

"I'm fine." Everyone was gathered around, staring at him. Fen didn't like it. He tried to get up again.

Flint held up two fingers in front of his face. "How many fingers am I holding up?"

"Two."

"Follow my fingers with your eyes." He moved his hand side to side.

"Can I get up now?"

Flint stood and helped him up. "Why don't you sit out for a bit?"

But Fen had seen that there was a new arrival in the practice yard. Barik was standing over by a weapon rack, watching.

"I'm fine, I told you. I want to spar some more." Fen pulled away and looked around for his sword.

"Everyone take a break. Go get some water." Flint walked over to Barik.

Strout fell in beside Fen as he headed to the water bucket.

"If you think this means I'm going to take it easy on you next time, you're wrong. Next time I'll hit you twice as hard."

"Maybe next time I'll crack *your* skull."

"Sure, like that will ever happen." Strout looked at the side of his head. "You sure have a hard head, though."

Strout pushed his way through the other boys clustered around the water bucket and grabbed the ladle from Lukas. Cowley moved over next to Fen.

"You really okay? I saw how hard he hit you."

"It's just a bump. It hardly even hurts." Fen touched the spot, expecting to find a large, tender lump there. But there was nothing. Except...

There was something hard stuck in his scalp. He pulled it out and looked at it.

"What's that?" Cowley asked.

It was a little shard of stone, about the size of his fingernail. "Nothing," Fen said. "A piece of rock. It must have gotten stuck in my hair when I fell down."

Cowley took it and looked at it. "Huh. Maybe Flint's right. Maybe your head *is* made of stone." He made as if to toss the stone aside but Fen took it from him and stuck it in his pocket.

Strout finished drinking, but instead of handing the ladle back to Lukas he dumped the rest of the water in it over the chubby boy's head, then held it up in the air where Lukas couldn't reach it.

"I really hate that guy," Cowley said. "I hope when I finally start growing I get bigger than him. I can't wait to make him pay for how he treats us."

While waiting to get some water, Fen surreptitiously looked over at Barik and Flint. Flint was talking and Barik was listening intently. At one point both men looked up and right at Fen, who quickly turned his eyes away. His face burned at the thought that Barik had seen him get knocked down like that. He wanted to spar again, right then, to show Barik that he really could fight.

But by the time they were done getting water, Barik was gone.

"No more sparring for today," Flint said. "I want to start teaching you some wrestling."

"Wrestling?" Strout said with a sneer. "What are we, farmers?" He had his sword in his hand and he held it up. "We fight with these."

Quick as a wink Flint's blade shot out and rapped Strout on the wrist, hard. Strout yelped and dropped his blade.

"It's the middle of a battle and you just dropped your weapon," Flint said, tossing his sword down. "What are you going to do now?"

Holding his wrist, Strout looked at him, confused, and Flint acted. He took two quick steps forward. One hand grabbed Strout's wrist, the other his shoulder. Then he did something Fen couldn't quite follow and suddenly Strout was lying on his back and Flint was on top of him, his knee planted on his chest.

"You don't want to be helpless without your blade, do you?"

"I wasn't ready," Strout said sullenly.

Flint hopped up and turned to the boys. "That, right there, is perhaps the most useless excuse in the world. The point of being a fighter, a real fighter, is to always be ready. Those who aren't ready end up dead."

The rest of the afternoon was taken up with learning about leverage, arm locks, hip throws and so on. Fen had done some wrestling with other boys while growing up—who hadn't?—and thought he knew a few things, but he soon realized he knew nothing at all.

When they finally stopped for the day the sun was just going down. "Buckle on your swords, boys," Flint said. "From now on the swords, and the mail shirts, are part of you. Unless you're sleeping or I tell you to take them off, you'll wear them constantly."

As the boys trudged wearily toward the mess hall two young servant girls hurried by, carrying baskets. They eyed the boys, one whispered to the other, and they both giggled.

Cowley strutted toward them. "Hello, ladies. You want to see my sword?" The grin on his face and his tone made it clear he wasn't talking about his weapon.

This brought forth a fresh wave of giggling and then the braver of the two, a girl with long, red hair, said, "Nope. We hear it's rusted and nearly useless."

They hurried off and the other boys broke into howls of laughter at Cowley's expense. Cowley stood there staring after them, a half smile on his face.

Shaking his head, Fen grabbed Cowley's arm and pulled him toward the mess hall. "You'll say anything, won't you?"

"I think they like me," Cowley said earnestly. "Did you see the way the red-haired one looked at me?"

"You never stop, do you?"

"I try not to," Cowley said with mock seriousness.

"Come on. Let's get some food. I'm starving."

"Don't worry," Cowley told him. "I'll let you have the dark-haired one."

Chapter 12

After dinner a few nights later, Cowley pulled Fen off to one side. He looked around to make sure no one was listening, then in a low voice said, "I need your help."

Fen pulled his arm out of Cowley's grasp and eyed him critically. He'd known Cowley long enough to be suspicious when he acted like this. "With what?"

"You remember those two servant girls awhile back? The ones we spoke to that night on our way to the mess hall?"

"I remember."

"One of them—the red-haired one—has agreed to meet me later."

"Good for you. Let me know how it turns out," Fen said. When he tried to head for the barracks Cowley blocked him.

"No," Fen said firmly.

"But you haven't even heard what I was going to ask you yet."

"It's still no. I'm tired and I'm sore. Tomorrow's another long day of training and I want to go to sleep."

"You know what you are, Fen? You're an old man, that's what you are. An old man who's forgotten all about how to have fun."

"That's okay with me." Fen tried to leave again and Cowley grabbed his arm.

"Please, Fen? Just do this for me? She won't meet me unless she can bring her friend. You remember, the pretty girl with the black hair?"

"We're not supposed to leave the barracks after lights out, you know."

"But it's not like there's a lock on the door. Who will know? Come on, you owe me one."

"For what?"

"I don't know. For…stuff. Look, we're just going to get together with them for a little while. If you don't like her, we'll leave. I promise you."

Fen hesitated and Cowley pushed on. "So you miss an hour of sleep. What difference does it make? Are you really such an old man that you can't give up a little sleep?"

"One hour? You promise?"

Cowley grabbed him around the neck and dragged him close. "I knew I could count on you, Fen."

Cowley told him they'd be sneaking out of the barracks about a bell after lights out. All Fen knew was that he fell asleep almost immediately and it seemed like no time had passed before Cowley was shaking him awake.

Fen stumbled after him to the door. Cowley opened the door a crack and peeked out, then motioned Fen to follow him. Two of the other barracks were dark and silent, but there was a lamp burning in the third and low voices coming from it. There was no one out and about though and they snuck across the yard with no problem.

They passed the mess hall and the smithy and circled around the stables, which were quiet except for the occasional stamp of a horse's foot. Beyond the stables they entered onto the wide lawns of the palace grounds. Always perfectly manicured in the past, the lawns were showing signs of neglect. Weeds grew up through the grass. Some of the flowers had died and hadn't been replanted. The hedges were untrimmed.

The Fist had no interest in such things and the men who once tended the lawns had been reassigned, most put to work expanding the castle gardens. A whole section of manicured lawn had already been dug up and planted with fall potatoes and wheat. The functional was what mattered to the Fist, not the beautiful.

When Fen realized they were heading for the palace he grabbed Cowley's arm and stopped him. "We're not going in there. Tell me we're not going in there."

"Of course we are. Where did you think we were going to meet them, in the stables?"

"Why not out here?" Fen hissed. "There are benches we could sit on."

Cowley patted his shoulder and shook his head. "Poor Fen. There's still so much you don't know about girls, isn't there?"

"Oh, knock it off. Like you know anything about them."

"I know that you have to woo them if you want them to let you touch them. These aren't scullery maids that will let you paw at them under a bush, Fen. These are real quality girls, handmaids for the fancy ladies. They expect a little more."

"That's it. I'm out." Fen turned and started back the way they'd come.

Cowley practically tackled him. "You can't leave! You promised me!"

"I did *not* promise you."

"Well, you implied…"

"You misled me."

"I did *not* mislead you. I may have forgotten to mention where we were meeting them, but you didn't ask either. Really, Fen, when you think about it, isn't this actually *your* problem, rather than mine?"

At first Fen could only stare at him. "You're unbelievable, you know that?"

"Thank you. I'll take that as a compliment."

"It wasn't a compliment."

"So, now that we got that out of the way, shall we continue?" Cowley gestured toward the palace. Only a few lights burned in the place.

"If we get caught, we're going to be in so much trouble."

"But we won't get caught. Why? Because you're with me. If you were on your own, sure, you'd stumble around like a lead-footed bull, probably knock over a couple of vases and wake up the whole place. But you're not. You're with me and no one knows that big old pile of rock better than I do. I will get us in and out and no one will ever be the wiser."

For all Cowley's bravado, Fen still had a bad feeling about this. But he also knew if he backed out now he'd never hear the end of it. It was easier simply to go along and get it over with. And he had to admit that he didn't hate the idea of getting to know the black-haired girl. She seemed nice and she was awfully pretty.

"You better not get us in trouble," Fen said.

"Of course I won't get us in trouble. Now let's hurry. We don't want to keep the ladies waiting."

They hurried across the lawns, but instead of circling around to the front doors of the palace, Cowley led Fen to a small side door.

"It's a servants' entrance," Cowley said. "It'll be dark inside so hold onto my shirt."

Beyond the door was a darkened hallway. Once the door closed behind them Fen couldn't see a thing but Cowley moved ahead confidently. Holding onto Cowley's shirt, he was able to follow. They walked for a couple minutes, then Cowley opened a door. Dim light came in. He stuck his head through.

"All clear," he whispered.

Fen found himself in a wide hallway with a high ceiling covered in mosaics and gilt-framed paintings on the walls. Shadowed alcoves were spaced along the sides. As they passed the first one, Fen glimpsed an armored form standing inside it and he stopped, his heart speeding up.

"Don't worry. It's only decoration. It's not a guard," Cowley said. The armored form's hands were gripping a double-bladed ax, the head of the weapon resting on the ground between its feet. "I call this one Charlie." Cowley rapped the figure on the head softly. The alcove behind the suit of armor had a thick curtain hanging in it. "I've hidden back there many times to get out of work. Charlie's never betrayed me. We can trust him."

They went around a corner. This stretch of hallway had doors all along one side. Cowley opened the second one and drew Fen inside. The room was dark except for a tiny bit of light leaking out around the edge of the floor-length drapes that covered the window. Cowley closed the door and then fumbled around in the dark until he got the lantern lit.

When Fen saw how richly-furnished the room was he started shaking his head. "We can't be in here. This room looks like it belonged to the king." There was a huge, canopied bed, two wardrobes, a pair of chairs flanking a low table, and a doorway leading into another room.

"Relax. It's not the king's bedroom. Besides, the king's dead, remember? We have a Fist now and he sleeps on one of the upper floors of the palace."

"How do you know that?"

"I know all the servants, remember? Servants know everything and they like to talk."

"That doesn't mean it's okay to be here. If we get caught, we could end up in the dungeon." All his life Fen had heard horrible stories about the dungeon that was supposedly built underneath the palace.

"We'll be in trouble, you're right about that. But they won't put us in the dungeon."

"How can you be sure?"

"Because old King Doderick had the dungeon converted into a wine cellar. Not just wine, either, but casks and barrels of ale and rum and brandy. They store food down there too."

"Oh." That helped some, but not that much. Fen paced around the room, wishing he'd never agreed to this.

"You're making me nervous, you know. Here, have some of this. It will calm you down." Cowley handed Fen a flask.

"What is it?"

"It's brandy. Drink some."

Fen pulled the cork and sniffed it. "It smells awful."

"Tastes awful too," Cowley said brightly. "But don't let that stop you. Drink up. I can't have you sweating nervously all over the ladies."

Fen took a little sip. It burned and it tasted worse than it smelled. He handed the flask back to Cowley, who took a gulp and gasped. Tears started in the blond boy's eyes and he said roughly, "Ah, that's the good stuff."

"It's terrible."

"I know." Cowley put the cork back in.

"Then why'd you say 'that's the good stuff'?"

"Because that's what you're supposed to say."

The door opened then and Fen whirled, his heart instantly in his mouth.

It was the two girls. The red-haired one led the way. Behind her came the black-haired one. They closed the door behind them and the four of them looked at each other.

The red-haired girl looked both boys up and down frankly, a mischievous smile on her face. The other girl had her arms clasped over her chest and her face turned down.

Cowley broke the silence. "Ladies, this is my friend Fen. He's shy and more than a little dull, so don't expect much out of him."

"Hey!" Fen protested. "I'm not dull!"

The red-haired one laughed out loud and a grin crept over the dark-haired girl's face.

"Fen, the red-haired beauty before you is Amma, and her equally radiant friend is Ravin. Say hello, Fen."

"Hello, Fen," Fen said without thinking, then clamped his hand over his mouth. The girls giggled some more and he felt his face go red. Silently he vowed to get Cowley back for embarrassing him.

"Sadly," Cowley continued, "I only just now realized that this room has only two chairs in it. That means we either have to double up or, well, I guess we could sit on the bed." He winked as he said the last part.

Fen was mortified. How could Cowley say such a thing? He looked at the girls, expecting them to be outraged, to storm off and never speak to them again.

But Amma laughed and wagged her finger at Cowley. "I was warned about you, Cowley, you and your smooth tongue. I'm ready for you." Next to her Ravin was wide-eyed, her hand over her mouth.

"I can only speak the words that are in my heart," Cowley said, sketching a quick bow. "And your beauty has swept me away."

To Fen's surprise, Amma began clapping slowly. "Those are quite the fancy words, young Cowley. Did you practice them long?"

Cowley grinned. "That depends. Did you like them?"

"Hmm." Amma turned to Ravin. "What did you think?"

"I think he's a rogue," Ravin said. Her voice was small and clear and instantly Fen thought it was the most wonderful sound he'd ever heard. "Mama told me to avoid men who spoke like that."

"Good advice." Amma turned back to Cowley and with mock sternness said, "She called you a rogue, but I think a better word would be knave. Be warned, sir, we are onto you. Your tricks will not work here."

Cowley hung his head and gave her a crestfallen look. "I don't have any more fancy words right now, anyway."

"Then let's have a seat, shall we?" Amma and Ravin sat down together in one of the chairs. "Well?" she said, when the boys just stood there.

Fen and Cowley exchanged a look. Then they looked at the remaining chair. The chair had arms. It was maybe big enough for both of them, but they'd be sandwiched together pretty tightly.

"I don't feel like sitting," both boys said nearly simultaneously.

"And I won't have you looming over us like guards," Amma said. "Shall we go, Ravin?"

Another look passed between the boys and then they sat down in the chair. They were wedged in uncomfortably close to each other. Fen was glad they hadn't worn their swords.

"What's that in your hand?" Amma pointed at the flask Cowley was holding.

"Just a bit of brandy to take the edge off the night air," Cowley said. He didn't sound so cocky anymore, as if a bit of the air had gone out of him.

"Toss it over and let us have a taste." Cowley flipped the flask to her and Amma snatched it out of the air one-handed. She took a sip and wrinkled her nose. "I've had better."

"But Tevin promised me this is the same brandy that the lords drink."

"Tevin is a liar and he told you what he needed to so that you would give him your coins. This is probably the brandy they use in the kitchen for cooking." She handed the flask to Ravin, who took a tiny sip and grimaced.

Amma recorked the flask and tossed it back to Cowley, who misjudged it and dropped it. "You'll need to do better than that, knave."

Cowley picked up the flask and tried to recover his earlier aplomb. He really tried hard and Fen had to give him credit for his effort. But the confident, smooth-talking boy had lost his place and he stared down at his hands. Fen cleared his throat and tried to say something, but he found he had no words at all so he fixed his gaze on the tapestry that hung on the wall behind the girls, pretending to be fascinated by it, though it depicted an old woman sitting beside a stream.

Only Amma seemed comfortable. She spoke of this and that, sharing palace gossip and waving her hands as she talked. She had a little smile on her face the whole time and Fen could tell she was enjoying herself.

He didn't know about Ravin, though. He snuck several looks at her. The first few times she had her eyes turned down. The last time she caught his gaze and he felt his face get instantly hot and he quickly looked away.

Amma had subsided and they were sitting there in awkward silence when the door suddenly opened.

All four of them bolted up off the chairs in alarm. The open door blocked their view of whoever had opened it. From the other side of the door came a male voice.

"Come on, sweetie. Just come in here with me for a few minutes. No one will find out. I…hey, why is the lamp lit in here?"

The door swung closed and Fen and the rest found themselves staring at a surprised guardsman and a servant girl. For a few seconds all of them stared at each other in shock. The guard found his voice first.

"You kids aren't supposed to be in here," he growled. "You're going to get in lots of trouble."

A tiny squeak came from Ravin. Fen wished there was a hole nearby that he could crawl into. Even Amma seemed at a loss for words.

It was Cowley who came to their rescue. "You think *we're* going to be in trouble? We're only kids. I think you're the ones who are going to be in trouble."

The guard frowned. The woman grabbed hold of his arm.

"What do you think your sergeant will say when he finds out you were derelict in your duty? That you left your post to take a woman to bed in one of the rooms?" Cowley slapped his forehead as a new thought struck him. "Forget your sergeant. What do you think the *Fist* will say?"

Guardsman and servant both turned white. The guard seemed to be having trouble breathing all of a sudden. "Maybe no one needs to find out about this," he croaked. "It could be like it never happened."

"You think it's that easy?" Amma said. "I report directly to Hanneh who, if you are unaware, is in charge of all the female servants. Same as Dineh here does. Yes, Dineh, I know who you are."

When she said the name the young woman shrank behind the guardsman, as if he could protect her.

Amma continued. "If Hanneh finds out I knew about this and didn't tell her, she'll have my hide as well. Why should I risk that?"

"I'll never tell!" poor Dineh wailed. "I won't say a word!"

"Like she said," the guardsman added. "No one tells. No one ever knows."

"You must be new here then," Amma said. "This is the palace. Every wall here has ears. Secrets have a way of spilling out," she said ominously.

The two looked guiltily around as she said this, as if they might see watchers right then.

"You can see why this is a problem," Cowley said.

Dineh turned on the guardsman. "I never want to speak to you again, Kerl," she hissed, slapping him on the arm. "If you get me thrown out into the street…"

"Hey, hey, that's not going to happen." He turned a desperate look on Fen, who felt almost sorry for him. "Is it?"

Cowley and Amma shared a look and Fen caught something that passed between them. They were clearly enjoying this.

"What do you think?" Cowley asked her.

"Maybe just this once," Amma replied. She looked at Ravin, then at Fen. "How do you feel about it? Are you willing to take this risk?" Fen and Ravin nodded quickly.

"Kerl, Dineh, we'll keep this between us," Cowley said.

"That would be great," the young guardsman said in relief. "The sergeant said one more misstep and I'd be down walking the wall all night long. I won't forget this."

"I won't either," Cowley said. "Believe me."

Guardsman and servant fled from the room. After the door closed behind them Cowley thrust his fist into the air and cried out softly, "That was *incredible*!"

"That's what you think it was?" Fen exclaimed. "I think the word is terrifying. Do you know how much trouble we would have gotten into?"

"Nope," Amma said. "Incredible is the right word." To Cowley she said, "Did you see the look on his face when you said, 'You're the ones who are going to be in trouble'? I thought his jaw was going to fall off!"

"And then you said 'Every wall here has ears'! I thought they were going to run right then."

While the two of them continued talking excitedly, Fen and Ravin exchanged incredulous looks.

Ravin clutched Amma's sleeve. "I want to go back to my room now, please."

Fen took that as his cue and turned on Cowley. "It's time to go before we get caught for real."

"Okay, okay, I guess it is a little late," Cowley said. He bowed to the girls. "Until next time, my ladies?"

Amma returned a little curtsy. "With breathless anticipation, my good sir."

⁜ ⁜ ⁜

They had barely left the palace when Cowley started talking excitedly. "Wasn't that great, Fen? Wasn't that the most fun you've ever had?"

"I don't think you and I have the same idea of what fun is," Fen grumbled.

Cowley continued as if he hadn't heard him and, knowing Cowley like he did, Fen guessed he probably hadn't.

"Isn't Amma the most amazing girl ever? So pretty and so sharp!" He caught himself and hastily added, "And Ravin, wasn't she amazing as well?"

"I wouldn't know, since you and Amma hogged all the words," Fen said.

"I think I'm in love," Cowley said, putting his hand to his chest. "I think I've met the woman of my dreams."

"Keep your voice down," Fen said, catching hold of his arm. "We still have to make it back to the barracks without getting caught, you know."

Cowley pulled away from him and jumped up on the lip of a fountain they were passing by. He flung his arms outward and said, "Love!"

Fen grabbed the hem of his shirt and yanked him down. "You're an idiot, you know that?"

"Whatever you say, Fen."

"Where'd you get all that stuff from, anyway? 'I can only speak the words that are in my heart'? 'Your beauty has swept me away'? Who talks like that?"

"I listened, Fen. I learned."

"What? How?"

"One thing I learned early on is that to high-born people servants are invisible. We're like moving pieces of furniture. If you keep your mouth shut and your head down, they forget you're even there. You wouldn't believe the things I've seen and heard."

90

"I never thought of that." Grudgingly, Fen added, "I have to admit, that was pretty clever the way you turned it around on that guardsman. I thought we were doomed."

"I'm quite proud of that myself. I'll tell you, I was worried at first too. But all at once the words popped out of my mouth. I'm not quite sure where they came from."

"That's a problem you have a lot of the time."

"And did you see the way Amma picked up on it, how quick she was? What a girl she is!"

Fen sighed. He had a feeling he was going to have to hear a lot about Amma in the coming days.

"Let's get back to the barracks, okay?"

Chapter 13

Fen and Cowley were walking into the mess hall at the end of another long, grueling day when Ketrick, the ancient chamberlain, appeared and caught hold of Fen's arm. "You'll be dining with the Fist tonight."

That caught Fen by surprise. He hadn't been called in to eat with the Fist since he'd started training to be a soldier. There'd been so much going on that he'd kind of forgotten that the Fist had said he would call him in now and then.

"Should I clean up first or...?"

"You know the Fist," Ketrick said. "What do you think?" He limped away. Fen followed. He knew better than to keep the Fist waiting.

As before, there was no one in the room other than the Fist and a single servant. Barik looked up from his plate and motioned Fen to approach. Fen started to bow when he got close but stopped when Barik scowled. "Don't do that," he said. "Not when it's just the two of us."

There was a plate set at the table to Barik's right and Fen sat down there. The food looked good—a large slab of meat resting in a pool of brown gravy, roasted potatoes, a chicken leg and a wedge of cheese—and he suddenly realized how terribly hungry he was. The Fist was already eating so he dug in. They ate in silence. When the food was gone the Fist spoke.

"How is the training going?"

"It's going good. I've learned a lot."

"What about the rest of your squad?"

"They're doing good too."

"We learn best when we're young. Every year we get older it's harder to change our thinking and learn new things, don't you think?"

Fen considered this. "I don't know, sir. I'm still pretty young."

The Fist regarded him. "That you are. But you're getting older every day. Someday you'll know what I mean." He crossed his arms. "It was a good idea that you had."

"Sir?"

"Training boys to be soldiers. In order to make this nation strong again we need to get rid of the bad habits we've learned and bring in new habits. Teaching new habits to people who are already grown and set in their ways is hard. Many of them never get it. With young people you don't have that problem. Young people are flexible, easy to mold. I should have seen that right away, but I didn't, because I'm stuck in my ways just like everyone else my age. But you're not. You saw past what has always been done to what needs to be done."

Fen thought about this and how he should respond. He wasn't sure if the Fist was testing him or not, looking for a specific answer. Finally, not knowing what to say, he simply told the truth. "I don't know about that, sir. I only wanted to be a soldier and I didn't want to wait. I wasn't really thinking about that other stuff."

"See? That's what I'm talking about. If you were older, you would have tried to seize that opportunity. When your liege congratulated you on your accomplishment your first thought would have been to try to use it to your advantage, to better your own situation. But instead you spoke truthfully. You don't know how rare that is among adults."

Fen found himself a little confused by what Barik was saying. All he could think to say was, "I'm glad I could help."

"We're going to make this nation into something special, Fen, you know that?"

"I hope so, sir."

"I know so. I already have enough boys to form a dozen more squads. All of them are orphans. They have the most motivation to fight, don't you think?"

"Yes."

"Those squads will be officially formed once I have a place to put them. That won't be much longer."

There was something in his tone of voice that sounded faintly ominous, but Fen couldn't figure it out.

"They don't say it aloud, because every one of them is afraid to say anything that they think might upset me, but I can tell that most of the officers think I'm crazy. What fool trains boys? But that's because they have no vision. They can't see down the road."

Barik stood up and began to pace, his hands behind his back. He was wearing simple leather breeches and a white, sleeveless tunic. His arms bulged with muscle. His mustache was oiled and the ends hung down past his jaw. The light reflected off his bald head and cast his eyes in shadow.

"They can't see what I can see. They can barely see past the ends of their own noses. They're as bad as the late king and the nobility. They only think of themselves. There's no thought of anything larger." He paused in his pacing and fixed his piercing gaze on Fen. "That's why we lost this war, Fen, never forget that. We lost because our leaders failed us. It was not the army that failed, it was those who led us." His face twisted with bitterness as he spoke and heat crept into his voice.

"They thought only of themselves and their own pleasures and forgot that our enemies are implacable, unyielding, ever watching for their opportunity. They allowed us to grow weak. The number of soldiers—real soldiers, with training, not conscripts—dwindled every year and you know why? Because soldiers cost money and they wanted that money for themselves. Nothing else mattered. You've stood on the wall with me. You've seen the shape it's in. For years I watched it slowly decay, whole sections crumbling away, and knew it would not hold up to a concerted assault. It wasn't just the wall either. The timbers in the gates should have been replaced long ago. They were riddled with termites and the only surprise is that they held up to the battering ram as long as they did."

He resumed pacing. His expression was bleak, even frightening. "All that changes now. Samkara will be strong again. It will take hard work and sacrifice. At times it will require ruthlessness, but it will happen, this I swear. I don't care what the cost is, either to myself or to others. One way or another, Samkara will be strong and safe from her enemies."

The Fist walked to the big window at the end of the room and stared out into the darkness. The window faced east and Fen had a vague idea that Marad lay that way, though he wasn't sure.

"I've been thinking about this. It may not be enough to conquer only Marad. We may have to conquer this entire island."

"The whole island?" Fen asked, surprised. There were a half dozen smaller nations on the island of Tarakand besides Samkara and Marad, most of whom were either allied with Samkara or neutral. "I thought only Marad was our enemy."

The Fist turned to him. "It's the only way to be safe. Otherwise we never know when one of them will turn on us as the Maradi did. You can understand that, can't you?"

Fen nodded slowly. "If you say it is what we must do, Fist, then that is all I need. I will march where you tell me to and fight who you tell me to fight."

The Fist's eyes gleamed and he walked back to the table and put his hand on Fen's shoulder. "It is people like you who are the heart of this great nation, Fen."

Fen's heart leapt and he swelled with pride. He could not have spoken if he'd tried.

Barik returned to his chair. "I spoke to you a moment ago of the need to be ruthless sometimes. Tomorrow is one of those times. You and your squad mates will be witness to it."

"What is going to happen?" Fen asked, curious.

"It's a secret. I've told no one, not even my generals." A hard look settled on his face. "Especially not my generals. I can tell you this much though. It is something no one expects."

⚓   ⚓   ⚓

The other boys were already in the barracks when Fen got out there. A few were already asleep and the rest looked close. Cowley was waiting for Fen.

"What happened? What did he want?"

Fen unbuckled his sword belt and shrugged out of his mail shirt before answering. Being rid of that extra weight felt heavenly. He rolled his shoulders while he chose how much of what the Fist had told him he could share and how much was in confidence. "He wanted to know how our training is coming. Other squads like ours are being formed."

"They won't be like ours, though. We'll always be the best."

Fen didn't answer. He laid down on his cot.

"Why you, Fen? Why does he talk to you?" Cowley asked.

"I don't know. I guess because I was there." He'd told Cowley about the battle in the square, how he and Barik were the only survivors. But he hadn't told him about what he saw—or rather, *thought* he saw—behind Barik, reaching out of the shadows. By now he'd mostly convinced himself that it was only his imagination anyway, and he didn't want to be teased about it.

Nor had he told Cowley about how he'd survived after the Maradi soldier struck him with his sword. That was something he tried not to think about either. He didn't want to be different. He just wanted to be a soldier, to defend Samkara against her enemies.

He pulled the shard of stone out of his pocket and peered at it in the dim light. How come he hadn't gotten seriously hurt when Strout hit him in the head? What was wrong with him?

"Lights out," Strout said, blowing out the lantern and plunging the barracks into darkness.

Fen put the shard back in his pocket, wondering. There was so much he didn't understand.

He was still wondering when he fell asleep.

Chapter 14

The next morning when they lined up outside the barracks Fen could see right away that something was going on with Flint. The sergeant seemed upset about something, snapping at the boys about little things, giving terse replies to questions they asked of him.

The boys followed him out the castle gates, which had already been rebuilt from new timbers, and down into the city. The light of the new day was growing in the eastern sky and the city was just starting to wake up.

Downhill from the castle, the boulevard led through an area populated by the nobility. High walls lined both sides of the wide, tree-lined street, broken here and there by spiked, wrought-iron gates, all of it protected by armed guards. Visible beyond the walls were the upper stories of grand mansions, symbols of unimaginable wealth and power.

It was a part of the city that Fen had never even ventured into before he followed Barik up here after the defeat. The lives of those beyond the high walls seemed something out of a dream. They'd taken a beating along with the rest of the city, it was true. A number of the fine mansions had burned and all of them had been thoroughly ransacked. Some of the inhabitants had been murdered.

But at the same time the nobility were recovering faster than the rest of the city. The mansions were largely stone and brick, and so this part of the city didn't burn as thoroughly as some parts did. Nor had the nobility lost very many of their number. Fen had heard rumors that many of them had secret escape tunnels and chambers carved out of the earth underneath their estates and it appeared those rumors were true.

All in all it looked as though the city's most powerful residents were going to survive the fall and sack of Samkara in fine shape.

At least until today.

When the running boys came up on the first of the grand estates they saw an unusual sight. Several dozen soldiers were clustered by the front gate, which was open. Lying on the ground outside the gate were the bodies of two dead guards, blood pooling around them.

Shouting came from the gardens on the other side of the wall and then a knot of soldiers emerged and spilled out onto the street. In their midst was a white-haired man wearing a richly brocaded sleeping gown. His hands were manacled in front of him and he was shouting angrily at the soldiers, telling them he would have all their heads. They paid him no heed.

Hustled along behind the nobleman was a white-haired lady, her hair in disarray, her face a mask of shock. She was manacled also. Two young men, clearly their sons, were also in chains, both of them shouting threats at the soldiers.

Fen expected Flint to stop, maybe tell them to turn back, and he slowed his pace. But the sergeant did nothing except alter their course to veer around the soldiers and their captives.

The same thing was happening at the next estate they came to. The recently-repaired gate had been knocked down with a small battering ram, the guards killed, and the nobles were being dragged out into the street. The man and his wife were crying and screaming, trying to grab onto anything they could—bushes, the remnants of the gate—while the soldiers dragged them by the ankles.

What made Fen's blood run cold was the sight of the two small children and the baby. The children were a boy and a girl, both around five or six. Soldiers had slung them over their shoulders and were carrying them, the children crying and reaching for their parents. The baby was crying as well. The soldier carrying the baby had it tucked under his arm like it was a piglet he was taking to the market.

Fen and Cowley exchanged horrified looks. "What's going on?" Cowley whispered.

Fen shook his head. He wondered if this was what Barik had been talking about last night after dinner when he said it was necessary to be ruthless sometimes. But what was he doing? Was he going to put all these people in prison?

Seeing the nobility dragged out into the street like criminals shook Fen to his core. In some ways it was more fundamentally shocking than the sack of the city had been. After all, even a child knew that enemies were out there, and that those enemies could and sometimes did conquer and pillage cities. But the problems that plagued the common folk didn't touch the nobility. They lived in a world apart, as remote and untouchable as the stars in the sky. They were above the law. They were never arrested. The common people never even laid hands on them. Seeing them treated this way was tremendously unsettling.

The scene was repeated again and again as they ran down the street toward the docks. Fen kept his head down and concentrated on his running, not wanting to see what was happening. He had no love for the nobility, but neither did he want to see them treated this way. Over and over he wished the sergeant would choose a different path—this wasn't the route they normally took on their runs—but Flint kept moving doggedly on, though there was a stiffness in the set of his shoulders that made Fen think he didn't like this either.

It occurred to Fen that the Fist had ordered Flint to take them this way. He'd *wanted* them to see this. But why? What reason did he have?

It was a relief when finally they passed out of the nobles' district. It was quieter down here, but there was an uneasiness in the air. People stood in groups on street corners, talking amongst themselves in low voices. There were no smiles. Everyone looked dour or fearful. No doubt there were many rumors, but although no one knew for sure what was happening, it was clear that something was happening.

The sun was up by the time they reached the docks. The boys stood in a loose group, breathing hard.

"Wait here," Flint said, and walked off into the milling throng of fisherman and sailors.

"What was that all about?" Lukas said. He looked a little pale. "What are they doing to those lords and their families?"

"What did it look like they were doing?" Strout sneered. "They were arresting them."

"But *why?*" the pudgy boy persisted. "What did they *do?*"

Strout didn't have an answer to that. None of them did.

"Did you know this was going to happen?" Cowley asked Fen.

"How would I know?" Fen replied.

"You had dinner with the Fist last night."

"Why would the Fist tell a boy his plans?" Strout said.

"What's going to happen to them?" Gage asked.

"That's not our problem," Strout said. "You want to be a soldier? Learn to not ask questions. Just do what you're told."

"I hope he puts the lot of them in the Gulach," Noah said angrily. The Gulach was the city prison. "Bloody nobles. They deserve whatever happens to them."

"Why do you hate them so much?" Lukas asked him.

"You don't? You never been whipped by one of their guards for looking at them when they go by in their fancy carriages? You never had one try to run you down on his horse for sport?"

"No."

"That's cause your parents were rich too. I heard you say they were merchants, didn't I?"

"They were merchants, but they weren't rich," Lukas protested.

"How many servants did you have?" Noah asked him.

"Only a few…" Lukas trailed off as he realized what he was saying.

"Like I said," Noah said. "You might as well be one of them."

"Maybe I was, but I'm not anymore." Lukas' face was getting red and there were tears in the corners of his eyes. "The Maradi killed everyone in my family and burned everything we had. I don't have anything anymore."

"None of us do," Fen said. "That's why we're here, isn't it?"

"Yeah, but some of us *never* had anything," Noah said belligerently.

"Let's all take a minute and cry for poor little Noah," Strout said sarcastically. "Why oh why did I forget my hankie today of all days?"

Noah looked like he was going to launch himself at Strout but Flint returned then. The sergeant was carrying a bag and he reached into it and started handing out something to the boys.

"Pastries!" Gage exclaimed, his eyes lighting up.

The boys jostled each other, trying to get theirs first. All except Fen. He waited until the rest had theirs, and then he took his. Flint gave him a look when he handed it over and Fen realized something.

They hadn't seen all of it. There was more to come.

The pastries weren't a random act of kindness. The look in Flint's eyes told Fen that the sergeant had been ordered to do something and he felt awful about it. The pastries were his way of softening it, whatever it was.

Fen barely tasted his. He watched Flint as he chewed, dreading what was coming.

When the boys were done with their treats, Flint gathered them around. "We're not going straight back up to the castle, boys," he said. Something in his tone got through to them and they went silent and stared at him, their smiles disappearing. "We have somewhere else to go first."

"Where?" Cowley asked.

"We're going to the Gulach."

The boys froze.

"Why are we going to the Gulach?" Lukas asked. "We're not in trouble are we?"

"No, you're not in trouble. You're going because the Fist wants you to see something," Flint said. His voice sounded like he was in pain.

"But why?" Lukas persisted. "What's going to happen?"

Right then a soldier on horseback, wearing a surcoat emblazoned with the red fist of Barik, blew three sharp blasts on the horn he was carrying. "Citizens of Samkara!" he yelled. "The Fist requests your presence at the Gulach." He repeated the message a couple times, then trotted off to tell others.

"I don't rightly know what's going to happen," Flint said grimly, "though I have ideas. There's no point in talking about it. We have our orders. Let's obey them."

They ran behind him, too-big mail coats flapping around them, cumbersome practice swords banging around their ankles, eight boys who were growing up fast. Heading for something that would change their world in a fundamental way.

⚏   ⚏   ⚏

The whole way to the prison Fen was gripped by a sense of foreboding so strong he felt he was choking on it. More than anything he didn't want to see whatever it was the Fist wanted them to see. He wanted to fall out of the line and hide until it was over.

But he didn't. Worse than whatever they were headed for was the thought of disappointing Barik. Ever since that terrible night when the city fell, he'd looked at Barik as the father he'd never

101

known. He craved the grim man's approval. He wanted to make him proud. He would endure anything he had to for Barik.

He steeled himself and continued on.

There was a large plaza in front of the Gulach. The more notorious criminals and others the king wanted to make an example of were executed there, for all to see. Public executions were a popular spectacle, with large numbers of people showing up to watch, vendors selling food and drinks, jugglers and musicians playing for the crowd, trying to earn a few coins. Fen had never seen one. His mother made sure of it.

So he was expecting to see some nobles executed. There could be no other reason for the Fist to tell the people to gather there.

But he never expected what he saw when he and the rest of his squad finally trooped into the plaza.

A wooden platform had been set up against the front wall of the prison, high enough that it could be easily seen by everyone in the crowd, which was swelling rapidly. It was long enough that it stretched across the entire front of the prison.

All along the platform people were lined up, kneeling before wooden chopping blocks, their hands manacled behind them. There must have been forty of them in all. Most were women and men, but there were also children of various ages. Some were still fighting to get away and they were bloodied and bruised. Others had resigned themselves to their fate and knelt there quietly, crying or praying. Men with axes stood beside them, waiting.

Ranks of soldiers were drawn up before the platform, all facing the condemned people. Flint led them through the crowd to a spot that had been left open for them near the center of the platform. The boys were dead silent as they took their places. Even Cowley for once had nothing to say.

Fen's knees were shaking but he fought to hide it. He was standing hardly more than an arm's length from a girl who was not much older than he was. She was wearing a green dress made of rich fabric with a lace collar. The dress was torn. Tears were pouring down her face and puddling on the platform. She looked up and her tear-stained eyes met his.

"Please," she whimpered. "Help me."

Fen tried to step back but other soldiers were pressed up behind him and he couldn't move away. He wanted to speak, to try and comfort her in some way, but he couldn't get any sound past his dry lips. The monstrousness of what was about to happen overwhelmed him. He was filled with shame and helplessness. There had to be a mistake. Surely this girl had done nothing wrong. Surely she would not be executed for whatever crimes her parents had committed.

The Fist emerged from the gates of the prison then and climbed the rough stairs up onto the platform. He walked to the front edge and looked out over the crowd. More people had arrived and the square was packed. The people went silent and every eye fixed on him.

"These people before you have been condemned to die for the crime of treason against the nation of Samkara," the Fist said. "It was because of them that we were defeated by our enemies. It was they who opened the gates and invited the Maradi butchers into our homes."

An angry murmur came from the crowd as he said the words. Scowls darkened faces and fists were raised. Several people shouted curses.

"They betrayed us with their greed. They stole everything from us and left us with nothing but scraps, so that we were too weak to resist the invaders when they came. Our numbers were too few. Our weapons were poorly made. Our walls were weak. And once the enemy was among us they hid while we were slaughtered!"

The angry murmur swelled, growing ever stronger. Around the boys most of the soldiers had joined in.

"They must be punished for this!" the Fist thundered. "They must learn that we will no longer stand meekly by and allow them to suck the life from our nation!"

The people met his words with mindless sound of rage and hatred. It was a hungry sound that could only be sated by blood. The citizens of Samkara had been through hell in the past months, first enduring the siege, then the rape and sack of their city. They were frightened and angry and they wanted someone to take it out on.

And the Fist had just given it to them.

"Kill them!" the Fist yelled above the growing roar. He dropped his hand in a slashing motion.

Heads were forced down onto the blocks. Weapons flashed downward. The girl before Fen screamed, or at least it looked like she did. He couldn't hear her over the roar of the crowd. Her blood spattered across Fen's face. Her head dropped from her shoulders rolled off the edge of the platform. The crowd went berserk, screaming and yelling wildly.

The bodies were kicked off the edge of the platform and more prisoners were dragged into place, forced to their knees in the slick puddles of blood and urine.

Fen could barely stand. He had his hands pressed to his ears but the roaring that filled his skull did not come from the crowd. His head was pounding with sudden, stabbing pains.

Barik gestured again and again the blades descended. Blood fountained and bodies jerked with death spasms. The executioners and front ranks of soldiers were splattered with blood. The crowd pressed forward in its mindlessness, their roaring like an angry sea.

Fen staggered backwards, the pain in his head rising to an unbearable crescendo. He thought he was screaming, but he couldn't be sure. The day pitched wildly around him but he saw none of it. His vision had gone red. Immense pressure was building inside him, rising fast to some kind of explosion. His whole body was shaking.

The last of the nobility were dragged forward and forced to their knees. Barik's hand fell and they joined their brethren in death.

At that moment, the pressure inside Fen exploded.

He shrieked, his cry lost in the sounds of the crowd. Something immense and uncontrollable burst out of him. It felt as if he were suddenly split open, from his feet to the top of his head.

The ground shook violently. There was a huge cracking sound and the ground split open right in front of Fen. The earth bucked upwards as the crack grew larger, longer.

The wooden platform was wrenched violently, wood splintering. People and bodies were tossed this way and that. The crowd screamed, in fear this time, and people fought to get away. Some fell into the crack.

There was one last, violent shudder and the stone wall of the prison split, all the way to the top. Pieces of stone cascaded to the ground.

Then Fen fell unconscious and knew no more.

Chapter 15

"Hey, Fen. Are you okay?"

Fen opened his eyes and saw Cowley crouched over him, a worried look in his eyes. People were milling all around them, talking excitedly.

"I think so. What happened?"

"I don't know. I really don't." Cowley helped him sit up.

What Fen saw seemed unbelievable. There was a huge crack in the ground, starting only a few feet away. It extended across the plaza clear to the wall of the prison. The wall of the prison had a wide split in it.

Did I do that? he wondered. He remembered the intense pressure in his head and the sudden release. The earthquake happened right at the same time.

He looked around guiltily, expecting to see people pointing at him, or backing away in fear. But no one was paying the slightest attention to him.

No one but Cowley. He was looking at Fen oddly. But before he could say anything a man pushed his way through the crowd to the edge of the crack. He was tall, with an imposing gray beard and thick eyebrows. He was wearing a brown robe and around his neck hung the symbol of Hentu, the god of storms and cataclysms.

"It's a sign!" the priest yelled. "Hentu has spoken!"

Nearby people broke off what they were saying and began turning towards him. He held up his hands. "Hentu has given his approval to what has happened here today. He smiles on our new king, the Red Fist!"

He whirled and pointed as he said this. The wooden platform had been torn in half. Only one part of it was still standing. Everyone on the platform had fallen off during the earthquake, but somehow the Fist was still there, above the crowd, looking down on them.

"All hail the Red Fist!" the priest shouted. "Beloved of Hentu! His is the fist that shall smite our enemies!"

106

The crowd picked up his intensity and they began chanting, only a few at first, but within moments every voice in the square was yelling, "Fist! Fist! Fist!"

With Cowley's help, Fen stood. The energy of the crowd was infectious and soon both boys were chanting as well. It was intoxicating, as if there were something in the air. People were jumping up and down. Women, and even a few men, had tears running down their faces.

The chanting ceased to be individual words and became instead a ceaseless roar, like the ocean during a storm, carrying all of them on its crest.

Then, when the intensity of the crowd was at its peak, Fen saw something. Or thought he did.

It was a shadow outlined in purple light. It appeared right behind the Fist. Something moved within its depths. He had an impression of a pale face, the features twisted with a mix of hatred and triumph.

Fen blinked and the shadow was gone.

Barik held up his hands and the crowd went quiet.

"People of Samkara! One more step has been taken today. The guilty ones have been punished. But there is still much work to be done before our nation is rebuilt, more challenges we will have to face. But I promise you this. We will face them. We will overcome them all. From the ashes we will rise, stronger than ever, and our enemies will regret the day they raised their swords against us!"

A wild cheer followed his words, a cheer that Fen joined in with, but at the same time he felt uneasy. What had happened here today? Did he really see the shadow? Was the earthquake caused by one of the gods, or did he do it?

And if he did do it, what did that mean? What was wrong with him?

Flint rounded up his charges. "Let's go. There's training to do." His expression was dark, a contrast to most of the people in the square, who still looked elated.

The pace he set as they ran towards the castle was faster than before, as if he sought to leave something behind. All the boys were staggering by the time they reached the castle, and Lukas was several hundred yards behind.

Flint gave them no time to recover, but started them straight into a brutal series of exercises as soon as they reached the practice yard, yelling at them whenever one of them faltered. By midday most of the boys had thrown up at least once and Gage passed out for a few minutes.

"Come on, sergeant," Strout finally said. "Ease off a bit."

"If you want easy, you're in the wrong place," Flint growled.

"We won't be much use to the Fist if we're all dead," Strout said.

Flint looked like he was going to yell at him, but then he relented. "Go get some chow. I expect you all back out here in half a bell."

When they had their food and were sitting in the mess hall, Lukas said to no one in particular, "What's wrong with the sergeant? Why's he so mad at us?"

"It's like he blames us for what happened at the prison," Gage said.

"What *did* happen?" Noah asked.

"He killed all the nobles, that's what happened," Lukas said. He sounded almost sad.

"That's not what I'm talking about, dummy," Noah said. "I'm talking about the earthquake. You think it was really a sign from the gods?"

"No," Strout said firmly, turning from his spot at the next table over. "The gods don't give two farts what happens to us. We're on our own here and that's all there is to it."

"I think it was the gods," Lukas said. "Maybe Hentu, like the priest said. It sounds like something he'd do."

"Maybe it was a sign from the gods that they didn't like him killing all those nobles," Gage said.

"I'm telling you, the gods had nothing to do with it," Strout insisted.

"So you're saying it was only a coincidence?"

While they were arguing Fen noticed Cowley looking at him, a hint of a frown on his face, and he quickly turned his face away.

He desperately hoped the earthquake had been caused by a god. He liked that answer better than the one that kept trying to push to the front of his mind. He'd spent the morning telling himself that it was only coincidence, the earthquake happening right when it did, when he felt the huge release of pressure inside his skull. He almost had himself convinced, too, just like he'd almost convinced himself that he hadn't actually seen a shadow behind the Fist. He was tired, that was all, what with all the training. He'd been hit on the head a few times too, which could make a person see and hear strange things, or so he'd been told.

Fen finished his food first and hurried back to the practice yard. Flint was there, sitting on a small barrel, his head in his hands. He looked up when Fen came over.

"What's wrong, sergeant?" Fen asked.

Flint gave him a strange, sad look. "It's the march to war, Fen. I've seen it before. It's stirring in the beginning, but it's never pretty at the end."

"But Marad is our enemy. We don't have any choice."

"There's always choices." Flint stood up and put his hand on Fen's shoulder. "Remember that."

⊥⊤　　⊥⊤　　⊥⊤

The afternoon wasn't as difficult as the morning had been. It was as if something that was burning hot inside Flint finally flickered and went out. There was still daylight left when he let them stop.

Fen was getting a drink of water when a servant came up and tapped him on the shoulder. "Come with me," he said.

The servant led him, not to the dining hall, but to a part of the palace that he hadn't been to before. There was a set of double doors with guards stationed before them. Waiting in the anteroom outside the doors were about fifty people. From the looks of them most were wealthy, not as wealthy as the nobility, but certainly far beyond the common person. Fen thought they looked like merchants to him.

They were clearly nervous. A number held handkerchiefs and were wiping sweat from their faces. They shifted uneasily from one foot to another and their eyes darted around the room. They watched Fen and the servant approaching with puzzled looks and that puzzlement only increased when the guards ordered them to make way and then opened the doors to allow Fen through.

The doors closed behind him and Fen found himself in a huge room. Running down either side of the room was a row of ornately-carved columns stretching upwards at least thirty feet to a vaulted ceiling painted gold. The walls were decorated with elaborate murals depicting scenes from Samkara's past. At the far end of the room, on a raised dais, was the throne. Barik was standing by the throne, talking to an officer.

Fen made his way across the room. Every step was difficult. He didn't want to be here. He didn't want to see Barik yet. It was all too fresh, too painful. He remembered the young girl in the green dress, dying under the executioner's blade. He remembered the children, the babies. The blood and the screams. He knew that when he closed his eyes tonight he would dream of the horrors he had seen today. He might always dream of them.

Fen stopped at the bottom step of the dais and waited silently. Barik dismissed the officer and turned to Fen.

"Come up here," Barik said.

Fen mounted the steps and stopped a few feet away, his eyes on the floor.

"Look at me."

Slowly, Fen raised his eyes. Barik's eyes were intense, almost painful to look into. They bored into Fen, seeing everything.

"You are upset by what you saw."

Fen nodded, blinking back the tears he felt in his eyes, wishing they weren't there, that he could be hard like the Fist was.

"I told you yesterday that ruthlessness is sometimes necessary, didn't I?"

Fen swallowed and nodded again.

"But right now in your heart you question me. You wonder if I am, perhaps, not the leader you chose to follow, but a monster instead. You wonder if you have made a mistake."

"No, Fist," Fen whispered.

The skin around the Fist's eyes tightened. "Don't lie to me, Fen. Never lie to me. I get enough of that from the rest of them. Tell me the truth when you speak to me. I will never punish you for that."

Fen could no longer keep the tears back. Through blurred vision he stared up at the man and asked, "Why did the children have to die too?"

Barik nodded as if he'd been expecting the question. He answered it with one of his own. "Do you know why I executed the nobility, Fen?"

Fen wiped at his tears, ashamed of them. "You said they were traitors."

"I have a confession to make, Fen. That's not really why I executed them. If that was my only reason I would have just executed the men, maybe some of their wives. I would have left the children alone. A child isn't capable of being a traitor, not really."

Fen swallowed. He was confused. Too much had happened today and he couldn't keep up with it all. "Then why?" he asked, his voice cracking. "They were so *young*."

Barik went to the throne and sat down. "I did it because now I can seize their wealth. All of it. Their gold, their lands, their houses. It all belongs to me now."

"You did it for *money*?" Fen was stunned. He thought there was nothing Barik could have said that would have surprised him more. "I thought you didn't care about money?"

Barik frowned. "I don't." He gestured at the richness of the room. "I care nothing for this," he said dismissively. "Look at how I'm dressed if you don't believe me." He was dressed as a common laborer in stout boots and rough breeches with a simple tunic. His clothes were dirty and there was a smudge of soot on one cheek, proof that he'd once again spent much of the day in the hard work of rebuilding the city.

"No, I need the coin for all of Samkara. To rebuild this nation. To make our army strong once again. Such things take a great deal of money. Money that the nobility had. Money that they had stolen over the generations, from all of us. Now that money will be put to good use. Instead of rich homes and lavish parties, it will buy swords and spears and horses. It will build machines of war.

"That is why I killed them all."

Then he waited silently, staring at Fen, waiting for his reaction.

Fen lowered his head, no longer able to look him in the eye. He wanted to run away. He wanted to lie down and sleep and never wake up. Nothing made sense anymore.

"Ruling is a difficult job," Barik said, his tone rough, almost angry. "It requires difficult decisions, decisions that can be hard to live with. But if I do not make those decisions, who will?"

"I...I guess so."

"No!" Barik barked, startling Fen. "Don't do that!"

"Do what?"

"What you just did. You are troubled by what I have done, but instead of speaking up, instead of challenging me, you simply went along with it. Understand this, boy, I get enough of that already." He waved his arm to take in the entire palace. "There's one thing I never realized before I took over, something I never even considered, and that's how everyone changes. Everyone bows and scrapes. They say, 'Yes, Fist,' and 'No, Fist,' but they don't mean it. They're always watching me, trying to guess what I want them to say and then jumping to say it.

"It's not only the servants and the merchants who come for an audience either. It's the officers in my own army. They have no thoughts of their own. They only want to be the first to agree with whatever I think." He regarded Fen again. "Can you see why that is a problem, the danger that lies there?"

When Fen hesitated, he said, "Speak up, boy. Speak your mind."

"There's no one…no one to tell you when you're wrong."

"Exactly!" Barik boomed. "In the days since I took power I've spent a lot of time thinking, trying to figure out what went wrong so I could see how to steer Samkara clear of the mistakes that were made before. And it's clear to me that one of the biggest was this culture of fear that permeates our whole city. The officers in the army all saw what was happening as well as I did, but they were all afraid to speak up, afraid of what would happen to them. And because of that, the rot was allowed to spread unchecked until it reached its logical, final conclusion in our defeat at the hands of our enemies.

"I won't let that happen again. I don't want to make the same mistakes. When I'm wrong, I want people around me who will tell me so. It's too late for most of my officers. I've told them to speak their minds and they nod and agree but they're only saying that because that's what they think I want to hear. They're too old. They've been doing it the old way for too long and they can't change now. I'll have to replace them, raise up new officers who will think for themselves and speak up when they think things are going wrong.

"Can you be one of them, Fen? Can you speak your mind to me?"

Fen drew himself as straight as he could and forced himself to meet Barik's gaze. "I think…I mean, I can. I will."

Barik nodded. "Good. Now, stand off over to the side and pay attention. I want you to see something."

Fen moved off to the side, wondering what was going on. The Fist called to the guards to open the doors.

The merchants who had been waiting outside filed into the room, nervously looking around. Like lambs surrounded by wolves they stuck close together as they approached the throne. When they reached the foot of the dais hats were removed and they all sank to their knees, staring fearfully up at the Fist.

For the longest time the Fist said nothing. He simply sat there and stared at them, his gaze fixing on one man for long seconds before slowly moving to the next. Fen noticed that most of them could not meet his eyes and looked away. Only a couple, near the front, stared back at the Fist and he saw that it cost them to do so.

As the silence dragged out, the merchants became more and more uncomfortable. More hands plied handkerchiefs across sweaty brows. As he stood there watching, Fen realized what the Fist was doing, how his silence was harder on them than any words could be. The Fist had them thoroughly cowed before he spoke.

When he realized this, Fen relaxed somewhat. If the Fist wanted them cowed, that meant he wasn't planning on killing them. At least not today. He wasn't going to have to witness another slaughter.

Abruptly, the Fist stood and walked to the edge of the dais. The merchants, surprised by his sudden movement, shrank back.

"Do you know why you're here?" the Fist asked. His voice was soft, but there was menace in his tone. He did not like these men gathered here before him and he didn't care if they knew it. In fact, he wanted them to know it.

One of the merchants who had managed to meet his gaze earlier, a stout man in rich robes, his wrists jangling with gold bracelets, spoke up.

"I assume you have something you wish to tell us, Fist. We are, of course, happy to answer your summons. I believe I speak for the rest of my brethren here when I say that we are eager to comply with whatever it is you need from us."

"Of course you are. Haldric, isn't it?"

The merchant nodded. "Yes, sire. At your service."

"You're one of the ones I especially wanted to see, Haldric."

The man's eyes grew very wide. Fen noticed the way the others near him subtly shifted away, leaving him on his own. "W…why?"

"Under the late king, your company had the contract to supply the weapons for conscripted soldiers, right?"

"We…we did, sire."

"Were you aware, Haldric, that many of those weapons were absolute shit? That many of them broke the first time they were struck by an enemy weapon?"

Haldric tugged at his collar and had to lick his lips before he could speak. "I'm…well, that is, sometimes mistakes are made in the manufacturing process. Errors creep in." An idea struck him and he held up one finger. "Sometimes subcontractors are engaged to help with the process, other interests brought in to, say, supply the steel. It is possible that one of those I bought the raw steel from was not supplying the quality I had counted on." His own words seemed to have encouraged him so that his voice was stronger by the end.

"Is that the excuse you're going with, Haldric?" the Fist asked. His voice was now so soft Fen could barely hear it, and yet that made it even more frightening. "Think carefully now. Much depends on what you say next."

Haldric turned green. His mouth opened and closed like a fish thrown on the bank. No words came out.

"Since you are at a loss for words, let me give you a suggestion, Haldric, that may help you at this important moment in your life. I am a man who values the truth above all. I have no tolerance for lies. They enrage me, make me want to hurt people."

A definite space had opened up around Haldric. Sweat was pouring down his face and he was shaking.

"I think what you meant to say, Haldric, is that you've been terribly greedy, that you knowingly sold the army inferior weapons to pad your profits and while doing so you and your equally greedy friends and co-conspirators patted each other's fat backs and congratulated each other on what smart businessmen you are. Am I correct in this?"

Haldric managed a nod, though he still could not speak.

"And what you want to say next is how sorry you are."

Haldric found his voice. "I am, sire," he babbled. "Terribly sorry!"

"But, alas, you know that mere words are not enough, so you'd like to make a grand gesture to prove your sincerity."

"A...grand gesture?"

The Fist motioned and an aide hurried forward, carrying a parchment, which he gave to Haldric.

"Read it. It contains a full accounting of all the weapons you mean to replace, for *free*, to prove how sorry you are."

Haldric did so, his eyes widening in alarm. "But...sire," he said in a strangled voice. "I'll be *ruined*."

"Yes, but you'll have the gratitude of your Fist rather than his rage. And you'll still be alive. That's worth something, don't you think?"

Haldric clutched the parchment to his chest. "It will take some time."

"You have four months."

The last of the air went out of the man and he slumped over. "Yes, sire," he said in a barely audible voice.

The Fist looked out over the rest of them. "I have pointed Haldric out as perhaps the worst example of selfish greed, but he is by no means the only one. You have all fed on the blood of Samkara like ticks on a dog. Before you leave the palace, each of you will receive a similar list of goods or services which you will happily replace and replace promptly. Failure to do so will result in you and your entire family being executed and all lands and wealth seized by the state. Are there any questions?"

Chapter 16

"You boys take a break," Flint said. It was mid-afternoon and the boys had been practicing wrestling since lunch. "Have some water. I have something I need to take care of." He looked into the water bucket, then at Eben. "The bucket's empty. Go refill it."

Without a word Eben went over to the bucket, picked it up, and left the practice yard. Flint left to take care of his business. Noah and Lukas flopped on the ground. Wallice went off by himself and leaned against the wall.

Fen sat down against a rack filled with practice weapons, leaned his head back and closed his eyes. Cowley sat down beside him.

"I wonder what their story is," Cowley said.

Fen opened his eyes. "Who are you talking about?"

"I'm talking about Wallice and Eben. I mean, after all this time and we still don't know anything about them."

"We know they're brothers." They looked too much alike to be anything but brothers. Both were thin and wiry, with long, straight black hair that looked like it had never been cut a single time in their lives. They both had the same dark, expressionless eyes and closed faces. Wallice was half a head taller than Eben, so he was probably the older of the two.

"Has either of them ever talked to you? I mean, something besides 'give me the salt'?" Cowley asked.

"No. I don't think I've ever heard a complete sentence from either of them."

Lukas chimed in then. "I think there's something wrong with them. I knew this boy, lived down the street from my father's shop. He got kicked in the head when he was real little by a mule. It did something to him. When you looked into his eyes you could see there was nothing inside there anymore."

"I don't know," Cowley said. "I don't think that's it. I think it's something deeper."

"What else can it be?" Lukas said. "They don't talk. Either of you ever see one of them laugh or smile? They're simple, that's all there is to it."

"But both of them?" Cowley asked. "How does a mule kick both of them in the head? That doesn't make sense."

"It doesn't have to be a mule that kicked them," Lukas said. "It could be something else that happened to them."

"We don't know what happened to them when the city was sacked," Fen said. "We don't know what they went through, what they saw. Maybe that's what made them the way they are. Maybe in time they'll get over it."

Fen didn't realize that Strout was listening in until the older boy made a disgusted sound and said, "That's horse shit."

"What is?"

"Saying they're like that because of what they went through. Don't make excuses for them. It wasn't like the rest of us were having milk and cookies that night. We all went through it, but we don't sit around sulking about it."

"That's it?" Cowley asked. "You think they're sulking?"

"I think I'm tired of the silent act. It's time someone made them talk." Strout was staring at Wallice as he said this. His face was dark with sudden anger and his fists were clenched.

Fen saw what was coming first. "Leave him alone, Strout," he warned, but Strout was already moving.

Wallice was leaning against the wall, staring at the ground. Strout walked up to him and said, "Say something."

Wallice glanced at him but didn't speak. His face showed no expression.

Strout shoved him. "I said *say* something!"

Wallice's jaw tightened a little, but still he was silent.

Fen wanted to stop what was coming, but he didn't know what to do. He moved closer and the other boys followed. Lukas looked worried. Noah looked excited.

Strout put his hand to his ear. "What was that? I can't hear you. Come on. I know you can talk. Say something!" He shoved Wallice again.

And Wallice exploded.

He head-butted Strout in the chest, catching the bigger boy off guard and knocking him back a step. Then he lowered his shoulder and tackled him. He made no sound. His attack was frightening in its silent ferocity.

117

At first Wallice had the upper hand. He straddled Strout and began punching him in the face and chest, swinging wildly, furiously.

But with a heave Strout threw the smaller boy off. The two rolled around on the ground, scratching, punching, neither able to gain the advantage. The other boys ran up and circled around them.

"Hit him, Wallice!" Noah yelled. "Punch him in the face!"

Gage and Lukas, no fans of Strout, yelled similar encouragement to Wallice.

But then Strout's superior size and strength showed through. He punched Wallice in the stomach hard enough that Wallice gasped. Then he got him in a headlock and started punching him in the face. Wallice fought and twisted like mad, but he couldn't get away.

"We have to stop this," Fen said. "He's going to hurt him." No one paid any attention to him, their attention all fixed on the fight. Fen realized that if anyone was going to do anything, it would have to be him.

However, just as he started forward, he heard a feral cry from behind him and turned to see Eben, just entering the practice yard, struggling with the heavy bucket of water.

Eben dropped the water bucket and charged, the whole time still making the sound. It was somewhere between a scream of rage and a cry of pain and it was the eeriest sound Fen had ever heard. It chilled him to the bone.

Eben jumped on Strout's back, but instead of punching him, he grabbed him around the neck and bit down hard on Strout's ear.

Blood spouted and Strout howled in pain. He twisted, trying to knock the younger brother off him, but he couldn't quite reach him and the whole time Eben was biting down, snarling and jerking his head around as if trying to bite his ear completely off.

Which, Fen realized with heart-stopping clarity, was exactly what he was trying to do.

Fen grabbed Eben and tried to pull him off, but Eben had his teeth locked tight and all he succeeded in doing was causing Strout to cry out. At the same time, Cowley and Gage tackled Wallice, who'd gotten up and was about to launch himself at Strout again.

What would have happened next, Fen didn't know, because right then Flint got back. The sergeant took in what was happening in a glance and ran across the practice yard. He shoved Fen out of the way and took hold of Eben's face in his gnarled hands.

"Let go, lad. It's time to let go." He worked his powerful thumbs into the boy's jaws, slowly forcing them open.

Once free, Strout rolled away and came to his feet, his hand clamped over his ear. Blood streamed down the side of his face and his eyes were wide with shock.

"What's wrong with you?" he yelled at Eben.

Flint was crouched on the ground, holding Eben down. Eben was going berserk, trying to get away from Flint, all the while still making the strange, feral sound. Flint yelled at the boy to stop and shook him a couple times but it had no effect.

"Let me go!" Wallice shouted, and Fen turned to look at the older brother, who Cowley and Gage were still holding down. "Let me go! I can help him!"

The boys looked at Flint, who nodded.

When they let Wallice go he ran to his brother and knelt by him. He leaned down close to his face. "Stop it, Eben! It's Wallice! I'm here! I'm okay!"

He kept shouting the words at the boy. After a minute his words must have gotten through because the wildness gradually left Eben's eyes and he went still.

"Wallice?" he said in a small voice.

Flint let go of Eben and Wallice grabbed him in a fierce hug. The two sat there on the ground then, Wallice rocking Eben while silent tears streamed down the younger brother's face.

Flint went over to Strout, who was looking pale. Blood was running down his neck. "Let me see." Strout pulled his hand away and Flint inspected his ear. It was a bloody mess, half bitten away. "It's not good, but you should be able to keep it. Go see the stitcher, boy. You know where his office is?"

Strout nodded and ran off, taking a wide circuit around the two brothers, who were still on the ground.

Flint turned to the rest of them. "What happened?"

"Strout was trying to make Wallice talk," Fen said. "He shoved him and yelled at him. Wallice attacked him. They were fighting and then Eben showed up."

Flint looked at the others and they nodded. "Well, I think Strout learned his lesson. What about the rest of you? Did you learn anything?"

"Don't mess with them brothers," Noah said somberly. The small boy was looking at them with respect. "They'll tear you up."

"That's part of it," Flint agreed. "But that's not what I'm looking for."

"We don't turn on our own," Fen said. "Whatever happens, we stick together. Or we're nothing." They were words that Flint repeated to them nearly every day, in one form or another.

"That's right. You boys are looking at this and you're thinking, what happens now? I'll tell you what happens now. Nothing. Because you're brothers. Brothers fight. It gets ugly sometimes. But you put it behind you because you're family. If you want to survive as a soldier, you have to know that no matter what happens, the man beside you will protect your back."

He stared at them while they absorbed this. Then he waved them away. "Take the rest of the day off. Get some rest. We'll continue training again in the morning."

They filed out of the practice yard. On the way out, Fen looked back over his shoulder. Flint was kneeling beside the two brothers, talking to them in a low voice.

⚜ ⚜ ⚜

The boys went back to the barracks and sat or lay down on their cots. No one talked, each of them thinking with what had happened, what Flint had said. The brothers didn't reappear.

After a time Strout entered. He had a big bandage on his head and he looked angry. "Did he kick them out of the squad?" he said. "Are they gone?"

Fen sat up and looked at him. "No, he didn't."

Strout scowled. "After what they did, they're still in the squad?"

"What about what you did?" Fen asked him. The other boys were watching intently.

"What did I do?" Strout said sullenly.

"You turned on one of your brothers," Lukas said quietly.

Strout glared at him. "What are you talking about?"

"You provoked Wallice without a reason," Cowley added.

"What?" Strout pointed at his ear. "You all saw what they did to me, right? You weren't asleep or anything while it was happening?"

"We saw," Lukas said. "You turned on your brother for no reason."

Strout spun on the chubby boy. "Quit saying that! Those two are animals. They aren't my brothers."

Gage spoke up. "They're my brothers. And so are you, Strout."

His words shook Strout a little so that for a moment he couldn't reply. Then he said, his voice rising, "Are you telling me you believe that garbage Flint is always spewing about us being a family?"

"I don't think it's garbage," Fen said calmly.

"I don't either," Cowley added. Lukas and Gage both nodded.

"You all aren't much of a family, that's for sure," Noah said, "but I guess you're better than nothing."

Strout had become very agitated. He was breathing hard and his face was flushed. "Well, I'm not your family and you aren't mine! My family is dead, you hear me? Dead!"

"Which is why we're family," Gage said. "None of us has anyone else."

"I don't need anyone else," Strout snapped. "You hear me. I don't need anybody!" He stomped out the door and left.

⚓ ⚓ ⚓

Strout didn't come back for the rest of the afternoon. But not long after they'd eaten dinner the barracks door opened and the brothers came in. Wallice had his hand on Eben's shoulder, almost like he was guiding him. Neither boy looked up as they passed down the aisle between the row of cots to the far end of the barracks, where they slept off by themselves. The boys all looked at each other. Fen felt like he should say something—he wanted to let them know it was okay, that he didn't hate them—but he didn't know what or how to say it.

Surprisingly, it was Noah who broke the ice.

Noah got up off his cot and took an apple out of his pocket. He walked over to the brothers, who were sitting side by side on Eben's cot. Wallice looked up, his expression guarded. Eben kept his eyes down.

121

"Here," Noah said. "I saved this for you. I don't know if you got dinner or not."

Wallice took the apple, a strange look on his face.

Lukas got up and rummaged around in the chest at the foot of his bed. He took out a bun and went over and gave it to Wallice as well. "I was going to eat this later," he said sadly. "But I can't let a brother go hungry."

Wallice looked at the food in his hands, then at the other boys. Fen thought he looked bewildered, like something had just happened to him that he'd never experienced before. His mouth opened and closed a few times. Then he nodded and whispered something that might have been thanks. Eben never looked up at all.

Chapter 17

The months passed. Fall turned into winter, which was slowly turning into spring. The training had continued mostly nonstop, with only the rare day off. It became more difficult, and yet easier at the same time as they grew stronger and fitter.

It was morning when Fen and the rest of the boys ran through the open castle gates, headed down to the docks. Flint wasn't running with them this morning. He only ran with them sometimes now.

Everywhere there was bustling activity. The city had changed a lot over the months. Most of the burned buildings had been torn down and hauled away and new buildings erected in their place. The farmland around the city was being plowed and spring crops planted. The docks seethed with activity, as Samkara pursued trade with the small nations up and down the coast.

The boys ran by the estates that used to belong to the nobles. A number of them had been converted into barracks. The first one they passed housed only boys. A dozen more squads like Fen's had been created, some with boys as young as seven and eight in them. Fen's squad was the only one quartered in the castle. The city had grown used to the idea of seeing boys training to be soldiers, and they no longer drew curious looks when they took their morning run.

The boys reached the docks and turned to run back up the hill. None of them were breathing hard. Running was almost easy now. It was amazing to Fen how much they had all changed.

Lukas had lost the layer of fat he carried. Gone was the baby face and in its place someone different, leaner and harder, was emerging. Noah had grown noticeably taller, though he was still the shortest among them. He still retained his savage intensity and the other boys had learned that if they went too far teasing him, he was prone to blow up and attack them. He seemed utterly fearless.

Gage had grown the most, four inches at least, so that he was almost as tall as Strout now, and his shoulders had broadened, muscle filling in. He was still prone to clumsiness and the others ribbed him about it, but Fen had a feeling that once he got used to his size that would go away and he'd be a man you wouldn't want to tangle with.

Eben and Wallice, the quiet, black-haired brothers, were no longer as thin as they had been. They still barely spoke except when necessary and kept to themselves most of the time. Fen had learned a lot about the other boys' pasts, but where the brothers were concerned it was all a blank.

Strout was still the tallest and the strongest among them, though the gap was not as wide as it had once been. Of them all, he was the only one Fen truly disliked. The boy's arrogance and casual cruelty made him grit his teeth.

Cowley was still the prankster, the one who made jokes and liked to laugh. He had filled out as well and as he matured the girls paid more and more attention to him. Even the women noticed him. His problem was that he loved the attention too much. He and Amma were still together, but that didn't stop him from flirting outrageously with practically every pretty woman he came across. Fen had seen girls fighting over him. He'd seen jealous lovers come after Cowley with fists flying. Cowley beat them all of course—after all, they weren't training every day to be a fighter like he was—and so those fights were fewer all the time. But if he hadn't encouraged the attention things would have been a lot simpler.

Every day when they ran, a different boy took the lead and chose their route to and from the docks. Today it was Noah, and he led them through one of the main market squares, which was already filling up with vendors hawking their wares—sausages, bread, withered apples stored from last year's crop, potatoes, a smattering of dried vegetables—and the first shoppers of the day.

On the far side of the square, Fen saw a priest standing on the steps of a temple. It was the same priest he'd seen in the plaza the day of the executions. He was waving his arms and preaching in a loud voice. It wasn't the first time Fen had seen him out there, preaching the same message. Ever since that day he preached the same thing. The Fist was beloved by Hentu, he said. He was the weapon Hentu would use to smite Samkara's enemies.

Fen wasn't sure he believed what the priest had to say. Mostly he was glad that everyone seemed to think the earthquake was caused by a god. He himself hoped it was true. That explanation was far better than the alternative, that he had somehow caused it himself.

As the event receded into the past it seemed more and more improbable that he had caused it. Why in the world would he have such power? It made no sense at all. There was nothing special about him.

Cowley dropped back to run beside Fen. He jerked his thumb at the priest.

"What do you think? You spend more time with him than anyone. You think the Fist has been chosen by a god?"

"I don't know what to think," Fen replied. "There's definitely something about him." No one could deny that there was a strange power around the Fist. He was possessed of a manic energy that was almost superhuman. He worked incredible hours, rising before dawn and working until long after dark. He seemed to be everywhere. It was no surprise to see him working with laborers who were repairing the city's defensive walls—working harder than them actually—and then see him a few hours later training soldiers.

But that was only part of it. The story of the earthquake spread across the entire city like wildfire, mutating as it went. By the end of the week there were numerous people who swore that the Fist simply pointed at the earth and ordered it to open and swallow the condemned prisoners.

Other events followed, fueling the fire. During the winter the Fist was working on some scaffolding four stories up, helping the stone masons move a large stone into position, when the scaffolding collapsed. The other three men working with him were killed in the fall, but the Fist walked away unscathed.

Just a few weeks ago the Fist was training with some soldiers, sparring with five men at once, so the story said. One of them got lucky and stuck a spear clear through his shoulder. But he simply pulled it out and walked away. By the next day there was no sign of a wound.

"There are a lot of stories," Fen said. "I don't know how many of them are true."

"I heard yesterday that some woman is going around saying her baby was sick with the crimson cough, but she held the child up when the Fist went by and it was miraculously healed."

As he had so many times before, Fen wondered if the Fist's powers were coming from whatever was in that shadow he'd seen twice now. He wanted to believe he'd only imagined it, but maybe that was some god, reaching through to touch the Fist. Maybe that was how the gods worked. What did he know about such things anyway?

They ran into the practice yard and Flint was waiting for them.

"We'll start out sparring today, boys," he said. "I thought our last session yesterday afternoon was sloppy."

"Which weapons?" Noah asked. They no longer practiced exclusively with the sword. They had spent time learning how to fight with spears, maces, axes, polearms and even staves. They still practiced wrestling also, and to that Flint had added hand-to-hand fighting and knife fighting.

"Let's start with the swords," Flint replied. He began pairing them up. Fen wasn't surprised when he was matched up against Strout. Four out of five times he went up against the larger boy. He understood now why he was so often matched against the blacksmith's son. Flint was challenging him, forcing him to improve, to reach the limits of his abilities. Nothing was better for that than fighting an opponent who outclassed him.

And it was working. He always lost—and he had plenty of bruises to show for it—but he was getting better. Strout was having to work harder to beat him. If Fen had been fighting someone weaker than him he wouldn't have been progressing as quickly. But while he was getting better by the week, it didn't seem like Strout was improving all that much. He stuck mostly to the same combinations of attack and defense.

Since he couldn't match Strout in size or strength, Fen had learned to rely on his speed, as Flint had told him to, way back on that first day of sparring. He'd also learned to study Strout. He watched him closely, picking up on his habits and tendencies. He was getting to the point where he almost felt he knew what Strout was going to do before Strout even knew it.

The problem was that the other boy was so much bigger and stronger that a lot of time it didn't matter. His attacks simply bulled through Fen's defenses.

Fen hefted his practice sword and faced off against Strout. He remembered when this sword had been so heavy, so unwieldy.

Now it felt like part of him, an extension of his own arm. He'd worn the sword at his side long enough that he hardly noticed its presence.

Strout attacked right away. With his size and strength, he preferred to be the aggressor. He spent most of his time working on his attacks and not nearly as much on his defenses, despite how often Flint rode him about it.

As expected, Strout led with his favorite attack, a frenzied series of feints and slashes that many times broke right through Fen's defenses and left him with a new bruise or two.

But Fen was ready for him. He parried the first blow, then danced away, keeping his weight on the balls of his feet, his body centered so that he could move, or attack, in any direction instantly.

Strout scowled and pursued him. Their blades rang against each other. Strout's attacks came too fast for Fen to consciously follow. Sword fighting was becoming more and more automatic for him. His thrusts and parries were more reflex than anything, happening before he had time to think of them.

Strout's blade slipped through and struck Fen hard on the upper arm. But he managed to return it somewhat, jabbing Strout in the shoulder while he was extended. It wasn't enough to hurt the older boy, but if he'd been using a regular sword, it would have cut into his flesh.

Strout came in high, swinging at Fen's head, then abruptly switching to hack at his knees. As he did so, Fen reacted without thinking. Instead of falling back and deflecting the two blows, he suddenly leapt forward, inside Strout's swing. He hooked his foot behind Strout's ankle and rammed his shoulder into his chest.

Strout, caught off-guard, couldn't react in time. He fell down onto his back. Fen followed up his advantage, jabbing his sword tip against Strout's throat.

"Yield," Fen said.

Strout gathered himself and Fen thought he was going to keep fighting, then he sagged back and nodded.

Elated, Fen stepped back. He'd finally done it. He'd finally beaten Strout.

He felt eyes on him then and looked to his right. At the edge of the yard stood Barik, his arms crossed over his chest, watching.

Then Strout was charging at him again and there was no more time for looking around. This time he was a fraction too slow and Strout's sword slipped through and struck him in the chest hard enough to hurt, even though he had on his mail shirt and a padded jupon underneath it.

A few minutes later Flint called a halt and sent them to get water. He grabbed hold of Fen before he could follow the rest.

"I saw that. It was good work. I knew you'd beat him sooner or later."

Fen swelled with pride, but he tried to hide it. "He's stronger than me, but he's predictable."

"That he is. He's gotten lazy, too used to beating up on those smaller than him. But that's changing. The rest of you are catching up. Once he starts losing, he'll work harder at it. Defeat is a great motivator."

⚓ ⚓ ⚓

Flint stopped their training early that day, when it was only midafternoon.

"Go get cleaned up, boys. Put on a clean shirt and be out in front of the barracks in half a bell. Don't wear your mail shirts or your swords."

Puzzled, but happy for the time off, the boys took off for the barracks. Behind the barracks was a long trough filled with water. There were a few bars of hard, brown soap sitting on the edge of the trough.

Lukas stuck his hand in the water. "Brrr. Still freezing," he said.

"It's not that bad," Noah said, stripping off his shirt. "You just have to be tough." But he shivered when he stuck his arms in and goose bumps appeared on his skin.

The others stripped down to their breeches as well and started gingerly splashing water on their arms and chests, trying to get clean without getting too wet. The trough was constantly filled by a pipe that came from a nearby spring, and it felt to Fen like the spring must be nothing but a huge block of melting ice, the water was so cold.

Lukas was bent over, carefully dunking his head in the water, when it happened.

"That's no way to get clean," Cowley said. He bent, grabbed Lukas around the knees, then dumped him bodily into the trough.

Lukas bellowed and thrashed and the other boys all burst into laughter. "Cold, it's cold!" he yelled.

He came flying out of the trough and launched himself at Cowley, who was laughing so hard he couldn't defend himself. He was having difficulty dragging Cowley over to the trough when suddenly Strout pitched in, grabbing Cowley in a bear hug and throwing him into the water.

But when he did that he left himself exposed and Noah, always looking for a chance to get even with Strout, shoved him. His arms pinwheeled, but he couldn't keep his balance and he toppled in as well.

Wallice and Eben grabbed Gage, who was standing there giggling, and threw him into the water. Then Fen launched himself at them and managed to knock one of them in, though he went in at the same time.

By the end of it all everyone was soaking wet, shivering, and red from the cold. But they were the cleanest they'd been in months.

A bell rang, marking the time, and the rough housing ended immediately.

"We're gonna be late!" Lukas yelled, and they all took off running.

So it was that the eight of them were a few minutes late to line up in front of the barracks. They wore clean shirts, but their breeches and boots were wet and they were still dripping water and shivering.

Flint eyed them, but didn't say anything, either about being late or wet, though Fen thought he saw the corner of his mouth twitch in the beginning of a smile. "I have something for you." He motioned and a servant came forward, pulling a small hand cart.

"Noah, step forward."

Noah stepped forward and Flint took a new mail shirt and a padded leather jupon off the pile and handed them to him. He called the rest of the boys forward one at a time and gave them the same things. Fen stood there in line, staring at his with excitement.

"Well, what are you waiting for? Put them on."

Once they were all dressed, he said, "There's more." Each boy then received a surcoat. On each surcoat was emblazoned the Red Fist that was Barik's insignia.

"Just like the regular soldiers wear," Lukas said in awe.

"Today you *are* regular soldiers," Flint told them. "And now I have one more thing for you."

Another servant approached and what was in his cart made the boys stare and then grin at each other in excitement.

New swords, each one in a new scabbard and hanging from a new leather belt. Fen felt dazed as he buckled his on. He'd longed for this moment for what seemed like forever, sweated and bled and fought for it.

"You are no longer boys," Flint said. "From now on, you are soldiers."

They beamed at each other. Fen felt like he would burst.

"Go ahead, draw your swords," Flint said. "I know you're dying to."

They drew the swords from their scabbards. They glinted in the sunlight, straight and unmarred and pure.

"Remember what I told you," Flint said. "A sword is a responsibility. It is not a toy. It is not something to be played with. Don't draw your sword in public unless you intend to use it. Remember that you are official representatives of your Fist now. I expect you to act like it.

"Being a soldier is a big step. With it comes new privileges. But it also comes with new duties, new obligations. You are the Fist's men and you will behave like it. Am I clear on this?"

"Yes sir, sergeant!" they replied in unison.

"Good. Now go have some fun. You have the rest of the day off. Hit up the quartermaster before you go. I believe you all have some back pay coming."

Chapter 18

After leaving the quartermaster's, the young soldiers headed down into the city in a noisy, boisterous bunch. Spirits were high and they teased and joked and pushed each other as they walked.

"Real swords at last!" Strout yelled, drawing his and waving it around his head.

"Remember what Flint said about not drawing your sword," Lukas said worriedly.

"Stuff Flint! The old bag of wind isn't here now, is he?" Strout jabbed and slashed with the sword, his eyes following its glittering path.

A few of the others drew their swords as well. They whooped and began sparring in the street.

Fen wasn't one of them. This sword was noticeably lighter than his practice blade, yet it hung heavier on his hip, as if he could actually feel the weight of the extra responsibility Flint had been talking about. Somehow it all felt different now. It really wasn't a toy. It was a tool designed for one purpose: to kill people. That realization was not something he could easily shrug off.

"This mail shirt actually fits me," Noah said. His last had hung nearly to his knees. He fingered his new mail coat. It was much better quality than the old one, the links finer, stronger. It had been scrubbed with sand until it shone.

"New swords, free time and silver in our pockets," Cowley said. "What could be better?" He clapped his hand on Fen's shoulder. "What's wrong with you?"

"Nothing's wrong with me."

"Well you could've fooled me, walking along in your own dark cloud like that. We're on top of the world and you look like someone just killed your cat. Let it go and let's have some fun."

"You're right," Fen said. "It *is* time to have some fun."

"What should we do?" Gage asked.

"We should find women," Cowley said. "Beautiful women with large breasts and round stomachs!"

"That's Cowley," Strout said, grabbing him in a headlock and knuckling his head. "Only one thing on his mind."

Cowley twisted away and gave Strout a shove. "What else is there?" he laughed.

More good-natured ribbing followed as they made their way down the street, laughing, shouting, heedless of anything and anyone but themselves.

It struck Fen then. They spent almost every waking moment together. They slept in the same room every night. They fought and sweated and argued. Only this morning Wallice and Gage got into a fist fight and had to be dragged apart. But not before Wallice gave Gage a split lip. It was still swollen.

Yet now, when they could do anything they liked, they chose to stay together. They had become family.

And Fen had a moment where he could not clearly picture his mother's face.

"I know a place we should go," Noah said. "Down by the tanning pits."

"That's a terrible idea," Cowley said. "Simply terrible."

"It stinks down there," Lukas said, his nose crinkling as if he could smell it right then. "Like piss."

"I forgot that as a rich merchant's son you never smelled piss in your life," Noah retorted, putting his nose in the air and prancing around. "We're so rich our piss smells like rose water."

"And I forgot that you grew up bathing in piss," Lukas said.

A few of the boys guffawed, but Noah didn't give up on his idea. "Just listen to me for a second, you idiots. There's a place down by the tanning pits where they hold fights. Wild dogs. Rats. Sometimes they even get a rock badger in there. One of those can take on a half dozen dogs by himself."

"I've heard about those fights," Cowley said. "One of the servants talked about going down there. He said you can bet on the fights and win some real money."

"I'm not really interested in gambling with my money," Lukas said, putting his hand on his coin purse. "I was thinking about buying a pie."

"That's Lukas, always thinking with his stomach," Cowley said. "Come on. It's a special day. A time to try something new. I say we go and see what it's like."

"Count me in," Strout said. Gage chimed in and just like that it was decided.

"Lead on," Cowley told Noah.

Noah led them into a part of the city Fen had never been in before. The streets grew rougher and narrower as they went, the buildings meaner. They turned onto a narrow, winding street that wasn't cobblestoned. The buildings here were all three or four stories tall and they seemed to loom over them, blotting out much of the sky, leaving most of the street in perpetual shadow. The buildings slumped against each other like old men close to falling down and dying. Many of the walls showed large cracks. Garbage was piled against the buildings and the smell of raw sewage was strong.

"Don't walk too close to the edge of the street," Noah said. He pointed upwards. "You can get a chamber pot dumped on your head."

"People just dump their poop right into the street?" Lukas said, horrified.

"No public privies here," Noah replied. "Where else are they supposed to put it?"

Lukas looked like he was about to throw up. He got right into the middle of the street and craned his neck upwards, watching for anyone to appear at the windows. He was so fixed on that he didn't see the dead dog in the street and tripped over it.

"And they call me the clumsy one," Gage chortled. But his laughter sounded forced and no one else joined in. The atmosphere was starting to get to them.

In a doorway was what looked like a pile of old rags. But as they drew close to it Fen could see a pale hand and then a face, almost hidden in the rags. The mouth was open, and flies were crawling in and out.

"Is he dead?" Fen asked.

Noah shrugged. "Just stay together and don't slow down. It's not too much further."

An alleyway opened off to one side, so narrow Fen could have touched both walls at the same time. A man was in there, crouched over a body, going through the pockets. He looked up and glared at them. Noah ignored him and kept moving.

"I think he killed that man!" Lukas said in a loud whisper. "We should tell the city watch."

"The watch doesn't come down here," Noah said. "Keep moving."

"I don't want to do this anymore," Lukas said. Gage nodded his agreement. His usual loopy smile was gone and he was looking nervously side to side.

"We're close," Noah said.

"I still want to go," Cowley said. "We're soldiers, aren't we? We'll be okay." There were nods of agreement, but no one spoke up except Strout.

"I've come this far, I'm going the whole way."

Fen was glad they were all together. There was no way he would have come down here alone. He had his hand on his sword hilt and he wasn't the only one.

"You grew up in this area?" Lukas said. He was still whispering, as if afraid that if he spoke too loud something bad would happen. "I can't imagine how anyone could live like this."

"There's worse places to grow up," Wallice said, surprising them all. Though neither brother spoke much, Wallice was the most likely to say something. "You should see what it's like in Shantytown."

Outside the city walls was a huge open pit where Samkara threw its garbage. On the edge of the pit was a huddle of ramshackle structures built from discarded bits of this and that. That was Shantytown. Its residents lived off the garbage that the city dwellers threw away.

"You guys grew up in Shantytown?" Lukas' eyes got very wide. "I didn't know…how could…?"

"I don't want to talk about it," Wallice said, and closed off once more.

Fen was surprised. Those were probably the most words he'd ever heard from either of the brothers at one time. He'd guessed from the number of scars both boys had that they'd come from a tough background, but he'd never guessed it was as bad as Shantytown. The people living out there were basically wild animals, from what he'd heard. He'd always thought there were no children there at all.

How did they survive? he wondered. Did they have a mother or a father who looked after them, or did they do it on their own? He shuddered, suddenly really grateful for his childhood. They'd always been poor and they had to work hard to survive, but his mother had been kind and she'd made sure he was always taken care of.

He looked around at his companions, wondering what other secrets they kept. Where did they come from? What shaped them? The only thing he knew that they all had in common was they were all orphans. Cowley had always been an orphan, but the rest, at least those whose story he knew something of, had been orphaned when the city fell to the Maradi.

He wished, as he had so many times before, that he knew his own father. At least something about him. But he didn't. His mother had refused to speak of him and always retreated into sadness when he asked. Now, with her dead, he'd never know.

The stench of the tanning pits began to overtake the smell of sewage. It was so strong it made Fen's eyes water.

"Oh, god, that's awful," Gage said, holding his nose. Cowley was making gagging noises. Lukas had his surcoat pulled up over his nose and mouth.

"You get used to it," Noah said. "Don't be such babies."

It was funny, Fen thought. Noah was the smallest and youngest of them all, and yet he was the only one who didn't look overwhelmed by all this. Actually, he thought, looking at Wallice and Eben, they weren't overwhelmed either. But the rest of them were, though Strout was doing a good job hiding it.

Up ahead now they could hear men's voices. There was shouting, harsh laughter, then a ragged cheer mixed with shouts of rage and frustration.

"This is a bad idea," Lukas said, but no one answered him. They'd come this far. They couldn't turn back now, not until they saw what they'd come to see. Every boy had his hand on his sword.

The street ended suddenly and they stumbled out into a large open area. Fen could see the defensive wall of the city just a couple hundred paces ahead. The only buildings in this area were low, wooden shacks. There were a number of large pits where the animal hides were soaked in urine as the first step in the curing process.

There was a sizable crowd of men, probably fifty of them, crowded around a pit looking down into it. As the boys approached cautiously, a wild shout went up from the crowd. Money changed hands as bets were made.

Fen and the others looked at each other nervously. Lukas looked closed to panicking. Cowley had a half-smile on his lips, but Fen knew him well enough to know it was an expression he got when he was nervous. Strout looked like he was gritting his teeth. Other than Noah, only the brothers looked unperturbed, but they were such closed books anyway that it was hard to tell.

As they got close to the crowd a man turned and caught sight of them. He noticed first the uniforms and his face grew alarmed, but then he took in their age and alarm was replaced by something sly. He walked toward them.

"Hello, Rat," Noah said.

Rat was skeletally thin and twitchy. There was a large mole that covered most of one side of his jaw. He drew up when Noah addressed him, squinting at the boy. Then he smiled, a crooked thing that made Fen think of a wolf.

"Is that little Noah? It is! I haven't seen you in forever. Thought you were dead for sure, but now I see you up and joined the army. One of those kiddie soldiers we've been hearing so much about."

Whatever was happening in the pit seemed to have ended and the men were turning away, collecting bets, arguing with each other.

"Look, everyone!" Rat cried. "We got special guests today! Some of Samkara's army of the future!"

The boys all came to a halt as every eye turned on them.

"I knew we shouldn't have come here," Lukas moaned.

"Don't let on you're afraid," Noah whispered. "They get worse when you do that."

He strode boldly forward. After an instant's hesitation, Fen and the rest followed him. Fen tried to keep his expression hard, like he'd seen too much to be frightened by some rabble.

"We came to see the fights," Noah said. "What's next?" As he spoke he saw a couple men he recognized and he nodded to them. After a moment they nodded back.

"C'mon, make room," Noah growled. "Or do I have to shove this sword up someone's arse?"

136

Grudgingly, the crowd parted, shifting to allow them access to the pit. Noah moved into the opening and the others followed.

The pit was about twenty feet across and about eight feet deep. Strewn across the bottom were the carcasses of dozens of rats—big things with fat, pink tails and yellow teeth—and one dog who was almost dead. Bleeding from dozens of wounds, it was holding itself up with its forelegs only, its rear legs no longer working.

A man jumped down into the pit. Drawing a dagger from his rope belt, he dispatched the dog with a swift slash across the throat. Then he began throwing carcasses out of the hole. He tossed out the dog last, then jumped up, caught an outstretched hand, and was pulled out of the pit.

There was a commotion on the other side of the pit and the crowd parted as two dogs were dragged forward, one a brindle, the other solid black. Ropes were tied around their necks and they were snarling and snapping at anyone who came close. Men grabbed them, held them still, and the ropes were untied. The dogs were tossed into the pit.

They regained their footing and faced each other, hackles rising, teeth bared. Both dogs were painfully skinny and the brindle had an open wound on its hip that looked infected. Fen felt sick. He wished he'd never agreed to come. He liked dogs. He always had. He didn't want to watch these dogs fight for the entertainment of these men.

"If you want to stand and watch, you have to bet," Rat said, pushing in next to the boys. "The fights ain't free."

Noah was studying the dogs. "What are the odds on the brindle?"

"Three to two."

"Five coppers on the brindle," he said.

"Five from me too," Strout added.

"Like taking baby birds from the nest," Rat said with a grin, taking the money. "Didn't you notice the brindle's limping?"

"I noticed," Noah said. "It doesn't matter."

The crowd parted again as a man came through carrying a piece of bloody hide, chunks of meat still stuck to it. He tossed the hide down into the middle of the pit.

The dogs, who had been growling and circling each other, went instantly berserk, charging at the food. A moment later they were tearing at each other in a writhing mass of snapping teeth and snarling.

The black dog had the early upper hand, using its greater size to knock the brindle down and tearing a large flap of skin away on the brindle's neck.

More money changed hands.

But then the brindle twisted and got away. The men shouted and cursed, exhorting the dogs. Punches were traded. The boys were all silent, watching in horrified awe. To Fen it was like something from a nightmare. These were not men around him, they were wild beasts. Yet even wild beasts fought only to survive. This was madness and cruelty, such that only men could dream of.

The brindle ducked under the black dog's attack and bit down on the larger dog's hind leg.

Just like that the fight turned.

With that flash of teeth, the brindle severed the tendon in the black dog's hind leg. The black dog lost its balance and went down. The brindle went for its throat and the fight was over.

By unspoken agreement the boys backed away from the pit. Fen knew there was no way he was going to ever watch another one. He was getting out of here and never looking back. Then he realized something.

Not all of them had withdrawn.

The others realized it about the same time and they turned back to see Noah and Strout facing off against Rat.

"Pay up, Rat," Noah said. "You owe us fifteen coppers."

Rat's beady eyes swung from one boy to the other. A gray tongue came out and licked his upper lip. "I don't think so, boys."

"It was a fair bet. You'll pay."

Rat shook his head. "Call it the price of admission."

"You're not keeping my money," Strout said, putting his hand on the hilt of his sword.

Rat's eyes narrowed. "You think to come *here* and threaten *me*? This is *my* house."

He gestured and a number of men stepped out of the crowd and flanked him. There were ten of them altogether.

"Now that you've angered me, it's going to cost you. We'll be taking those flashy blades from you children and then you'll scamper on out of here and be glad we didn't gut you like a fish."

Chapter 19

"You want my blade?" Strout said, drawing his sword. The rest of the boys were only a fraction of a second behind him.

Fen's heart was racing, but his thoughts were remarkably clear. As he stood there, in the moments before the battle began, words that Flint had pounded into them so many times came to him.

Watch your enemy. What weapons does he have? Does he move like he knows how to use them? How is his balance? Is he right- or left-handed?

And, most important of all, *Look in his eyes. What do you see in his eyes?*

Every clue he could gather might be the difference between living and dying.

What he saw made him feel slightly better. The weapons the men had were crude at best, nothing to match the swords he and the others carried. Only one of them had a sword and it was a short sword. The rest had clubs or long daggers.

And they were overconfident. He could see it in the way they swaggered forward. It was in their eyes too, which showed greed and lust for violence, but no caution, no measuring of an unknown foe.

These men had no training. They were nothing more than common thugs. The one with the sword wasn't even holding it properly.

Right then, Fen knew they would win this fight. And he knew his brothers knew it too.

The men charged them. As they came they howled curses, probably thinking to frighten the boys, stampede them, whereupon they would be easy prey.

None of the boys so much as flinched. They held their fighting stances, swords up, as the men closed in.

One of the men with a club came at Fen. He had long, greasy hair and he was wearing a stained smock. With a grunt, he swung the club hard at Fen's head. Fen leapt back and the club missed his face by several inches. Before the man could recover he lunged.

The tip of his sword struck the man in the chest and slid between his ribs. It was surprisingly easy.

Then he was pulling back. Flint had warned them many times about the dangers of driving the blade too deep, the risk of getting it stuck in the foe's body and not being able to pull it out in time. He reset his balance and attacked again.

The man yelped and looked down at the wound in surprise. When he looked back up, he saw Fen's blade descending on him once again. He tried to block it with the club, but he was too slow.

The blade slashed across his bicep, not a deep cut, but deep enough to hurt. Fen didn't want to kill him. He only wanted to drive him off and it worked. The man screamed and dropped his club. Before Fen could attack again, he whirled and ran.

Fen took in the battle at a glance. Strout's man was down and bleeding. The brothers had one body at their feet and were swinging at the man with the short sword, who appeared to have some skill with it and was desperately trying to disengage without getting killed.

Cowley slashed his attacker across the face and the man fell backwards, howling. The man attacking Gage took off running just as Lukas coolly slapped aside a dagger thrust and cut deep into his attacker's thigh. The man dropped his dagger and went down, holding his hands over his head in surrender.

Only Rat still faced them, and he was bleeding from the stomach. His eyes fixed on Noah's blade as the boy approached him and he dropped his dagger.

"It was all a misunderstanding," he hissed, showing his teeth. "There's no need for violence."

"Where's our money?" Noah demanded. He was a head shorter than the man, but he looked taller at that moment. His expression was utterly hard and cold and Fen had no doubt he would kill Rat without blinking if it was necessary.

Look what we've become, he thought.

Rat started digging through his purse with shaky hands.

"We'll take the whole thing," Strout said.

"No," Fen said. "We're not thieves."

Strout looked like he was going to argue with Fen, but then he shrugged and backed down.

Moments later Noah had their coins and the boys were hurrying back the way they'd come. As soon as they were around a corner and out of sight they turned to each other, everyone talking at once, amazed and excited by what they'd just done.

"Did you see the way they ran from us?" Gage said. "They *ran*." He sounded like he couldn't believe it.

"I can't believe how easy it was," Lukas said, and then repeated it.

"Me either," Cowley said. "It was like everything slowed down and also happened really fast, all at the same time."

"It was a lot easier than fighting you," Fen said to Strout.

"It's all that training," Strout replied.

"Gentlemen, gentlemen!" Cowley said loudly, cutting through the din and finally getting their attention. "I want to propose two motions." They all looked at him. "One, I propose that we are awesome."

"I second that motion," Lukas cried. Other voices joined in.

"And two, I propose that we adjourn to a tavern I know where there is ale to be had." He gave a mischievous grin. "And buxom wenches!"

"Ale and girls!" Gage yelled.

They followed Cowley through the streets of the city. The sun had fallen and night was coming on. They walked confidently. They walked like real soldiers, Fen thought. Afraid of nothing. Filled with wonder at what they were capable of now.

He thought of his mother then and repeated the vow he made anew every day. *I couldn't protect you. But I promise I will protect others.*

Cowley made a couple of wrong turns and had to ask for directions finally, but just as it was growing dark he pointed at a tavern across the street and shouted, "There it is! The Rusty Cock!"

The sign had a badly painted rooster on it. A tiny amount of the red paint was still visible. Several men were just going inside.

"I thought you grew up in the palace," Fen said to Cowley. "How'd you know about this place?"

141

"Wilferd," Cowley said, without looking at Fen. His attention was fixed on the tavern and a smile was on his face. "He's one of the gardeners. He talks about this place all the time."

"It looks pretty seedy," Fen said dubiously. The building was in a general state of disrepair. The sign hung crookedly. Trash was piled by the door and someone was lying on it, passed out. Several men stood at the corner of the building, talking. One passed something furtively to another, then all of them glared at the boys.

"The places that aren't seedy we can't afford. Besides, Wilferd says it's not such a bad place once you get past the crust." He slapped Fen on the back. "Trust me. Have I ever steered you wrong?"

"You mean other than the time we almost got caught in that room in the palace? Or how about the time you thought it would be a good idea to sneak into Flint's quarters and *borrow* one of his shoes as a joke?"

"Those were minor missteps," Cowley said. "They have no bearing here."

Cowley opened the door. The tavern was really loud. Music, laughter and shouting poured from the place.

"Couldn't we go somewhere a little quieter?" Fen asked.

"Quiet places are dull," Cowley assured him. "And we have to celebrate. We became real soldiers today. How often is that going to happen?"

So saying he confidently led them inside.

Inside it was even louder. The place was packed with men and every one of them seemed to be shouting. Lanterns hung from the rough-hewn beams overhead, their dim light further weakened by the smoke from numerous cigars and pipes being smoked. A bar lined one wall, a stout man behind it pouring glasses of ale as fast as he could, while barmaids whisked the mugs away to customers. In the corner on a tiny raised platform a musician was playing a guitar while a woman accompanied him on a drum. It was hard to hear them over the din, but they sounded pretty awful to Fen.

There were no open tables, so they wedged themselves into a corner and Cowley disappeared into the crowd to find them a barmaid. The boys huddled together and stared wide-eyed around them.

Fen had been in taverns lots of times before, of course, while helping his mother clean, but they'd been nicer ones than this and he'd only been in them during the day, when at most they had two or three customers in them.

"It looks like we made it through the brambles only to fall into the ditch," Lukas shouted.

"We'll just have one or two ales and then leave," Fen replied.

Cowley returned and with him was a barmaid with a tray of clay mugs, brimming with foamy ale. She handed the mugs around and Cowley paid her. Then he leaned in close and said something in her ear.

"You're only a boy!" she cried in mock horror. She was easily twice Cowley's age, her cheeks round, her curly hair cut short. "I'd hurt you and then I'd feel bad."

Cowley said something back, his words lost in the noise of the tavern and she pinched his cheek and slid away into the crowd.

"Here's to us!" Cowley shouted, holding up his mug. "Last one to finish buys the next round!"

Fen had only had ale once before and he remembered hating it, but this one tasted surprisingly good and it went down easily. At least he managed not to be last. That was Lukas, who complained that he'd had to burp in the middle and it wasn't fair but the others shouted him down and when the barmaid reappeared a few minutes later with more mugs of ale he dug into his coin purse to pay her.

This one went down even easier. Fen burped and looked around, realizing that he didn't feel worried or afraid anymore. In fact, he felt cheerful, confident. He could take on the world. There was nothing he couldn't do, no one he couldn't handle in a fight. Not that he needed to fight. The people in this tavern were his friends, all of them.

Gage shouted something to him and he shouted back. Neither understood the other, but they both laughed.

The next round arrived and Strout banged his mug against Fen's a little too hard, so that some of the ale sloshed out and over Fen's hand.

"Sorry about that!" Strout yelled.

"It's okay!" Fen shouted back.

Strout put his mouth up near Fen's ear. "You really believe all that stuff about us being brothers?" Fen nodded. "I always thought it was garbage, but when those men came at us I felt... It was good to have the rest of you there. We sure showed them."

Fen gaped at the other boy, wondering if he'd heard him correctly. He'd never heard Strout talk so nicely before. He shouted, "That's what brothers are for!" and gave Strout a big hug. Strout hugged him back and spilled half his ale down Fen's back but Fen didn't care.

That set off something and all the boys started hugging each other—all of them but Wallice and Eben—though even they gave out a few pats on the back.

"We have to have more ale!" Cowley shouted. "More ale, more ale, more ale!" It caught on and soon all the boys were chanting the words over and over.

More ale arrived. Fen took a big drink and some sloshed over the rim and down his chin. He wondered briefly why he'd never gone to a tavern before. Taverns were a lot of fun. He tried to share his epiphany with Noah, but Noah was too busy shouting about something else to listen.

A man came over to them and gave a small bow. He had frizzy red hair and sunken cheeks. He looked them over, licked his lips, then said something. His words were lost in the din.

Lukas looked owlishly at Fen. "What'd he say?" He seemed to be having trouble standing and had to grab onto Fen's arm to catch his balance.

"What?" Fen replied.

"That's what I thought." Lukas let go of Fen's arm and promptly fell on the floor.

Gage started laughing so hard that he dropped his mug. Ale sprayed everywhere.

Fen turned his attention back to the frizzy-haired man. He was saying something into Cowley's ear and Cowley was nodding vigorously, a big smile on his face. Fen took an unsteady step toward Cowley and grabbed his shoulder.

"It's only two pieces of silver!" Cowley cried, turning to Fen. "I have that!" He reached for his coin purse, opened it and peered inside. "There's two of everything." He closed one eye. "That's better." He took a couple of coins out and held them up to peer at them.

"What's that for?" Fen asked.

Cowley threw his arm around Fen's neck and pulled him close. "He says he knows where some girls are. You want to come with me? I have more money." Without waiting for an answer he let go of Fen and started after the man who was motioning for him to follow.

Fen grabbed Cowley's arm. "Don't do it." It was strange how hard it was to make the words come out right. Why was it suddenly so hard to talk? "I don't trust him."

"Don't worry," Cowley said cheerfully. "I'll only be..." He waved vaguely. "...over there somewhere. I won't be long." He pulled away from Fen's grasp and stumbled after the man.

Gage watched Cowley walk away. "Where's he going?" Gage asked.

"Girls," Strout said. "He's going to find girls. I should go with him. I have money too." But he made no move to follow, only stood there weaving, a vacant grin on his face.

"Maybe we should have another ale," Gage said. "Mine's empty already." He looked around. "Hey, where did my mug go?"

That brought fresh howls of laughter from the others but Fen didn't join in. It bothered him that Cowley had gone off without the rest of them. There was something wrong with that, though he couldn't quite put his finger on it right then.

"What's wrong?" Noah yelled.

"I don't trust that man," Fen replied.

Noah blinked at him. It looked like he was having trouble getting his eyes to work. "What man?"

"The one who was just here."

Noah turned to look around and nearly fell down. Strout had to catch him. "There was a man here? I didn't see him," Noah said.

"Cowley left with him," Strout said. "He's going to see a girl."

For some reason that caused Gage to start giggling again and soon Lukas and Noah joined in.

"What are we laughing about?" Noah yelled, stumbling and falling to his knees, which made the other boys laugh even harder.

"I'm going to find him," Fen said. "We're supposed to stick together."

"We'll come with you," Wallice said. Eben, standing beside him, nodded. Neither one of them was holding a mug.

145

"So I…so I better find someone to hold my ale," Fen said. He held it out to Lukas, who promptly dropped it.

The three of them pushed through the throng, elbowing and fighting their way toward the door Cowley and the man had disappeared through. A man stepped on Fen's foot, and another one cursed and shoved him after Fen bumped into him and caused him to spill some of his ale, but the place was so crowded that Fen didn't fall down.

Mumbling apologies, he finally got through the press and reached the door. He swung it open and stepped through.

At first what he saw didn't make sense to him and he blinked, trying to clear up his vision.

Cowley was kneeling on the floor and two men were bent over him, one of them the frizzy-haired man. It looked like they were tugging on his shirt and it took Fen a moment to realize one of them was trying to pull Cowley's mail shirt up over his head while the other was trying to unbuckle Cowley's sword belt. There was blood on Cowley's face and he was trying to fight them off but his efforts were feeble.

Fen figured all this out about the same time one of the men looked up and saw him and the brothers in the doorway. He snarled and reached for a short sword that hung from his belt.

Fen yelled and charged him, trying to draw his sword as he went.

But he couldn't get his sword free and then his feet got tangled up with each other and he ended up crashing into the man. His momentum was enough that the man was knocked backwards and tripped over the frizzy-haired man who was still wrestling with Cowley.

All of them went down in a tangle. Fen felt someone punch him in the eye, but strangely it didn't seem to hurt. He countered by punching back and throwing an elbow. He couldn't seem to get any force behind the blows and the man hit him again, then grabbed him in a headlock.

All around him was thrashing and grunting and swearing and he fought to get free but he couldn't get a hold of the man's arm to pull it off his neck.

Then, suddenly, the man let go of him. Fen rolled free and came to his knees. Wallice and Eben were there. One of them was kicking the man who'd been holding Fen in the ribs and the other was punching the frizzy-haired man in the face over and over.

A door opened further down the hall and Fen looked up and saw two more men emerge from a room and come running toward them. Both had wooden cudgels in their fists and one was wearing leather armor.

"Look out!" he yelled, fighting to his feet and trying to get his sword free once more.

The brothers broke off their attacks and grabbed onto Cowley, dragging him back towards the doorway. The four of them almost made it through the doorway when the thieves hit them in a rush.

Fen fell backwards into the tavern room. Someone caught him before he fell and he realized a moment later it was Strout.

"Thought you might need some help!" Strout yelled, and threw himself at their attackers, his fists flying. Behind him came the rest of the squad and with howls they launched themselves into the fray.

The melee spread quickly. Strout, trying to punch one of the thieves, missed and hit a bystander, a short man with a bald head, knocking him backwards into another man with a long beard. The man with the beard roared and punched the bald man in the stomach.

The bald man's companions yelled and threw themselves at the bearded man, picking him up and throwing him on top of a table, which splintered and collapsed. The men sitting at the table charged the bald man's companions and from there it was just chaos.

Fen could no longer find the men who'd tried to rob Cowley. He saw Cowley once in the sea of cursing, fighting men, but when he reached for him the sea tugged him in the other direction and he lost him in the crowd.

Someone punched him in the ear and he turned but there was no way to tell who'd done it. He saw a man with a pock-marked face standing there. Somehow, in the midst of the chaos, the man was still holding his ale and drinking it as if nothing was happening. Strangely, the man winked at him and raised his mug in a toast.

Then someone tackled Fen from behind and he went down. He kicked and thrashed until he was able to make it back to his feet.

He looked around and saw Wallice and Eben standing back to back, fighting people off. It struck him as odd how steady they seemed. Their kicks and punches seemed to go where they wanted them to. Every time he tried to hit someone he missed.

Suddenly the tavern door burst open and a handful of armed men wearing leather armor forced their way in. One of them was blowing a whistle over and over and another was yelling, "City watch! Stand down!" The rest began laying about them with truncheons, clubbing men senseless left and right.

As they came toward him, Fen put up his hands. Most of the rest of the tavern's patrons also quit around that time. They broke off, nursing split lips and bruised knuckles. Those nearest the door began to slip away.

The big man who had been pouring ales earlier pushed his way through the rapidly-thinning crowd. "It was them!" he yelled, pointing out the boys. "They're the ones who started this! And now my tavern is trashed." He pushed his angry face right up close to Fen's. "You'll pay for this," he growled. "You and your young pup friends."

"It wasn't us!" Fen protested. "It was them! They tried to rob our friend!"

The sergeant in charge of the watch was a big-bellied man with gray hair. "Who did?" he asked Fen. "Who tried to rob your friend?"

"Those men..." But Fen faltered as he spoke, realizing he couldn't see the frizzy-haired man or his companion. The rest of the boys looked around them but found nothing.

"They must have snuck out the back," Fen said.

"Sure they did," the sergeant said sarcastically.

"They always do," another one of the watch added and several of the onlookers chuckled.

"He's telling the truth," Cowley said. "They knocked me down in that hallway and were trying to steal my mail shirt and my sword when my friends came to my rescue." He was swaying and slurring his words badly as he spoke. "We have to go after them! They're getting away!"

He tried to run for the doorway but right away tripped—or was tripped—and fell heavily.

"Are you boys going to come peacefully to lockup, or do we get to do this the hard way?" the sergeant said, smacking his truncheon in his open hand.

"I think you should try to run," one of the watch said, a cold smile on his face. "It's more fun that way."

"No," Fen said. "We'll come peaceful."

The boys were relieved of their sword belts and iron manacles were clamped on their wrists. While this was being done the tavern keeper kept pestering the sergeant. "I want them to pay. I want the army to pay. Don't let them get away with this. I run an honest establishment. I pay my taxes to the king. I demand protection."

"You'll get your ounce of flesh, don't worry," the sergeant told him, clearly irritated. "Stop your yapping."

"I just want what's coming to me."

"Come down to the lockup in the morning and talk to the clerk. He'll put your name on the docket." When the tavern keeper opened his mouth to continue the sergeant held up one thick finger.

"One more word, just one more, and I'm dragging you down too. Interfering with the lawful duties of the night's watch, that's what this is and I'll write you up."

The tavern keeper gave up then, but he followed them out into the street, glaring at them the whole way. Once they had started down the street he raised his fist and bellowed, "You'll pay for this!" one last time.

The ale seemed to have mostly worn off. Fen's eye was aching and starting to swell shut and about a dozen other places hurt as well, especially his ribs on the right side, though he didn't remember getting hit there. With the return of sobriety it was hitting him how much trouble they were in.

He wasn't the only one. Now that the excitement was over the boys were looking at each other sheepishly. Fen knew they were all thinking the same thing: *What's Flint going to say when he finds out?*

The lockup was a grim, dirty building, low and squat, wedged in between two taller stone buildings. It had no windows, only a thick, iron-bound door. The sergeant banged on the door and after a moment there was the sound of a key in the lock and the door swung open.

The boys were herded through the door and into a low-ceilinged, dingy room. There was a rough wooden desk with a clerk sitting behind it. He was a wizened, wrinkled little thing, dried up and stringy as old boot leather. He was wearing thick spectacles that made his eyes look very large. On the desk in front of him was a large, leather-bound ledger. While the sergeant told him the charges against the boys he stared unblinking at them, his face betraying no emotion.

"Drunk and fighting," the clerk said, dipping his quill in ink and writing in the ledger. "Names?"

One by one the boys gave him their names and he wrote them down. After the last one he said, "What was damaged?"

"I don't know," the sergeant said. "The place was a dump before the fighting started so it's hard to tell what they caused and what was already that way. You'll have the tavern keeper in here in the morning, though. No doubt he can tell you."

The clerk turned his spectacled gaze on him. "Your estimate is important to the resolution of such matters, sergeant. I believe I've told you that before."

"I know." The sergeant scratched his thick neck. "I'll get it better next time. Can we get on with checking them in? I'm due to get off duty soon."

"You said you would do better last time," the clerk said. "And the time before that."

"Okay, okay! Let's see, two broken tables and maybe four or five chairs. A dozen mugs. I think."

"You *think*? The fact that these boys are in the army makes it especially important that you be sure. You know how the Fist feels about waste. Inaccuracy leads to waste."

"I liked this job better before you came along," the sergeant grumbled. "Back then all we had to do was crack heads and drag away the bodies."

"You have my deepest sympathy, I am sure," the clerk said, though his face betrayed no emotion. He glanced at the items he had written down in the ledger, then spun it around and held the quill out to the sergeant. "Sign here, please."

The sergeant got a pained look on his face.

"A simple X will do."

The clerk waved to a guard who was standing by the door leading to the cells. The guard pulled a ring of keys off his belt, unlocked the door and the boys trooped through.

He led them down an ill-lit hallway, past several other doors, then stopped at one and unlocked it. He swung the door open and motioned them inside. Once they were in, Strout held up his manacled hands and said, "Hey, are we going to get these off?"

"Maybe if you change your tone, pup," the guard said. He was an older man, his hair pure white and his teeth stained brown from tobacco, but his eyes were sharp and corded muscle showed in his forearms.

"Please?" Fen asked, and several others chimed in.

"I have your word you boys won't cause any troubles?" he asked.

"We promise," Fen said and the others nodded.

"They'll be sending word to your sergeant," the guard said as he began unlocking their manacles. A couple of the boys groaned and he grinned. "I imagine he'll have words for you, not pleasant ones either."

He left. The only light in the cell was from a sputtering oil lamp hanging in the hallway outside, casting its weak light through the small, barred window. The room stank of urine and excrement. The straw on the floor was moldy and sticky. There was no furniture of any kind.

"We're really in for it," Lukas said, leaning against the wall and holding his head in his hands.

Strout turned on Cowley and gave him a shove. "This is your fault. You had to go chasing after a wench and now we're all in trouble."

Cowley shoved him back. "I didn't tell you to come after me. That was your choice."

"So we were just supposed to leave you?" Lukas asked.

"That would have been the smart thing to do," Strout growled. "I should've never gone with the rest of you idiots tonight. You're nothing but trouble."

"We didn't want you to," Noah said, advancing on Strout with his fists clenched. "No one asked you to. No one likes you."

"You think I care about that?" Strout retorted. "I wish I never had to look at any of your faces ever again." He drew his fist back.

Quickly Fen got between them. "Knock it off. Turning on each other will only make things worse."

"Shut up," Strout told him. "I'm sick of hearing you say things like that, like Flint says. You think you're in charge of this squad without him around? Is that what you think?"

"I never said that."

"But you sure act like it. You're always chiming in, acting like you know what's best for everybody. But you don't. You don't know anything about anyone."

"I know what would be best for everybody," Noah piped up. "If you quit the squad, Strout. We don't want you with us."

Fen whirled on the smaller boy. "Don't talk like that, Noah. We're all in this together."

"Not him," Noah said belligerently.

"There you go, doing it again," Strout said to Fen. "You think just because you're the Fist's pet that makes you special."

"Lay off him, Strout," Cowley said tiredly. The blood on his face had dried and he looked haggard. "Don't forget I'm the one you're mad at."

"I'm mad at all of you." Strout glared around the room. "I may be stuck in the same squad with you, but that doesn't mean I have to like you. And it sure doesn't mean that we're brothers. We're soldiers and that's it. Everybody just leave me alone." He stomped off to the other side of the cell and threw himself down.

"Are we done fighting now?" Lukas said. "I'm tired. I need to sleep." He yawned and sat down on the floor. "Ugh. The floor is all sticky. The worst part is, I'm going to be lying in it soon."

Chapter 20

The next morning they were awakened by the cell door opening. A voice they knew all too well boomed, "Up and at 'em, soldiers! There's work to be done!" It was Flint, holding a lantern. He poked the nearest boy in the ribs with the toe of his boot.

Stiffly, the boys got to their feet. Fen's eye had swollen the rest of the way shut during the night. He ached everywhere. On top of that, he had a splitting headache and his stomach was doing flips. He was certain he would be throwing up soon.

From the moans and groans, the other boys weren't doing any better. The exception was the brothers, who looked pretty much normal. They didn't even seem beat up.

Flint led them to the outer office where the same clerk was still sitting behind the desk. Fen wondered if he had a home or if he just lived there. Flint signed them out and they buckled on their sword belts and followed him outside.

Outside, Flint didn't say a word, he simply took off running. Groaning, weary and sick, they took off after him.

It was the worst run of Fen's life. His mouth and throat were parched. Every step pounded inside his skull. His feet didn't seem to work right and he kept stumbling on the cobblestones. Except for the brothers, none of the others were doing any better. Cowley threw up in the first five minutes, and Noah and Lukas weren't far behind him. Gage fell down twice.

The run lasted an eternity, but finally the walls of the castle loomed up before them. Fen thought nothing had ever looked better in his life. Beside him he could hear Lukas softly gasping, "Thank the gods," over and over.

A dozen paces from the gates, Flint turned around and headed back down the hill. The boys staggered to a halt and gaped at him in disbelief.

"You have got to be kidding," Strout wheezed. His face was pale and sweat plastered his curly black hair to his head.

"I can't do it," Gage whimpered. "I can't run another step."

Flint stopped and looked back at them. "No one's forcing you to. If you can't handle the *responsibility* of being a soldier, then quit." With that he took off running again.

"I'm going to kill him," Strout said. "That's all there is to it."

Groans came from the boys but they all started after their sergeant. Except for Lukas, who stood bent over, his hands on his knees.

"Come on, Lukas," Fen said, going back and tugging on his arm.

Lukas gave him a tearful look. "I can't do it. I've got nothing left."

"I don't care. I'm not letting you quit."

Fen had to practically drag him, but he finally got Lukas going again.

Fen wasn't sure how he made it. He wasn't sure how any of them made it, but somehow they finished the run and finally, mid-morning, stumbled into the practice yard. Most of them collapsed right away. Noah curled up on the dirt on his side, his hands over his face. Lukas flopped onto his back.

Flint gave them a minute, then said, "Okay. Enough lying around. Get your practice swords out and let's do some combinations."

"What about breakfast?" Cowley asked. "You can't work us this hard without some food." Others chimed in in agreement.

"It's too late. You lads missed breakfast."

A chorus of cries greeted his words. "We have to eat!" Lukas wailed.

"You can't do this to us!" Gage added.

"Get up," Flint snapped, his voice hard and cold. "Get *up* and get in formation!"

The boys pulled themselves to their feet and got into line. Flint began stalking up and down the line.

"Let's get one thing straight," he said, biting off each word. "I did not *do* anything to you. You did this to yourselves. You did this when you chose to get drunk and get into a fight in that tavern."

"We couldn't just—" Strout began, but Flint cut him off.

"Silence!" he roared. He was the angriest Fen had ever seen him. "Don't speak until I tell you to. I see now that I have gone too

154

easy on you. Clearly you've learned nothing that I've been trying to teach you. Do you think this is a game? Is that it?"

He stabbed a finger at them. "*This is not a game!*" he yelled. "You are learning to be soldiers. You are learning to kill. And if you don't learn it, if you treat it like a game, it is you who will be killed.

"You are not children anymore. You're soldiers and you need to start thinking like soldiers. You need to understand that your choices have consequences." He began ticking off the points on his fingers. "One, you shouldn't have gone into that tavern. Any idiot could see a place like that is trouble. All you had to do was look around. Thieves and cutthroats everywhere. That was your first mistake. Then you compounded that mistake by getting drunk. Ale dulls your wits and kills your coordination. You are bright enough to understand that, right? When you drink, you can't fight. So, not only did you go into enemy territory, but then you let your guard down. You made yourself a target."

He glared at them for a moment, letting the words soak in.

"Then you committed the worst error of all. *You split up.* Your strength lies in each other. Once you start going your separate ways, that disappears. You become vulnerable, easy to pick off one by one."

Flint's tone changed abruptly, most of the anger leaving it. "Understand this. What I am teaching you is for your own good. Whether you learn it or not has no effect on me. I don't get paid any more or less no matter what happens to you. My purpose here is keeping you alive. That's it. Maybe I'm an old fool, but I don't want to see you dead."

Along with the rest, Fen stared at the ground, unable to meet his sergeant's gaze. He realized then why Flint was so upset. He wasn't mad at them, not really. He was worried about them. He didn't want to see them hurt or killed.

He looked up and met Flint's eyes. "I'm sorry, sergeant," he said.

The other boys mumbled their apologies as well and Flint nodded.

"Now go get your practice swords."

⚜　　⚜　　⚜

155

"That was the longest day of my life," Cowley said at the end of the day as they trudged out of the practice yard. It was after dark. Fen was so tired he could barely put one foot in front of the other. At the end, the sparring had been a joke, the boys stumbling against each other, their swings slow and unwieldy. A child could have defeated any one of them.

"Hey! What's the matter with you?" Cowley yelped as Strout suddenly slammed him up against the wall.

"This is your fault," Strout snarled, shoving his face right in close to Cowley's. "None of this would have happened if it wasn't for you."

"I think you said that already, last night," Cowley said.

"I hate how smug you always are. I ought to kick the smugness out of you right now."

Cowley gave him a little half smile. "So why don't you?"

"Because I'm too tired." Strout turned away and trudged toward the mess hall.

"That guy has a real attitude problem," Cowley said.

"Maybe this time he has a good reason for it," Fen said.

"What? You're mad at me too?"

"Yes, I'm mad at you! What you did was stupid and selfish."

"Okay, maybe it was a little stupid," Cowley admitted. "But still—"

"It was more than a little stupid. Those men could have killed you. Don't you get that?"

"You're being dramatic."

"No, I'm being your friend. I don't want to see you die, Cowley."

"I was only having a little fun," Cowley protested, but he looked a little sheepish.

"Why did you go with that man anyway? What about Amma? Don't you care about her at all?"

Cowley looked away. "Of course I care about her. This doesn't have anything to do with her. I was just messing around and it got out of hand."

"That's the problem with you, Cowley. You're always messing around. You treat everything like it's a game. Well it's not. We're not little kids anymore. You have to start taking this seriously or…"

"Or what?"

"Or you don't belong in the squad."

Fen walked away then. He could feel Cowley's eyes on his back, but he didn't look back. Cowley was his closest friend. He would do anything for him. But if he couldn't see how his reckless actions endangered the squad, then he didn't belong there.

Chapter 21

"We're going to start something new today," Flint said. "Come with me."

He led them out of the practice yard and across the castle grounds, towards the stables. In front of the stables was a row of saddled horses. When he saw the horses, Gage's eyes lit up and he hurried forward to the front of the group.

"Horses, sergeant?"

Flint nodded. "Your father raised horses, didn't he?"

"He did." Gage's eyes were fixed on the animals, a big smile on his face.

None of the other boys looked anywhere near as eager as Gage did. Fen looked around at their expressions, which ranged from distrust to veiled fear. He'd never been on a horse and he was willing to bet none of them had either. Horses in his experience either belonged to the wealthy and were therefore strictly off limits, or they were work animals, pulling carts and wagons, and the drivers of those tended to be free with their whips if anyone interfered with their work.

"It's time you learned to fight from horseback," Flint said. "But to do that, you'll first need to learn to ride, right?" He gestured to Gage. "You want to start them off?"

Gage nodded eagerly. "Which one is mine?"

"Whichever one you want."

Gage walked down the line, looked the animals over carefully, then chose a tall roan. He untied her and led her out in front of the boys. "Horses are amazing creatures," he said. "But you have to be careful with them. The important thing to remember is that they spook easily. And when they do, they go kind of crazy. That's when you can really get hurt."

As he spoke he was stroking the horse's muzzle. To Fen's surprise he actually pressed his face against the horse's neck for a moment and when he continued talking his voice was husky with suppressed emotion.

"If you treat your horse well, take good care of him, he will never let you down. You won't find a truer animal in the world."

"Now we know why Gage isn't interested in girls," Noah said. "He's in love with horses."

The boys laughed and Gage's cheeks turned red.

"Okay, knock it off," Flint said, striding forward. He stood by the horse's hindquarters and pointed at its feet. "See those things down there? They hurt when they hit you. If you walk up behind a horse when he's in a bad mood, or if you come up behind him and startle him, he'll kick you and believe me when I tell you there's nothing like it. Nothing and no one in your life will ever hit you that hard. Remember my words and save yourself a whole lot of pain. Now, everyone pick a horse and let's get started."

Fen chose a spotted horse—Gage told him it was called an appaloosa—and patted it gingerly on the neck. Up close the animal seemed awfully tall. "Is it a boy or a girl?" he asked Gage.

"How old are you now?" Noah asked. "And you still don't know the difference between boys and girls?" More laughter greeted his words.

"She's a mare," Gage said.

"Don't just stand there looking at them," Flint said. "Mount up and let's get started." He and Gage climbed on. They made it look easy.

It was harder than it looked, but Fen made it up onto the mare's back. It felt really different, up there so high. Awkward too, but overall he liked the feeling. Around him the other boys were getting on also. Lukas' eyes were very wide and he had a death grip on the pommel. Noah missed his first try at getting on and fell on his back. Cowley made it on the first try and held one hand up in a flourish.

The brothers, Wallice and Eben, got on without much trouble, then looked darkly around them, as if expecting it to all be a trick somehow. For all his bold words, Strout looked the most ill at ease on his horse. He sat on its back like he was ready to jump off at a moment's notice.

Gage sat his horse like he'd been born there. The smile on his face was radiant.

"Let's move out," Flint said. They followed him across the castle grounds and toward the main gates.

Fen was relieved when his horse turned and followed the sergeant's with only a little bit of nudging from him. Right then his whole focus was on not falling off and making a fool of himself. He didn't know what he would have done if his mare had refused to move, or decided to head back into the stables.

It was really strange at first, sitting on the horse's back. The animal moved with a sort of rocking motion, unlike anything he'd ever experienced before. When he didn't fall off right away he decided that riding a horse wasn't too bad. It was a lot easier than walking, that was for sure. And when they got into the city and started moving through the morning crowds, he liked how different everything looked. He could see so much more than he could when he was on the ground. He could see a man slouching in a doorway and noticed the knife he was holding in his hand, down by his leg. He could see a woman wrestling with the turkey she was carrying slung over her shoulder, and knew before she did when the bird got its legs free of the twine she'd tied them with and with a sudden flapping of wings got away. She cursed and started chasing it through the crowd, while people around her called out advice and insults.

Cowley was watching the woman too and when she turned a corner and disappeared out of sight, he looked over at Fen with a grin on his face. "I could get used to this," he said.

"I think horses are great!" Lukas said out of nowhere. "This is lots easier than walking or running. No one can step on my toes up here!"

"I think there's something wrong with mine," Strout said, a dark look on his face. He was still gripping the pommel of his saddle with both hands. "This beast has already tried to buck me off two times."

"You're imagining things," Flint called back to him. "These are the oldest, gentlest horses in the castle. That horse you're riding is at least twenty years old. She wouldn't buck if you waved a flag in her face."

"You're saying that to make me feel better," Strout said.

"Not interested in making you feel better, lad. Just stating the facts."

"Look! She just did it again!" Strout said. "She started to buck."

Gage was riding beside Strout and he laughed. "She didn't try to buck. It's just a horsefly is all. It landed on her butt and she's trying to get it off. Here, I'll take care of it." He reined his horse closer and then swatted at the large blue-green insect the next time it landed.

"What are you doing? Don't do that!" Strout yelped.

"Take it easy. I almost got it." The horse fly landed again and this time he killed the thing. "There. Now you don't have to worry about your wild beast bucking you off."

"I wasn't worried about it. I was just being careful, that's all."

"I like how people get out of your way when you're on a horse," Noah said. "I feel like a king." He waved at some young boys who were rough housing in the street in front of him. "Make way there, boys. Make way."

One stuck his tongue out at him and the other made a rude gesture. But they did get out of the way as the horse bore down on them.

Noah twisted in his saddle to look back at them. "Can you believe the cheek?" he said. "When did people quit teaching their children respect?"

Fen looked back at the brothers. They were riding side by side, their heads turning constantly, eyes darting, as they tried to watch in every direction at once. "If I had to guess," he said to Cowley, pointing at them, "I'd say they're not enjoying this too much."

Cowley looked back at them. "It's too exposed for them. They don't like being noticed."

"There *are* a lot of people looking at us," Fen said.

"Including those girls over there by that vegetable stall," Cowley said. "You saw them, right?"

"I saw. I'm just not going to stare at them like you are."

"What's wrong with a little staring?" Cowley asked, winking at the girls, who smiled and looked shyly away.

"I don't know. Why don't we ask Amma about it?"

"I don't think there's any need to tell Amma," Cowley said hastily.

"Still sore from the last lump she gave you?" Fen asked innocently. A few days earlier Amma had caught Cowley flirting with the daughter of a merchant who was delivering a wagon load of saddles to the castle. She'd marched over and pulled his hair good and hard, then added a slap for good measure.

Cowley rubbed his cheek. "She hits hard."

"Maybe because you give her reason to."

"And you're so perfect, I guess."

"It's called loyalty. You should try it sometime."

"Speaking of Ravin…"

"I wasn't talking about Ravin," Fen said defensively.

"No, but I can tell you want to. Do you still talk to her?"

"When I can." Fen lowered his voice so the others couldn't hear. He didn't like being teased. "We're going to go down into the city one of these nights after I'm done training."

"You mean like on a date?" Cowley asked, putting his hand over his mouth in mock surprise.

"I don't know. Why does it have to be called anything? Can't we just be friends going out on the town?"

"I can't believe you actually worked up the nerve to ask her." The smile playing on Cowley's lips made Fen want to slug him.

"Actually," Fen admitted with a wince. "She kind of asked me."

"Ha! I knew it! I told Amma, I told her."

"You told her what?"

"I told her you were too shy to do anything. I told her if Ravin didn't make the first move you'd both die of old age before you asked her out."

"You what?" Fen said, horrified.

"I told Amma you were sweet on Ravin but too scared to do anything about it."

"And then she told Ravin. I'm going to kill you, Cowley."

"Why? It worked, didn't it?"

"She must think I'm the saddest excuse for—"

"Really? Then why did she ask you to go out?"

Fen had no answer to that but he still wasn't happy with Cowley. "Stay out of my business from now on."

Cowley held up his hands. "Sure. Get angry at the friend who saved you from a life of loneliness. This is the thanks I get."

"What did you do, Cowley?" Lukas asked, overhearing the last part.

"Nothing," Fen told him.

"I saved him from a life of despair and emptiness, that's what I did," Cowley said loftily. "But there's no pleasing some people."

Lukas spurred his horse closer. "What did you *do*?"

"Don't tell him," Fen said. "I'm warning you."

"I'm sorry, Lukas, but fear of Fen's wrath has sealed my lips. You'll have to get it from him."

"I bet it's something to do with that black-haired girl I've seen you talking to. She's so pretty," Lukas said dreamily. "I wish she'd talk to me."

"See?" Cowley crowed. "Other people, *normal* people, would be happy to have my help."

"I'm done listening to you," Fen grumbled and spurred his horse forward, leaving the two boys laughing behind him.

They left the city and rode out into the countryside. The rains had been kind that year and the fields were fat with crops. Tomatoes, corn, squash, lettuce, beans and other vegetables grew in profusion. Fen remembered what Barik had told him during one of their talks, about the foundation of a nation's wealth being its agriculture, and he looked on the crops and saw what they meant to Samkara's future, to her strength and rebuilding.

"Okay, lads, since it looks like you've mastered the difficult art of staying on a walking horse, let's see how you do with a little trotting," Flint said, and spurred his horse forward down a dirt lane that led between two fields.

The boys followed. It didn't take long for Fen to realize he didn't like this nearly as much as walking. It was like being in a wagon that was going fast down a very rocky road. He had to hold onto the pommel to keep from falling off.

"It feels like my teeth are going to rattle right out of my head," Lukas said.

"My butt's already getting sore," Noah added.

"You'll get used to it," Gage called back over his shoulder. "Stand up in the stirrups a little bit. Let your legs absorb the shock."

Fen did what he said and felt immediately better. It still wasn't a pleasant feeling, but at least he didn't feel like he was being shaken to pieces.

They trotted for what seemed like forever, then stopped at a small stream to let the horses drink.

"I officially hate horses," Strout said.

"That was the worst," Lukas moaned. "Why do people do that?"

"Because it's a lot faster than a walk and a horse can keep it up for hours," Gage said. "You start galloping around and you'll wear your horse out in no time."

"He's right," Flint said. He and Gage were the only ones who didn't look like they were in pain. "When you need to cover a lot of ground and you don't have the option of swapping horses every couple hours, a trot is the way to go."

"We could always just fight on foot," Noah said. "That's what most soldiers do."

"You're not most soldiers," Flint said. "You want to be part of the Fist's elite troops, you have to be able to ride. You're not saying you want out, are you?"

"No, I'm not saying that," Noah moaned. "But I'm going to need a new butt when this is over. The old one is just about ruined."

Despite how sore he was, Fen chuckled at that and most of the others did too.

"If it makes you feel better, that's all the trotting for right now," Flint said. A ragged cheer went up from the boys. It died quickly when he added, "But..."

"Why is there always a 'but'?" Cowley groaned.

"But, we're going to start learning to fight from horseback."

Flint led them off into a nearby meadow and had them break into pairs. "Go to it. Spar."

Naturally, Fen was paired off against Strout, who looked thoroughly angry about the day's events. Strout spurred his horse straight at Fen and swung at him.

It was awkward, fighting on a horse. Fen jerked on the reins but his horse didn't move much at all and so he took the blow awkwardly on his sword. Strout spurred forward so that he was somewhat behind Fen and swung at him again. Fen couldn't turn far enough in the saddle and this one hit him hard on the shoulder, numbing his whole arm so that he nearly dropped the weapon.

He dragged on the reins and managed to turn his horse before the next swing and was able to parry this one and launch a counter that landed on Strout's arm. Strout jerked back and when he did so he lost his balance and had to grab wildly at the pommel. A quick thrust against his ribs with the blunted practice weapon and Fen was able to shove him hard enough that he fell off.

Strout snatched up his weapon and charged at Fen. Fen parried the first two attacks but then Strout surprised him by jumping up and grabbing onto his sword arm. Before he knew it, he was pulled out of the saddle and landed hard on the ground.

Next, Fen sparred against Gage. Right away he realized he was in trouble. Gage was a decent swordsman when they fought on foot and Fen usually defeated him pretty quickly. But this was not the same old Gage. He and his horse moved like they'd been doing this for years. Most of the time Gage wasn't even holding onto the reins, but his horse did what he wanted it to anyway. Every time Fen swung, Gage's horse danced away and then while he was trying to recover to swing again, Gage darted in and scored easy hits on him.

After a while, Flint called a halt. Every one of them but Gage had hit the ground at least once and Wallice was nursing a sore wrist that he'd hurt when he landed awkwardly on it.

"How did you do that?" Fen asked, breathing hard. "How did you make your horse go where you wanted it to?"

Flint overheard and said, "Go ahead, Gage. Tell him."

Gage sheathed his sword and looked them all over. "I just used my knees and my feet to let him know where I wanted him to go," he said, patting his horse on the neck.

"That doesn't make any sense," Strout groused. "This nag barely moves when I jerk the reins. No way I can move it with my knees."

"Can I tell them the rest?" Gage asked the sergeant, who nodded. "This will sound silly, but it's because your horse doesn't respect you."

"That's crazy," Strout said, and Fen had to agree with him. It was only a horse, wasn't it?

"Horses are a lot smarter than you think," Gage said. "By the time you've gotten on and ridden across the road your horse can already tell whether or not you know what you're doing. Once your horse figures out you're green, he knows he can put things over on you. Mostly, horses are lazy, just like we are, so what he tries to do is make things easier on himself. If he can tell that you're really clueless, he'll refuse to obey you at all. He might take you straight back to the stables."

Gage leaned forward and scratched his horse between the ears. "But once your horse knows that you're in charge, that you know what you're doing, then it all changes, especially if his training has been even halfway decent. Then, with a firm hand and a little kindness, he'll do anything for you."

Suddenly Gage seemed to realize that this was the most he'd ever said to the squad all at once and he looked around nervously. "Sorry," he said, lowering his head. "I got a little carried away."

"No, you did good," Flint said firmly. "I couldn't have said it better myself. You lads need to listen to what he said. Be firm with your horse. Let it know you are in charge. But don't be cruel. Cruelty brings obedience, but you lose the animal's heart that way. Any questions?"

No one said anything, so Flint said, "Let's head back then." He gave them a wicked grin. "Who's up for some more trotting?"

They started back to the city. Fen made sure he rode right behind Gage and he did his best to copy him. He would learn from the other boy until the day when he could ride like Gage did.

By the time they got back to Samkara, Fen's legs ached and his butt and thighs felt like they were on fire. When he slid out of the saddle he staggered and almost fell down, his legs felt so weak.

"I won't be able to sit down for a week," Noah moaned.

Lukas crumpled when he hit the ground and lay there, making little noises to himself. Fen limped over to him and helped him stand up. "Look at the bright side," he said. "At least we didn't have to run today."

"I'd rather run than ever get on that awful creature again."

Fen walked stiffly toward the barracks. How come he was so tired when the horse did all the walking today? he wondered. It didn't make sense. He thought he was in excellent shape, but he had sore muscles he'd never known existed before now. All in all, he wasn't sure he was any more of a fan of horses than Lukas was.

Chapter 22

"Gather around," Flint said the next day after they were done training. "I have an announcement to make. It's time you had a squad leader."

The boys looked at each other, wondering who it would be. Fen hadn't even thought about it before. He caught Strout giving him an angry look and it surprised him. Did Strout think he would be chosen as squad leader?

Flint took the cloth badge of a corporal out of his pocket and handed it to Fen. "Congratulations, corporal. You're the new squad leader."

Strout exploded immediately. "What? Why'd you pick him? I'm a better fighter than he is."

Flint was unperturbed by his outburst. "That may be true. But there's a lot more to leading men than fighting ability."

"We're soldiers. What could be more important than how good you are at fighting?" Strout said sullenly.

Flint scratched his ear. "We all have weaknesses. I have them. You have them. Even the Fist has them. You want to know what one of your weaknesses is, Strout? You only care about yourself. You don't care about your squad mates. It doesn't matter to you if one falls. You just keep on going. After your little adventure in the tavern when Lukas fell during the run and couldn't get up, what did you do?"

Strout glared at the sergeant but didn't say anything.

"You did nothing. But what did Fen do? He went back for his squad mate and tried to help him. There was a time when Gage was thinking about quitting. What did Fen do? He talked to him." He looked at the boys. "The reason I chose Fen as your corporal is because he's always looking out for you. That's what a good leader does. He looks out for his men."

Fen felt awkward, being singled out like that, but he felt proud too.

"Now go get your dinner. I'll see you tomorrow. Fen, one of your new duties is making sure all the practice weapons are racked properly at the end of training every day."

Fen saluted. "Yes, sir."

"Congratulations," Gage said after he'd put his axe on the rack, patting Fen on the shoulder. "You deserve it."

"The sergeant is right you know," Lukas added. "You're always looking out for everyone. You kept me from quitting a few times."

"Does this mean we have to salute you now?" Cowley asked with a mocking smile.

"Of course we do," Noah said, snapping off a salute that was picture perfect except for the rude gesture he added at the end. "Sir!" he cried.

Even Wallice and Eben nodded at Fen after they put their axes on the rack.

Strout was last. He deliberately took his time, getting a drink of water first, and the others were already gone by the time he was done. Instead of putting his weapon on the rack, he tossed it on the ground.

"It should have been me," he growled, giving Fen a dark look. "You only got it because you're the Fist's pet." Then he stomped off.

Fen picked up the weapon and put it on the rack, wondering if he was right. Was he being favored because of the Fist? He'd seen Flint talking with him a few times. Maybe Flint figured if he didn't want to get into trouble with the Fist he should promote Fen. He was still worrying about it as he left the practice yard. Cowley was waiting for him.

"I heard what Strout said."

"Do you think it's true?"

"I think Strout is a selfish idiot, that's what I think."

"But he's right. I do know the Fist. Maybe Flint promoted me because—"

"That's horse shit. You know Flint better than that. He does what he thinks is best. If he chose you it's because he thinks you're the best one for the job. And he's right. You are the best one. I mean, who came looking for me that night in the tavern?"

Fen smiled. "I was only trying to keep your dumb ass out of trouble."

"Which is what the sergeant just said. You're the one always looking out for the rest of us. So stop being such a dolt. You earned that promotion. Enjoy it. Go order someone around."

"Why don't I start with you?"

"Five minutes in power and it's already gone to your head?" Cowley said with a grin. "I can tell this isn't going to end well."

"I have a feeling you're going to have some extra running to do tomorrow."

Cowley's smile disappeared and he turned serious. "You know you're going to have to fight him, don't you?"

Puzzled, Fen asked, "What? Fight who?"

"Strout, you dummy."

Fen sighed. "Do you think so?"

"He's going to brace you every chance he gets. He's going to try to make you look weak. If you let it pass it's only going to get worse and worse."

"Maybe he'll get over it if I give him time."

Cowley snorted. "Stop fooling yourself. People like Strout don't get over things. Trust me on this, Fen. If you don't lick him, he'll tear away at you and never stop."

They were in the mess hall, waiting in line to get food, when a servant came up and told Fen he would be eating with the Fist that night. Strout, ahead of them in line, turned and gave Fen a foul look.

"Like I said," he growled. "Nothing but a pet."

"The other children never really liked you, did they, Strout?" Cowley asked.

"You need to watch your mouth, funny guy," Strout said, "before I put my fist in it."

"Thanks, but no. Hungry, but not that hungry. I think I'll stick with whatever slop the cook is dishing up."

Some of the other boys heard the exchange and were watching intently. Fen could feel their eyes on him, waiting to see what he'd do.

"What are you staring at, Fen?" Strout said. "You have a problem with something I said? The truth hurts, doesn't it?"

"Don't take that from him," Noah said. "Pop him in his fat mouth."

"So that's it, Fen?" Strout said, his lip curling. "You're going to let other people fight your battles for you?"

The servant tapped his foot impatiently. "The Fist is waiting."

"We'll talk about this later," Fen said, and turned to follow the servant out of the mess hall. Behind him he heard Strout make a mocking sound and his ears burned.

☩   ☩   ☩

Fen walked into the palace dining hall. Barik, sitting at the head of the table, looked up as he walked over. His eyes fell on the corporal badge that Fen was holding wadded up in his hand. "Looks like you made corporal. Well done."

Fen looked down at his hand. He'd forgotten he was still holding the badge. "Thank you, Fist."

Barik motioned for him to sit down. "You don't seem very happy about it."

Fen sat down. There was already a plate of food and a mug of water waiting for him. "It hasn't sunk in yet is all." He put the badge in his pocket. Barik gave him a curious look and returned to his meal. Fen started in on his. The meal was stew, bread and cheese. Not very different from what he'd be eating in the mess hall right now. Barik clearly wasn't interested in royal fare.

Barik finished his stew and wiped out the bowl with the bread. His dark eyes turned on Fen. "I heard about your adventures in town."

Fen looked up into Barik's gaze. "I'm sorry about that, Fist. We shouldn't have gone."

Barik waved it off. "You're young. You got some freedom and got carried away. It happens. It was you who went after your friend, wasn't it? Who found him being robbed?"

Fen nodded.

"Why? What made you go after him?"

"I don't know. I just had a bad feeling."

"Learn to trust those feelings, Fen. They'll keep you alive. In this case they might have saved your friend's life. How is the horseback training coming?"

"It's getting easier. We started practicing archery today."

"It's not the same as shooting arrows on foot, is it?"

"It's not. You have to time your shot, plan it around the horse's movements, so the horse doesn't throw you off."

"None of the other young squads are nearly as advanced as yours is."

"Flint is an excellent sergeant, sir."

"He's the best. That's why I assigned him to you." Barik sat there looking at him, drumming his fingers on the table. Then he surprised Fen by asking, "Can you do your letters? Sums?"

"No, sir."

"I'll speak to the chamberlain and have him arrange it. When you are a captain, you'll have to be able to read missives in the field and write reports to send back."

Captain? The thought stunned Fen. The most he'd ever hoped was to make it to sergeant. Officers came from the nobility, occasionally from one of the wealthier merchants. At least they did before Barik took over.

"You think you're up to it? It won't be easy, I promise you."

Fen nodded. "I can do it." The thing was, he actually believed that. In the last year he'd learned that he was capable of far more than he'd ever imagined he was.

"But…"

"Sir?" Fen asked.

"There's something bothering you. What is it?"

Fen's first thought was to deny it, but he knew how much Barik disliked dishonesty so he summoned his courage and spoke his mind.

"Did I get this promotion because of you?"

Barik's expression darkened and Fen wondered if he'd made a mistake.

"You ask that? After all this time? Haven't I made it abundantly clear that my new army will be based on merit rather than birth or wealth? I had nothing to do with your promotion. If Flint promoted you it was because he believed you are the best man for the job."

Fen lowered his eyes, chastened. "You're right." He hesitated, wanting to say more, to ask something that he'd wondered about for a long time, but not sure if now was a good time.

"Spit out the rest of it, Fen. I told you to speak your mind. Do so."

Fen took a deep breath. "Why, Fist? Why me?" He waved his hand to take in the room. "You have me in here to eat with you. You tell me things. I don't understand why."

Barik went very still. Fen could see he was thinking. At last he said, "You were there. In Victory Square. You survived as well. I took that as a sign."

"But I was just a little kid."

Barik stood up so suddenly he knocked over his chair. Fen flinched, afraid that he'd gone too far. Barik walked to the big window at the end of the dining hall and stared out into the darkness. In a soft voice he said, "I had a son. He was about your age."

He stayed motionless in front of the window without speaking for so long that Fen began to wonder if he should get up and leave. But he also knew that he couldn't leave until his Fist sent him away. It was agony sitting there. He wished he'd kept his mouth shut.

After an eternity Barik spoke again.

"He died during the siege, early on. A catapult stone landed on our home. Both he and my wife were crushed." His voice was strangled, seething with painful emotions.

Fen could hardly breathe. "I'm sorry," he said, his voice barely a whisper.

Barik whirled away from the window and walked back to the table. He put his big hands on the table and leaned on them. The look in his eyes was painful to see. "Thousands died at the hand of the Maradis. That is what drives me, Fen. I will never allow that to happen again. Never. Do you understand?" As he spoke it seemed the air around him grew darker, the shadows wrapping about him.

"I do," Fen said honestly.

"It matters not the cost to me. It matters not the cost to this nation. We will be strong again. We will avenge their deaths, all of them."

"I will do anything I can, give my life if necessary," Fen said, and he meant every word of it.

"Then you have your answer. That's why you're here. I saw something in you that night, Fen, something you yourself didn't know was there. I saw someone who had suffered as I had and who would stop at nothing to fix it. This is why I have taken an interest in you. It is my dream that you lead my armies someday. Mine is the fist, and you shall be the sword that I wield to crush our enemies forever."

Fen's breath caught in his throat. He wondered if he'd heard Barik right.

"I can see my words shock you," Barik said.

"I...I never imagined..."

"Maybe I'm wrong. Maybe you're not the one for this task. It will be hard, harder than you can imagine. You're worried that you've been promoted because I favor you, that advantages are being handed to you that you haven't earned, but the truth is the opposite. Because of what I see in you, I expect *more* from you. Not expect, *demand*. Can you manage that?"

Fen had to fight back the tears when he raised his face to look at Barik. "I can," he said.

Barik released him then and Fen left the room. He hardly saw anything around him as he left the palace and headed for the barracks. Did the Fist really mean what he said? Was it possible? Would he someday lead Samkara's armies? It seemed impossible. What was he but another orphan? How could he ever be capable of such a thing?

But he remembered the look in Barik's eyes when he spoke and he knew that Barik believed in him and he resolved that he would not let his Fist down. He would show him that his faith had not been misplaced.

Chapter 23

"What are you getting all cleaned up for?" Lukas asked.

Fen had just come from the trough out behind the barracks. His hair was wet and he was still dripping. "No reason. I felt dirty." He didn't look up at the other boy but continued digging around in his foot locker. He pulled out his spare shirt.

"You're putting on a clean shirt." Lukas said it like it was an accusation. "That's not nothing. You're going somewhere. Where are you going?"

Fen turned on him. "Can't you leave it alone?" If Lukas kept it up others would notice and then he'd never hear the end of it.

But it was already too late.

"I bet he's going to meet that girl," Gage chimed in, showing his gap-toothed grin.

"What girl?" Lukas asked.

"You know what girl. The black-haired one."

Fen felt his face getting red. "It's none of your business, either of you. Just let it go already."

But there was no going back now.

Lukas flopped down on Fen's cot and gave Fen a big smile. "Are you gonna kiss her?"

"What I'm going to do is punch you," Fen replied. "That's what I'm going to do."

"Who is Fen going to kiss?" Noah asked, walking into the barracks.

"See what you've done?" Fen said to Lukas. "You had to go and open your big mouth and now everyone knows."

"Not me," Noah said. "I don't know yet. Who is Fen kissing?"

"I'm not kissing anyone!"

The door opened again and Cowley came in. He saw the boys all clustered around Fen's bed and came over to join in. "What's going on?"

"Fen's kissing some girl," Noah said. "But no one will tell me who."

"It's Ravin," Cowley said. "That's who it is, isn't it? Unless you're even slyer than I thought, you dog." He leered at Fen.

"You're terrible people, all of you," Fen said. "Why don't you shut up and leave me alone?"

"For once I agree with Fen," Strout put in. He was sitting on his cot, leaning up against the wall, trying to thread a needle to repair a rip in his breeches. "All of you shut up or go somewhere else. I'm sick of listening to you."

"That's our Strout," Cowley said. "Always with a cheery word." Strout flipped him a rude gesture and Cowley laughed. He turned back to Fen. "Where are you taking her?"

"Who says I'm taking her anywhere? Who says I'm even going to meet anyone?"

"You pretty much just did," Cowley said. "Come on. Spill."

The other boys closed in, sitting on Fen's cot or the nearby ones. "We're not going until we get what we came for," Noah said.

"You might as well give up," Gage added with mock seriousness. "We have you surrounded."

"So if I tell you, then you'll leave me alone?"

"If we like the answer."

"I'm taking her to the puppet show down in Rippon Park."

Groans and boos greeted his words.

"A puppet show? Those are for little kids!" This from Noah.

From Lukas: "That's the dumbest idea ever!"

Fen glared at them. "I hate you all." All that brought was more laughter. Fen groaned inwardly. This was exactly what he'd hoped to avoid.

"Now hold on," Cowley said, holding his hands up to silence the others. "I think the puppet show is actually a pretty good idea." The others gave him surprised looks, but didn't shout him down, Cowley being their resident ladies' man. Fen gave him a grateful look. Maybe they would all leave him alone now.

"Lots of private places to be found in Rippon Park," Cowley added with a knowing smile. "There's a good spot behind the statue that comes to mind." He doffed an imaginary cap. "My hat is off to you, sir."

Fen had had enough. He shoved Cowley off his cot onto the floor. The boys all howled with laughter. Noah laughed so hard he fell off the cot.

"I'll get you for this," Fen told Cowley.

From his seat on the floor, Cowley looked up at him. "I hope so. It's more fun when you do."

Fen pulled on his surcoat, buckled on his sword belt, and fled. The door closed behind him, mercifully cutting off most of the noise. He stood there for a moment in the darkness, straightening his clothes, running his fingers through his wet hair. He remembered that he'd wanted to borrow Cowley's comb and he'd also meant to put a fresh shine on his boots. For a moment he considered going back into the barracks but a fresh round of laughter—no doubt a new joke had been made at his expense—put an end to that idea.

He double checked to make sure he had his coin purse, then started across the castle grounds. It felt like there were butterflies in his stomach, fluttering around. He'd spoken with Ravin a number of times since that first night when he and Cowley snuck into the palace, but this was the first time they'd done anything together and he was a lot more nervous than he wanted to admit even to himself. His palms felt strangely sweaty, but no matter how many times he wiped them on his breeches it made no difference.

Halfway to the spot where they'd agreed to meet he lost his nerve and stopped completely. This was a mistake. He never should have asked her to go out with him. What in the world was he going to talk about all night? And why had he asked her to a puppet show? Noah was right. Puppet shows were for little kids. He clapped his hand to his forehead. He was the world's biggest idiot.

A thought occurred to him. He might still get out of this. Ravin probably talked to Amma and told her about the puppet show. He'd heard girls shared everything. Amma no doubt laughed and then Ravin realized that this whole date was a terrible idea. At this moment she was probably in her room, getting ready for bed and feeling relieved that she'd skipped the whole nightmarish event.

It was all for the best, Fen told himself. He was a soldier now. Soon he'd probably be off patrolling and such. He'd be gone all the time. He might even get himself killed. It would be cruel to put Ravin through all that. It was best to break things off now. He'd still see her around now and then and he'd be nothing but nice, but he'd keep his distance. Maybe someday they'd even laugh about the silly date they almost had.

He felt a lot better now. He also felt really sad, but that part was unimportant. What was important is that he'd narrowly avoided making a really big fool of himself. Well, he'd better at least go to the meeting point, to make sure she hadn't showed up.

It was with a much lighter step that he made his way toward the palace and the bench underneath the willow tree where they'd arranged to meet. He even whistled a little to himself as he walked down the brick path between the privet hedges. The path curved around and the hedges opened up right where the empty bench was sitting.

Except that it wasn't empty.

Ravin was sitting there, stray light from the palace spilling across her face and hair.

Fen stopped as if he'd run into a brick wall. His whistle died in his throat.

Ravin, hearing his footsteps, turned and smiled at him. As he stood there, rooted to the spot by sudden terror, her smile faded and was replaced by concern and a little confusion.

"Fen? Is that you?"

Fen knew then how the fox felt when the hounds closed in. There was no escape. His eyes darted around, a dozen foolish plans raced through his mind, and all of them led to naught. Somehow he forced himself to walk toward her, though his legs felt numb and very far away.

"Oh, it *is* you," she said, relief evident in her voice. "I wasn't sure at first. You were standing there so still. I thought there was something wrong." A small frown. "*Is* something wrong? You look pale."

Fen blurted out the first thing that came to mind. "I think I ate something bad at dinner." Instantly he cursed himself for saying it. Gods, was he the dumbest person ever?

She got up and came toward him. "Oh, I'm sorry. Will you be okay? Do you...do you still want to go to the puppet show?"

Fen swallowed. His mouth was so dry. He should have drunk more water. "Do you still want to go?" he croaked.

She smiled. It was a beautiful smile. Suddenly the light from the palace seemed to flare brighter. "Of course. I love puppets.

177

They make me laugh." The smile faded, the concern returning. "But if you're not feeling well, we could…go another time."

Suddenly, to his mortification, Fen realized he was grinning stupidly, a smile that felt like it was stretching from one ear to the other. He tried to tone it down, but it didn't seem to be working. All he could think was, *She likes puppets!*

Ravin blinked. Her smile started to creep back, then faded. "Are you starting to feel better?" she said hesitantly.

"Actually, I'm feeling lots better," Fen said. "Suddenly."

"You're sure?"

"You like puppets."

A pause. "Yes, I do. I already said that. Are you sure you're feeling okay?"

"I feel better than okay."

"Let's go then," she said, smiling again. "Oh, you wore your sword."

Fen realized that he hadn't even made the decision to do so. Putting it on had become a habit. "You want me to put it back?"

"No, I think it makes you look very dashing." She put her hand over her mouth, her eyes widening. "That was very forward of me. Maybe too forward."

"Not at all."

"I've been spending too much time around Amma, I'm afraid. She's starting to rub off on me."

They started for the castle gates. Fen felt like he was walking on air. She was so close. He could smell some kind of flowers on her. Her dress was a sort of peach color and it seemed almost to glow.

"I like your dress," he said, then winced. He really needed to start thinking things through before speaking.

"Do you? Amma got a hold of the fabric—I don't know how and I don't think I want to know—and she helped me sew it. We were up half of last night getting it finished in time for tonight."

Fen was staggered by that. "You…worked that long just to get ready for…for…"

She gave him a shy smile. "No one ever asked me to a puppet show before."

"I thought…the others said puppet shows are silly."

"Well, they're the silly ones. They obviously don't know anything."

"I guess, I mean, you're right. What do they know?" He wanted to ask her then if she would take his arm, the way he'd seen other couples do, but he couldn't think of any good way to ask her so he stayed silent.

They reached the castle gates. Lamps mounted on the wall provided light. Fen realized that he knew one of the two soldiers who were manning the gates. His name was Shinn and he was old for a soldier, with a large, bushy beard and a belly to match. One of Shinn's ears was mostly gone, lost to a sword many years ago and he walked with a limp. Shinn was a friendly man who liked to talk and Fen had chatted with him a few times.

Shinn's bearded face split in a big smile when he saw the two of them. "What's this, then? Is that you, Fen? Who's the lovely young lady with you?"

"This is my friend Ravin."

"More than just a friend, I bet," the other soldier said with a leer. He was a young man with a scruffy beard and he was openly looking Ravin up and down.

"Mind your manners around the lady," Shinn said, elbowing him in the stomach and doubling him over. "My apologies for his behavior, my lady." He sketched a rough bow.

Ravin smiled at him and returned a curtsy. "No apologies necessary, good sir."

Shinn pulled one of the gates open. "Where are you two off to this fine evening?"

"Down to Rippon Park for the puppet show," Fen said, then winced, expecting to be teased.

The other soldier opened his mouth to say something but caught the warning look Shinn gave him and closed his mouth again. Shinn scratched the rubble that was his ear and nodded sagely. "A wise choice, corporal. May I suggest you try the lemonade they sell there? No doubt the young lady will enjoy it."

"Thanks," Fen said. "I'll keep it in mind." He and Ravin passed through the gates.

"Mind you're back by twelve bells, Fen," Shinn called after him. "The gates are barred then."

⯑ ⯑ ⯑

The street leading to Rippon Park was well-lit and had quite a few people on it. A handful of businesses were still open and there were a number of street vendors, selling everything from sweetmeats to flowers. One of them, an elderly lady, lit up when she saw them. Taking a rose from the basket on her stand she moved out to intercept them.

"The lass will be wanting a rose," she told Fen, holding the flower up to him. "I've seen that look in many an eye. You don't want to disappoint her, do you?"

"I don't..." Fen stammered. He looked at Ravin. "Do you?" She smiled and that told him all he needed to know. He bought the rose from the old woman and was shocked at the price but didn't have it in him to haggle. It would only make him look cheap, he thought. Besides, what did mere coin matter tonight?

One of the businesses that was open was a dress shop. In the window several dresses were displayed, along with some inexpensive jewelry and some women's shoes. "Oh," Ravin said, heading over to look closer. "They're so beautiful, don't you think?"

"Not half as beautiful as your dress," Fen said gallantly and then immediately worried he'd said too much.

"That's so sweet," she said, linking her arm through his. It all happened so quickly and so naturally that Fen didn't quite know how to react. He could feel her bare arm on his and he was afraid to move, afraid she would pull away. "But those are so much nicer. This old thing couldn't compare."

Fen thought no dress ever made could look better than what she was wearing, but he couldn't for the life of him find any way to say it that didn't sound foolish so he settled for shaking his head. The shopkeeper came out then, his sales pitch already starting. When he saw who they were the words died on his lips. Fen had no doubt that the cheapest of the dresses was far beyond anything that he could afford.

"Don't crowd the window so much. I don't want you blocking the other shoppers," the shopkeeper said, then went back inside.

"How rude!" Ravin exclaimed. "Just for that we're not buying any of your overpriced dresses!" she called after him. When he stopped and turned back, scowling, she and Fen hurried away laughing.

They heard the city bells ringing, marking the time. "Nine bells already?" Ravin said. "We have to hurry, the first show is starting!"

They half-ran down the street and a few minutes later arrived at Rippon Park—which sat beside the Heron River, just downstream from Hangman's Bridge—breathless and laughing. Fen thought that he'd never felt so happy in his entire life. His mouth opened to say so, but at the last moment reason prevailed and he clamped his mouth shut, keeping the words inside. If he'd learned anything from Cowley, it was that you had to take it slow with girls. They didn't like boys who were too head over heels.

The puppet show had already started and they joined the crowd gathered around on the grass. Afterwards, Fen could never say what the puppet show was about, only that he had the most wonderful time. Ravin laughed over and over and he laughed with her. That was what mattered.

When it was over he put a coin in the cup one of the performers carried around. From one vendor he bought a cup of lemonade and from another skewers with spiced, roasted lamb and onions on them. They sat side by side on the grass, eating and drinking, talking about the show. When they'd used that up he asked her about herself, where she'd come from.

"I was born down in the Distillery District, you know, where they make all the liquors? But I don't remember much about it. I was only four or five when I was sent to the palace."

"Your parents sent you away so young?"

She shrugged. "It's pretty common. People have too many kids to feed. They have to go somewhere. I went to the palace."

"Do you ever see your parents?"

"I wouldn't know where to find them." She leaned forward and patted his hand. "Don't look at me with those sad eyes. I don't miss them. The servants in the palace, they're my family, Amma and the rest. I don't like all of them," she made a face "but isn't that normal? You don't like all your family, but they're still family and you look out for each other."

"But to go there at four. You were so young. What jobs could you do then?"

"I didn't go there to work, not at that age anyway. I was there as a playmate for the king's children and the children of the nobles who sometimes stayed in the palace. As I got older I stopped being a playmate and became more of a maid for the young women. Amma was too. That's how I got to know her."

Fen remembered then that terrible morning when the Fist executed all the nobles and their families. Vividly he remembered the young woman in the green dress. She was so close to Ravin's age. Ravin probably knew her.

"What's wrong?" Ravin asked, touching Fen's shoulder. "A shadow just came over you."

"I was thinking of when the Fist executed them all. You must have had friends there."

She put her hands in her lap and looked down. "You're right, I did know a number of them. That was an awful day, one I won't forget." She bit her lip, then looked up at him. "But you must understand, they weren't my friends, not really. Even the girls I'd known the longest, the ones I made mud pies with and played dress-up with, they were always separate from me. They never forgot who they were and who I am. That line was always there."

She stopped and looked off into the darkness, as if seeing something in the distance. "Some of them were quite cruel, actually. When they were angry they would slap me or pull my hair. Or they would blame me for things they had done. I was whipped more than once."

"They had you *whipped*?" Fen could hardly imagine it. The thought of someone whipping a person as wonderful and kind as Ravin was terribly upsetting.

"It didn't happen too many times. And it happened to the other maids as well."

"That doesn't matter. Whipping someone for something they didn't do is *wrong*."

"I agree. But that doesn't change anything. At least it's different now that the Fist is our king. I mean, he's a hard man, it's true, but he's fair. He won't tolerate cruelty or injustice. He found out that one of the painters was beating his apprentice for no reason and he had the man whipped and driven out of the castle altogether."

"It still makes me angry."

"That's sweet. It really is." Ravin took a deep breath and wiped at her eyes. It took Fen a moment to realize that tears were running down her face.

"What is it?"

"The whipping wasn't the worst of it," she said in a small voice. "There were other...things that were worse." Her shoulders were shaking and Fen wanted to put his arms around her, tell her everything would be all right, but he didn't know how and he didn't have the words, so he just took hold of one of her hands.

She squeezed his hand hard and it seemed she took something from him that helped, for she found the strength to continue on. "The fathers and brothers of the girls we waited on were worse. They..." She had to stop and get hold of herself. "At first it was only crude comments, maybe a pinch or a squeeze here and there. But one day the father of one of the girls I was waiting on found me alone in her rooms and he...he pushed me down on the bed." She was crying hard now, her words nearly lost in her tears. "I tried to get away, but he was too strong."

Sitting there, hearing her sobs, feeling her pain as his own, Fen became enraged. His blood pounded in his ears and his muscles ached from restraining himself. He wanted to draw his sword and run until he found the man who'd done that and make him pay. Even knowing the man was probably dead now didn't make him feel any better.

"I'm sorry," he said. The words were so small and inadequate, but they were all he had. He felt so helpless and angry.

She leaned into him then, shaking hard, and he put his arm around her and held her tightly. How long they sat like that he didn't know, but gradually her shaking ceased and she sat upright once again, wiping the last tears from her cheeks.

"Thank you," she said. "That helps." She looked up at him and tried to smile. "I'm sorry. I didn't mean to do that."

"Don't be sorry," he said fiercely. "*Never* be sorry. It wasn't your fault what happened." No woman should ever have to endure that, he told himself. If he was the Fist he'd make rape punishable by death. He'd make Samkara safe for all women.

"How about we talk about something nice for a while?" Ravin said.

"Okay," Fen said. Forcing himself to sound cheerful again he asked, "What do you do now? With all the ladies gone?"

Ravin shook her head. "It's been a big adjustment. I work in the kitchens part of the time. I also work out in the gardens, like that one day you saw me out there. It took a while to get used to the work. I realize I was pretty pampered before, when the hardest thing I had to do was braid a girl's hair. You should try scrubbing clean one of those big cookpots after the cook let food burn in there. I practically have to climb in there to get it all out." She gave a small chuckle.

"But I don't want to only talk about me. What about you? It must be terribly difficult, the training you do. I've only seen bits of it but I can't imagine how you survive."

"At first I thought I would die. We all did." Fen shrugged. "It's still hard, but it's gotten easier too. We've started riding quite a lot. We go out into the countryside to train. I like getting out of the city, seeing all the trees and the flowers. You can't imagine how many flowers there are this time of year..." He broke off, hoping he hadn't given away too much. Girls probably didn't like men who talked about flowers.

But Ravin didn't seem to notice. "I would *love* to ride a horse someday," she said, her voice dreamy. "They're such magnificent animals."

"Someday I'll take you, I promise," Fen said stoutly.

They heard the bells chiming in the distance and all at once Fen realized how late it was. He looked around and saw that the park was nearly deserted. The puppet theater was gone. All the vendors had long since packed up and gone home. The only people left were a small group of men sitting on a bench, drinking and talking loudly.

"We have to go," they both said at the same time and got quickly to their feet.

Fen remembered what Shinn said, about the gates being barred at twelve bells. It was that time now. He only hoped he'd be able to convince them to open the gates and let the two of them in. He didn't relish the thought of spending the night out on the streets, not to mention how much trouble he'd be in from Flint in the morning.

They hurried out of the park and back the way they'd come. The shops were all closed and tightly shuttered now and the street was dark except for the occasional street lamp burning every few blocks. Their footsteps sounded very loud in the quiet emptiness. Ravin pressed in close to Fen and took his arm.

Fen kept his eyes moving, constantly scanning the street before them and now and then looking over his shoulder, alert for any signs of movement. A dog slunk across their path, growling at them before darting down an alley. A cat yowled from on top of a building and another one answered. He was glad he'd worn his sword.

Ahead he saw a lone figure going the same way they were. He was weaving and stumbling. The smell of liquor was strong as they caught up to him. He looked at them as they hurried by, mumbling something that Fen didn't catch.

The attack, when it came, caught him off guard, despite all his efforts at vigilance.

They were passing an alleyway on their right when a man suddenly burst from it. At the same time another man, who'd been standing concealed in a doorway just ahead, jumped out and came at them.

Fen tried to draw his sword but Ravin was holding onto his right arm and in the moment it took to free himself the men had already closed the distance.

The man coming out of the alleyway had something dark in his hand and as he swung it Fen just had time to shoulder Ravin out of the way so that it missed her.

It was a sap, a small leather bag filled with lead shot, and it hit Fen on the temple hard. Lights burst in his vision and he staggered to the side, losing hold of his sword.

The other man was carrying a truncheon and he swung the weapon at Fen's head. Only Fen's stagger saved him from being brained. As it was the short club glanced off his skull and he dropped bonelessly to the ground, unconsciousness claiming him.

☩   ☩   ☩

Fen's eyes opened and at first he had no recollection of where he was or what had happened.

Then he heard a woman's scream nearby, the scream suddenly muffled, and it all returned to him.

Ravin!

He came to his feet and stood there, trying to clear his vision, so dizzy he almost fell down again.

There was another muffled cry and he realized it was coming from the alleyway.

Thoughtlessly, he charged into the dim recesses of the alley, wanting nothing but to rescue Ravin before it was too late. As he ran he at least retained the presence of mind to reach for his sword but his scabbard was empty. Whether the weapon had been taken from him or he'd dropped it in the street he didn't know, but it was too late either way. He was committed and there was no thought of going back to look for it.

Ahead in the gloom he saw the struggling form of Ravin, sprawled on her back on a pile of refuse. One assailant was holding her down, while the other was tearing at her dress.

Fen went berserk then. What exactly happened next he was never sure.

With an inarticulate cry Fen launched himself at them. Hearing him, the one holding Ravin down let her go, picked up his truncheon and swung.

As the weapon swung down toward him, Fen blocked it with his forearm. There was pain, but it was dim and unimportant. In the same instant he pivoted and swung his right fist at the man's head with all his strength.

There was a sickening crunch and the man was thrown backward.

The other man straightened up and there was a dagger in his hand. As Fen turned toward him he swung the dagger, stabbing Fen low in the side…

Except that, instead of penetrating, the blade skipped off.

Stunned, the man froze, unable to comprehend what had just happened.

And that was all the opening Fen needed. He hammered the man twice in the body, knocking him backward, the breath expelling from him with each blow. Then he ripped the dagger from the man's hand and sank it up to the hilt in his chest.

The man's hand went to the weapon, but his fingers couldn't seem to close on it. With a sigh he collapsed and died.

Fen stood there for a moment, breathing hard. He realized then that the ground was heaving underneath him. A piece of brick dislodged from the side of one of the buildings and fell to the street with a crash.

Then the heaving stopped—if it had actually happened at all and he didn't simply imagine it—and Fen turned to Ravin.

She had rolled onto her side and was lying there, weeping. He gathered her up in his arms.

"It's okay," he kept whispering to her over and over. "It's okay. It's okay."

She clung to him as he carried her back out to the street. He saw the glitter of his sword and stopped next to it.

"I have to set you down for a minute," he whispered to her. "I have to pick up my sword."

She nodded and he set her down and sheathed his sword. When he went to pick her up again she shook her head.

"I can stand. Hold me for a minute." She wrapped her arms around him and held him tightly.

Over her shoulder Fen could see the dim forms of the two men sprawled where he had left them. He had a feeling they were both dead, even the one he had punched in the head. He'd felt the way the man's skull caved inwards when he hit him. How was it possible that he'd been able to punch him that hard? And how come his hand wasn't broken?

He touched his side where the man stabbed him. There was no blood. It wasn't even sore.

Just like that terrible night in Victory Square when the soldier tried to kill him with his sword, he'd emerged unscathed when he should have been badly wounded or killed.

And had there actually been a small earthquake? Was it possible he caused it?

Why did these things keep happening? What was wrong with him?

It scared him. He didn't want to be different. He just wanted to be a soldier and do his duty.

"I can walk now," Ravin said. "I want to go home."

Fen kept his left arm around her as they walked, making sure his right was free in case he needed to draw his sword.

The castle gates were closed, but Fen pounded on them with the hilt of his sword until the spy hole opened. He was relieved to see that it was Shinn who looked through.

"The gates are closed—" Shinn began, but he broke off when he saw who they were, and the condition they were in. The spy hole closed and his voice could be heard ordering the gate opened.

"What happened? Are you two all right?" Shinn asked worriedly, holding up a lantern to get a closer look at them. "Shall I call a healer?"

"No, we'll be okay," Fen said. "We're a little shook up is all."

Still holding Ravin close he guided her to one of the servant's entrances into the palace. A lamp burned there and in its light he could see that her new dress was torn and there was a scratch on the side of her face.

"I'm sorry," he said as she let go of him and reached for the door handle. "I'm so, so sorry."

She turned back to him and gave him a wan smile. "You were there. You saved me." She touched the side of his face briefly, then opened the door and hurried inside.

Fen walked away from the palace in a daze. He stopped when he was beside the mess hall and leaned against the side of the building, suddenly so exhausted he wasn't sure he could take another step. He relived that terrible moment when he heard Ravin scream. Desperation and fear washed over him as he fully realized for the first time how close Ravin had come to being badly injured or killed, to say nothing of the horror of rape. He started shaking as the stress of what had happened, delayed by his need to care for Ravin, caught up to him.

Mixed in with that was fear of what was inside him. He could no longer completely deny that there was something wrong with him. Too many strange things had happened that couldn't all be explained away. But what was it? Where did it come from?

For the first time he considered the possibility that this illness or whatever he had came from his father. His mother had never really told him how his father had died, but from the few scraps of information he gleaned from her he'd gotten the impression that it was something unusual and frightening. Fragments of a memory came to him then, his father lying on a bed, his skin strangely gray, but they blew apart and quickly faded away.

Was he sick? Was he some kind of monster?

And, most important of all, what would happen if other people found out?

He might be dismissed from the army. He might be locked away as a danger to others. He would lose everything, the squad, which had become his family, Barik, Flint, Ravin, his future as an officer. He'd have nothing, be nothing.

He realized then that he would have to be always on guard. All of the incidents had happened when he lost control of his emotions. He would have to learn how to control them from now on. He couldn't let whatever *it* was slip out again. Who knew what would happen if it did, how many people he might hurt?

No matter what it cost him, he had to hide this strange, frightening thing about himself. He had to make sure no one ever found out about it and that it never escaped his control.

Chapter 24

"You came in late last night," Cowley said the next morning.

Fen rolled over with a groan. He was completely exhausted. He felt like he hadn't slept at all. What sleep he'd gotten had been an uneasy sleep, filled with nightmarish images he couldn't remember.

"I'll take that groan to mean you had a good time," Cowley said.

Fen sat up, rubbing his eyes. His whole body felt like it was filled with sand. "Mostly, anyway."

"What does that mean?"

Fen's first thought was to keep the attack to himself. But then he realized that Ravin had surely told Amma about it and Amma would inevitably tell Cowley. "A couple of thugs attacked us on our way home."

Cowley's eyes went wide. "Really?" He looked Fen over. "No blood. No missing parts. That means you won, right?"

"I guess," Fen said, wishing Cowley would let it drop and knowing he wouldn't. He felt sick at the thought he had killed two people. It didn't feel like winning to him. It felt awful.

"Good thing you had your sword, then."

Fen hesitated. It would be easier to simply let Cowley believe he'd used his sword to fight them off. But he didn't like lying. "Actually, I lost my sword right in the beginning."

"How'd you fight them off?"

"You were in a fight?" Lukas asked, overhearing them.

Fen pulled on his mail and reached for his sword belt. "It wasn't much of a fight."

"Listen to Fen being modest," Cowley crowed. "He fights off two thugs then claims it was nothing."

"You fought off two men?" Noah said, jumping right into the conversation. "What happened? Did you kill both of them?"

Fen winced. Why did they have to act like this was some amazing thing? He could still remember how it felt when the dagger sank into the man's chest. It was a horrifying feeling. He should have lied from the beginning. "I didn't kill anyone. It was a couple of cutpurses is all. I ran them off. They were practically kids."

"Kids?" Noah said scornfully, though he was barely thirteen. "That doesn't sound like much of a fight."

"It wasn't. Let's stop talking about it. We're going to be late."

The others went back to getting ready, except for Cowley. He leaned in close and spoke in a low voice. "Later you're telling me everything."

"You're not going to let this go are you?"

Cowley shook his head. "There's more to this than you're letting on."

"Not really."

"Okay." Feigning disinterest, Cowley turned away and picked up his sword belt. "I guess I'll have to get the story from Amma then."

Fen groaned. "You're impossible."

Cowley turned back and gave him a sly look. "Wouldn't it be easier to tell me the story yourself?"

"I wonder if I can get you transferred to another squad."

"I expect a complete report at the end of the day," Cowley said.

As Fen was leaving he saw something lying on his bed and bent closer to see what it was.

Several shards of reddish stone were lying on his blanket.

He picked them up. They looked like the same kind of stone he'd found in his hair after Strout clubbed him during training that one time. He touched his head where the assailants had struck him and wondered.

He looked around to make sure no one was watching him, then put the shards into his footlocker.

⚎ ⚎ ⚎

Training had barely ended for the day when Cowley cornered him and pulled him aside. He waited until the others had left for the mess hall, then said, "Tell me."

Fen had been preparing for this moment, planning what he would say, yet still he wasn't sure. "You were wrong about one thing. She liked the puppet show."

"I don't care about the puppet show and you know it. I want to know about the attack."

Fen looked around, making sure no one was listening. "I'll tell you, but you have to keep it to yourself. You promise?"

"Cut me down if I leak a word," Cowley said, licking his thumb and drawing a circle over his heart.

"We stayed in the park too late."

Cowley grinned. "You sly dog, you!"

"It wasn't like that," Fen said irritably. "We were just talking. Do you want to hear this or not?"

"Sorry, sorry. Go on."

"It was after twelve bells. The streets were empty. Everything was closed up. One of them jumped out of an alley at us. The other was hidden in a doorway."

"What weapons did they have?" Cowley asked. "Did they know how to use them?"

"One had a sap, the other a truncheon and yeah, they knew how to use them. They knocked me out for a few seconds."

Cowley's eyes lit up. "Is that when you lost your sword?"

Fen nodded. "When I woke up I heard them." He swallowed. "They'd taken Ravin into the alley and they..." He couldn't make himself say the words. "I went berserk and attacked them."

Cowley's face had gone dark while he talked and now he said, "I wish I would've been there. I'd have killed them both. Scum like that don't deserve to live."

Fen looked around again. "I think maybe I did," he whispered.

Cowley's eyes fairly bugged out. He grabbed Fen's arm and pulled him off behind the mess hall. "You *killed* them?"

"I think so. I didn't check."

"But you said you lost your sword."

"One of them had a dagger. I took it away from him. I don't really remember all that happened. I went a little crazy. Remember, you said you wouldn't tell anyone."

"And I won't. But I wish I could. You're a hero. Those men got what they deserved. I'm glad you killed them."

Fen didn't feel like a hero. The truth was he felt sick about the whole thing. All day long he'd relived those moments over and over. Whether they deserved it or not, the fact was that he'd killed at least one, and likely two men. Ended their lives. His rational mind told him he'd had no choice, that he'd had to do it, but in his heart he felt awful.

He'd learned firsthand that no matter what anyone said, killing another person was a terrible thing to do. Doing so had marked him, changed him forever. He would never be the same again.

"I don't know why you want to keep it a secret," Cowley was saying, jarring Fen out of his thoughts. "If it was me I'd tell everyone."

I'm not you, Fen thought. *I'm not sure who I actually am.* "You promised, Cowley."

"And I'll keep that promise. But that doesn't mean I understand. Heck, you might even get a promotion."

"I already got a promotion," Fen pointed out.

"So that means you don't want another one?"

"I'd like to get used to this one first."

They started for the mess hall. "Are you going to see her again?" Cowley wanted to know.

"I don't know. She probably hates me now."

"I bet you're wrong. In fact, I'm sure of it."

Fen barely managed to sit down before the other boys were all over him, Lukas and Noah leading the charge. Gage was right behind and even the brothers, Wallice and Eben, looked over at him with interest. Only Strout acted like he couldn't care less, but Fen noticed he wasn't sitting too far away.

"Did you kiss her?" Noah asked. When Fen shook his head a collective sound of disgust rose from them.

"Did you at least hold hands?" Lukas wanted to know.

"Some handholding," Fen admitted. "Some hugging too."

"Ooh, hugging!" Noah cried, wrapping his arms around himself and pretending to hug himself. "Maybe some squeezing too?" he asked hopefully.

"What are you guys, six years old?" Cowley said, shaking his head.

"Quiet, you," Noah said to him, then turned back to Fen. "Tell me about the squeezing. I hear girls are awfully soft."

"There was no squeezing," Fen said. "And I wouldn't tell you if there was." Despite how awful he felt about what he'd done he found himself grinning at Noah's antics.

"I say she stood you up and you spent the night wandering around the streets crying to yourself," Strout said out of nowhere.

"Sure, Strout," Cowley said. "That's what happened. Why don't you go back into your cave now and let the adults talk." Strout gave him a murderous look, which he ignored.

"Don't listen to him," Lukas said. "He's just jealous. Did she like the puppet show?"

"She did. In fact, she loved it. You were all wrong."

Noah's face showed how he felt about puppet shows. "But puppet shows are for little kids."

"The problem is, you don't know anything about girls. At all," Cowley pronounced.

"I do too," Noah protested, but the others shouted him down.

"Could we talk about something else now?" Fen asked, noticing that other soldiers at nearby tables were listening in with big grins on their faces. He knew whatever he said would spread everywhere nearly instantly. There were no secrets in the castle, not really.

╬   ╬   ╬

After they ate, Cowley disappeared for an hour. When he came back he found Fen sitting on one of the benches outside the barracks, using the fading light to sew up the hole in his surcoat, caused when the assailant tried to stab him in the side. If he had any doubts about what had really happened, that hole cleared them up for good. He remembered how hard the impact was. That dagger would have sunk up to the hilt. He should be dead now.

"I talked to Amma," Cowley said without preamble.

Fen put the needle down, sewing forgotten. "What did she say? How is Ravin?"

"She says she's pretty shook up. She begged off work today, told them she was sick."

Fen's day crashed down around him. What little cheerfulness he'd managed to gather fled instantly. "I knew it. She blames me. And she should. I was supposed to keep her safe and I failed."

"Stop it already," Cowley said, cutting in, "before you drown in all that self-pity. Let me finish first and then you can go jump off Lover's Leap if you want to." Lover's Leap was a cliff overlooking the ocean off the southwestern corner of the city. No broken-hearted lovers had actually jumped off it in anyone living's memory, but that didn't stop people from using the name.

"What else did she say?"

"Well, she's shook up—"

"You said that already."

Cowley frowned. "Maybe that's it. I can't exactly remember." There was a ghost of a smile at the edges of his mouth.

"I will break your arm."

"Aren't you the violent one all of a sudden? What happened to Fen the gentle?"

"Maybe I'll break both arms."

"No need," Cowley said hastily, realizing suddenly that Fen sounded pretty serious. "I remember now. According to Amma, Ravin can't stop talking about you. She says it's terribly irritating." In a high-pitched voice he said, "'Every other word it's Fen this and Fen that.'"

"Amma didn't really say that."

"Every word."

"You're a liar."

"Okay, maybe I made up a tiny bit of it."

"But the part about Ravin talking about me? You didn't make that part up, did you?"

"No, I didn't make that part up. Why would I? It's boring and so predictable."

Fen let out the breath he'd been holding. "I don't see how it's predictable."

"Girl gets attacked. Boy saves girl. Girl swoons and proclaims everlasting love. Blah, blah, blah. It's the oldest story in the book."

Fen hardly heard him. He was thinking about Ravin. He wanted to go to her right then.

And do what? Throw himself at her feet and tell her he loved her? She'd laugh at him for sure. Only a real sap would do that.

Suddenly Cowley had a hold of his head and was shaking it. "Are you still in there, Fen? Can you hear me?"

"Let go. What did you do that for?"

Cowley laughed. "I thought I'd lost you. Glad to see you're back."

"I wish I could go see her right now."

Cowley shook his head. "Terrible idea. If you start chasing her around like a puppy, she'll run away from you for sure."

Chapter 25

"I won't be going with you this morning," Flint said. The squad was getting ready to leave on their morning run. "I have some work I need to do. I'll see you back here in a bell."

"Are you sure that's the real reason, sergeant?" Noah asked, giving him a slow wink. "Maybe the real reason is that you're getting too old and you can't keep up with us anymore." A couple of the boys laughed at his remarks.

"Any time you think you're ready to challenge me, on anything at all, you let me know, okay?" Flint replied, a hint of a smile on his face. "Why don't we start right now with a little wrestling?" He started toward Noah, who backed up quickly and retracted his statement. None of them had ever succeeded in throwing their sergeant. He was too wily, too experienced for that.

Flint looked at Fen. "Corporal, you're in charge." With that he walked away.

Fen saw the dark look that appeared on Strout's face when Flint said that and inside he groaned. He was mortally tired of the older boy. Ever since Fen was promoted to corporal Strout's attitude, never very good, had gotten worse and worse. He never passed up a chance to confront or belittle Fen. Just the night before at dinner Fen had made an offhand comment about the weather—it had rained on them all day—and Strout started mocking him and calling him a baby who couldn't handle a little water.

"All right, then," Fen said. "Let's head out."

He started running across the castle grounds. The others fell in behind him. He looked back over his shoulder and saw Strout standing there with his arms crossed. For a moment he thought Strout was going to refuse to run. What would he do then? Tell Flint? He couldn't do that. He'd lose any chance he had of being an effective leader if he did. But how much authority did he really have? What could he really do if Strout refused?

But when he glanced back again, he saw Strout running after them. He felt relieved. The problem was pushed back for a while.

The run was uneventful until they were heading back up toward the castle, nearing the end of the run. Noah, who was running right behind Fen, suddenly fell hard. Almost instantly Noah was back on his feet. He charged Strout and tackled him. The two went down, fists flying, Noah shouting about how Strout had tripped him.

Fen turned in time to see Strout get Noah in a headlock and punch him solidly in the eye.

"Stop!" Fen yelled.

Both boys ignored him.

Fen jumped in then, grabbing Strout's arm when he pulled it back to hit Noah again. Strout looked up at him, his face twisted with anger.

"Stop!" Fen yelled again.

At first he thought Strout was going to ignore him, but then the boy stopped fighting him and let go of Noah. Noah rolled away. Fen let go of Strout's arm and stepped back. Strout stood up.

"He tripped me!" Noah yelled. He had a cut on his chin and his eye was starting to swell.

"I did not," Strout replied.

"You did too!"

Lukas spoke up then. "I saw what happened. You did trip him."

"Why don't you mind your own business, fat boy?" Strout snarled.

"Did you trip him?" Fen asked.

"So what if I did? What are you going to do about it?"

"I asked you a question. Did you trip him?"

Strout shrugged. "It was an accident. He was running too slow. He needs to learn to stay behind if he can't keep up."

Cowley grabbed Noah before he could charge Strout again.

Fen stared at Strout and Strout stared back defiantly. Once again Fen wondered what he should do. "Watch where you're going, Strout," he said. "Come on. Let's finish this."

When they ran into the practice yard a few minutes later Flint was waiting, sitting on a wooden keg. His eyes went to Noah, taking in the cut, then to Strout with his stormy expression. Last he looked at Fen, but his expression was unreadable and Fen couldn't tell what he was thinking. Though he saw nothing on Flint's face he understood one thing:

Flint was leaving this for him to handle.

He was on his own.

‡   ‡   ‡

The morning passed uneventfully. No more problems cropped up until midafternoon. Flint called a break and the boys headed for the water bucket. As usual, Strout got there first. He took his time, drinking several ladles full of water, ignoring the complaints from the other boys.

When he was done, he dropped the ladle back in the bucket. As he turned away, his elbow hit the bucket. The bucket tipped over, spilling the rest of the water on the ground. Strout looked down, a look of feigned surprise on his face. "Oops. Guess I spilled the water."

"You spilled it on purpose," Noah said angrily.

"I did not," Strout replied. "It's Lukas' fault. Piggy couldn't wait his turn and pushed me."

"I did not!" Lukas protested.

"Are you calling me a liar?" Strout pushed Lukas.

Spots of red rose in Lukas' cheeks and his fists clenched. Strout grinned mockingly at him.

Gage, ever the peacemaker, stepped forward. "I'll refill it." He picked up the bucket and headed off.

Strout gave Fen a triumphant sneer and swaggered off. Fen stared after him, anger and frustration boiling inside him. He realized then that Flint was watching and had seen the whole thing. But when Fen turned to look at him, Flint pretended to be inspecting a rack of halberds.

"You're going to have to do something about him," Cowley said to Fen in a low voice.

Fen sighed. "Yeah. I know."

"Just so you know, I have your back."

"Thanks. But this is something I have to do myself."

Cowley gave him a crooked grin. "I know." He clapped Fen on the shoulder. "But I'm there for you anyway."

After the break was over, the boys lined up, waiting for their next orders. Flint called Fen forward. "I have to meet with the captain. I'm leaving you in charge. Lead them in halberd drills until I get back. I shouldn't be much more than a bell."

A groan rose from the boys as he said it. No one liked halberd drills. The weapons were long, heavy and unwieldy. The drill consisted of standing in a line and then, on order, stepping forward, stabbing, stepping back, stepping forward to swipe, stepping back. On and on.

It was monotonous and tiring. Unlike swords or battleaxes, there was no real technique to it. It was unlikely that they would even use halberds in battle. Halberds were largely for untrained soldiers, those conscripted to fight against an invading enemy. But Flint wanted them to be familiar with every weapon out there. As he told them over and over, a soldier never knew when his weapon might break or get torn from his hands. He needed to be able to fight with whatever he could get his hands on.

Flint left the yard. "You heard the sergeant," Fen said. "Grab a weapon and get ready."

Grudgingly, the others all went to get a halberd. All except for Strout who instead went over to a bench and sat down.

Fen took a deep breath. This was it then. "Was there some part of that order you didn't understand, Strout?" he barked, trying to put as much authority as he could into his voice.

"Oh, I understood it all right," Strout said, leaning back against the wall. "I'm choosing not to follow it is all."

Fen could feel every eye on him as he walked over to Strout. He wished so much this didn't have to happen. He'd tried so hard to be reasonable, to find another way. "You don't get to choose which orders you follow," Fen said.

"Real soldiers don't fight with halberds. You know this as well as I do. I'll never use one. That means I don't need to practice with one. You boys carry on, though. I'll sit here and watch." He grinned insolently up at Fen, daring him to do something.

Fen had a feeling that Flint didn't have a meeting right now. He knew the situation was coming to a head and he'd left so that it could. Flint was testing Fen, wanting to see how he would handle this. One thing was for sure. He couldn't expect Flint to solve this for him.

"Get up and pick up a halberd."

Strout stood up. He pressed in close to Fen and gave him a hard stare. "Make me."

Fen head-butted him, catching him right on the chin. Strout's head snapped back and he fell back a step. Before he could recover, Fen hit him twice in the ribs, as hard as he could, knocking Strout back another step.

But it wasn't going to be that easy. As much as Fen had grown and gotten stronger, Strout was still six inches taller and he'd gotten stronger too.

He blocked Fen's next punch, then caught him with a hard right to the jaw. Fen tasted blood.

After that Fen was on the defensive. Strout's punches came too fast and too hard for him to do much more than try to survive. He kept his fists up and elbows in as Flint had taught them, protecting his face and body as much as he could while blow after blow rained down on him. Most of them landed on his forearms, but now and then one got through. He took a punch in the eye that made him see stars for a second.

Dimly he was aware of the other boys gathering around, calling out encouragement. The whole time he kept his feet moving, ducking and bobbing. And always he kept his eyes open, watching for his chance.

At first there didn't seem to be any, the blows came with such speed and power. But as the fight wore on, he noticed something. All those furious punches were taking their toll. Strout was starting to tire. His punches slowed down and Fen could hear him breathing hard. Fen realized that he himself was not breathing hard at all.

He noticed something else too. Strout was getting frustrated. He'd thrown his hardest punches and Fen was still on his feet. His mouth hurt and his eye was sore, but other than that he felt pretty good.

Strout muttered a curse under his breath and waded in to throw another flurry of punches, none of which got through.

When he fell back after a moment, Fen saw something he'd never seen in Strout before: uncertainty.

He was beginning to realize that he could lose.

At the same time, Fen had become calmer and more confident. He saw now how all this time, sparring against Strout nearly every day, he'd always felt inferior to the bigger boy. He'd always felt like he couldn't measure up.

That was what had been holding him back. His own self-doubt.

Fen smiled.

Strout gritted his teeth and waded in once again, swinging with wild abandon. Fen didn't even duck or dodge this time, just kept his guard up and took the punches as they fell. Watched and waited.

And there it was.

Strout threw a sloppy punch that flew wide and at the same time his off hand dropped too low. Fen took a half-step forward and threw his left, swiveling his hips as he did so to put all his power behind it.

The punch caught Strout square in the nose and Fen heard it break. Blood spurted and Strout's head flew back.

Before he could recover, Fen followed with the right, burying his fist deep in Strout's stomach. Strout folded forward and Fen hit him in the ear, then chopped down with the blade of his hand on the back of his neck.

Strout dropped to the dirt.

Fen stood over him, his heart singing. He'd beaten Strout. Not by trickery or luck, but by taking the best he had to offer and withstanding it, then returning the same.

"Wow," Cowley said. "I do *not* want to fight you."

Lukas kept saying, "I can't believe you beat him," over and over. The brothers were looking at him with open respect. Gage was wide-eyed.

But it was Noah who stood over Strout. "Finally!" he shouted. When he drew back his foot to kick Strout in the ribs, Fen grabbed him and tossed him aside.

"We're a squad. We don't do that to each other."

He crouched down next to Strout. "Come on, Strout. Get up."

Strout groaned and rolled onto his side. Fen took his hand and pulled him to his feet.

"Line up!" he barked at them. The boys hurried to obey, and even Strout limped into place.

"We're not always going to get along," he told them. "We're not always going to like each other. But we're a squad. We stick together. No matter what. Is that clear?"

"Yes, sir," they replied. Even Strout appeared to mumble the words. Blood was still running from his nose but he didn't wipe at it.

"Pick up your halberds and let's practice."

When Flint came back he looked at Strout, then at Fen. He didn't say anything, only nodded slightly at Fen and started them on a new drill.

At the end of the day, after he dismissed them, he called Fen to wait behind. He put his hand on Fen's shoulder and looked him in the eye.

"Do you want me to tell you what happened?" Fen asked him.

"I don't think so. I think I can guess what happened. Strout defied you and you stomped him. Then he decided to listen to you. But I do have one question: Did you learn anything today, corporal?"

"I did."

"Care to share it with me?"

"I learned more than one thing."

"Well?"

"It wasn't Strout holding me back, it was me."

Flint raised an eyebrow. "You don't say?"

"I had it in my head that I couldn't beat him. Not without getting lucky anyway."

"So this wasn't luck?"

"No. This was months of hard work and training."

"Is that it?"

"No. It was also me keeping my head. Strout lost his and he made key mistakes."

"Being a leader isn't as easy as it looks."

"It's not."

"And what are you going to do with Strout now?"

Fen thought about this. "Noah was going to kick him in the ribs. I stopped him."

"Why?"

"Because we're brothers." Fen thought some more. "I'm going to make sure Strout knows his place is with us. That hasn't changed."

"You're going to be good at this someday, you know?"

"Someday?" Fen said with a smile.

Flint smiled back. "Don't get too cocky, lad."

⚖   ⚖   ⚖

The others in the squad were mostly done eating by the time Fen got into the mess hall. All of them but Strout looked up at him when he came in. Cowley gave him a thumbs up. Noah gave him two thumbs up. Strout, sitting off at another table alone, kept his face turned down.

Fen got his food and then went and sat down across from Strout. Still Strout didn't look up. Fen took a small clay jar out of his pocket and slid it across the table to Strout.

"The healer says this will help with the swelling. He also says you should come see him so he can reset your nose. It'll heal faster that way."

Slowly Strout raised his head and looked at Fen. There was dried blood on his face. His eyes searched Fen's face, looking for any sign of mockery or triumph, but Fen was careful to keep his expression neutral.

Strout picked up the jar and turned it over in his hand. When his eyes came back up to Fen's they were confused.

"Why?" he said at last.

"You're part of the squad. That makes us family."

Something unreadable passed over Strout's face then. For an awful second Fen thought he was going to cry. Then his habitual scowl settled back into place. He put the jar in his pocket and stood up.

"It was a lucky punch."

"Are we going to have to do it again?" Fen asked him.

Strout considered this, then shrugged. "Maybe." He walked away.

⚓ ⚓ ⚓

"What did you say to him?" Cowley asked Fen after dinner. He and Fen were back at the trough behind the barracks. Fen had pulled off his shirt and was washing his face and chest. A couple new bruises were already starting to show.

"Not much."

"Really? I'm your best friend and that's all you're going to give me?"

"What else do you want?"

"I don't know. Something juicy. Did he swear vengeance or anything?"

Fen pretended to scan his memory. "I don't think so."

"So, what? You talked about the weather?"

"He said something about the bread being stale I think."

203

"You're a terrible friend, you know that?"

"Who said we were friends? I can barely tolerate you."

Cowley groaned and punched him in the arm.

"Hey," Fen said. "I'm a little sore, you know."

⚔ ⚔ ⚔

The next morning Strout ran at the front of the squad the entire way down to the docks and back. Not just in front, but way in front. He ran like he was pursued by personal demons, his head down, arms pumping.

When it came time to drill, he worked harder than anyone, even though the first drill was with halberds. He stabbed and slashed as if fighting an actual foe.

He kept his mouth shut the entire day, no mocking comments, no complaining. Fen kept looking at him, wondering, trying to read him. He noticed Flint watching him too, though the sergeant said nothing.

When it was time for lunch, Fen went and sat by Strout. Strout gave him a dark look, then returned to his food. "What do you want?" he mumbled.

"You know a lot about blacksmithing," Fen said.

"So?"

"It's the guard on my practice sword. It's coming loose and it pinches my hand."

"Take it to the weaponsmith."

"I could. But I also know he's busy so he'll probably tell me to come back later. I thought maybe you could at least take a look at it. Maybe it's something you can fix easily."

"Don't think I don't know what you're trying to do."

"Which is?"

"I don't want to be your friend. I don't need friends."

"Who said anything about friends? We're squad mates. I need help with my gear and you might be able to give me that help. Why wouldn't I ask you?"

"I'm busy."

"Look, Strout. You don't have to like me and I don't have to like you. But out there, facing the enemy, we have to be able to count on each other. We have to help each other. That's how we'll survive."

Strout met his eyes. "That's all this is?"

"I promise."

"Let me see it."

⚏   ⚏   ⚏

"I don't know why you bother," Cowley said later. "Everyone hates him."

"He's in my squad. That's why I bother. And maybe there's something else there, something else to him. I'm the corporal. I have to at least try."

"Well, if that's the price of being corporal, I'm glad Flint didn't name me. I can't stand that guy."

Chapter 26

"That's it for the day," Flint said.

It was early afternoon. A couple of the boys whooped. Free time was always popular.

"Not so fast. I want you to spend the rest of the day getting shiny. That means a bath and use soap. Shine your boots. Shine your mail. Shine your sword. Everything you've got, if it isn't nailed down, I want it to shine so brightly I can't look at it. The only thing you don't have to clean is your clothes. Someone from the laundry will be by to pick them up. That way we can make sure they look good. You lads lack decent laundry skills."

"What's going on, sergeant?" Fen asked.

"They finished the work on the wall today and the Fist is going to get up and give a speech. He wants all his soldiers there, looking neat and proper for the big event. For some reason he wants your squad front and center. I won't have you making me look bad."

Flint left and the boys put their practice weapons away, then headed for the trough behind the barracks.

"I was beginning to think they'd never finish that wall," Gage said. "What's it been, almost two years now?"

"Has it been that long?" Lukas asked, frowning as he thought about it.

"It has," Cowley said. He ruffled Noah's hair. "Why, when we all started training together two years ago, Noah here was just a little pipsqueak. Now he's grown all the way up to a runt."

Noah threw his shoulder into Cowley, knocking him sideways as Cowley laughed. They'd all grown so much, even Noah, though he was still the shortest among them and it looked like he was staying there. Of course, anyone who confused his size with his ability would soon be sorry. Noah fought with fierceness and intensity. Coupled with his quickness, it made him a formidable opponent. Fen had accumulated a lot of bruises and a couple of scars to prove it.

They'd all changed so much, he reflected as they stripped off sweaty tunics and dirt-stained breeches and started cleaning up. Strout was growing into a tall, broad-shouldered young man. His beard was coming in and there was hair on his chest. He was still the biggest and the strongest among them. He'd grown in other ways too. While still acerbic and often irritating, somewhere along the line he'd finally settled into his place in the squad and only occasionally complained or questioned Fen's orders.

Cowley was nearly as tall as Strout, but not nearly as broad. He still had a devilish grin that said he was planning some kind of trouble, but the boyish look on his face was toughening, becoming a man's face. He was rangy and strong, the fastest runner among them, with the greatest endurance. When he cared enough to put in the effort. He still had a lazy streak and was always looking for the easy way.

Lukas had probably changed the most. The pudgy, moon-faced little boy was gone, replaced by a serious-looking young man with thick brown curls. The baby fat he'd carried when they started was all muscle now. He was a deliberate, methodical fighter, not the flashiest among them, but rarely did he make mistakes.

Gage still had his gap-toothed grin and he was still the first to try and smooth things over when tensions boiled over and fights started—which they did fairly frequently. There was a gentleness to him that belied his burgeoning skills. While he could handle any weapon, he excelled with a bow and his horsemanship skills far outstripped the rest of them. On horseback he was a different person than he was on foot, more confident. On foot his old clumsiness still sometimes resurfaced, but on horseback his balance was flawless.

Then there were the brothers, Wallice and Eben. Eben, the younger, was now slightly taller than his brother. They still reminded Fen of half-starved wolves, with a lean, hungry look about them. They were more sinewy than muscular, lean and whip-thin. They fought together like two parts of the same person. They still barely spoke, but they sat with the others at meals and they watched closely, their intense eyes taking everything in.

The boys were cleaning up, most with soap all over them, when Lukas, who was scrubbing his hair, looked up and yelped. Instantly he jumped into the trough and crouched down in the water so only his head was sticking out.

"What's wrong with you?" Cowley asked, turning to see what he was looking at.

Amma was standing there, a large basket in her hands. Behind her was Ravin. Ravin was trying to avert her eyes, but Amma was taking it all in, a big smile on her face.

Like the rest of them, Fen was still wearing his smallclothes but he felt his cheeks burn red and he snatched up his breeches and held them before him. Noah and Gage jumped in the trough as well, while the brothers ducked behind it. Strout grabbed his boots and covered himself.

Only Cowley seemed to be enjoying the whole thing.

"Well, ladies, you see anything you like?" he said with a leer.

Amma pretended to be peering about. "I can't see much of anything at all," she said. "Nothing worth noticing anyway."

"Oh, now, you don't mean that," Cowley said. He then proceeded to strike a few poses, flexing for them, turning this way and that. "How about now?"

By then both girls were laughing. Ravin glanced up and caught Fen's eyes. He felt himself grow still redder and took a step back. Trying to get some kind of hold on the situation, he said, "I guess you've come for our clothes?"

"That's what we're here for," Amma replied cheerfully. She came forward then, Ravin trailing her, and they started picking up clothes off the ground and putting them in the basket.

"You'll be wanting these too," Cowley said, making like he was going to remove his smallclothes. Ravin's eyes widened and she turned away, but Amma faced the young man boldly.

"Sure," she said, holding out her hand. "Hand them over."

His bluff called, some of Cowley's smile faded. "Uh…maybe they're not that dirty?"

"Oh, they're that dirty, all right. Worse, even." Amma laughed. She turned to Fen. "Well?"

"Well…what?"

"Your breeches. That's the only thing we're missing."

Remembering the hole in his smallclothes, the hole he'd been meaning to sew up but somehow had never gotten around to, Fen went scarlet. "Yeah, maybe I can wash them myself."

"My orders are to collect your clothes and wash them. *All* of them. You don't want us whipped for not doing our jobs, do you?" she asked innocently. Behind her Fen could see a smile on Ravin's face, though she had her face partially averted.

208

"Okay, but...maybe less staring?"

That brought a hoot of laughter from those crouched in the trough and Amma's smile got even broader. "Come on, Fen. We have work to do," she said.

Reluctantly he handed the breeches over, quickly covering the hole with one hand. With a last look back the two girls took the laundry and left.

"Oh my god!" Lukas yelled. "I can't believe that just happened!"

"I can't believe you stood there and faced them," Gage said to Cowley. "I thought for sure you were going to take *everything* off."

"Too bad you chickened out," Strout said. "I wanted to see them react when you did. I bet they would have run."

"I did not chicken out," Cowley said. "I merely behaved like the proper gentleman that I am. I did not wish to embarrass the ladies."

"In other words, you chickened out," Lukas said.

"Coming from the man who's crouching in the trough like a scared child," Cowley scoffed.

"They surprised me, that's all," Lukas said, climbing out of the trough. "I had soap in my eyes. I couldn't see."

"At least none of us had to stand there with a hole in our drawers like Fen did," Noah said. "Way to impress the ladies."

"It's not that big of a hole," Fen protested.

"But it doesn't have to be, does it?" Cowley said with an evil grin. "Not for you."

Fen threw a bar of soap at him.

⚏　⚏　⚏

Later, while they were eating, Lukas said, "Now that the wall is finished, do you think we'll march on Marad?"

"What makes you say that?" Fen asked.

"I heard some of the other soldiers talking. They said the Fist has been waiting until he's sure the city is secure before he attacks them."

"That's just talk," Gage said. "Soldiers always talk. You should know that by now." He looked at Fen. "Right?"

"I think Gage is right," Fen said after a moment. "It's only talk. We're not anywhere near strong enough to attack Marad yet. I think it will still be years before we are."

"That's too bad," Noah said. "I'm sick of training. I'm ready for some action." A couple of others chimed in with their agreement.

"You cubs got no idea what you're talking about," a soldier at the next table said. He was middle-aged, with more than a few scars and a missing finger on his left hand. "You think war is a game. But you end up in the middle of one and you'll find out soon enough it's not a game." Having said his piece, he gathered up his plate and left.

"Don't listen to him," Noah said. "He's just old and that's the kind of thing old people say."

"He doesn't know what Wolfpack squad is capable of," Lukas added. He and Noah banged their forearms together and exchanged growls. Noah had come up with the name Wolfpack a few months earlier. He repeated the name whenever he could, trying to get it to catch on with the others, though Lukas and Gage were the only ones reliable about it. The growling and the forearm thing were much more recent.

Fen kept his mouth shut. He still had nightmares now and then about that night in Victory Square, the sounds of men screaming, the clashing of steel, the smell of blood and bile. He remembered that battle as being ugly and terrifying. The thought of going through such a thing again, and this time actually fighting in it, turned his guts to water. He only hoped when the time came that he'd have the nerve to stand and fight, that he wouldn't turn tail and run.

Chapter 27

Their clothes were ready for them the next morning, all clean and folded, sitting in the basket outside the door of the barracks. The squad dressed and then busied themselves with last-minute touchups, putting more bootblack on their boots, scouring their chain mail until it shone, oiling scabbards.

Then Flint called and they trooped outside to form up with all the other soldiers quartered in the castle. There were seven or eight hundred of them, Fen estimated. All of them together made up what was now called the Castle Regiment. There were four other regiments in the city, all of them forming up and getting ready to march down to the main gates. The Fist wanted the citizens of Samkara to see the full might of their rebuilt army.

From what Fen knew, there were still fewer than five thousand soldiers all told, smaller than the army had been when the city fell to the Maradi two years before. The difference now was that every one of them was a trained, professional soldier. The previous army had been mostly made up of conscripts, with very little training and poor quality weapons. Once the gates fell, they had no chance of standing against the better-trained and better-equipped Maradi.

He'd heard soldiers talking about desperate hours after the Maradi entered the city. There were stories about entire regiments throwing down their weapons and running, about weapons that broke the first time they were struck by the enemy.

The Fist was going to make sure that never happened again.

The order came and the regiment marched out of the castle and down into the city. As they went, other regiments fell in behind them and the entire army marched down to the main gates, all glittering steel and waving flags.

The entire city had turned out and the atmosphere was of a massive holiday. The streets were lined with the citizens of Samkara, cheering, throwing flowers. At one point a young woman burst out of the throng of onlookers, ran up to Cowley and gave him a kiss on the cheek, all to a huge cheer from the citizens and soldiers alike.

Street vendors were out in force, selling sweetened drinks, roasted nuts and skewers of fried meats. One enterprising vendor had made a cartload of small flags, dyed with the red, clenched fist and he was doing a brisk business, selling them to people who waved them as they cheered.

"Not bad, is it!" Cowley said to Fen, nearly having to shout to make himself heard. "A man could get used to this."

Fen had to agree. He found himself standing up straighter, sticking out his chest. He felt proud of who he was, proud of the Wolfpack squad that marched with him. They were the strong wall that would stand between this nation and its enemies. They would keep these people safe and ensure that they never went through the suffering and destruction that they did last time.

He'd done the right thing, when he told the Fist that he wanted to be a soldier. This was what he was meant to do. Nothing he could do with his life could possibly measure up to this one, simple thing: keeping his fellow citizens safe. He thought of Ravin, with her lustrous black hair and shy smile. For her, for all of them, he would make sure the city never fell again.

The great square inside the main gates of the city was filled with a cheering throng of citizens, in their excitement threatening to overwhelm the thin line of city watch whose job it was to make sure that the area in front of the wall remained clear for the soldiers to assemble in.

Repairs and improvements finally finished, the wall of Samkara was impressive to behold. It was almost twenty feet taller than it had been. The areas that had been damaged by the enemy catapults had been replaced with fresh stones. But that was only part of it. Two tall, round towers had been built flanking the main gates, guarding the approach. No future enemy would easily march up with a battering ram to assault the gates.

The gates themselves were easily four feet thick, solid oak sheathed completely with iron. And if a besieging army got through the gates, they'd find their fight had only just begun, because then they'd have to pass through the barbican where they would be exposed to fire from all four sides by the defenders. On the far side of the barbican was a heavy portcullis.

The crowd parted and the regiments marched through and took up their positions. Sergeant Flint, resplendent in his uniform, led

Wolfpack squad up to the very front and center, right before the broad platform where the Fist would stand and address the crowd.

Fen and the rest of his squad, conscious of the very great honor being given them, wheeled smartly and took up their positions, shoulders back, eyes fixed firmly forward.

The Fist appeared, riding on a white horse, surrounded by his personal guard wearing full armor and helmets. The crowd cheered harder, people screaming at the tops of their lungs. The crowd parted for him and as he rode through their midst he held up one clenched fist. The crowd roared and held up their fists as well. When he reached the first regiment and began to pass through their ranks, he lowered his fist and pressed it to his chest. The soldiers returned the salute with a cheer.

This was repeated with each regiment and when it was Castle Regiment's turn Fen slammed his fist to his chest, his pride so strong that his eyes blurred momentarily with tears. He would do anything, give anything, for his people and his Fist and he knew every man around him felt the same.

Fen was positioned beside the stairs that led up onto the platform and when the Fist dismounted to climb the stairs he gave Fen a nod. The Fist's eyes burned with intensity. He wore a simple white robe with the red fist emblazoned on it. An iron clasp held it closed at his throat. His clothing was simple too, leather breeches tucked into knee-high leather boots, a plain white tunic. There was no crown on his head. He'd had the old one melted down, the gold used for the repair of the city. His head was bare, his bald scalp gleaming in the sun. His long mustache was freshly oiled.

His horse was led away and his personal guard followed him up the stairs, then arrayed themselves behind him. The Fist stepped up to the edge of the platform and held his clenched fist over his head.

The crowd erupted anew, screaming his name, pressing forward.

He brought his fist down and the crowd went silent. Every voice stilled as the people leaned forward, straining to hear his words.

"In our darkest hour, when I stepped forward to lead this nation," the Fist began, "we were a torn and bleeding people. Our heart had been ripped from us. Our homes were ashes, our world in ruins. We were badly beaten and down.

"But we did not stay down! We stood up, determined to fight again!" Again he thrust his fist into the air and again the crowd cheered wildly, the soldiers joining in.

He lowered his fist and the crowd went silent again.

"I've called you here today to see the results of our hard work. You see behind me the stone wall that protects our city. You see before me the army, the human wall that protects our city. But that is not the only reason I called you here. I also called you because I want to renew the oath I made to you on that day, the oath to do whatever it takes, to make any sacrifice necessary to defend Samkara from—"

Suddenly his words broke off. A gasp came from the crowd.

Fen whirled and what he saw was something from a nightmare. For a heartbeat he could only stare in stunned disbelief.

The Fist was staring down at a sword tip that protruded from his chest. Blood was running down his tunic.

For what seemed like an eternity he stood there, the soldiers around him frozen, the crowd staring.

Then chaos broke out. People screamed. Soldiers fought to draw their weapons.

The Fist turned, staggering as he did so, and Fen could see a man behind him, backing away. It was one of the personal guards. There was a look of disbelief on his face. He took another step back, shaking his head in denial, his hands held up.

Blood was pouring down the Fist's back. His knees were starting to buckle. Somehow he stayed on his feet. His face twisted in a mask of hatred and he reached out with his right hand, his fingers grasping as if to close around the assassin's neck, though he was too far away to reach him.

And that's when Fen saw something unbelievable.

Writhing tendrils of what looked like smoke emerged from the ends of the Fist's fingers. The smoke was black, tinged slightly with purple. The smoke tendrils homed in on the assassin and wrapped around his throat. The assassin's eyes bulged with horror as he was lifted into the air. He began choking and spittle ran down his chin. He clawed at his throat and his legs kicked in the air.

All at once a beam of white light shot out of his mouth and went into the Fist's mouth.

The assassin's cheeks hollowed. His eyes grew sunken. The skin stretched tight across his face. His very flesh appeared to be melting away.

Within seconds he was dead. He stopped struggling and went limp. The beam of light went out. The smoke tendrils withdrew back into the Fist's hand and the assassin's body collapsed.

The Fist lowered his outstretched arm. He flexed his fingers. He turned so that he was facing the silent, watching crowd. He reached back, managed to take hold of the sword, and slowly pulled it free. The crowd gasped as the wound sealed up quickly. There was blood on his clothing still, but the Fist was perfectly healed.

The Fist held the assassin's blade aloft.

"Nothing will stand between me and my vow to protect this city!" he thundered.

The crowd stared at him in stunned silence, hardly able to breathe.

"Even death itself cannot stop me!" the Fist yelled. "*Nothing* can stop me!"

Still the crowd stared in silent awe, until the silence was broken by one voice.

"All hail the Fist, chosen of Hentu!" It was the gray-haired priest who so often preached on the steps of Hentu's temple. "Hentu has sent him to Samkara as a sign of his favor! All hail the Fist!"

As if his words had released a torrent of pent-up emotion the crowd suddenly found its voice. A roar rose from it, echoed by the soldiers. The Fist joined in, throwing his head back and howling at the sky.

Only Fen was silent, struggling to grasp what he had just seen.

When the cheering stopped, the Fist descended from the platform. His personal guard moved to follow him but he waved them back. "I no longer need you," he told them.

As he walked into the crowd his people pulled back, opening a lane for him to pass through. They went to their knees, heads bowed. The chant at first was only a few people, but others quickly picked it up until the entire square boomed with one word, repeated over and over.

"Fist. Fist. Fist…"

Chapter 28

The squad gathered in their barracks after they got back to the castle, unable to stop talking about what they'd seen.

"I still can't believe that happened," Lukas said. "No way could anyone survive a wound like that."

"Then he pulled the sword out and the wound was gone," Noah said, his voice filled with awe. "That was incredible."

"What about the way he killed that assassin?" Lukas said. "He lifted him into the air and strangled him but he wasn't even touching him."

"The Fist was at least ten feet away from the assassin," Noah said.

"It has to be like the priest said," Gage put in. "The Fist is the chosen of Hentu, or some other god. Only a god could do that."

"However he did it, I know one thing for sure," Strout said. "If I was Marad I'd be pretty scared right now. With the Fist leading us there's no way we can lose."

While the others talked Fen sat quietly. It was clear no one else had seen the smoke tendrils or the white light. They didn't realize that the Fist was alive because he had stolen the assassin's life. They thought the Fist was the chosen of a god. Only Fen knew differently.

He remembered back to that night in Victory Square, when he saw the hands reach out of the shadow and touch the Fist's head. Smoke had come out of those hands and gone into the Fist, the same smoke—or whatever it was—that the Fist had just used to steal the assassin's life. Who, or what, was in that shadow? What did he want? Why had he given such power to the Fist?

One thing Fen felt sure of: that was no god he had seen in the shadow. It was someone dark, someone evil.

And he was using the Fist.

But why? What did he want with Samkara? Did the Fist know he was being used?

And one final question: how come no one else but Fen saw what happened?

"Why are you so quiet?" Cowley asked, leaning over from his cot to look into his eyes. "Are you okay?"

Fen lowered his voice and looked around to make sure the others weren't listening in. "This may sound weird," he said softly, "but did you *see* anything strange?"

"You mean, other than our Fist pulling a sword out of his back?" Cowley said sarcastically. "Other than that, no."

"Not that. I mean, did you see how the Fist killed the assassin?"

"He, uh, picked him up by the throat and strangled him."

"From ten feet away?"

Cowley shrugged. "Like Gage said, there's a god involved or something."

"So you didn't see black smoke come out of his hand?"

Cowley's look was puzzled. "Black smoke? What are you talking about?"

It was as he feared, Fen thought. No one else had seen what he'd seen. Unless, of course, he was going crazy and seeing things. He rubbed his eyes.

"You don't look so good," Cowley said.

"I don't feel so good."

"Tell me more about this black smoke you saw. What did it do?"

Fen shook his head. "I must have imagined it." He tried a wan smile. "You know how I get carried away sometimes."

"No," Cowley said, all seriousness for once. "I don't. Because you don't. You're the most level-headed person I know. You're so level-headed I don't know how you don't die of boredom. You saw something. I want to know more about it."

Fen stood up and motioned Cowley to follow him outside. No one paid any attention to their exit. He leaned against the wall of the barracks and ran his fingers through his hair. He recounted what he'd seen. When he was done, Cowley was shaking his head.

"I didn't see *any* of that."

"Like I said, maybe I imagined it," Fen said shakily.

"Or maybe you had a vision. There's an old woman who works in the laundry in the palace. She claims to have visions."

"But that's crazy."

"Is it really? Our Fist just pulled a sword out of his back and walked away smiling. What could be crazier than that?"

"I don't know."

"It's not too outlandish, you having visions," Cowley said. "I've always known you were different."

A thrill of fear went through Fen. Did Cowley suspect his secret? "What do you mean? I'm not different."

"Come on, I've seen you take hits to the head that would put anyone else out. And then your story about defeating two attackers that night, *without* your sword? Who does that?"

"I was lucky."

"Or maybe you're touched by the gods too. Maybe that's why the Fist is always calling you in, taking such notice of you."

Fen froze. Could that be it? But he didn't want to be touched by a god. He just wanted to be a soldier. "Do me a favor, okay? Don't talk about any of this with the others."

"Sure," Cowley said. "Whatever you say." But he looked wonderingly at Fen.

⚖ ⚖ ⚖

Fen wasn't surprised when the servant showed up and beckoned him to follow. He didn't want to do this. He needed time to sort through what he'd seen and figure out how he felt about it. But his Fist summoned him and so he went without hesitation. He could do nothing else.

The servant led him to one of the upper floors of the palace, across a large, silent room and out onto a balcony that afforded a view of the city. Barik was pacing restlessly back and forth, muttering to himself and waving his hands in the air.

He turned to Fen as soon as he heard him approach. His eyes were alight with some kind of fey energy.

"Look," he said, pulling his shirt open. Where the sword point had emerged there was only a faint, purple mark. "That's all that's left." His eyes searched Fen, as if he were looking for something.

Fen felt dread and hope mixed together inside him. "I thought you were dead."

"I know. So did I. I could feel my life leaving my body. I knew I only had seconds to live. All I wanted, before I died, was to kill the one who'd killed me."

He resumed pacing, stalking the balcony like a caged cat. He started muttering to himself again and gesticulating.

This went on for a minute and Fen began to wonder if Barik had forgotten he was there. Finally, he ventured, "Sir?"

Barik spun on him. At first, when his gaze fell on Fen, there was no sign of recognition. It was like he'd never seen Fen before. Then the moment passed and he continued talking as if nothing had happened.

"I remember reaching out, wishing only that he was closer, that I could kill him before I died. And then…and then…I could *feel* his life. I could feel it draining out of him and rushing into me. I could feel it healing me. It was incredible. There is no way to describe it."

Fen just stared at him. Too many emotions roiled around inside him. He couldn't choose one to focus on. Fear, love, despair, wonder. All that and more.

"What happened to me down there?" Barik asked him.

Fen recoiled from the question. "I don't know. How could I?"

Barik gave him an odd look. "Don't lie to me, Fen. You're holding something back, I know it."

Fen's mouth felt very dry and it was hard to get the words out. "I thought I saw some black smoke or something come out of your hand and wrap around the assassins' throat."

Barik looked puzzled. He raised his right hand, spread his fingers, and looked at it. "Smoke came out of my hand?"

"I probably imagined it," Fen said.

"That's a strange thing to imagine."

"It was probably nothing."

Barik gave him a searching look. "But you don't think so."

"I don't know what to think."

"Maybe it's like the priest said. Maybe the gods have chosen me for some reason."

"It could be. I don't know much about the gods, Fist." A forgotten memory came to Fen then. One day he and his mother passed by a temple with a statue of a sad-looking god outside it. There was something intriguing in the statue's eyes and he asked if they could go inside. But his mother grew visibly angry at his request and told him she would never set foot in a temple again as long as she lived. "We tried every temple in the city when your father became sick, but none of them did the slightest good. I won't turn to them again."

After that he'd asked her what his father was sick with, but she'd refused and hurried him away from the temple without saying another word.

Barik went to the railing and leaned on it. His forearms were corded with muscle. He was a powerfully built man. Fen remembered how hard he'd fought in Victory Square before he was pulled down. Now that he thought about it, it was strange that Barik had emerged from that pile of dead soldiers unscathed. Was he being protected by someone or something even then?

And for what? What purpose did this all serve?

As if reading his thoughts Barik turned his head to look at him. "I've been trying to figure out why. The whole afternoon, since the attack, I've been asking myself one question over and over. This isn't the first time I've survived something which should have killed me. Something out there is watching over me. But why? Clearly I'm meant to do something, but what?"

"Protect Samkara?" Fen said. "Keep us safe from our enemies?"

Barik shook his head. "I think there's more. I think I'm meant for bigger things."

What could be bigger than keeping your people safe? Fen wanted to ask. What could be more important than that?

"Everything changed today, Fen," Barik said. "Nothing is as it was. We are about to embark on something unlike anything this world has ever seen. I can feel it in my bones. Something incredible is happening and it is centered right here, around me. I've been chosen by the gods to carry out some grand plan that I can't yet see. Something bigger than just Samkara. Something that affects the entire world." His gaze was intense. His eyes were practically glowing.

Fen was aware that he was sweating profusely. It was running down his back underneath his shirt. He could feel it running down his face. He felt like he was burning up inside. He had a vague sense of strange energies running through him. A world that had settled into predictable patterns had suddenly upended. Nothing made sense any more.

"The future starts now," Barik said.

Part Two: Aislin

Chapter 29

Netra set the bowl of porridge down on the simple wooden table and stirred a spoonful of honey into it. Next to the bowl she set a mug of steaming herbal tea.

"Aislin, your breakfast is ready."

Aislin was still in the bedroom and when she didn't appear, Netra went to the curtain that hung in the doorway and pulled it back. The cottage Netra lived in was small, just the two rooms, and she and Aislin shared the only bedroom and the only bed.

Aislin was lying on the floor peering closely at something. She didn't look up when Netra spoke to her again, but she did stand up. She walked by Netra without looking up at her or acknowledging her in any way.

She sat down at the table and took a bite of the porridge. Netra came and stood by her, stroking her hair. Aislin's hair was white-blond and silky to the touch. She twitched slightly away from Netra's touch, but continued staring out the window at a seagull wheeling in the sky as she ate.

"I'm going to the Jansen farm today," Netra said, sitting down on the other chair. "Their horse is foaling and they are worried about it. Do you want to come with me?"

Aislin didn't reply. She simply continued eating and staring out the window. She ate mechanically, neither unhappy with the porridge or happy with it, as if it were something she was required to do but had no feelings about one way or the other. All her attention stayed fixed on the bird, wheeling in the cloudy sky.

"Aislin. I asked you a question. Look at me."

After a moment the little girl turned her face to Netra. She showed no expression at all. Netra was struck, as she often was, by the color of her eyes. Today, with the wind picking up and clouds building in the sky, her eyes were a deep, fathomless green, like the depths of the sea. But on other days her eyes were a light green, dappled with flecks of gold like captured sunlight.

As she always did, Netra looked for something in the little girl's eyes, some spark, a sign that there was someone in there, looking back at her. But that spark was not there today. Today her eyes were bottomless and distant.

"Do you want to go to the farm with me? See a baby horse?"

After a moment, Aislin shook her head. It was a tiny movement, almost imperceptible.

"Words, Aislin. Remember what I said? Use your words." Netra had spent a lot of time trying to get Aislin to use her words, with only limited success. The child was fully capable of talking, she just chose not to. It was one more thing that set her apart from the other children in the village. Frankly, it made people nervous.

Aislin blinked and seemed to be searching inside herself for the proper response. Seconds passed, and then she said, "No, Mama."

Netra cupped her cheek. "See, Aislin? That wasn't so hard, was it?"

Aislin turned away and resumed staring out the window. Netra sighed and stood up. She was doing the best she could but it didn't seem to make any difference. As she had so many times before, she considered taking Aislin and going to Qarath, a day's walk to the north. Qarath was the capital and also the headquarters of the Tenders of Xochitl, an order of women dedicated to healing and nurturing all living things. Netra had grown up in the order and she was still a Tender, she supposed, but after the terrible events with Melekath and his Children—events which had come so close to destroying everything living in the world—she'd retired here to this small village, wanting nothing more than a quiet life away from everything.

It was possible that one of the Tenders in Qarath would be able to help Aislin. Even if none of them could help, it would still be a relief to discuss the child with Cara, Netra's childhood friend who had been chosen as FirstMother in the aftermath of the events.

But then, maybe there was nothing wrong with the child at all. Maybe this was simply how she was and would always be. She was no ordinary child, that was for sure. Netra had only to listen with her inner senses to hear the strains of Sea force mingled with her LifeSong. The thought that Aislin would always be this way tore at Netra's heart, for she had come to love the child deeply in the eight years that she had cared for her.

More than anything, Netra longed to connect with Aislin, to share her childhood, to talk and laugh with her. But always there was this wall between them and no matter how hard Netra tried, she could not seem to get through it.

Hanging from the ceiling of the cottage were a number of bundles of herbs and plants, drying. Against one wall was a long set of shelves. The shelves were covered with jars, pots and small boxes containing the herbs and salves Netra used to aid her healing. Her ability to manipulate LifeSong was, of course, her primary tool for healing, but the herbs and such helped as well in a limited fashion.

The herbs and salves also helped the local villagers and farmers feel more comfortable with Netra's healing. The events surrounding Melekath's escape from his prison, and the important role the Tenders had played in defeating his Children, had done a great deal to improve the way Tenders were viewed by most people. Certainly they had come a long way from the days when they were almost universally hated and feared. In Qarath, for instance, they were honored and respected and there was no shortage of girls and young women seeking to join the order.

But the village of Seaside was not Qarath. The people here were still suspicious of Tenders and the powers they had. So to help them feel better Netra downplayed that side of her healing and used the more traditional tools of normal healers.

Netra packed her travel bag, put on her old brown cloak and went to the door. A gust of wind blew in when she opened it and she turned back to Aislin. "It looks like rain. Stay out of the sea if it rains, okay?"

There was no response and Netra wondered why she worried anyway. The child was like an otter in the water, which made sense, considering where she'd come from. But if Netra had learned one thing about parenting, it was that being a parent meant worrying about your child, even when there was no need to. Her fear for Aislin wasn't something she seemed to be able to control, no matter how much she tried to reason with it.

Unfortunately, the child's affinity for the sea only made the villagers even more uncomfortable around her. They fished in the sea, it was true, but only from the shore. There were no boats. No one swam in the ocean. It had been thousands of years since the cataclysmic wars between the gods of the sea and land, but people still feared the sea enough to stay away from it.

"Just be careful." Netra gave Aislin a hug, then went out the door and left.

Chapter 30

A few minutes after Netra left, Aislin stood up from the table. She left the half-eaten bowl of porridge on the table and went to the door. A stiff breeze swirled her hair around her face and lifted the edge of her thin dress. It was chilly outside, the last vestiges of winter still in the air and the storm pushing cold air before it, but she didn't take her cloak down off the peg where it hung from the wall, or put on her shoes.

The cottage sat in the lee of a small hill a quarter of a mile or so from the sea. Aislin followed a narrow path that took her to the top of the hill, where she sat down cross-legged and looked out over the sea. The rising sun was trying vainly to pierce the thick clouds that were building far out to sea. The crashing of the breakers could be heard over the wind. Seagulls cried and pelicans dove into the water, scooping up struggling fish. She smiled as she looked at it.

Later, she took another path that led down to the village. Seaside wasn't much, a few dozen one-story, wood and stone houses set well back from the sea. A small stream ran down through it. On the edge of the village was the road that led between Qarath to the north and Thrikyl to the south. There was a small inn for traders and others who passed along that road, but most people chose to stay in Hempsted, which was only a couple hours to the south. Which was fine with the residents of Seaside, who mostly wanted to be left alone.

She walked down the town's only street, oblivious to the other people, most of whom moved out of her path as she approached. A few smiled and spoke to her, including an elderly woman who was sweeping her front step, but Aislin paid no attention to them either. The old woman stopped her sweeping and stared after the child, shaking her head sadly.

A spate of rain fell and Aislin stopped in the middle of the street to tilt her face up at the sky, closing her eyes, letting the raindrops land on her face. A farmer with a small cart full of potatoes pulled by a sway-backed old horse muttered under his breath and led the horse around her.

The rain let up and Aislin continued on. In front of one of the homes several children were playing with a leather ball. The ball bounced away from them and came to a stop in front of Aislin. She picked it up and examined it closely.

"Throw the ball, Aislin!" one of the children, a girl about Aislin's age, called.

Aislin ignored her, her attention fixed on the ball.

"Throw the ball!" another child called.

"That won't do you any good," a boy said. He was a couple years older than Aislin and wore a perpetual scowl. He ran over to Aislin and took the ball from her hand. A flash of emotion, perhaps irritation, passed across her face when he did so, but it was quickly gone.

"You're nothing but a freak," the boy told her.

"Don't say that, Kerl!" the first girl called. She had long, sandy hair and freckles across her nose and cheeks. "It's mean."

"It's true, Dariana," Kerl said. He stuck his face up close to Aislin's. "Isn't it true? That you're a freak?"

Aislin turned away and continued walking down the street.

"Why do you always have to be so mean?" Dariana said.

"Why does she have to be so weird?"

"She can't help it."

Kerl grunted. "You're probably right. She's what, half-fish?" All the children knew the story of how Aislin had come to live among them, though none of them were old enough to remember it.

"Are you blind, Kerl? She's not a fish."

"Then how come she spends so much time in the sea? Isn't that where fish live?"

"You're nothing but a big dummy, Kerl."

"And you're bossy."

Still arguing, the children went back to playing while Aislin walked on alone.

She walked along the beach, staring at the sand. Dozens of starfish had washed up during the night and she spent a few minutes picking them up and putting them gently back in the water. She crouched by a small hole in the sand and waited until a tiny crab scuttled out of it, then watched its progress across the beach.

Further along the sandy beach gave way to a rocky shelf and there were dozens of tidal pools. On her hands and knees she stared into the biggest one, watching the snails, crabs and tiny fish make their way around their miniature world, a faint smile on her face.

In one of the pools she found a dead fish floating on its side. Her smile faded, replaced by sadness, and she picked the fish up, holding it tenderly as if afraid she would hurt it. She walked to the edge of the rocky shelf and set the fish in the water, then waved goodbye to it as it sank beneath the surface.

By midmorning the wind had grown stronger, the waves bigger. Aislin walked out into the surf. Soon she was chest-deep in water, but she did not stumble or lose her footing when the waves struck her, as if she were too much a part of the water for that to happen.

She spread her arms and let the water take her.

On land Aislin was a graceful child, but it was in the water where she really came into her own. She swam with the grace of a dolphin, moving nearly effortlessly. The waves seemed to help her, even when she swam against them. Out beyond the breakers was a family of sea otters. They did not scatter at her approach but swam and played around her as if she were one of their own.

Unnoticed by Aislin, Dariana had followed her down to the beach and was sitting on the sand, watching her. For a long time she sat there, her eyes alight as she watched Aislin swim. She envied the natural way Aislin moved through the water and wished she could do the same. One day when she was younger she followed Aislin into the water, but the water pulled her under and her mother had to run in and drag her out. After that she was forbidden to go into the sea and even now she had to sneak away if she wanted to go down to the beach and watch Aislin swim.

⚜ ⚜ ⚜

Near midday Netra returned home to find the door open, flies gathered on her daughter's breakfast. She shut the door and headed for the beach, knowing exactly where she would find her.

As she passed through town the elderly woman who had spoken to Aislin got up from her tiny garden and walked with her.

"Kerl was picking on her again," the elderly woman said.

"I've given up talking to his parents about it, Mirrim," Netra replied. "I think they actually encourage it. Not everyone in Seaside is as understanding as you are, unfortunately." She gave the old woman a sad smile.

"She's just different, is all, and folks around here don't always handle different all that well."

"You're telling me," Netra said. Most of the locals accepted her—won over mostly by her healing skills. It was amazing how curing a sick child broke the ice with people—but there were still a few who avoided her and spoke in low voices behind her back.

"The child moves to a song only she can hear," Mirrim said. "She'll come around when she's ready. You'll see."

"I hope so," Netra said. "I really do." She appreciated Mirrim's constant efforts to help her feel better about Aislin, but in her heart she doubted.

They walked to the beach and watched Aislin swim.

"At least she's stopped taking her dress off," Netra said and the old lady chuckled. It was only recently that Netra had been able to get through to Aislin on that. So many times she'd explained to the child that it upset people, that she was too old to run around naked.

"I worry about her so much," Netra said. "I never know what to do."

"That's the way it is with kids," Mirrim said, patting her arm. She'd raised seven of them herself. "You never know. Not for sure. You muddle along and hope it will all turn out right."

"If there was only something I could do to get through to her." Netra felt her throat tighten. She always felt sad when she talked about Aislin. "There are times when it seems like I'm close, when I think I can see her in there, looking out at me. She looks lonely and I get the feeling she wants to come out, but she doesn't know how. But then it passes and it's like there's no one there at all." Her voice broke slightly. "It's hard."

"I know it is, dearie," Mirrim said, putting her arm around her.

⚕ ⚕ ⚕

Aislin came out of the water an hour or so later. Mirrim had already left, gone back to her garden. Netra had brought a towel from the cottage and she wrapped it around Aislin, then rubbed at her hair, drying it.

"How was your swim?"

Aislin didn't answer. She was looking at a sandpiper running along the beach. Rain spattered around them.

Netra looked at the sky. Lightning flashed and thunder rumbled offshore.

"It looks like it's really going to rain hard. What say we go home before it does?" Aislin started to follow the sandpiper but Netra caught hold of her hand and stopped her. The little girl didn't resist as she led her up the beach and back into the village but she looked over her shoulder at the bird until it was out of sight.

They walked without speaking. The street was mostly empty, most people having gone inside to get out of the coming storm. The children had left the leather ball on the ground and Aislin pulled away from Netra to pick it up.

On impulse, Netra said, "Kerl was mean to you again today, wasn't he?"

Surprisingly, Aislin looked up at her.

Netra's breath caught in her throat. Most of the time, when Aislin looked at her, the little girl didn't really look *at* her, so much as *through* her. But on those rare times, like now, when she actually did look at Netra, the force of her gaze was almost palpable. Netra froze, afraid to move and shatter this precious moment.

"Why, Mama?" Aislin asked in a small voice.

Netra crouched in front of her and took the child's hands in hers. "Why what, Aislin?"

"Why does that boy push me and speak to me in a loud voice?" Aislin cocked her head to one side. "I don't understand."

Netra's heart soared. In a shaky voice she said, "I don't know for sure. I think he's frightened of you."

Aislin frowned.

"You're not like him and that scares him."

Aislin nodded. "I come from the sea."

That surprised Netra. Aislin had never said anything like it before. "In a way. I don't know for sure. But I know that the sound of the sea is inside you."

"I belong to the sea."

The way she said it, so straightforward, so calm and certain, somehow it made Netra's heart drop. *No*, she wanted to say. *You belong to me!* But she knew that Aislin didn't, not really.

"I don't think so," Netra said. "I think you belong here, with us."

"But I only feel right when I'm in the sea."

Netra had never told Aislin about her origins. She's always assumed the child was too young. She decided to take a chance. "When you were a baby, you were brought here by a...man. He said there is something special about you, that you are important. He brought you to me because you need to be here. He said there is something you will do someday to help everyone."

But by the time she'd finished speaking, Aislin had stopped listening and was looking at the ball again.

"I don't care," she said in her small, high voice that sounded like birds crying in the distance. "That's why he does those things. Because I don't care. About him or anybody. That's why I'm different."

She said all this without looking at Netra, more as if she were speaking to herself. Like she was just realizing something that she had been puzzling over. Then she let the ball drop and walked up the street.

Netra stared after her, her hand over her mouth, tears in her eyes. The loneliness of that statement cut her clear to the bone. What was it like to be in there all alone, surrounded by people you didn't understand and who didn't understand you?

Netra thought she had never felt so helpless in her entire life. She, who had stood against those beings who people called gods, who had entered into the River where no one had ever gone before and emerged unscathed, now stood confronted by one little girl and she had no idea what to do, how to help her.

All her knowledge of herbs and healing, all her ability to manipulate the raw power of LifeSong, and yet here she could do nothing. She didn't even know where to start.

She hurried to catch up to Aislin. The little girl had stopped and was crouched by a dead bird. She flipped it over, intently watching the tiny insects underneath the carcass, the way they raced this way and that, frantic for cover.

"Let's go get something to eat," Netra said, as the first fat raindrops began to fall in earnest. When Aislin didn't respond, she took hold of her hand. It was cold, still clammy from the sea. The little fingers did not close around hers. When she pulled, Aislin stood and followed without resistance, but she kept her eyes fixed on the dead bird as long as she could, staring back over her shoulder at it until it was swallowed by the rain.

⌇⌇   ⌇⌇   ⌇⌇

It was raining hard by the time they reached the small whitewashed cottage. Netra hung her cloak on the peg by the door. Then she got a fresh dress and a pair of warm socks from the trunk in the bedroom, pulled off Aislin's wet dress and pulled the dry one on over her head.

She put the little girl on the chair. "Let's get these socks off you, shall we?"

It always bothered her, how cold Aislin's skin was after she had been swimming in the sea. As cold as a fish. She always felt the urge to bundle her up tightly afterwards, even though Aislin never shivered, never took a chill or a fever, regardless of the time of year or how cold the water was.

The whole time she was dressing Aislin the little girl stared off into space, singing one of her strange little songs, as she often did, especially when Netra was dressing her or bathing her or combing her hair. Netra had often wondered if being so close to another person like that made Aislin uncomfortable, that maybe the singing was a way to push it all away, but she had no way of knowing.

The songs themselves were beautiful, in a haunting, ethereal sort of way. They made Netra think of deep places, of vast creatures that moved through the sea. The words to the songs made no sense to her. She wasn't sure if Aislin was making them up, or if they were an actual language that was innate, something she carried imprinted deep inside her.

When she was done dressing her, Netra took Aislin's hands in her own. "That's a beautiful song, honey. What's it about?"

Aislin just kept singing and staring over Netra's shoulder. Netra moved so that she was in the child's line of sight, but her eyes—a darker, stormier green now—looked right through her without seeing her.

Netra sighed. The tenuous connection she'd had with the child only a short while ago was already gone and in its place was a wall that seemed even thicker than before.

She built a small fire in the fireplace as the rain began to come down even harder. Raindrops hissed and sizzled on the flames and the wind clawed at the thatch roof. Lightning flashed and thunder grumbled as sheets of water poured from the sky.

Rain began to leak through the roof and Netra got a pot to put under it. She'd been meaning to speak with Ned about the leak and ask him to fix it. She'd helped his two children through a terrible cough last winter and he'd promised her he would work on her roof in return.

She laid some vegetables out on the table and began to chop them for soup. "You want to help chop, Aislin?" Sometimes the little girl would help with preparation. She seemed fascinated by the glitter of the blade. But instead she got up out of her chair and went and crouched by the pot, watching the water stream down into it.

"The foal was born healthy," Netra said to Aislin's back. "You should have seen it. You'd have liked it. It was awfully cute." The truth was that it was just as likely Aislin would have completely ignored the colt. She showed little interest in land animals for the most part, preferring birds and the denizens of the water.

As she chopped and added seasoning to the soup, Netra talked about her day, things she saw on the way to the farm, a funny story the farmer had shared with her, the way the colt looked taking his first, wobbly steps. Aislin didn't respond to any of it. Most times she didn't. But Netra did this every day anyway, partly in hopes that something, somehow, would get through to the child, but also because she needed to, because it was hard to live alone with another person.

"You're like Shorn, you know," she said at one point. "Like you, Shorn could never stop talking either. It was always jabber, jabber with him." She chuckled a little at the thought. For the longest time Shorn said almost nothing to her, even though they spent all day every day together. Even after he began to open up a little he still said very little. She felt closer to Shorn than almost anyone alive, yet she still knew so little about him. How often she missed him. How often she looked down the road that led north from the village, hoping to see his broad figure approaching. The world seemed a safer place when he was around. She hadn't seen him for over ten years now.

When the soup was on the fire, Netra walked over to check on Aislin, who was still crouched by the pot of rainwater. As she approached she saw that Aislin was doing something with her hands, but she had her back to her and Netra couldn't see what it was. She also realized that the child was singing again, a different song than she'd been singing before.

Then she got close enough to see what was happening and she came to a stop, her hand going to her mouth.

Under Aislin's hands a small waterspout had risen from the pot, a thin column of water about a foot high and swirling slowly.

Netra stayed motionless, afraid to make any sound or movement that might interfere with what she was seeing.

The pace and tone of Aislin's song changed. As it did, the water changed too, and began sparkling with different colors, reds and greens and yellows. It was beautiful, mesmerizing.

After a bit, Aislin's song changed again. Shapes appeared in the water. Netra saw dolphins and different kinds of fish, cavorting in the water spout, leaping and swimming. At one point she even saw a sea turtle and was reminded of the time Ya'Shi had summoned one for her and Shorn to ride on back to shore.

Wanting to know more about what was happening, Netra stilled her thoughts and listened with her inner senses. Underneath Aislin's song she could hear—though not with her ears—the strange and powerful Song of the Sea. It sounded like deep currents and seething, colorful, vibrant life. She remembered the first time she had heard that unusual Song, underneath the buried city of Kaetria. She'd touched Sea Song herself and been awed at the raw power it contained. It was a power that, while not exactly inimical to life, was certainly not friendly to it either. It was a power that could easily destroy any living creature who came in direct contact with it. Yet here was this little girl, molding that awesome power as if it were nothing.

Aislin stopped singing and sat back. The waterspout and the colorful creatures all vanished. It was only ordinary water once again.

"That was beautiful, honey," Netra said softly. Aislin didn't look at her or respond, lost in her own world once again.

They ate dinner and the rain slackened, the storm's fury moving further inland. When her bowl was empty, Aislin got up from the table and went to her bed, where she pulled the covers over her.

Netra cleaned up and followed her into the bedroom. She stood there holding a candle, looking down at the small form underneath the blanket, her chest rising and falling with each breath. She put out the candle and crawled in next to her. She ached to wrap the child in her arms and hold her close, but she knew better than to do so. Aislin usually didn't respond well to sudden touching, especially if she was asleep, thrashing and making an odd wailing sound as she fought to get away.

Netra stared up into the darkness for a long time before she finally fell asleep.

Chapter 31

The next morning Netra woke up early from restless sleep. She lay there in bed for a while, unable to shake the sense of foreboding that had settled over her during the night. She had a feeling that something bad was coming, something that would bring an end to their time living in this quiet village. She enjoyed living here. After the chaos and suffering she had endured during the time of Melekath's escape from his prison, Seaside had offered a welcome respite, a place to step back and gather herself. A place to rest and heal wounds that would probably never fully be healed.

She mourned this loss of her sanctuary keenly, though what she feared had not yet come to pass.

In the dim light of the early morning she looked at the sleeping form of Aislin. The child looked so peaceful in sleep. She had no idea of the troubles that lay ahead of her. Netra ached at the thought of what she would endure, and cursed Ya'Shi for his prediction, as if it were he who was responsible for what was to come or Aislin's place in it.

If she could, she would take Aislin and flee. Find some place far away where her daughter could be safe. But she already knew that was impossible. When vast struggles come, nowhere is far enough, nowhere is safe. What has to be faced can only be faced.

She rose and prepared breakfast, forcing her thoughts down more cheerful paths, and when Aislin emerged, stumbling and sleepy-eyed, Netra greeted her with a smile that if not completely genuine, was at least partly so.

She set a wooden bowl filled with steaming porridge in front of Aislin, then touched her hair gently. Aislin flinched away from the contact.

"How did you sleep? Did you have sweet dreams?"

Aislin didn't answer and Netra sat down across from her. "That was beautiful, what you did with the water last night."

Aislin didn't respond, but the spoonful of porridge stopped halfway to her mouth.

"How long have you been able to do that?"

The tiniest shrug, then the porridge resumed its passage and Aislin continued eating.

"Tell me about it, honey. How do you do it?" Then Netra waited, her heart in her mouth, hoping. She was about to give up when Aislin looked up. The little girl didn't look into her eyes, but over her shoulder.

"There's music in the water. It wants to come out." She tilted her head, as if she was listening to it right then. And maybe she was. "I let it out."

"It's a wonderful gift you have," Netra said. "It's something special. Something precious."

Aislin went back to eating as if she hadn't heard.

Netra reached across the table and took her hand. Aislin twitched, but didn't pull her hand away. "But you need to do something for me, something very important." She waited for a response, and when there wasn't one, she continued. "You need to keep it hidden. Keep it our little secret. Just between us. Can you do that? Can you do that for Mama?"

Then she waited with bated breath. There was still so much distrust and fear among the villagers. Some barely tolerated the little girl as it was. If they saw her controlling water like that…

Aislin frowned. "I don't want to."

"I know, honey, and it's not forever. It's just for now. That's all."

Aislin peeked at her, saw Netra looking at her, and quickly averted her gaze. Staring at the table top, in a dull voice she said, "It's because I'm different. I scare them."

"They're afraid because they don't understand. But if we give them time, if we go slow, they'll have a chance to get to know you as I do." But did she *really* know her daughter? "Then they'll see there is nothing to be afraid of."

Aislin pulled her hand away. "They make me mad sometimes."

Netra sighed. "They make me mad sometimes too. But we have to be patient and give them time. Can you do that?"

But Aislin had already gone back to eating and nothing Netra said got any more responses out of her and finally she gave up and ate her own breakfast.

⚓ ⚓ ⚓

237

Later there was a knock on the door. Netra opened it and found a man on the other side she only knew by sight but had never met. He had the weathered features and knobby hands of one who has worked hard in the sun his whole life. His clothes were homespun and old; stitches showed where they had been mended many times. All she knew about him was that he lived on one of the outlying farms, tucked up in the folds of the small inland mountain range to the west.

"Can I help you?" she asked him.

He was holding a shapeless hat in his big hands and he twisted it, uneasy at being here. He only briefly met her gaze before looking away.

"I have a shatren down. She's one of my best milkers. I'd hate to lose her."

Netra looked at him, knowing what it had cost him to come here, to ask her for help. The few times she'd encountered him in the past, he'd given her a dark, suspicious look and hurried away. He must be truly worried about the animal to come fetch her now.

"Of course," she said. "I'll come straight away. Only let me fetch my things." She started to go back inside, then paused. "I need to bring my daughter along, if that's okay. I don't want to leave her alone today."

She saw his face tighten and knew right away that whatever his misgivings about her, they were double for Aislin. On any other day she wouldn't bring Aislin, not wanting to put him or his family through any greater strain. But after what she'd seen last night…it might be some time before she felt comfortable leaving Aislin alone. If this man wanted her help, he would just have to put up with her daughter as well.

"Aye," he said. He gestured with a calloused hand. "I have the cart, down to the bottom of the hill. I'll wait for you there." He turned and lumbered away.

Netra went inside and began packing her bag with everything she thought she might need and then whatever else she could fit in as well. Often she was called out to help with one problem, only to find there were others that needed looking after as well. It was best to be as well-prepared as she could.

"Get dressed, Aislin," she said as she packed. "We're going to a farm. Won't that be fun?"

Aislin sat at the table, her legs swinging under the chair, staring out the window. Netra spoke to her again and again got no response, so once her bag was packed she went to Aislin and took her hand. The little girl didn't resist as she pulled her up and led her into their bedroom.

Aislin stood there lifelessly while Netra dressed her, less a child than a very large, upright doll. She didn't resist, but she didn't help either.

Once Netra had her dressed, she took her back into the front room and put her cloak on her, tying the drawstring snugly with a double knot. Aislin had a way of "accidentally" untying knots when she didn't want to wear her cloak and then "accidentally" losing it. It looked like rain again today and, Sea power in her veins or not, Netra wasn't going to let her get wet and chilled if she could help it.

Next came the child's shoes and then they were ready to leave the house. They stepped out into a brisk, chilly wind. The sky overhead was filled with scudding clouds and the ground was muddy.

Netra pointed down the hill, where the farmer waited beside his cart. "We're going to ride in a cart. We're going to have fun today."

"I don't want to go," Aislin said sullenly. "I want to go to the sea."

"When we're done I'll take you there. I promise. But right now we're going with the farmer. He has a sick cow shatren and he needs our help."

Aislin didn't say anything more. She didn't resist Netra when Netra started leading her down the slope, but neither did she help. Instead she plodded along woodenly and when Netra stopped and let go of her hand to take a rock out of her shoe, she stood there without moving, not even looking around.

Netra didn't miss the uneasy look the farmer gave Aislin when she led her up to the cart. Nor did she miss the way he moved a step away from them, though he pretended that the harness on the horse needed to be adjusted.

Aislin stood motionlessly when Netra told her to climb into the cart, so Netra simply picked her up and set her in the back.

Whereupon the child huddled in the depths of her cloak, withdrawing until only a pale smudge of her face was visible.

The cart had only the one seat, so Netra sat in the back with Aislin and let her legs dangle over the edge as the cart bounced along the rutted road that led from Seaside and wound back into the hills. The farmer made no attempt at conversation and so Netra had plenty of time to sit and look around.

The rain had washed everything clean and the countryside looked fresh and new. The hills were low and gentle here and lightly forested with pine, scrub oak and aspen. Down by the small stream there was a good deal of fertile bottomland, rich soil deposited by floods over the years, and it was there that the farms were situated, one tucked away in each bend of the stream.

The farmers were all hard at work, plowing their fields, preparing them for seeding. Spring was coming quickly and there was much to be done in preparation. Up on the hillsides small flocks of goats and sheep grazed, watched over by children and dogs. Beaver dams dotted the stream, creating ponds here and there where fish jumped and birds called from the trees.

It took quite a while to get to the man's farm. The road had nearly petered out by then, and was cut by deep ruts and jutting stones that made riding in the cart an uncomfortable proposition at best. His farm was one of the last before the slopes of the low mountains began in earnest and the land became too steep for farming. The farmhouse and barn were built together, as was usual around here, where the winters could get quite cold, both made of thick logs chinked with clay. Most of the land around the farmhouse had already been plowed. Netra could see the plow sticking out of the ground at the edge of the last field before open ground turned to woods.

The farmer pulled the cart up in front of the house and set the brake. Two brindled dogs came racing out barking to check out the newcomers, followed closely by three young children. They all stopped and stared at Netra and Aislin with big eyes. Aislin was still unresponsive so Netra simply lifted her out of the cart and set her on the ground. As limp and passive as Aislin was, she thought she might just fall down when she set her down and she'd decided she didn't care if she did. If the child wanted to carry it to that extent, then let her. But Aislin got her feet under her and stood on her own, studiously ignoring the three children, who were staring openly at her.

The oldest of them was a boy about Aislin's age and in a loud voice he said, "It's the fish girl, all right, but I don't see any fins or nothing."

There was a girl a little younger than he and she said, "Maybe they're hidden under her cloak."

Just then their mother came striding up. She was wearing an apron and drying her hands on the corner of it. She cuffed the two children. "Keep a civil tongue in your heads," she snapped. "That's no way to treat guests."

She came over to Netra and held out her hand. "I'm Mattie and I'm sorry for them."

"I'm sorry too," Netra said.

"It's just, we're pretty isolated up here and we don't often get visitors. They don't get much chance to practice manners." Mattie was probably thirty, her face lined from years of motherhood and eking out a living here on the edge. Her brown hair, tied back in a neat bun, was already shot through with gray and her hand, when Netra shook it, was roughly calloused.

"I understand," Netra said. "Children have a way of doing what they want rather than what they are told to do."

Mattie cast a glance at Aislin as Netra said this and Netra could see the woman's curiosity. Like everyone, she had heard about the mysterious child that came from the floating island and she knew also about that child's unnatural—and doubtless unhealthy— fascination with the sea. Like the children, she was probably wondering if the child had gills or something else unusual, but she was hiding it better than they were.

It was a reaction Netra had seen over and over during the years and there were times when she thought she was used to it. But then there were other times, like today, when it angered her. Couldn't people see that Aislin was only a little girl? However different she might be, she was still a child. There was nothing to fear, nothing to point at. Emely and Jiff's son had a dent in his skull you could put your fist into and he talked and shrieked at people no one else could see, but people had given up staring at him years ago. When would they stop staring at Aislin?

"There's a cow shatren that's ill?" Netra said, not wanting to stand there any longer. She just wanted to heal the animal and leave. She wanted to be alone. She turned and realized that the farmer had already walked away. She caught only a glimpse of him as he disappeared into the barn.

Mattie broke off staring at Aislin guiltily and nodded. "There is. You'll want to follow Daren into the barn. I won't hold you up longer. I only came out because I wanted to ask you something. I've a wee one inside, a little girl, and her cough is back. I wanted to ask if you could have a look at her. As long as you're here."

And with that Netra's irritation vanished, washed away by her concern for the little girl. She knew what it cost Mattie to come ask her and that meant the child was sicker than she was letting on. Her healing nature was triggered and everything else vanished before it.

"I'd be happy to." Netra took her bag from the cart with one hand and with the other she took Aislin's hand, not wanting to leave her alone with these children.

The inside of the barn was dim and warm from the bodies of the shatren lined up in their stalls. It being the end of the winter, most of the hay was gone, only a small pile still remaining in the back of the barn.

Netra heard Daren in one of the stalls and went over to find the cow lying on her side. She set her bag down and knelt beside the animal.

"Can I get some more light in here?" she asked. Daren moved to the door of the stall and swung it open so daylight poured in.

The cow was in obvious pain. Each breath was tortured and her tongue was sticking out, her eyes wide and glassy. A puddle of drool had gathered in the dirt under her head. Her belly was huge, bloated badly. Netra knew right away what it was. The cow was colicky and it was a serious case of it. Untreated, the animal would likely be dead in a few hours.

Fortunately, Netra knew she could heal the cow. It wouldn't really be all that difficult, either. But it wasn't something she could reliably treat with herbs. She would have to use her other healing ability, the one that made people like Daren so uncomfortable.

"I'm glad you got me here in time," she told Daren. "I can cure her."

She saw the sigh of relief that escaped him as he knelt by the cow's head and stroked her face. In that moment she saw his real fondness for the cow that went beyond her monetary value.

"I have just the thing to put her right," she said, reaching into her bag. "Can you bring me a bucket about half full of water, please?"

While he was getting the water, she dug around in her bag and found a pouch containing beetleswort powder. It wasn't actually helpful for colic, but when put in water it bubbled and turned the water an impressive shade of green. In other words, it looked good and that was what counted. The farmer would see the cow drink it and he'd go away thinking that was what healed her.

Once he brought the bucket back she mixed the powder into it. While she was doing so Aislin wandered off but it seemed like she was only looking around the barn so Netra left her alone and let her go. Maybe she would find something to interest her.

They were able to get most of the liquid down the cow's throat. Then Netra knelt beside her and put her hands on the cow's side. This was when the real healing would happen.

"One more thing," she told Daren. "If you could find some sprigs of hensbane. There should be some sprouting by now. That will aid her recovery. I shouldn't need more than a handful."

Daren grunted and left. The hensbane had no healing properties that Netra knew of. It was simply a way to get the farmer out of the way while she healed the cow.

Once he was gone, Netra closed her eyes and went *beyond*. *Beyond* wasn't a place. It was a state of heightened awareness that Tenders were able to access, generally after much time and practice. While *beyond*, a person could *see* the flows of LifeSong. Not with the physical eyes, but with the inner senses.

As Netra went *beyond*, the familiar mists rose up around her. She pushed deeper, passing through the mists and into the clear darkness on the other side. The first thing she *saw* was the flow of Song attached to the cow shatren. It appeared as a shining, golden thread floating in the blackness. If she was to follow it back, she would see that it branched off a larger flow, then an even larger one. Followed the whole way back she would come upon the River itself, the source of all LifeSong, a vast, golden river of pure energy.

The flow of Song was attached to the cow's *akirma*, which appeared as a glowing white light laced with brown and amber colors. Every living thing has an *akirma* and every living thing has a flow of LifeSong attached to that *akirma*. It is the constant flow of Life-energy into the *akirma* that keeps things alive. Sever that flow, or tear the *akirma* far enough that too much of the creature's Selfsong leaks out, and life is replaced by the silence of death.

Netra focused her attention on the cow's *akirma*. On the surface of the *akirma*, just over the animal's stomach, was a reddish blotch, showing the location of the cow's illness. With the right application of more Song, she could heal it.

Shifting away from the cow's *akirma*, Netra looked deeper *beyond*. The glow of numerous other flows of Song appeared in the darkness. Netra laid the touch of her will on them and knew instantly which ones attached to the different members of the farmer's family and which ones were attached to animals, plants, insects and so on. With a little effort she could *see* the glows of their *akirmas*. Those of the people were a dazzling white, those of the animals more brownish, the plants more greenish.

Then, ever so gently, she began gathering Song from those flows, siphoning it off and gathering it to her, focusing it on her hands, which began to glow brightly, though the glow would only have been visible to someone who was *beyond*.

She only took a small amount from each flow, small enough that no harm would come to any of the living things. Small enough that most would not notice it at all. Sometimes animals would flinch and look around, as if sensing the approach of something unfamiliar and some people were sensitive enough to feel it. Those who were usually described it as being like a tug, something gently pulling at them inside.

The only one she avoided taking Song from was Aislin. Her flow of Song had the power of the Sea mixed in with it and she wasn't sure what would happen if she was to use some of it for healing.

The Song she siphoned off was strong and pure and with it came the familiar rush. It energized her in a way that nothing else possibly could, flowing through her, filling the empty spaces, pushing back fear and darkness. She loved this feeling, loved it more than anything.

Loved it too much.

And so she was careful not to hold onto it for very long. Too well she remembered the dark days during the war when she had bloated herself on stolen Song and the harm she had caused others with the hunger she'd developed for it. A hunger that had never completely gone away.

She pressed her hands to the cow's side and then gently released the borrowed energy into the animal's *akirma*. The golden Song flowed from her hands, spreading out through the cow and as it did, the reddish blotch grew fainter and finally disappeared completely.

Netra released the last of the borrowed Song and then rocked back on her heels and left *beyond*, feeling, as always, the sense of emptiness that followed contact with pure Song. She wanted so badly to take just a sip off it, only a tiny bit to push away the emptiness, but she knew the almost-inevitable consequences if she did.

She opened her eyes and was surprised to see Daren standing there, looking down at her, a bunch of hensbane clutched in one hand. "Oh, I didn't hear you come in," she said, wondering how long he'd been there, how much he'd seen. She wiped her mouth with the back of her hand, feeling oddly guilty as if she'd been caught doing something wrong.

"I've brought the plant," he said gruffly and in his tone—and in the echoes of Selfsong that radiated from him—she could hear his suspicion and discomfort. He knew she'd been doing something that went far beyond mere herbs and medicinal plants. He'd have heard of it from others, but this was the first time he'd seen it himself.

"Good, good," she said, getting to her feet, noticing that he took a step back as she did so.

Both were distracted then by the cow, which sat up and looked around. Her brown eyes were once again clear. The bloating had already noticeably receded. She craned her neck to try and reach the hensbane, thick tongue curling out for it.

"She's...she's going to be all right," Daren said, giving the animal the plant and scratching her behind the ear. "Just like that."

This was the part Netra loved, when their fear of her fled, chased away by their joy at the healing. With some the fear returned later on, but others gave it up forever, grateful for what she'd done for those they loved.

"She should be fine now," Netra said.

"Thank you," he said simply, his voice again gruff but this time from suppressed emotion. "I've…" He rubbed the cow's forehead. "She's a fine cow, the finest."

"I'm glad I could help."

"I've no coin," he said as she picked up her bag. "But we'll see you well provisioned. Still a fair number of vegetables in the root cellar, some eggs, a chicken if you like and more to come once the crops start coming in. It's not much, but it's all I have."

Netra saw from the look in his eyes that he would be one of the latter, for whom gratitude was stronger than fear.

"That would be lovely," she said. "Except for the chicken. I'm afraid we don't eat meat."

"Whatever you want, you just let me know," he told her earnestly.

╫   ╫   ╫

Netra took Aislin's hand and headed for the house. The three children were breaking up kindling and they stopped in their work to stare and whisper. Snickers followed but when Netra looked down at Aislin, the little girl seemed as if she hadn't heard. Maybe she hadn't. There was no way to tell.

Mattie greeted them on the stoop and led them inside. The home was low-ceilinged, simple, but clean and homey. Coals glowed in the fireplace and a large iron kettle sat on the wood-burning stove. There were two bedrooms and Mattie led her into one of them, where an infant lay in a crib that had been lovingly carved, sanded and polished.

"She's had a bit of a fever for a few days," Mattie said, "but I didn't think much of it. Just a childhood thing, you know? But today she seems worse and with you being here already I thought, well, it can't hurt to have you take a look at her, can it…?" She trailed off with a little laugh as if at her own foolishness, but the worry in her face was evident and she was twisting the edge of her apron nervously in her hands.

"I'm sure it's nothing," Netra told her reassuringly. "Would you get me some water to wash my hands before I examine her, please? Who knows what I picked up in the barn."

246

"Of course, of course." Mattie hurried off.

Mostly Netra wanted a moment alone with the child to examine her, to get an idea of how sick she really was. But when she bent over the crib she knew there was something very wrong before she even touched the baby. She could hear it in the Selfsong emanating off the child, feel it tingling in her fingertips.

She put a hand on the child, closed her eyes and slipped *beyond*. What she *saw* there shocked her.

It was the size of her thumb, pulsing with an unhealthy yellow color. She probed around it with her inner senses for a minute, determining the full extent of it, then withdrew.

When she opened her eyes she saw that Mattie was back, standing there with a basin of water in her hands, her eyes wide. "It's bad, isn't it?" Her hands began shaking and Netra took the basin from her, afraid she would spill it.

"It is," Netra said. Mattie put her hand over her mouth and her eyes brimmed with tears. "It's a tumor, I'm afraid. On her lung."

"Oh..." Mattie said in a low voice. She put a hand on the infant, stroking her cheek. The baby grabbed her finger with tiny hands. "Will it...will she live long?"

"I think I can heal her," Netra said.

Mattie turned on her, grabbing onto her arm like a drowning woman. "You can?"

Netra nodded. "But not with any ordinary means. You know, don't you, about my...abilities?"

"I've heard stories, but I was never sure if they were only that."

"They're true. But I keep them from most people. Most people are frightened of them. They still remember the stories of how the Tenders used to be." Until the recent war against Melekath and his Children, Tenders had been hated and feared almost everywhere in Atria. That fear went back a long way, to the days of the old Kaetrian Empire, when the Tenders were at the height of their powers. Unfortunately, they lost their way and abused those powers, using them to increase their own wealth and power, instead of for healing the way their god, Xochitl, intended. When the Tenders' power finally failed, during the collapse of the Empire, people turned on them, killing most of them, destroying their temples.

Things were better now. The Tenders were healers once more and they were regaining their standing in the eyes of the people, but old fears died hard.

"That's why Daren didn't want to call on you," Mattie said. She lowered her head. "I didn't want to either. But he knew the cow would die without your help and so…" She looked up at Netra. "I *am* afraid," she said stoutly. "I won't deny it. But I'll do anything to save my baby."

"That's what I needed to know," Netra said. "Now, the first thing is, I need to make sure I won't be disturbed while I'm doing this. It's very delicate, what I'm going to do, and having someone barge in and disrupt my concentration could be deadly."

Mattie strode to the front door of the farmhouse and dropped the bar into place. Then she came back into the room and barred that door as well. She went to the room's lone window and closed and latched the heavy shutters. "What else?"

Netra took a deep breath. "There is an energy that flows through all living things. That is Song. To heal the child I will need more Song than what she has within her. Normally I would gather some from nearby flows and use that, but that is raw Song, what we call LifeSong, but it is a blunt tool and if I use it to cut away the tumor I will probably hurt her. In her weakened state it would likely be too much.

"What I need to use for this is Selfsong. When raw LifeSong passes through the *akirma*—which is like a glowing field surrounding the body—it is refined and becomes Selfsong. That's why—"

"I don't need to understand," Mattie said, cutting her off. "Take it from me. Take as much as you need."

"I must warn you that it will not be pleasant," Netra said. "You'll feel a coldness and a despair such as you have never known. You may feel like you are dying."

Mattie's lip quivered but she bit it almost fiercely. "I don't care."

"Okay," Netra said. "Pull up that chair and sit down. You won't be able to support yourself while I do this."

Mattie pulled the room's only chair up close to the crib and sat down. She leaned into the crib and stroked the baby girl's tiny face. "Her name is Lea, after my mother."

"It's a beautiful name."

"It'll be okay, my precious baby," Mattie cooed. "Mama's here and this woman is going to help you." Lea caught hold of her thumb and tried to suck it. Mattie looked up at Netra. "What do I need to do?"

"Nothing. Sit back and try to relax. Closing your eyes will probably help. Whatever you do, try not to move. We don't want to break contact while I'm in the middle of this." Mattie nodded and took a deep breath.

Netra closed her eyes and went *beyond*. She passed through the mists and down into the velvet darkness on the other side. To her left was the glow of Mattie's *akirma*, and to her right was Lea's much smaller *akirma*. Unlike the colic, which had been visible on the surface of the cow shatren's *akirma*, the tumor was deep inside the child, frighteningly close to the brighter glow that was her Heartglow. She would have to be absolutely sure that when she cut the tumor away she didn't nick the Heartglow.

Summoning some of her personal Selfsong, Netra spread it like a balm over the top of the baby's head, soothing her, pushing her down into a deep, dreamless sleep. She needed to make sure the baby didn't move during the procedure.

Next Netra laid both hands on Mattie's *akirma*. Her hands began to tingle and the hunger she had wrestled with for so long flared into sudden life. She pushed the hunger aside and focused some of her own Selfsong into her hands, making of it a sharp edge to cut a small opening in Mattie's *akirma*. She had to make sure she kept the cut small; too big of a cut and Mattie's Selfsong would pour out in a sudden rush and she would die.

Mattie gasped and jerked as Netra made the cut and Selfsong began to spill from her. Quickly, Netra put her hands over the cut, catching the Song before it could radiate away. As the energy flowed into her, the spark of hunger roared into sudden flame, so strong that it staggered her. The feeling of power and warmth and euphoria swept over her and she wanted nothing more than to keep feeding that feeling, to draw and draw on Mattie's Song until there was nothing left.

Netra had to fight hard to control the urge, but control it she did. Aware that she was breathing hard from the effort, she directed a tiny bit of Song onto the cut in Mattie's *akirma*, sealing it shut.

Then she turned to the child. For what she needed to do she had to make a larger cut. Once she did, the baby's Selfsong would drain away very rapidly. She would have to use some of the Song she'd taken from Mattie to replenish what was draining away, to keep Lea alive.

At the same time, she needed to also use some of that Song to cut the tumor out and destroy it. She would have to work quickly, before the borrowed Song was depleted, and she would have to work carefully, so that she didn't harm the baby. Never had she tried an operation so delicate and she felt a sudden surge of fear. If she failed, what then? How would she face this family? How would she face herself?

There was no time for self-doubt. She had to act and she had to act now.

She laid her hands on Lea's *akirma*. Channeling a tiny stream of the Song, she sliced through her *akirma*. Despite how deeply Netra had put her under, the baby cried out and twitched. Netra had to stop and hold her hands over the cut, slowing the outrush of Selfsong, waiting for the baby to go still once again.

Once the child had settled back down, Netra went to work. Trying her best to ignore the Song that was now pouring steadily from the child, she summoned all her will to focus a tiny stream of the borrowed Song into something like a fine blade. With that blade she cut around the tumor, careful to avoid the Heartglow. Once the tumor was free, she concentrated on it, wrapping it in pure Song, using the power to dissolve it.

A long minute passed, Netra putting everything she had into eliminating the tumor, conscious of how quickly the Song she'd borrowed from Mattie was diminishing. At last the tumor was gone, broken down into its individual cells which the child's body would gradually reabsorb. Netra withdrew quickly. Between the effort of replenishing the child's dwindling Selfsong and the energy needed to deal with the tumor, she'd used up all the Life-energy that she'd taken from Mattie. To close the opening in the child's *akirma* she was forced to draw on her own reserves of Selfsong.

When she was done she was shaking badly and she felt weak. She stepped back from the crib, rubbing her arms. She felt so cold, so drained. She was acutely conscious of the woman and the child so near to her, their Songs bright warm fires in the cold darkness.

She moved away from them, going to the window and opening the heavy shutter. "It's done," she told Mattie.

Mattie opened her eyes and stood up. She swayed and had to grab onto the crib to keep her balance. She scooped up the baby and held her to her chest.

"Is she…did it work?"

Netra nodded. "She's going to be okay."

"Thank the gods," Mattie breathed, tears running down her face. She buried her face against the child and cried for a moment.

Netra wanted to go to her, to comfort her, but she still didn't trust herself. The hunger was too strong. "She will sleep for some time still and she will be weak for a while, but she should be back to herself in a couple of days."

Mattie raised her tear-stained face. "How can I ever thank you for what you've done?"

"Just seeing you hold her is enough," Netra said honestly. She wasn't making it up either. The sight of mother and daughter was a beacon pushing back the darkness she felt crowding around her.

Suddenly something occurred to her and she looked around.

"Where's Aislin?"

⚏   ⚏   ⚏

Aislin wasn't in the bedroom. She wasn't in the front room either. Now that she thought about it, Netra realized that she couldn't remember seeing the child since shortly after entering the farmhouse. She'd let go of her hand when she went to examine the infant and then she'd forgotten all about her. Aislin must have slipped out then.

"I'm sure she's just outside playing with the others," Mattie said, but Netra barely heard her. She was fumbling at the heavy bar holding the front door closed, afraid that at any moment she would hear screams from outside.

She got the door open and hurried outside, blinking at the sudden brightness of the sun after the dimness of the bedroom. At first she didn't see Aislin anywhere and fear bloomed in her chest, but then she saw her slight form down by the stream, the other

251

three children nearby. They all looked unhurt and she took a deep breath, glad there'd been nothing to worry about.

"There they are," Mattie said. "Down by the beaver pond. Nothing to worry about."

"I'll go get her," Netra said. "I'll be right back."

She hurried toward the children. As she drew close, she could hear them talking.

"Come on," the boy said to Aislin. "I want to see your gills. Show them to me."

Aislin was looking down at the ground, not responding.

"What's wrong with her?" the girl said. "Why don't she talk?" The youngest of the three, barely old enough to be out of diapers, stood watching with his thumb in his mouth.

"It's cause of the gills, I bet," the boy said. With one finger he poked Aislin in the shoulder. "Hey, fish-girl. Can you breathe underwater?"

For the first time Aislin looked at him and whatever he saw made him take a step back.

"Can *you*?" she said.

The boy was standing with his back to the beaver pond and when Aislin said those words Netra saw the water in the pond start to swirl. Tiny waves lapped up on the shore around the boy's feet.

"Stop it!" Netra cried, running the last few steps and grabbing Aislin by the shoulders.

"I wasn't doing no harm," the boy said sullenly.

"I'm not talking to you," Netra said. The water was still moving. She gave Aislin a little shake. "I said stop it."

The swirling ceased and the waves receded.

"What's wrong with her?" the little girl said.

"She's just different," Netra replied. "Isn't that enough?"

She took Aislin's hand and led her away. "Never do that again," she hissed in a low voice. "*Never.*"

"I was tired of him," Aislin said, not looking at her.

"That's not a reason," Netra said. "It's never a reason." As she said this, she could not help but think of the terrible things she had done, the ways she had abused her power. "Did you hear me? Tell me you heard me."

But Aislin had lapsed back into silence and nothing Netra said could draw her out.

"Is everything okay?" Mattie asked when she saw the look on Netra's face.

"It's fine," Netra said. "I...I've been having some problems with Aislin's behavior lately."

"I know how that is," Mattie said. "I can't ever get through to that boy of mine. His head's like a stone. Whatever happened, I'm sure he was to blame and I'm sorry for it."

Netra gave her a weak smile. "Fortunately, nothing happened. I probably overreacted."

"Children do that to you." Mattie gave Lea another hug and touched her cheek. "I want to thank you again. I don't..." Her voice broke. "The last one died just about this age, almost two years ago. I couldn't go through that again, not so soon."

"Bring her to me anytime you need to. Any time. I mean that," Netra told her sincerely.

"You better count on it. You've made a believer out of me this day." Mattie came forward and took Netra's hand. "I don't know what you did in there, but I'm grateful. Anything you ever need, and I mean anything, all you need to do is ask. I'm sorry we don't have any coin for you, but you won't want for food for you and the little one for a good long time."

"That's enough," Netra replied. She looked around and saw Daren emerging from the barn, heading their way. "If you don't mind, I think we'll walk back home."

"You sure you don't want Daren to take you in the cart? It's no trouble."

"Thanks, but I think I feel like walking."

"If you say so. He'll come by your house later and bring you some vittles, so you don't have to carry anything."

A few minutes later Netra and Aislin were walking down the road toward home. When they were well away from the farm, Netra stopped and crouched down in front of Aislin.

"Look at me, Aislin," she said, moving into the child's line of sight. Aislin turned her head to look away. "No, you're going to look at me." Netra put her hands on the child's face and turned it to face her. Aislin turned her eyes down.

"What were you planning on doing to that boy?"

No answer. Netra wanted to shake her until her teeth rattled. She had to grit her teeth until the feeling passed.

"If you don't talk to me, I won't let you go down to the sea."

Aislin flinched slightly.

"I'm sorry to have to threaten you with that," Netra said, "but this is serious. That frightened me, what you did back there. I thought maybe you were going to harm that boy."

She waited to give Aislin a chance to respond and when she didn't she continued. "When you hurt someone, it leaves a mark inside you. That mark never goes away. Believe me, I know this. The things I've done…I'll never be free of them."

Still no answer.

"Talk to me, Aislin. Tell me you understand what I'm saying." Her voice cracked and she paused.

"I don't know what I was going to do," Aislin blurted out suddenly, her face darkening. "But I'm tired of it. Maybe it's time to be scary. Maybe that will make them leave me alone."

Netra's heart broke a little when she heard the words. She gathered the child up in a fierce hug, tears streaming down her face. "I know it's hard. I know you're angry and you don't understand. But you can't do that, honey. You can't ever strike out at anyone that way. If you do I'm afraid they'll take you away from me. I'm afraid they'll put you away somewhere and we won't be together anymore. I love you so much and I don't want to see that happen."

She pulled back and stared into the child's eyes, willing her to understand.

For the first time, Aislin looked at her rather than through her. "They'll take me away?" she said in a small, lost voice.

"I'm afraid they will. I'm afraid they'll put you somewhere so you can't harm anyone else."

"We won't live together anymore?"

"No," Netra said, fresh tears starting in her eyes.

"That would make you sad." It was a statement, not a question.

"Sadder than you can imagine."

"Okay," Aislin said. Then she pulled away and started walking alone down the road.

Netra stood and stared after her, not sure what, exactly, had just happened. Despite how many times she'd told Aislin she loved her, the child had never told her back. She wasn't entirely sure the child was capable of feeling love. This was the closest she'd ever come to showing Netra that she did.

Netra wiped at her tears. It occurred to her that Aislin's acquiescence might have less to do with anything approaching love and more to do with a discomfort at having her living situation changed. Aislin did not handle changes well and often grew very agitated when they happened, such as the time when she broke her mug and Netra had to get her a new one that was a different color. Whatever it was, she would take it and call it a small victory. Living with Aislin for this long had taught her to count every victory she could.

Chapter 32

"How about we go on a picnic today?" Netra asked Aislin. The little girl was sitting on the floor staring out the window, watching the clouds roll overhead. She hadn't spoken since they got back from the farmer's a few days ago, as if she'd used up all her words for a while and needed to wait for some more to build up.

Netra went over and sat beside her. She stroked her hair, marveling at the softness of it. It was so thin and wispy, as if it were made of the clouds Aislin was staring at.

"We'll go down to the beach and you can swim in the sea. You'd like that, wouldn't you?"

Nothing at first, then Aislin nodded, almost imperceptibly.

Netra got up and went to the shelves where she stored their food. "We'll bring some of the cheese that Mattie made and the rest of that loaf of bread. There's also apricot jam we haven't opened yet. What do you say to some of that? Won't that be good?"

She continued talking as she packed the food into the bag she usually carried herbs and salves around in. It was habit by now, after nearly eight years, like narrating her life for someone who couldn't see.

While she was packing, Aislin went to the front door and opened it. She stepped outside and looked up at the sky.

"Don't leave without me!" Netra called after her. "And put your cloak on."

Aislin made no move to get her cloak so Netra got it for her once she'd put hers on. But then she looked at the sky, saw that it was mostly clear, felt the gentle breeze, and put it back. They could always come home if the weather turned bad later on. It also meant one last thing she'd have to keep track of, since Aislin would ditch it at the first opportunity and make no effort to pick it up.

Aislin started down the path to the village and Netra hurried to catch up with her. "Take the left fork when we come to it, honey. We'll go a different way today. I want to go to a different part of the beach." The left fork of the path led around the village to the north. The truth was she didn't want to go through the village yet. She was still a little shaken by what almost happened at the farmer's. She wanted to keep Aislin away from other people for a while until she was sure there wouldn't be a repeat.

As they circled around the village, Netra looked down and saw Mirrim out in front of her home, standing at the edge of her garden, leaning on a spade. Mirrim saw them and waved and Netra waved back. At the sight of the older woman Netra felt a sharp pang. Right then she wanted nothing more than to go talk with her. Talking to Mirrim calmed her, helped her regain her perspective.

She briefly considered trying to get Aislin to go by Mirrim's for a half hour or so, but she quickly gave up on the idea. The little girl was walking with the firm steps and determined look she got when she was heading to the sea. Trying to divert her now would be next to impossible. Netra would probably have to drag her, and then she'd spend the whole time trying to sneak away anyway. No, Mirrim would have to wait.

Netra picked up the pace to keep up with Aislin, who was already getting out ahead of her. The path wound through the low hills then into a band of sand dunes and finally out onto the beach where there was a small bay. Netra eyed the sea uncomfortably. Considering the mildness of the weather, the waves seemed awfully high. Maybe there was a storm out to sea that was out of sight. She looked south, toward the village. Oddly, the waves seemed smaller over there.

"What do you say we start by building a sand castle?" she asked Aislin, knowing the question was pointless as soon as she asked it. Only once had she ever gotten Aislin to show the slightest interest in sand castles and that was the time the child stomped the one Netra had spent an hour building.

Aislin ignored her and made a beeline for the sea. She paused briefly at the edge of the surf to kick off her sandals and then dove out into the next wave. Netra sighed and hurried to pick up her sandals, which were already being sucked out to sea. Sometimes she felt like raising Aislin was a constant tug-of-war between her and the sea, with Aislin as the rope. The sea kept trying to pull her child away from her, and she kept trying to pull her back.

Netra backed away from the surf and chose a small dune to sit on where she could keep an eye on her child. Not that there was really any need to. Aislin swam with all the ease and grace of a fish. It seemed so effortless, the way she knifed through the water. She hardly moved her arms at all, and then mostly just to steer it looked like. She kicked with her legs but nothing like hard enough for the speeds she attained. Netra had only tried swimming a couple times in her life, in beaver ponds, and she'd barely been able to move in the water at all.

As the minutes passed and the sun grew higher and warmed the air, Netra began to relax. It was a beautiful day, after all, only a light breeze, the feel of spring in the air. Sandpipers ran along the beach and seagulls wheeled overhead. The steady roar of the waves had a soothing, almost meditative quality. She began to feel sleepy and wondered if she could nap.

She glanced out at Aislin, checking on her out of habit, but this time what she saw made her heart pick up. She jumped to her feet to get a better look. Was that…?

A shark fin, cutting the water only a dozen feet or so from where Aislin was floating on her back.

"Aislin!" Netra called, running toward the beach, now thoroughly frightened. She'd seen the remains of seals that washed up on the beach and knew what one of those cold-blooded predators was capable of. "Aislin, get out of the water!"

Now there was another fin, then another and another. Soon there were at least six of them, swimming in a circle around the little girl. Netra splashed into the sea up to her knees, screaming Aislin's name. Still Aislin did not respond. Netra had no way of knowing if she could even hear her.

Desperately, Netra went *beyond*, pushing through the mists and into the velvety darkness. There was Aislin's *akirma*, circling it were the glows of the sharks' *akirmas*. In the distance she could see several more sharks swimming closer.

Netra gathered herself. The sharks were well within her range. From here she could reach out with her will and snatch the flows of Song that sustained the creatures. Fear for her daughter lent her strength and she would be easily able to rip those flows away. Bereft of the Life-energy that sustained them, the sharks would quickly die.

The danger lay in how many of them there were. She might not be able to get them all before one of them was able to attack Aislin. Already one of them was gliding right toward the child.

She focused and reached for it…

But as she did, she saw with her normal vision as Aislin finally reacted. As the shark neared the child she rolled over and swam toward it. The shark, instead of attacking her, slowed and, even as Netra grasped its flow, it bumped the child gently with its nose.

Netra watched in amazement, moments from killing the creature, as Aislin stroked the top of its head. The shark slid by her and she grabbed hold of its fin and gave it a tug.

Then the others closed in. The water around the child fairly seethed with sharks. They seemed to be seeking her out, crowding in close but without bumping into her. Aislin petted them all as if they were puppies rather than dangerous predators, a smile on her face the whole time.

Netra could only shake her head in disbelief. Gradually, she backed out of the water and went to sit down, though she continued to keep a close eye on things.

The child and sharks played together for nearly an hour, then one by one the creatures slipped away. Aislin swam to shore and emerged from the sea, dripping wet and still smiling. Netra went to meet her.

"Did you see?" she asked, looking straight at Netra for once.

"I did," Netra said. "How did you…I didn't know you could do that."

"They know I am their friend. I'm hungry."

With that Aislin opened the bag, dug into the food and started eating ravenously. She was always extra hungry after swimming in the sea.

Nibbling on a heel of bread, Netra watched her eat, still stunned by what she had witnessed. Curious, she slipped *beyond* and examined the child more closely. This time she *saw* something she'd never *seen* before.

There was another flow attached to her *akirma*. Unlike the normal flow of LifeSong, which was golden, this was green. But not the green of a plant. Rather it was the emerald green of the sea. And it was pulsing softly.

Had it always been there but she'd just never noticed it before? Or was it new, something appearing as the child's powers awakened?

Netra reached out with her inner senses and brushed up against the flow, then quickly pulled back. Whatever that flow was, and it had to be some kind of Sea power, it was not pleasant to touch it.

Netra left *beyond* and laid her hand on Aislin's shoulder. What are you? she wondered. Where did you come from?

When Aislin was finished eating she looked longingly at the sea once again, but Netra stopped her before she could head back in. "Can you do something for me first?" she asked her.

Without looking at her, Aislin said, "All right."

"Can you do what you did the other night, when you made the shapes and the colors in the water? I'd like to see it again."

Aislin opened her mouth and began to sing. It was the same eerie melody, though pitched differently. Netra guessed that the words were in the same language as before, but she had no way of knowing for sure. Whatever they were, they seemed to hiss over her skin like the surf, washing over her, then withdrawing, washing over, withdrawing, over and over. It was simultaneously soothing and frightening.

Netra found herself wanting to get up and pace, and also to lie down in the sand and close her eyes. It was very peculiar.

Instead she slipped back *beyond* and observed. The first thing she noticed was the way the odd green-blue flow attached to Aislin was thicker now and pulsing more strongly. Then she looked out into the sea and forgot about the strange flow.

Before, all she'd *seen* in the water were the golden flows of the various fish and other creatures that lived there. Now, though, she could *see* so much more. Thick, powerful currents of emerald green in constant motion. Even more surprising, they seemed to be moving in time to Aislin's strange song. Even from this distance Netra could feel how much power was there, moving to the call of one little girl. When she'd fought Melekath and his Children she had taken hold of vast quantities of power several times, but except for the River itself, she'd never touched anything on this scale.

Awed, she slipped out of *beyond*. The waves were even larger now, rising in gray-green walls that seemed almost to tremble in place for a moment before crashing onto the beach. Within those temporary walls of water could be seen brightly colored, glowing shapes of fantastic creatures, darting and frolicking.

This went on for several more minutes and then all at once the next wave collapsed and the colored shapes winked out. Surprised, Netra turned and saw that Aislin had toppled over on her side.

⚏ ⚏ ⚏

Alarmed, Netra bent over her. "Aislin!" The child's skin was cold, but that in itself didn't mean much, since her skin was always cold after she had been swimming. She seemed to be breathing normally. Netra laid her hands on her and probed with her inner senses. There was no inner damage to be found. It seemed most likely that she had overexerted herself and simply passed out.

That was what the analytical healer side of Netra said anyway. The mother side of her wanted to panic and shake the child until her eyes opened. She wanted to grab all the Song she could and pour it into the child until she fairly glowed.

Netra forced herself to sit back, though she kept a hand on Aislin and her inner senses stayed alert. As she sat there she thought of how close she'd come to killing herself the first time she touched a trunk line, which was one of the thick lines of LifeSong that the smaller flows branched off of. It had held so much more power than she'd imagined it would. What if Aislin had just done the same thing? How close had she come to truly hurting herself?

A few minutes later Aislin stirred and sat up. Happy to see that she was okay, Netra hugged her hard. Aislin squirmed until she let her go.

"You scared me," Netra said.

"I'm getting stronger."

"You have to be careful. You can hurt yourself."

Aislin shook her head. "The sea will never hurt me. It's my mother."

That hurt. Much more than Netra would have thought it would. She wanted to say *But I'm your mother!* But she held the words in and she held the sudden tears in too. She wiped at her eyes, thinking that she should be used to such pains by now. Aislin didn't connect like normal children did. She had no sense of the feelings of others and because of that she could be suddenly, shockingly cruel. But it wasn't her fault. It was how she was.

"I'm going back in the water." Aislin got up and Netra didn't try to stop her.

She was staring after her when she heard the crunch of footsteps on the sand and turned to see Mirrim approaching.

"You couldn't have picked a closer spot?" Mirrim asked, sitting down on the sand with a sigh.

"I wanted to be out of sight of the village," Netra confessed.

"What's gotten into you recently?" Mirrim asked. "I haven't seen you around. I was beginning to think you were sick."

Netra hesitated, wondering how much she should tell. She trusted Mirrim, far more than anyone else in the village, but she wasn't sure how far that trust extended. "I'm worried about Aislin," Netra confessed, the need to share her burden outweighing her other concerns. "I've been keeping her close to me."

Mirrim's next words surprised her. "Her power is awakening, isn't it?" When Netra started stammering out a denial, Mirrim shook her head. "Come now. You know I'm sensitive. I told you I passed the Testing." Testing was something Tenders did to see if a girl was sensitive to LifeSong. Mirrim had told her that when her parents found out what she did, they forbade her to join the Tenders.

"How long have you known that she has power?" Netra asked.

"All along, I think. But at first I wasn't paying attention."

"Yet all this time you said nothing."

"I figured you would tell me when you were ready to. Or you wouldn't. Either way, it was your business not mine."

Netra made a sudden decision. "Ya'Shi—he's the one who brought her to me when she was a baby—he said that there is some kind of cataclysm coming and that she will be instrumental in defeating it." It was the first time she'd said the words out loud and she was surprised at how good it felt to get them off her chest. She'd been carrying the weight of them alone for so long.

"What sort of cataclysm?"

"He didn't say."

"Do you believe him?"

"I wish I didn't, but I do."

"So your daughter is supposed to save the world."

"That pretty much sums it up."

Mirrim looked out at Aislin, playing in the water. "What can she do?"

Netra told her about the shapes and colors in the rainwater. "Today she did the same thing in the sea."

"That's impressive. She's not doing that with LifeSong," Mirrim said.

"No, it's not LifeSong. Her power is different. It comes from the sea."

"That probably explains why she loves the water so much."

"Today I think she was controlling the waves too. They were higher here than anywhere else. How much power does it take to do something like that?"

"If she wasn't powerful, Ya'Shi wouldn't have gone to all the trouble to bring her to you now, would he?"

"I guess not."

"So you knew all along this was going to happen someday, and now that it's happening you're afraid."

"I'm terrified," Netra said.

"Of what?"

"It's a terrible burden, being responsible for saving the world."

"You sound like you know from personal experience."

"I've never really told you what I did during the war. I made so many mistakes. I did terrible things and caused so much suffering. It did something to me. I'll never be the same. The thought that she is going to have to go through the same things I went through…it makes me crazy."

"But they won't be the same things, will they?"

"I don't know. I've been hoping all along that Ya'Shi was mistaken about her, that she didn't have any power and now that I see it awakening I'm afraid for her. I'm afraid of what she'll go through. I don't want to see her suffer."

"You're her mother," Mirrim said patiently. "A mother loves her child so much it hurts. She wants nothing but to keep her child safe and she'll do anything, move the world if that's what it takes, to keep her that way."

The look she turned on Netra was sad. "But here's the painful truth. *You can't.* You can't keep your child perfectly safe, no matter what you do, and if you try too hard, you'll only make things worse. It's a hard truth to swallow, but there's no getting around it. You cannot shelter your child from her mistakes any more than you can shelter her from the ones you made. All you can do is stand there with your heart in your hand and hope."

Netra took a deep breath and closed her eyes. "I hate you for saying that."

"I know."

"Because I know it's true."

"I know that too."

Netra opened her eyes. "I don't know if I can stop myself from trying, though."

"Most of us mothers can't," Mirrim said. She wrapped an arm around Netra's shoulders and drew her in close. "And I fear it's going to be even harder for you. You see that child out there? She's not yours, not really. She belongs to the world. Your job is to take care of her until the world needs her."

Chapter 33

Netra was grinding dried roots with a mortar and pestle one morning when there was a knock on the door of the cottage. Aislin was sitting on the floor in the sunshine that came in through the open window and she showed no signs of hearing the knock. Netra walked over to the door and opened it.

Dariana stood there. She smiled up at Netra. "Can Aislin come out and play? I brought her a doll too." She showed Netra the dolls she was carrying. They were made from corn husks twisted together and bound with rough twine. One's dress was made from a scrap of red cloth, the other's was blue.

"I made them myself. The blue one is for Aislin because she likes the sea so much."

Netra turned to glance at Aislin. The child still had not so much as looked up. "I don't know," she said. She searched for a suitable excuse. "She hasn't been feeling well so I've been keeping her close to home until she's better."

"Please?" Dariana pleaded. "We'll stay right here by your house while we play. I promise."

Netra thought about it. On the one hand, she was still worried about what Aislin might do and didn't want her out of her sight. On the other hand, it had been weeks since the incident at the farm. Aislin was becoming increasingly irritable at the restrictions on her. Yesterday she pushed her cup off the table in a fit of pique and it smashed on the floor. Twice Netra had caught her trying to slip away and go to the sea. She couldn't keep the child cooped up forever. At some point she was going to have to loosen her grip.

"I wish I could be more like her," Dariana said wistfully.

"You do?" Netra asked, startled.

"She's so beautiful and free." Dariana was staring at Aislin, whose white-blond hair was fairly glowing in the sunlight. She looked back at Netra. "Can she? Please?"

"I don't know if she wants to play," Netra said. "She's been in a foul mood all morning." But then she heard footsteps and turned to see that Aislin had gotten up and was walking toward them.

"Here," Dariana said, holding out the doll with the blue dress. "It's yours if you want it."

Aislin ignored the proffered doll and instead grabbed the other one out of Dariana's hand.

"Aislin!" Netra snapped. "You don't do that! It's rude."

"It's okay," Dariana said. "I'm happy with either doll."

"I'm glad you feel that way, but it's still not okay for her to take things without asking."

"I should have let her have her choice," Dariana said.

Netra crouched down in front of Aislin. "If I let you go, will you play nice?" Aislin didn't look at her. She was staring at the doll, stroking its dress with one finger. "Aislin, look at me." She took the child's chin in her hand and turned her face up to her. "I won't let you go out if you don't answer me."

Aislin stared fixedly at Netra's chin. She mumbled something. Netra sighed. It was probably all she was going to get. She stood up. "You'll stay close by?" she asked Dariana, who nodded eagerly. "Okay, then. But no going down to the sea. Not without me."

"We won't," Dariana assured her. She took hold of Aislin's hand. "Come on! Let's play."

To Netra's surprise Aislin let herself be pulled outside. It even looked like she quickly glanced at Dariana for a moment. Dariana was already talking excitedly to Aislin, telling her the names of the dolls and starting in on a story about how they were sisters from a faraway kingdom.

Netra, watching them, wondered if maybe she'd been too strict with Aislin. Maybe this was what she'd needed all along, some time with a friend her age. Maybe Dariana could crack through the shell that she had so long been trying to get through. Certainly Aislin looked more cheerful than she had been the last few days. The dark frown she'd worn all morning was gone and while she was not looking Dariana in the eye, she was following the doll that Dariana was moving about, acting out some story, and it at least looked like she was listening.

Netra watched them play for a few more minutes. Dariana was building a little house out of sticks for the dolls and Aislin even added a couple sticks of her own when Netra decided that she could leave them alone and get back to what she'd been doing.

She left the door open and went back to the mortar and pestle, trying to get the dried root as fine as she could. She had an idea that if she mixed it with feverfew she could end up with a mixture that was good for a spring cough that a lot of the children seemed to develop around here. But she wanted to be very careful. Feverfew could be quite strong and she wanted to get the mixture just right.

At first she checked on the girls every few minutes, but when everything seemed to be going fine she finally left them alone and immersed herself in her task.

Then she heard shouts, followed by a girl's scream.

Netra dropped what she was doing and ran for the door, her heart in her mouth. The girls were not where she'd last seen them. The makeshift dollhouse had fallen down. Girls and dolls were gone.

She looked around frantically. There was another shriek and she looked down the hill. The girls were down by the stream, by the big beaver pond just upstream from the village. Both of them looked okay. But there was something wrong with the beaver pond. The water in it was thrashing wildly.

She took off running.

Dariana was standing at the edge of the water. The little girl was waving her arms and yelling, "No, Aislin! Let him go!" Aislin was nearby, standing rigidly, her arms at her sides, tiny fists clenched.

Waves crashed and foamed in the pond as if it was in the grip of a huge storm, though there was no wind. Dark, ominous-looking shapes raced in the water. As Netra got to the children she saw that there was a boy in the pond, trying to get out. But each time the waves knocked him back. A wave bigger than the rest struck him and he lost his footing and went down.

Netra grabbed Aislin and shook her. "Aislin! Stop it right now!"

Aislin's face was dark with rage and she pushed Netra. The strength behind the push surprised Netra and she staggered and nearly fell down. She could barely see the boy anymore through the foaming waves. He was completely underwater.

He was drowning.

Netra grabbed Aislin by one shoulder, spun her around, and slapped her hard in the face. "Let him *go!*"

Aislin's hand came to her cheek and she looked at Netra in stunned disbelief. Then her face darkened further and her eyes narrowed.

Netra felt the power around Aislin build. In moments it would break free. She and Dariana would be hurt, maybe even killed.

"Please, Aislin," she pleaded. "Don't do this. You're hurting him. You'll hurt others."

Aislin blinked and glanced over shoulder at the foaming pond. The boy was no longer visible in there at all. Confusion passed over her face and she looked back at Netra.

"I didn't mean to."

Her small shoulders slumped and just like that the power dissipated. The foaming waves collapsed.

A moment later the boy burst up out of the water, choking and gasping. He stared at Aislin with wild eyes, then with a cry he splashed out of the pond and took off running for home.

Dariana was standing there, sobbing loudly. "It's not her fault!" she cried to Netra. "Kerl took her doll and he…and he pulled its head off and threw it in the water. I told him to stop but he wouldn't listen to me. I'm so sorry. It's not her fault."

"It's okay," Netra said. "You did everything you could. But you should go home now. Your mother will be worried about you."

Still weeping, the little girl stumbled away. Netra turned back to Aislin and was surprised to see tears in her eyes. "Mama?" she said uncertainly and held up her arms.

Netra wrapped her in a hug. Aislin was trembling and she squeezed her tightly and kissed the top of her head.

After a minute the child's shaking eased and she pulled away. She picked up the body of the doll, lying by her feet.

"We have to go," Netra said.

⚱️ ⚱️ ⚱️

Netra pulled Aislin along behind her and hurried up the hill toward the cottage. As she went she made plans, thinking about what they should take with them and what would have to be left behind.

Because she saw, clearly, that they could no longer stay in Seaside. Not after this. The villagers wouldn't stand for it. They might even try to harm Aislin, a thought which caused Netra a strange feeling that was part fear and part rage. The rage frightened her. She didn't want to know what she might do if her child was threatened.

When they got to the cottage she started hurrying around, throwing food, clothes, and a few other items into her pack. It was the same pack she'd carried so long during the war and she'd hoped to never need it again. Now she was glad she hadn't gotten rid of it.

She was tying the drawstring on Aislin's cloak when she felt them approaching. At least a half dozen people, coming up the path to the cottage. She could hear the anger and fear in their Songs. She knew what a lethal combination those two emotions were, how they could make otherwise-sensible people act in awful ways.

She was standing in the doorway when they got there, Aislin behind her.

"We're leaving," she said. "We won't be back."

Their leader was a thick-shouldered man with a heavy jaw and short-cropped black hair. It was Tenus, Kerl's father. He had a pitchfork in his hands. The rest were all carrying some kind of weapon, mostly clubs but one had an old short sword. "The child has to pay for what she done," he growled.

"She's only a child," Netra said. "I'm taking her away."

"She's a demon, that's what she is," one of the other men said. He was the village blacksmith and he was holding a large hammer. "She's a danger, I've always said so."

Netra felt her face grow very hard. She took a step forward, which surprised them. They were expecting her to fall back before them, maybe duck inside the cottage and bar the door. "You're not touching her," she said coldly.

"You're only one woman," Tenus said, pointing the pitchfork at her.

"We don't want you around here neither," one of the others said, hefting the club he carried.

The men exchanged glances and Netra knew, she could feel, what was coming. They were gathering their fear and rage, checking in with each other, making sure they were all of the same mind. Once they felt that group will they would act. There would be blood and violence.

But they didn't know who they were up against. They didn't know what Netra had been through, what she was capable of.

Reaching out with the power of her will, she clamped down on their flows, pinching them off. The men froze in place, their eyes bulging. Mouths opened but no sound came out. Then she reached for their *akirmas*. It would take only a moment to shred them and the men would die in seconds.

Then she felt a small hand in her own. She glanced down and saw Aislin looking up at her. "No, Mama," Aislin said. "Don't."

Suddenly breathing hard, Netra stepped back from the brink. She withdrew the power she'd been so close to using and let go of the men.

They staggered back, hands going to throats, faces pale. In their faces was the knowledge of how close they'd come to death.

"Get out of here," Netra snarled.

The men turned and practically ran down the hill.

Netra looked down at Aislin. She realized she was shaking, from adrenalin, but also from fear at how close she'd come to killing those men.

"Thank you," she said to Aislin.

"We're going now?"

"We're going."

Netra picked up her pack, closed the door of the cottage, and they walked away, heading north for Qarath.

Part 3: Karliss

Chapter 34

Karliss crouched behind the wheel of the wagon and watched as the women carried another round of *progis*—fried pieces of goat flesh sweetened with honey and baked in a flaky pastry—on wooden paddles from the clay ovens to the table to cool. There were close to a hundred of the tasty pastries on the table already and more coming out every few minutes. The women of the Spotted Elk Clan had been hard at work making the pastries all morning in preparation for the feast that night.

Karliss meant to get himself a sack full of those pastries and he had a plan in place to make it happen. He peered around the wheel at his friends, Batu and Hulagu, who were crouched behind a different wagon, each holding a small cloth sack, their hoods pulled over their heads to hide their faces. He tugged on his ear—the signal they'd come up with to indicate all was going well—and Batu did the same.

He turned his attention back to the pastries. What made swiping the pastries so difficult, and so much fun, was the old woman guarding them. To Karliss' youthful eyes Henta was older than the hills. The skin of her face was the color of old leather and covered with deep seams, her eyes narrowed down from decades of wind and sun. Her hair was completely white and done up in a pair of long braids that hung down nearly to her waist. Shells brought by the Olarmi traders decorated her braids. The hemp jacket she wore stretched to mid-thigh, the alternating pattern of reds and greens dyed into it denoting her clan and status within that clan.

Old she undoubtedly was, but she was in no way feeble or slow. The *janu* she wielded was proof of that. The *janu* was a long scarf that the Sertithians wore that could be wrapped around the neck to keep the cold wind out, or around the face and head to keep out the blowing dirt and sand. Hers was fringed with beads made from polished stones and she wielded it expertly, snapping the tip regularly over the cooling pastries to keep the flies away.

She was also very effective at using the *janu* on boys, as Karliss had found out the year before at the annual Gathering, when he tried to swipe a *progi* and got snapped on the ear with it. His ear hurt for two days after that and Henta still laughed at him about it.

But not this year. This year he had a plan and he was certain it would work.

The long table the *progis* were cooling on stood up against two wagons that had been placed end to end. Parallel to those wagons were two more, about fifteen feet away and also placed end to end. The wagons were used by the nomadic Sertithians to carry their possessions as they moved about the high steppes where they lived, seeking the best grasslands for their herds of horses, goats and yaks. The wagons had high wooden sides and had been placed this way to provide a measure of protection from the winds that swept the high steppes nearly continuously.

They also provided protection from watching eyes and hiding places for boys with plans to carry out.

Two more women made their way from the clay ovens where the *progis* were baking, carrying a fresh batch of pastries on wooden paddles. They placed the *progis* on the table and headed back to the ovens. This was the moment Karliss had been waiting for. The cloth they had been placing the *progis* on was now full. Another one would need to be laid down.

Henta reached into the wagon and took out a fresh cloth. She shook it out and laid it out on the table. When she turned to reach for the small stones she would use to weight the cloth down, Karliss acted.

Cupping his hands around his mouth, he pursed his lips and whistled, very softly, the sound only audible from a few feet away.

Instantly the wind responded. A sharp gust whipped up and Karliss directed it just so...

The cloth lifted up off the table and wrapped around Henta's face, completely blinding her. She staggered back a couple of steps, clawing at the cloth, which seemed almost to be clinging to her like a living thing.

Karliss whistled again and a small whirlwind rose up just beyond Henta. It swept the ground, picking up loose dirt and bits of plant matter. He pointed and the whirlwind raced toward the clay ovens, engulfing the women working there, effectively blinding them.

Seeing their opportunity, Batu and Hulagu broke from cover and raced to the table, where they began scooping *progis* into the sacks they carried. In seconds the small sacks bulged and they ducked under the wagons and ran off. Karliss let the wind die down and raced off after them.

⚏   ⚏   ⚏

A few minutes later Karliss joined his friends behind the large rock they'd chosen as their meeting point. The rock sat beside the stream that wound across the wide, shallow valley where the annual spring Gathering was being held. It was big enough for them to hide behind and far enough from the sprawl of the camps of the various clans that they wouldn't be disturbed while they enjoyed their ill-gotten booty.

"That was incredible!" Hulagu said when Karliss sat down. Like Karliss and Batu, his pants were tucked into his soft, knee-high felt boots with leather soles. He wore a cotton shirt and hemp jacket that went to mid-thigh and was tied closed by a belt dyed red and green, the colors indicating they were members of the Spotted Elk Clan. A short, curved knife was stuck in his belt.

"I'll never forget the sight of old Henta with that cloth wrapped around her head," Batu chortled, his words muffled by the *progi* he had stuffed in his mouth. Batu tended toward chubbiness and if there was food around, some of it was generally stuffed in his mouth. He waved his arms around, mimicking Henta fighting with the cloth.

"I was hoping the old goat would fall down," Hulagu said, picking up another *progi*. He was big for his age, with a gentle nature, but he'd felt the business end of Henta's *janu* several times and he had no fondness for the woman.

"Give me one of those," Karliss said, snatching up one of the sacks and pulling out a pastry. He bit into it and savored the flavor, simultaneously salty from the goat meat and sweet from the honey.

"That's the first time I've seen you raise a whirlwind," Batu said. "I didn't know you could do that."

"It's nothing," Karliss said with feigned modesty that fooled neither of them. If there was one thing Karliss enjoyed, it was showing off. "Just a little thing I've been working on."

"Well, it worked perfectly," Batu said, holding up a fresh *progi*. "Here's to the first successful raid of the week."

273

"May we have many more!" Hulagu crowed.

It was only the first full day of the annual Gathering, with five more days still to come. Once a year, to mark the spring equinox, all the clans of the Sertithians gathered here, in the heart of the high steppes where they lived. All feuds were put aside during the Gathering, as were the raids. For one week harmony mostly reigned. It was a week of feasting, horse racing, sword-fighting, wrestling, and archery competitions. It was also a time for young people of different clans to court. A large number of young women would leave the Gathering as a member of a different clan than the one they'd arrived with.

Most importantly, the annual Gathering was a time to make sacrifices to, and hopefully placate, the gods of the four winds. The Sertithians' world was inhabited by spirits—there were spirits in the streams, lakes, mountains, the infrequent copses of trees and, most especially, the wind—but they were minor entities compared to the wind gods. The wind gods carried the power of life and death. Which was why the most important event of the whole week was the ritual of appeasement, when the *tlacti*—the wind shamans—of every clan joined together to direct the pleas of tens of thousands of Sertithians skyward in the hopes of ensuring a bountiful year.

The three friends were too young for most of the competitions and much too young for courting, not that any of them had any interest in that yet. Nor were they likely to do well even in the ones they were eligible for. As a shaman's apprentice, Karliss spent very little time practicing with a bow or any other weapon and he didn't much like horseback riding, which was highly unusual amongst a people who practically lived on horseback. And neither of his two friends were very good at any of the martial arts either. Batu far preferred eating to fighting, and Hulagu's gentle nature held him back.

That was why this year Karliss had declared they would make their mark on the Gathering in their own way. Today's raid was only the beginning. They planned to conduct a different raid each day on a different clan and to cap it all off with one spectacular raid on the final night. The details of these raids were still hazy, but Karliss was confident he would come up with something.

"I hope we do this good with the Angry Bear Clan," Batu said, licking his fingers. "No one makes better mince pies than they do. I can't wait to stuff myself on them."

"I've been thinking about that," Karliss said, "and I think that if we—"

Unfortunately, the other two didn't get to hear what Karliss thought because he broke off suddenly and yelped as his ear was seized and given a sharp, painful tug.

"Oww!" he cried, turning to see the angry face of his mother looming over him. Right behind her were the other boys' mothers and neither of them looked happy. Batu and Hulagu leaped to their feet but they didn't get far before they were rounded up as well.

"You're coming with me," Karliss' mother snapped.

Still holding onto his ear, she began striding quickly back toward the camp and Karliss had to run to keep up, afraid that if he fell she would pull his ear clean off.

"I warned you," she said. "I told you to stay out of trouble. Wait until I tell your father."

At the mention of his father, Karliss wilted. His father was a fairly calm man, even-tempered, steady and slow to anger. Even when he was drinking *achai*, fermented yak's milk, he never lost control and beat his family as so many other warriors were prone to do.

But when his father *did* lose his temper…? Karliss would be lucky if he saw the light of day for the whole Gathering. Especially since his father had made an extra point of pulling him aside yesterday when they arrived and warning him about the consequences of making him look bad in front of the others.

"Please don't tell Ata!" he said, using the Sertithian word for father. "I'll be good. I promise."

"It's too late for that," she said. She let go of his ear, stopped and looked down at her son. "What do I have to do to get through to you, Karliss? How do I make you behave? Even Narantse behaves better than you do and she's only eight." Narantse was Karliss' sister.

Karliss rubbed his sore ear and tried hard to look remorseful but judging from the fact that her expression didn't change in the slightest, he guessed it wasn't working. Part of the problem, he realized, was that he wasn't *actually* remorseful at all. What had he done that was really so bad anyway? He was only having a little fun.

She took hold of his hand and continued on toward the camp. "You're twelve now, Karliss. It's time to start growing up and taking responsibility."

"I don't want to. Growing up is boring. I'd rather have fun." He realized he sounded childish when he said it but he didn't care. The lives of the adults he saw around him seemed terribly boring. They never had any fun at all.

"Really, Karliss? And what if we all did that, skipped our responsibilities and just had fun? We'd all starve. We wouldn't survive even a single winter. You do realize that, don't you?"

Karliss knew she was right, but that didn't mean he wanted to admit it. He settled for muttering under his breath.

"What was that?" she said sharply.

"I said I'll try to do better," Karliss replied quickly.

"Oh, I'm quite certain you will do better. Because you'll have the whole day in our yurt to think about it."

"What? The whole *day*?" It was still morning. There was so much of the day left to enjoy. The thought of spending all of it cooped up in their yurt filled him with horror. "You can't do that to me!"

"But I can." She shook a finger at him as he started to protest anew. "You might want to think carefully about the next words that come out of your mouth. You could find yourself spending tomorrow in there as well."

Karliss clamped his mouth shut. He knew that tone. When she used it she meant business.

"You get away with a great deal, Karliss," his mother said. "But not this time. You're not a baby anymore. I won't tolerate it."

"I'm sorry. I really am, Ana," he said, using the Sertithian word for mother. Now he actually *was* sorry, though mostly he was sorry because he'd been caught.

"I mean to make certain of that," she replied curtly.

"I'll apologize to Henta," he added. "And to the women working on the pastries."

"It's a start."

They had arrived at the family yurt by then and his mother undid the flap, pulled it open, and pushed him inside. Then she leaned in and shook her finger at him. "Stay right there. Don't do anything. Don't leave the yurt for any reason, not even to pee. Don't so much as stick one finger outside while I decide what your punishment will be."

"But I think I do have to pee," he protested.

"You should have thought of that earlier," she said, withdrawing and securing the flap.

Chapter 35

Karliss threw himself down on his sleeping furs after his mother left and stared up at the ceiling of the yurt. How long was he going to have to stay in here? If only he could sleep. The time would pass so much faster. He closed his eyes, but after a minute he sat up. There was no way he was going to be able to sleep.

He stood and began pacing. All the times he'd slept in here and he'd never realized how small the yurt was before. It was really tiny. How did five of them fit in here? Even worse, it felt like it was getting smaller. There didn't seem to be enough air, no matter how hard he breathed. He wiped his forehead and his hand came away wet with sweat.

What was wrong with him? he wondered. Was he getting sick?

He needed to calm down. He sat down cross-legged and forced his breathing to slow. Closing his eyes, he tried using the meditation technique that Ihbarha, the old *tlacti* he was apprenticed to, had taught him. In through the nose, out through the mouth, thoughts focused on a single flame that he pictured in his mind. He'd never been any good at this and the truth was that he'd never really put much effort into it, no matter how much Ihbarha berated him. He'd never seen the point to it. The world was filled with fascinating things to see and do. Why would he want to sit still and empty his mind?

Whenever he complained about being forced to practice meditation, the old man always told him the same thing: the meditation was necessary to develop mental control. Strict mental control was vital for a *tlacti*. Without that control, the spirits in the wind would get loose in the mind and run where they pleased. From that followed madness and death. This was the reality of the *tlacti*'s life. The *tlacti* spent his life in close contact with dangerous forces, where the smallest mistake could be fatal.

None of Ihbarha's endless warnings had the slightest impact on Karliss. The spirits in the wind were his friends. He had nothing to fear from them. But he'd learned not to say that to Ihbarha. It only made the old man angry and then he got punished. It was better to simply pretend that he was practicing meditation, even though he wasn't.

After a couple of minutes of trying to meditate Karliss gave it up and jumped to his feet. It was pointless. His mind was racing faster than ever. He actually felt worse than before. His heart was pounding hard in his chest and his hands were clammy.

He wondered why this was bothering him so much. After all, he slept in the yurt every night and it had never upset him before. It occurred to him that the difference was he'd never been confined to the yurt before. Somehow, knowing he couldn't leave was making it worse.

He went to the door flap and started to unfasten it, but then stopped. The yurt was in the middle of dozens of other yurts. There were people all around. They'd see him open the flap and one of them was sure to tell his mother. Then he'd be stuck in here tomorrow too. He didn't think he could stand that.

He let go of the door flap and went back to pacing. He felt like screaming. He couldn't take much more of this.

A sudden gust of wind shook the yurt and within the gust Karliss heard the voices of the wind, calling to him. Karliss had heard those voices his entire life and understood them as clearly as he understood his own kind.

What's wrong? Come out and join us! they called.

It wasn't the wind that was speaking, of course. It was the beings that lived in the wind, beings the Sertithians called spirits. Which wasn't accurate either. They called themselves *aranti*. Karliss often heard them. He wasn't surprised by their sudden arrival. Long ago he'd noticed that when he was upset or excited the *aranti* tended to cluster around, as if drawn to him.

Karliss replied to them, not in any human tongue, but in the language of the wind. To anyone else it would have sounded like the wind blowing, although perhaps a little oddly.

I'm trapped! I can't leave!

Karliss had never bothered to hide his unusual connection with the wind. It was who he was and he could no more hide it than he could hide the color of his hair. But there were exceptions to this, things he kept private, and one of those was his ability to speak to and understand the *aranti*. Communicating with the *aranti* wasn't something he'd had to consciously learn, any more than he'd had to try to learn the Sertithian tongue. He'd grown up around it, hearing it always, and simply mimicked it until he got it right. It was as natural to him as the Sertithian tongue. But he never spoke it around anyone else. It had always been his little secret, a part of him he didn't want anyone else to know about. He couldn't have said why—certainly he wasn't afraid of others knowing—only that he felt this was something for him alone.

The wind shook the yurt again and the voices intensified.

Let us in! they cried.

I can't! he replied. *I'm not allowed to open the door.*

An idea occurred to him then. He went to the back of the yurt and lay down on the ground. The yurt was securely staked down—it had to be to withstand the sudden gusts of wind that were so common on the high steppes—but he was able to work a little section of it free. It was only an finger-width or so, but it was enough.

A burst of cool, fresh air blew into the yurt and with it came one of the *aranti*. The *aranti* raced around Karliss, fluttering the sleeping furs and extra clothing, tipping over a small loom that his mother was weaving a jacket on. He could faintly see the *aranti* if he concentrated. It was a glowing, amorphous shape, constantly changing and flowing. Within that form was a section that glowed more brightly than the rest, with just a suggestion of a face to be seen there. Or maybe he was only imagining it. Either way, he always thought of it as a face.

Karliss felt some of his panic dissipate. At least he felt like he could breathe once again. But it wasn't enough. While he no longer felt like he was going to explode, he still felt awful. He didn't think he could manage to stay in here all day without finally doing something stupid that would get him in even more trouble.

Come with us! the *aranti* cried. *Play!*

I can't. I have to stay here.

The *aranti* raced around Karliss, faster and faster. It seemed to be tugging at him, but there was something strange about it. It wasn't pulling at his body so much as it was tugging at him…*inside.*

Karliss didn't resist. Why should he? He trusted the *aranti*. They were playful, friendly creatures. There was nothing malicious about them.

And then it seemed the *aranti* blew *through* Karliss. As it did, he let go of himself and embraced it. There was a moment of extreme disorientation, where he felt he was in two places at once, then he was flying through the small opening at the back of the yurt and soaring up into the sky.

Up and up they went. Karliss laughed with the pure joy and wonder of it. He'd never felt so free. His body and all its weaknesses were gone. He had no limits. Down below him stretched the vast camp of the Gathering, thousands of yurts, hundreds of wagons, tens of thousands of people and horses, a great welter of movement and activity. Higher and higher they went until people and animals became mere dots.

Then down they swooped, racing through the yurts, fluttering clothes, tipping over stools and drying racks, stirring up dust. The speed and freedom took his breath away. It was incredible, beyond words.

They lifted up into the sky once again and Karliss looked down and saw his yurt. It seemed so small and insignificant from above. So stifling too. Why did he spend so much time in there? Why did all of them spend time in such things? Out here was freedom.

Then he saw the figure of his little sister approaching the yurt. Probably his mother had sent her to check on him. He needed to get back right away. He didn't want anyone to know what he'd done here today.

Take me home, he asked the *aranti*.

Play! was the answer.

Home. He put all his firmness into it.

Reluctantly, the *aranti* swept down toward the yurt. His sister was unfastening the door flap when they got there. Under the edge of the yurt they passed and back inside. The wind blew through him and when it had passed Karliss opened his eyes to find himself lying on the ground, back in his own body.

Go, he told the *aranti* and it blew back through the opening. The air in the yurt went still.

He sat up just as Narantse opened the flap and entered.

"You're still here." She sounded surprised.

"Why wouldn't I be?" His words sounded strange to him. His tongue and lips felt weird and awkward. At first he wasn't sure he was making sense because his sister frowned and he had a sudden

281

fear that he'd spoken to her in the language of the wind instead of the language of people.

Narantse put her hands on her hips in a perfect, unconscious imitation of their mother when she was angry with Karliss. "Because you *never* do what Ana tells you to do. You *always* break the rules."

"That's not true, Narantse. You're exaggerating."

"Ana told me to check on you and make sure you weren't getting in any new trouble. I heard about the *progis* you stole."

"We only took a few."

"That's not what our mother says. Wait until she tells Ata. He's going to be sooo mad."

"Okay, you checked on me," Karliss said irritably. "You can go now."

"Yes, I can," she said. She stepped out of the yurt, then leaned back in. "*I* can come and go as I please because *I'm* not bad like you are." Karliss grabbed the first thing that came to hand—a wooden bowl—and threw it at her. He missed. She stuck her tongue out at him and shut the flap.

It was a good thing he returned when he did, Karliss thought. Who knew how his sister would have reacted if she'd found him lying still on the ground.

Karliss paced around the yurt after Narantse left, exhilarated by what he'd just done. He'd *ridden* the wind. Riding the wind was something *tlacti* could do, but they did it only in times of great need because it was so dangerous. And, at no time did a *tlacti* attempt to ride the wind without the assistance of other shamans, at least two of them. The other shamans were needed to hold onto the one who rode the wind. Without their help he would never have the strength to make it back to his body. The wind spirits would carry his spirit to the far corners of the world and leave him there, leaving his body an empty shell that would eventually die.

Yet here Karliss had done it and all by himself. And it was easy too. He hadn't needed anyone to hold onto him. He'd simply left his body behind, knowing the *aranti* would bring him back when he wanted it to. What *tlacti* had ever done that?

A scratching on the door flap interrupted his thoughts. Scratching was how visitors announced themselves. He walked over to the flap and unfastened it. Ihbarha stood there, dressed, as always, in his ratty old furs, a piece of felt wrapped around his head like a turban. On his cheeks were the tattoos marking him as *tlacti*. In his long braids were tied a number of small bones, colorful stones, and clay discs. Around his neck, on a leather thong, hung his *krysala*, a flattened bone disc that the *tlacti* used to summon and control the spirits in the wind.

"I'm not allowed to leave the yurt, Bagesh," Karliss said, using the formal term for his teacher. "You'll have to come in."

Ihbarha stooped to enter the yurt, tapping his forehead politely as was expected of a visitor as he did so. Karliss tapped his forehead in return. But then all politeness disappeared.

"I heard about the trouble you got into," the old man hissed, the lines in his face deepening. Quite a lot of white hair grew out of his ears—almost like horns, Karliss had always thought—and it quivered as he spoke. "What were you thinking, using the power of the wind for something as petty as stealing food?"

"I…uh…"

"No, don't answer. I *know* the answer already. You weren't thinking. You never do. You act with no thought to the consequences."

Karliss averted his eyes. He should have expected that Ihbarha would hear about his mischief and that he would react this way. He always got so upset whenever Karliss did anything with the wind outside the strict lessons and exercises the old man was always imposing on him.

"Have you listened to nothing I've tried to teach you?" Ihbarha continued. He was very agitated, almost shaking. He poked Karliss in the chest with a bony, arthritic finger. "Over and over I have tried to impress on you how dangerous the wind is, how fickle the spirits are which dwell within it. Yes, you are touched by the wind. Yes, you have a natural affinity for it, a power not seen for many generations. But you are still only a mortal man, nothing more than an insect against the vastness of the sky. One of these days you will go too far. One of these days the spirits will destroy you."

Karliss bit back the first reply that came to his lips, which was to tell the old man that the beings in the wind weren't spirits, they were *aranti*, and that there was no need to fear them like he did. But every time he tried to tell Ihbarha that he got clouted by the shaman's bony old fist. He was tired of that and so he said nothing.

"I know, *tlacti*," he said, trying to sound contrite, which wasn't easy because he was still awfully excited about what he'd just done. "I'm sorry."

Ihbarha shook his head. "No, you aren't. You're only saying that. You're not sorry at all."

"I'm not?"

"No, you're not. Look at you. You're practically smiling."

Karliss tried harder to look downcast, scrunching up his face as much as he could.

"You don't realize the honor the gods have paid to you or the responsibility that comes with it. You don't realize how close you've come so many times to angering them. Why they haven't struck you down yet is beyond me. You've toyed with them too many times."

Karliss had heard this lecture so many times before that he could practically recite it from memory. So he did what he usually did, which was tune the old man out. But this time he was snapped back into the present when Ihbarha clouted him hard on the top of the head.

"Don't *do* that!" the old man hissed. He gave Karliss a fierce, dark look. "You *listen* to me! You think this is all a game, boy, but it's not. It is the *tlacti's* sacred duty to protect his clan, to guide them with his knowledge and wisdom. It's his duty to placate the gods. The spirits are their servants, not your pets to play with whenever you want. If it was just your own foolish life you were endangering with your behavior I'd let you run off and get yourself killed. But you risk your entire clan, maybe all Sertithians! What if when the gods decide to punish you they punish all of us, huh? What then? When the drought and the pestilence come, when there is no food and locusts and fire cover the steppes, what then? Will you still be laughing when your people are dying?"

That shook Karliss. He hung his head. "I didn't mean to cause trouble," he said miserably.

"And always it's the same with you. 'I didn't mean to.'" The old man pretended to spit. "Bah! There's no getting through to you. Why did the gods saddle me with you instead of with a true apprentice, if not to demonstrate their own fickleness? Why can't there be anyone else in Spotted Elk Clan with even a hint of aptitude for me to train? Even that idiot, drooling lump Nergui would be preferable to you!"

"I'm sorry, *tlacti*," Karliss said, and for once he really meant it. "I don't know what's wrong with me. I try, but I just can't seem to change."

The old man made an irritated noise in his throat and waved away Karliss' words like they were flies. "Maybe it's not your fault," he growled. "The wind entered you at birth and it seems it never left." He turned and stomped out of the yurt.

Chapter 36

After Ihbarha left, Karliss paced the yurt, his emotions in turmoil. Much of the excitement he'd felt at riding the wind was gone, buried under Ihbarha's scolding. He didn't want to be *tlacti* for Spotted Elk Clan. Whenever Ihbarha went on about the scope and importance of his future duties he ended up feeling overwhelmed. His future as the clan *tlacti* loomed over him always, a heavy weight he must someday shoulder. Why did everything have to be so serious? Why couldn't his life be more like the life the *aranti* lived, filled with play and joy?

The flap opened again and Karliss looked up to see his father standing there. He winced and took a step back. "Ata, I can explain."

Ganzorig, Karliss' father, was a thick-bodied man with long, powerful arms and a heavy brow. There were a dozen polished discs of bone tied in his long braid, denoting his status as a respected warrior and clan captain. He crossed his arms and stared at Karliss.

"I should thrash you, I suppose," Ganzorig said. "It's what any father would do."

Karliss sensed a "but" coming and wisely kept his mouth shut.

"But it wouldn't do any good, would it?" His father let the flap fall shut behind him and sat down cross-legged on the ground. "It never does any good."

"I'm sorry, Ata." Surprisingly, Karliss actually *was* sorry. What Ihbarha had said had really shaken him.

"Ganbold won the wrestling contest, you know. Or you would if you'd gone to watch." Ganbold was Karliss' brother and he was everything Karliss wasn't, a budding warrior, a dutiful son.

"I forgot that was this morning," Karliss said.

"So the pride in one son saves the other from a thrashing he so deserves. Maybe," Ganzorig mused, almost sounding like he was talking to himself.

"Ganbold will be a great warrior."

"Or I've just gone old and soft. Your mother thinks so sometimes."

Karliss didn't know what to say. He sensed that he needed to be careful.

"Why can't you be like the other boys?" Ganzorig asked. It was a question Karliss had heard so many times.

"Because I'm not like them."

Ganzorig considered this, then nodded. "It's true. When the old shaman said you were touched by the wind spirits your mother was proud. For myself, I wanted a warrior, but I respect the will of the gods."

"Their ways are inscrutable," Karliss agreed.

"Did you really make the cloth wrap around old Henta's head?"

Karliss shot a look at his father and saw the glint in his eye. He nodded.

"I wish I could have seen that. Henta was ancient when I was a child," his father said. "I think she was born old. I don't think I've ever seen her smile."

"I don't think she can smile," Karliss blurted out. "Her face would crack and fall off."

Ganzorig gave him a stern look to let him know he wasn't old enough to speak that way about a respected elder. "You'll have to apologize to her. A real apology, too."

"I will. I promise."

"And then you'll help the women tend the ovens."

"How long?"

"Until they say you can go."

"But that could be all day!"

Ganzorig frowned at him. "Your mother thinks you should spend all day and maybe tomorrow here in the yurt."

"I'll help with the ovens," Karliss said hastily.

"It's the Gathering. A boy should be out taking in the sights, don't you think?" Karliss nodded. "But only if he stays out of trouble. Otherwise I *will* thrash you."

"I won't let you down," Karliss said earnestly.

Ganzorig sighed. "Probably you will, though." He stood up. "Go to Henta. Remember what I said."

⊥⊤   ⊥⊤   ⊥⊤

Henta was sitting on a stool by the cooling table, the beaded scarf in her hand. Her piercing eyes fixed on Karliss when he came into

287

sight and she stared unblinking at him as he approached. Her seamed old face showed no expression though her mouth tightened fractionally.

"A thousand apologies, revered elder," Karliss said when he was standing in front of her. He went to his hands and knees and pressed his face to the ground. Then he waited.

He didn't have long to wait. Suddenly there was a sharp pain in his right ear. He jumped up, his hand pressed to his ear. Henta had the *janu*, the long scarf, in her hand. "That hurt!"

"Good. It was meant to." She gathered the *janu* in her lap.

"I was apologizing."

"You're not done yet." She pointed at the ground in front of her.

"Are you going to hit me with your *janu* again?"

"I haven't decided. Every moment you delay makes it easier for me to decide though."

"Okay, okay." He prostrated himself once again. "I beg your forgiveness, revered elder, for my foolishness."

He felt her foot on the back of his head, pushing his face into the dirt. He resisted the urge to pull away.

She removed her foot. "Sit up." He sat up but stayed on his knees, sensing that he wasn't done yet.

"You're a worthless dung beetle of a child," she said, pointing a crooked finger at him. She was mostly toothless and her gums were yellow from the wortgrass she spent so much time chewing. Wortgrass numbed pain and produced a mild euphoria. "In the old days you would have been left for the wolves."

"Yes, revered elder," he said dutifully, keeping an eye on the scarf.

"I was there when you were born. I knew you were trouble then, but what could I do?" She seemed to be waiting for him to answer so after a moment he shrugged. Casually, so quickly he couldn't react, the scarf flicked out, the end snapping him on the cheek. Karliss put his hand on the spot, blinking back the sudden tears.

"Go," she said. "I don't want to look at you anymore."

Karliss jumped to his feet and ran off.

⊥⊤   ⊥⊤   ⊥⊤

By comparison, helping with the ovens was easier. No one hit him, for one thing, though it looked like some of the women wanted to. But they settled for ordering him about. He was sent to fetch more of the dried dung that was the primary source of fuel on the steppes where wood was so scarce. They put him to working the small bellows that was used to keep the fire hot. His arms were tired after a few minutes but whenever he slowed, one of them was on him in a moment. When they let him take a break from that it was to stir the batter for the pastry. After that he spent time standing over the hot oil, frying the goat meat for inside the pastries, getting burned when the oil spattered.

And so the hours passed. Morning became afternoon and Karliss began to wonder if he would ever be free or if they meant to keep him there forever. He'd had no idea that making *progis* was so much work. Finally, after what seemed an eternity, they let him go and he ran off to find his friends.

He found Hulagu watching the warriors get ready for a horse race. During the Gathering there were horse races every day. Some for speed, some for endurance. Next to the archery competitions, they were the most popular events, though they'd never interested Karliss that much. Horses were slow compared to the wind.

"How did it go for you?" Karliss asked him.

Hulagu pulled up the hem of his coat and showed him the bruise on his back. "How does it look?"

"It's turning purple already."

Hulagu twisted but couldn't quite see it. "I wish I could see it," he said wistfully. "It's going to be a good one. It hardly even hurt though." Hulagu was like that. Whenever he hurt himself, got a cut or a scrape or anything, he was oddly proud of it and showed it off to all the other boys like some kind of badge of honor. Karliss had never understood that about his friend.

"What did you get?" Hulagu asked him.

"I had to apologize to Henta. She practically stood on my head."

Hulagu laughed. "I wish I could have seen that."

"Then I spent forever helping with the ovens. But Ata didn't beat me. He's happy because Ganbold won the wrestling."

Hulagu gave him a horrified look. "You had to help with the ovens? I'd rather be beaten any day. It's over quicker."

That struck Karliss. He hadn't thought of it that way.

Batu came up then, chewing on a piece of yak jerky. "There you are. I've been looking everywhere for you two."

"What'd you get?" Hulagu asked him.

"Ana tried to beat me at first," Batu said, throwing away a piece of gristle. "But then she cried and hugged me." It was only what the other two had expected. Batu's father had died in a raid two years ago when his horse fell on him, and he had no brothers or sisters so his mother doted on him and let him do pretty much whatever he pleased.

"And then she gave you food," Hulagu said.

Batu grinned as he finished off the jerky. "I told her I did it because I was hungry." He held his hands up. "It's true, after all."

"You're *always* hungry," Karliss said.

"Also true," Batu agreed. He was a gentle, easygoing boy and it was difficult to dislike him.

The horse race started then with a loud cheer, a thunder of hooves and a cloud of dust. The boys made their way through the crowd. There were people everywhere. Young warriors, many of them already drunk on *achai*, laughed boisterously and told outrageous lies about their exploits. Maidens with the skin painted blue around their eyes, signifying their eligibility for marriage, laughed behind their hands and batted their eyelashes at the young men, who swelled under the attention and boasted even louder.

The old people sat on folding, three-legged stools, chewing wortgrass and watching everything. Small children scampered about, darting through the mass, chasing each other. The strains of music floated above it all as unseen men and women played their flutes and stringed instruments. The smoke of countless small fires, the smells of cooking food and the sweat of too many people too close together. There was so much to see and do, Karliss thought as he took it all in. Truly this was the greatest time of the year.

⚎　⚎　⚎

The afternoon passed quickly.

"I have to get back," Hulagu said, looking at the sun. It was just touching the horizon.

"Me too," Batu said.

"But the sun hasn't even set yet. It won't be dark for an hour at least," Karliss protested.

"My father said if I'm not at the communal fire by the time the sun goes down he'll send me out to help my older brother with herd duty tomorrow," Hulagu said. "The whole day."

"It only takes two minutes to get back to the camp," Karliss protested. "We have ten minutes at least. Let's go by Cloudfoot Clan's camp first. I heard they have a two-headed calf and I want to see it."

"Go by yourself, then. I'm not risking it," Hulagu replied.

"What about you, Batu?" Karliss asked. "We can make it if we run."

"I hate running. You know that," Batu said. "And they're making *sourlee* for dinner tonight. I want to be first in line. Maybe I'll get seconds if I eat fast."

"So you're both quitting on me?" Karliss said. "Just like that?"

"Just like that," Hulagu agreed and Batu nodded. Hulagu started toward the camp.

"It's only the first day," Batu said over his shoulder as he fell in behind Hulagu. "We can see the calf tomorrow."

"Unless it dies during the night," Karliss grumbled, shuffling after them. "You never thought about that, did you?"

"You don't think it will die during the night, do you?" Batu asked, suddenly worried.

"It's not going to die during the night," Hulagu said. "He's just saying that to get you to go with him. Karliss will say anything to get his way."

"I'm trying to help you see the wonders of the world before it's too late, that's all," Karliss said.

Still arguing, they made their way back to the camp. The sun was only partially down by the time they got there and Karliss pointed out that they would easily have had enough time to see the calf, but the other two ignored him. Batu grabbed his bowl from his yurt and was in the food line before the cooks called out that the evening meal was ready.

After the clan had eaten, the clan chief stood up by the fire and called forward those men and boys who had won or placed well in the day's contests. People cheered as each one was called forward, but Karliss paid hardly any attention. He was busy working his way through the crowd, getting closer to the table that was laden with *progis*. Once the day's winners had taken their pick of the pastries, he intended to be near the front to get one of the ones that was left. Naturally, Batu was there before him. There were a couple of women guarding the table and both of them were watching the boys closely.

"Not so fast," the chubby boy said when Karliss tried to move in front of him. "I was here first."

"Didn't you eat enough of them earlier?" Karliss asked.

"Didn't *you?*"

"I didn't eat nearly as many as you did."

"I was still here first. That's what counts."

The last winner the terl called forward was Ganbold, Karliss' brother. Ganbold was fourteen, with the stout build and long, powerful arms of their father, which made him well-suited to wrestling. He'd beaten a boy three years older to win first place.

Once Ganbold had his *progi* other people started moving toward the table to help themselves. But when Karliss stepped forward he felt a hand grab him by the shoulder. He looked up to see his mother frowning at him.

"No," she said.

"What? Why?"

Instead of answering, she swung him toward her, gripped his chin with her free hand and tilted his head back to stare into his eyes.

"What are you doing?" he asked.

"I'm making sure you're okay. I thought maybe you hit your head."

"Why would you say that?"

Before she could answer his sister, Narantse, blurted out, "How dumb are you? You stole *progis* this morning. You're not getting any more!"

"Narantse!" his mother snapped. "Don't speak to your brother like that!"

"But it's true!"

"Narantse," Munkhe said warningly.

"Sorry, Ana," Narantse said, but she didn't look sorry. She stuck her tongue out at Karliss when their mother wasn't looking.

"Go get your *progi* and stay out of this," Munkhe said to her daughter, pushing her toward the pastries.

"But I said I was sorry!" Karliss protested. "And I helped with the ovens almost the whole day!"

"So?" his mother said.

"So why am I still being punished?"

"You really don't understand, do you?" Munkhe said. "It's like talking to the wind."

Karliss looked at the table with the *progis* on it. They were dwindling fast. Soon it would be too late. "How about if I have only one?" he asked.

"No."

"But I—"

"Karliss, enough," his father cut in, walking up right then.

Karliss knew that tone. He bit back what he'd been about to say and instead shrugged. "Whatever. I'm not really hungry anyway." He started to walk away, but his mother grabbed him again.

"What now?"

"I don't want you wandering off. We're going back to the yurt soon."

"But it's so early! It's barely even dark!"

"You need your sleep," his father said. "You have a race coming up in a couple of days."

"What?" Karliss exclaimed. "I didn't enter a race!"

"I entered it for you."

"But I don't want to race!"

"Then you don't have to."

That was a relief. "That's good, because I—"

"I'll enter you in one of the wrestling contests instead," his father continued.

"I *hate* wrestling."

"You do?" his father said, acting like this was news to him. "What about archery? Or horseback riding?"

"I don't want to do any of those things."

"What do you want to do?"

"I want to have fun."

"Too bad there aren't any contests for fooling around," Narantse said, showing up with her *progi*. "I bet you'd win that every time!" Karliss scowled at her but she pretended not to notice, taking a big bite out of her pastry and smacking her lips to make him jealous.

"You're entering at least one contest this year," his father said.

"Do I have to?"

"No, you don't," his mother put in. "The women can always use help at the ovens."

"Okay, I'll do it," Karliss said hastily.

"Running it is, then," his father said.

"I think you should have at least asked me," Karliss grumbled.

"There was no need to. I already knew what you'd say," his father replied.

"I'm sure you'll do well," his mother said. "You like to run."

She was right. Karliss did like to run. Often when the clan was on the move Karliss ran the whole way. He was young enough that he could still ride in one of the wagons and old enough to have his own horse, but he preferred to run over either of them. He liked the way it felt, the freedom of it.

Ganbold came up then, finishing off his *progi*. "I will never understand that," he said. "Why would someone run when he could ride a horse instead? You should let me teach you how to wrestle, little brother." Before Karliss could answer, he grabbed him in a hold.

Karliss' response was immediate and unthinking. He twisted, writhed and a moment later he was free and standing a couple feet away from his bemused brother.

"How did you do that so easily?" Ganbold asked. "The boy I beat to win the title couldn't get out of that hold and he was the champion last year."

"I don't know. I just worked my way free."

"It was impressive. Seriously. If you'd let me teach you a few things I bet in no time—"

"No. I don't like people holding me." He didn't. It made him feel panicky.

"Even as a child you never liked being held," his mother said.

"The point of wrestling is to *not* be held," Ganbold pointed out.

"It seems to me there's no point to wrestling at all," Karliss said.

"I suppose you think there's no point to archery or riding either," Ganbold said.

"Not that I can think of."

Ganbold shook his head. His little brother was a complete mystery to him.

"Come on, Karliss, Narantse. Time for bed," Munkhe said.

"What about Ganbold?" Karliss asked.

"I'm going to go sit with the warriors around their fire," Ganbold said smugly.

"Ganbold is a man now," his father said. "He completed the trials. That means he can make his own decisions." Ganbold and several other boys from the clan had only finished the final trial during the last new moon, when they accompanied a group of established warriors on a raid of Angry Bear Clan. Before that they went through a half dozen other trials, including tests of skill with the bow and horseback riding, along with feats of endurance, food- and sleep-deprivation, and withstanding extreme cold.

That shut Karliss up. He'd seen what Ganbold and the others went through to pass into manhood and frankly, if that was the price of being an adult, he'd as soon stay a child.

Karliss accompanied his parents and sister back to the yurt. He was the last one to enter and stood outside for a moment, looking up at the sky, wishing he could simply sleep outside. He knew there was no way he'd be allowed too, though, so he didn't bother asking. His mother would lecture him about the many dangers roaming the steppes, from the plains bears to packs of wolves. She didn't understand that he didn't have to worry about any of those things, that the wind knew everything, all the time, and long before a predator approached him he'd know of its presence through the wind.

Munkhe stuck her head back out the door flap. "Come inside." With a sigh Karliss went into the yurt.

His parents went into their sleeping area and pulled the curtain which partitioned it off from the rest of the yurt. Karliss lay down on his furs, but he knew he was much too restless to sleep. A few minutes later he could tell from her breathing that Narantse was asleep.

Then something his father said made his ears perk up.

"Long-striding Antelope Clan still hasn't arrived at the Gathering."

Karliss nearly stopped breathing. Here was something fascinating. He hadn't heard anything about one of the clans not showing up. Clans never missed the Gathering. What had happened?

He settled in to listen for more information. He knew he shouldn't listen in. Sertithian culture was very strict when it came to privacy. In order to better defend against the many dangers of life on the steppes, the members of each clan erected their yurts close together. Such close proximity, combined with the fact that the hide walls of a yurt did almost nothing to muffle sound, meant that Sertithians had almost no actual privacy.

To combat this, the Sertithians practiced a sort of deliberate selective hearing. Nearby conversations, if they didn't include you, weren't to be heard. People who left the camp to relieve themselves or wash in a stream were not seen, even though of necessity people stayed close to the camp for safety. Most importantly, when clan members went into their yurts they essentially entered another world. What happened inside a yurt simply wasn't heard by the others. Family members could be screaming at each other at the top of their lungs and no one else in the clan would ever hear it, much less comment on it in any way.

This was doubly true inside the yurt. Once Karliss' parents closed the curtain on their sleeping space, they were gone. The children were not supposed to hear them. All Sertithian children learned this from an early age. They learned to simply tune out whatever happened on the other side of the curtain.

Except for Karliss. He'd never been able to not hear. Not only could he not tune out those around him, once they lowered their voices or began whispering his curiosity took over. Listening in wasn't a choice, it was a compulsion.

So when his parents began whispering, he went still and listened.

"What do you think happened?" his mother said.

Though she spoke very softly, Karliss had no trouble hearing her. He had unnaturally good hearing and probably could have heard her from much further away. It was something to do with his affinity for the wind. It was like the wind brought the sounds to him.

"I don't know. It's probably nothing," his father replied. "There was much snow this last winter. It's possible the rivers in their lands are swollen and they could not cross. Or maybe their terl is sick and could not travel. Terl Boke is quite old and he did not look well at last year's Gathering."

But Karliss could tell from the sound of his father's voice that his father didn't believe it was either of those things. His curiosity ratcheted up a few more notches.

"Could they have been attacked by outsiders?" his mother asked. "Their lands are on the border."

"No one has attacked out of the west for centuries," his father replied. "Besides, Terl Boke is too good of a leader to let his people grow complacent enough to allow themselves to be surprised. And to wipe out the whole clan? Impossible. Probably they simply came upon a herd of spikehorn and stopped to hunt. I'm sure they'll be here tomorrow."

They stopped talking then and Karliss lay in the darkness for a long time thinking about what he'd heard, wondering what had happened to the missing clan.

Chapter 37

It was the next morning and Karliss and his family were sitting in the yurt eating *birsch*—a thick paste made of ground barley and wild yams—scooping it out of wooden bowls with their fingers. Karliss put his bowl down.

"Can I go now?" he asked. The sun had only just risen but it felt to him like the whole day was getting away from him.

"Did you finish your *birsch*?" his mother asked.

"Mostly," Karliss said, surreptitiously pushing his bowl under his sleeping fur.

"What does mostly mean?"

Karliss rose part way. "I'm not really that hungry."

"But you will be later. Finish it. Every bit."

Reluctantly, Karliss sat back down and picked his bowl back up. Normally he liked *birsch*, but today it only stuck in his throat. He wanted to gobble the rest quickly and run out the door. Unfortunately, being as thick as it was, *birsch* wasn't the sort of food that could be gobbled. Not without a lot of water anyway and his water skin was empty. He ate another bite and then looked at his father.

"So I heard yesterday that Long-striding Antelope Clan hadn't showed up yet to the Gathering," he said casually, as if it wasn't something he'd spent half the night thinking about. "What do you think happened to them?"

As soon as he said the words he knew he'd made a mistake. Both his parents looked sharply at him.

"Where did you hear that?" his father demanded.

"Were you listening to us talk last night?" his mother said.

"What? No." Karliss tried to look as innocent as possible. "It was something I heard last night around the fire is all." He cast a hopeful look at his parents but neither's expression had softened so his innocent act probably wasn't working.

"You heard it around the fire," his father said flatly.

"I did!"

His father sighed and exchanged a look with his mother.

"You should beat him more," Ganbold said. His older brother had come in very late and until now was yawning and picking sleepily at his food. He looked a lot more alert now. "That's what I think," he added.

"Is it?" his father said. "Is that what you think?"

"Maybe it's not too late. He's only twelve."

"It was too late when he was born," Narantse chimed in.

"Quit talking about me like I'm not here," Karliss protested. "I can hear you, you know."

"Yet nothing changes," his mother said.

"I think we're getting off track," Karliss said. "The important thing here isn't how I heard about it. The important thing is what happened to them. Do you really think they were attacked by outsiders from the west?"

"Outsiders attacked one of the clans?" Ganbold said, the last of his sleepiness gone. His hand went to his bow, which he practically slept with.

"I never said I thought that," his father said.

"But it *could* have happened," Karliss persisted. "Or it could be something else. Something worse."

"What could be worse?" Narantse asked, alarmed.

"Stop scaring your sister," his father said sternly. "It was none of those things. Keep your crazy ideas to yourself. I won't have my son spreading foolish rumors." His dark gaze fell on Narantse, who was sitting there with her hand over her mouth. "I don't want to hear you talking about it either. This is going to upset enough people as it is. I don't want the two of you making it worse." Last he looked at Ganbold. "I trust I can count on you to behave like an adult about this."

"Of course," Ganbold said. "But maybe, to be safe, I should take a few of my friends and ride out this morning. You know, scout around a bit."

"You'll scout when your terl tells you to and not before, do you understand me?" The intensity from their normally-soft spoken father was enough to cow all three children into silence.

A few minutes later his father got up and left the yurt, and Ganbold went with him. Karliss finally finished the last of his food. "*Now* can I go?" he asked.

"Actually, I need your help with something for a bit," his mother said. "You and Narantse both."

"But I have things I have to do!"

"Trouble to get into, I bet," Narantse said.

"Whatever you have to do will still be there later," his mother said calmly. "Nasan's yurt has a tear starting and she needs dung for her fire. She's almost out. Narantse will help me sew the hole closed while you gather dung for her."

"I'm not going to do it," Karliss said, throwing his bowl down. "I gathered dung yesterday. I'm not doing it again today."

His mother slapped him. Hard enough to bring tears to his eyes.

"We tolerate a lot from you," she snapped, "but now you go too far. You know Nasan's husband died last winter and her only surviving son the year before. What would you have us do? Let her freeze? Do you care for no one but yourself?"

Karliss hung his head in shame. She was right. The clan was family. They took care of each other. It was how they survived the harshness of life on the steppes. "I'm sorry," he said miserably, wiping at a tear. Maybe there *was* something wrong with him. He genuinely liked Nasan. She always had a smile for him. She wasn't like Henta at all. He didn't want her to freeze.

"I try," he said. "But I just…it's like I forget. I can't seem to keep things in my mind. There's so much rushing around in there. There's always something that catches me and I have to chase it."

Munkhe's face softened and she touched his cheek. "It's the wind," she said. "I think you belong to it more than you do us. Promise me something, Karliss?"

Karliss brushed the last tears out of his eyes and looked at her. "What?"

"Be careful. I know you have a…connection with the wind that no one else understands. But I also know that it's dangerous. The gods and the spirits don't live in the same world we do. They tend to step on things without noticing. Don't let them step on you."

⚯ ⚯ ⚯

Karliss tried to be diligent and hard-working. He really did. When he set out with an empty sack to gather the first load of dried dung he told himself that he was going to stay focused. His mother had pointed out that if he worked hard, he'd be done sooner. Besides that, he felt bad about his selfishness and wanted to atone for it. He wanted to prove to his mother that he did care about others, that he could be a dutiful son.

But it didn't last very long. The great camp was stirring to life. The clans were up and moving, the second full day of the Gathering starting to pick up speed. The Sertithians were bubbling with the excitement of the Gathering and that excitement seemed to infect Karliss. He walked along slowly, over and over looking back at the camp. He found some dung and was bending over to pick it up when the wind suddenly brought him a snatch of conversation. He stopped, listening intently. The wind often did this, out of nowhere bringing him sounds from off in the distance. He often heard people who were far enough away he couldn't even see them.

The wind shifted a moment later and the conversation disappeared. Disappointed, he went back to his task. He'd gathered several pieces and was wishing he had a smaller sack when he very clearly heard someone say, "Qara says the *tlacti* might have to perform a ritual to find out about the missing clan."

Karliss froze, straining to hear more, but the wind had already shifted again. Though he could hear a number of snatches of conversations, he couldn't find the same one again. It was frustrating. If only he could force the wind to focus on what it was he wanted to hear, instead of blowing around so randomly.

He knew that Qara was the *tlacti* for one of the other clans, maybe Striped Badger Clan, though he wasn't sure. He'd met all the other *tlacti* at previous Gatherings, of course, but they were mostly dull and old and he'd never paid much attention to them.

Rituals could be dangerous, so if the *tlacti* were contemplating one that meant they were worried about the missing clan. It meant they thought something more than a flooding river or a herd of spikehorns was causing the clan to be late. Something serious was definitely happening. He couldn't wait to see his friends and tell them what he'd learned.

"Karliss! What's taking you so long?" his mother yelled.

Karliss hastily snatched up a couple more pieces of dung and took off running. "I'm right here, Ana!" he called. He emptied the sack beside the yurt. The pile was kind of small, he realized. He gathered the pieces and stacked them. There, that made the pile look bigger. Maybe that would be enough.

"What do you think, Ana?" he said. "That's probably enough, isn't it?"

His mother turned from where she was working on the yurt. She had the awl she was using to stitch the leather in one hand and was holding the rip closed with the other. "What, Karliss?"

"The dung. That's enough, isn't it?"

She looked at the small pile and shook her head. "Not even close."

"It's enough for today at least. I can always gather more tomorrow—"

"Go."

Reluctantly, Karliss headed out to collect more, grumbling to himself as he went. It seemed he would never be allowed to enjoy the Gathering. There would always be something in the way. Why was everyone else allowed to have fun but him? He'd be willing to bet that Hulagu and Batu weren't gathering dung right then.

It seemed like forever, but finally his mother said he'd collected enough. The words had hardly left her mouth before he was running to find his friends. Behind him he heard her call something to him but he didn't bother to listen. It probably wasn't important anyway.

He found his friends by Sharp-eyed Owl Clan's gamecock pens. Every clan raised chickens, turning them out during the day to scrounge for seeds and insects, then penning them at night to keep them safe from predators. Most of the clans also raised gamecocks for the sole purpose of entering them into the cock fights every year at the Gathering. The gamecocks used in the fights were proud birds with sharp beaks and even sharper spurs.

"Go on," Hulagu said to Batu. "Put your finger in there. I dare you."

"I already did," Batu said. "You saw me."

"Yes, but you pulled it right back out, before the gamecock even got close."

"Why don't you do it?"

"I will. You'll see. I'm faster than some dumb old bird."

Hulagu put his finger into the cage. The gamecock, a large bird that came nearly up to the boy's waist, with red-gold feathers and a nasty glint in his eye, darted across the cage and pecked at Hulagu's finger. Hulagu jerked his hand back, but not quite quickly enough.

"Ow!" he cried. A spot of blood was welling on his finger.

Batu laughed. "Not as fast as you thought, are you?"

"I want to try," Karliss said.

But before he could someone spotted them and yelled at them to go away and leave the gamecocks alone. The boys drifted away, Hulagu sucking on his injured finger.

"Where have you been?" Batu asked Karliss. "Did you oversleep?"

"No. I've been awake for hours. But I had to help my mother."

"Are you still in trouble?"

"More like trouble again."

"What did you do this time?" Hulagu asked.

"I sort of listened in while my parents were talking in their bed last night."

"Boy, you never learn, do you?" Hulagu said with a chuckle.

"I tried not to, but they were talking about the missing clan."

"There's a clan missing?" Batu asked.

"I heard something about that," Hulagu said. "It's Long-striding Antelope Clan, isn't it?"

"It is."

"But I heard it was nothing. They had some trouble getting here is all. They'll be here today."

"That's not what I heard," Karliss said, lowering his voice and looking around to make sure no one was close enough to hear. "The *tlacti* might hold a ritual."

Batu's eyes got round. "What kind of ritual? Do you think we'll get to watch?"

"They must be pretty worried," Hulagu said. "What else did you hear?"

"That's it," Karliss admitted. "But I'm going to try and find out more. I bet the *tlacti* are meeting to talk about it right now. I came to get you two first."

Hulagu gave him a knowing look. "You just want someone to get into trouble with you."

"We're not going to get into trouble. Not this time."

"That's what you always say," Hulagu replied, "right before you get us all into trouble."

"And I don't like that you said 'we'," Batu protested. "I haven't agreed to anything yet. Nor do I want to eavesdrop on the *tlacti*. They scare me. Ihbarha always looks like he wants to bite someone."

"You aren't going to abandon me on this, are you?" Karliss asked.

"It's not abandoning you if we never agreed to it in the first place," Hulagu pointed out. Hulagu was the reasonable one, the one who always saw through Karliss' fast talking to the heart of whatever he was trying to talk them into.

"It's completely safe, I promise you."

"Like the time we got caught by the horsemasters, trying to tie dried rattle gourds to the horses?" Rattle gourds were quite noisy once they dried out. A raiding party had been getting ready to go out on a raid and Karliss had talked his friends into going with him to tie the gourds to the raiders' horses as a prank. They got caught and it caused enough of an uproar that even Batu got a whipping.

"That was different. This is lots safer. There's no way we can get caught. You have to trust me."

"I don't know," Hulagu said, turning to Batu. "What do you say? Do you trust him?"

Batu shook his head. "I don't. Not at all."

"What are *you* worried about?" Karliss asked him. "You never get in any real trouble anyway."

"But *I* do," Hulagu pointed out.

"Come on. You two don't even have to do anything."

"Then why do you need us?" Batu asked.

"I don't *need* you, I just want to share it with you."

"Pretty generous of you," Hulagu said wryly.

"I think you just want to share the trouble," Batu said.

"Look, are you two coming or not?"

Karliss' friends looked at each other. "Maybe we should go and keep an eye on him," Hulagu said. "Who knows what trouble he'll get into without us?"

"You promise it's safe?" Batu asked.

"Of course. Perfectly safe."

Hulagu shrugged. "We're done here for a while anyway. He's watching us too close for us to get at the gamecocks now."

Karliss led the other two through the sprawling confusion of the Gathering. He needed to find Ihbarha and with this many people it could take all day. The *tlacti* could be anywhere. But Karliss had a mind to try something new. So he listened carefully as he walked, at the same time picturing the old man in his mind, concentrating on him.

It was hard to concentrate on Ihbarha. There were so many other interesting things to see in the camp, things that kept trying to distract him. A couple of times his friends started to talk to him. But Karliss put everything he had into it, and right about the time he was getting discouraged and thinking maybe this idea wouldn't work after all, he caught a scrap of Ihbarha's voice. He stopped and held his breath.

There it was again.

"...meeting with the others in five minutes..."

Karliss stuck his fingers in his ears and shut his eyes, trying to block out everything else. After a moment he heard Ihbarha's voice again. He wasn't sure why, but he had a feeling Ihbarha was off to his right.

"This way," he said, and continued walking. The others followed him to a point near the edge of the camp where they saw Ihbarha was standing with another *tlacti*, talking in a low voice. After a moment the two *tlacti* started walking.

"They're going to meet with some of the other shamans," Karliss told his friends excitedly. "They're going to talk about the missing clan."

"They're heading out of the camp," Batu said. "I don't want to follow them out in the open. They'll see us for sure."

"Don't worry about it. We'll stop far enough away. They're not paying attention to us anyway."

"Why are you so fascinated by this anyway?" Hulagu asked. "So a clan is late to the Gathering. It's probably nothing."

"But what if it's something. Don't you want to *know*?"

"Not especially."

"You can't quit now. We're so close."

"I can't?"

"Please don't," Karliss asked. "Look, there are some of the other *tlacti*, coming to meet them." He looked around and spotted a clump of small trees growing by a stream about a hundred paces away. "We can hide out in those trees while I listen. If anyone sees us, well, there's no rule against playing in the stream, is there?"

The other two looked at each other, then at Karliss. Batu was shaking his head. Hulagu looked resigned. "I'm in," Hulagu said finally. "After all, I haven't been in trouble since yesterday."

"What about you, Batu?"

Batu sighed. "I don't want to stand around by myself."

Karliss led them in a long arc toward the clump of trees, doing his best to make it look like they were wandering around with no real purpose in mind. As much as possible he resisted the urge to look over toward where the *tlacti* were gathering, though he did give in for a couple of quick peeks. Both times it looked like the shamans were paying no attention to them.

When they got into the trees he dropped to his belly and wormed his way to a spot where he was concealed by the leaves, but could look out and see the shamans sitting in a circle on the ground. There were eight of them now and they were a good hundred paces away. He stared at Ihbarha for a long moment, fixing him in his mind, then closed his eyes and listened. He listened harder than he ever had before, trying to tune everything out and focus only on Ihbarha.

After a minute a soft wind began to blow against his cheek and he could hear Ihbarha's voice.

"...don't think we should act too hastily. It's only been a day so far."

After that, there were some faint background sounds for a minute, then Ihbarha again.

"The ritual is dangerous, that's why. It's not something to rush into for no good reason."

This was no good. Karliss needed to be able to hear what the other *tlacti* were saying as well. He frowned, trying to expand his hearing, to see if he could hear more than Ihbarha. Batu started to say something but he quieted him with a gesture.

All at once it was like a barrier dropped and what had been faint background noises suddenly resolved into other voices.

"If we wait too long it may be too late," said a woman's voice that Karliss didn't recognize.

"And if the ritual gets away from us and one of us is injured or worse? Are you willing to risk that?" Ihbarha said.

"*I'll* do it if you're frightened to," the woman replied in a cutting voice.

"So now caution is to be confused with fear?" Ihbarha snapped. "Are we children to rush headlong into new danger thoughtlessly?"

"Don't start," said another voice, a man's. "We don't have time for it."

"I think we need to talk about what Qara saw in her vision," said another voice. She sounded like a young woman.

"It was a dream," Ihbarha said. "Nothing more."

"You're wrong," the first woman—presumably Qara—said. "This was much more than a dream."

Ihbarha started to speak again but a man cut him off. "Let her talk. Some of us haven't heard what she saw yet. Let us make our own decisions."

Qara spoke again. "I saw a monstrous, white-skinned figure. Gray flames roared around it, but they did not harm it."

"That's it?" Ihbarha said when she was done. "That's all?" Karliss knew the tone he was using and could picture the exact look on his face right that moment. It was a look of sarcastic incredulity. "You had a dream about a monster and we should panic and perform a ritual that could get one of us killed?"

"It wasn't a dream!" Qara snapped. "It was a vision brought by the spirits."

"Remember those traders that passed through a few years ago?" a woman's voice asked. "Didn't they have wild stories about soldiers who burned people alive?"

"The traders always tell stories," Ihbarha said. "Whatever they can make up to frighten the children."

"Are you sure they were only stories?" the woman persisted. "Have you forgotten when the plateau to the south exploded in fire and smoke? Bizarre creatures were seen fleeing across the steppes after that."

"And a few moons later, the day we all felt...whatever it was," a man's voice said.

What they were talking about had happened before Karliss was born but he'd heard stories about it. Everyone felt it when it happened. It was as if something vital had broken. And with it came a sense that awful things were now loose in the world. Those had been strange times, filled with dark portents everywhere. Then one day, out of nowhere, it was all over. No one knew what it was that had ended, or how, but they could feel that things had been put right. People still talked about it, but no one had any answers.

"That's still not enough reason to perform the seeing ritual," Ihbarha said. "I won't go along with it."

The *seeing* ritual? That was one Karliss had never witnessed. It was rarely performed because it was so dangerous. The seeing ritual was too difficult to be performed without the combined strength of all the *tlacti*. Which meant if Ihbarha didn't cooperate, it wouldn't happen.

"What will it take before you do agree?" Qara asked. "Does Erlik Khan himself have to show up?"

"More time, for one thing," Ihbarha said. "The missing clan might still show up. The ritual of appeasement is tomorrow night. We should at least wait until after that. We don't want to lose anyone right before the most important ritual of the year."

Several voices were raised, both for and against what Ihbarha had said, but all at once Qara cut them off. "Shh! Be quiet for a moment." The others subsided. "Someone is listening to us. I can feel it."

"There's no one anywhere near," Ihbarha protested. "You're imagining things."

"No, I'm sure of it."

Karliss didn't wait to hear anymore. He pulled back and opened his eyes.

"What is it?" Hulagu said when he saw the expression on Karliss' face. "What's wrong?"

"We need to get out of here. Quickly."

The boys pulled back through the trees and took off running in the opposite direction. In a few minutes they were back in camp and Karliss felt safe enough to stop. His friends caught up to him and the three stood in a circle, panting a little from the run.

"We're in trouble again, aren't we?" Batu said mournfully.

"No, of course not. I mean, I don't think so."

"Did one of them see you?" Hulagu asked.

"Not exactly."

"What does that mean?"

"One of them might have noticed me listening in. But there's no way for them to know it was us," he added quickly.

"You mean no way for them to know it was *you*," Hulagu corrected. "Batu and I didn't hear a thing. Isn't that right, Batu?" The stout boy nodded in agreement.

"What about being in this together?" Karliss asked. "We're a team, aren't we?" But neither boy budged and Karliss sighed.

"Did you learn anything at least?" Batu asked.

"One of them had a vision." Karliss told them what Qara claimed she'd seen. When he was done Batu's eyes were big and round. Even Hulagu looked a little pale.

"I don't want to know this," Batu said. "Next time don't tell me stuff like that."

"You asked," Karliss pointed out.

"But I didn't know it would be like that!"

"Let's talk about something else," Hulagu suggested, ever the practical one. "There's nothing we can do about it anyway."

"Yeah, let's find something to eat!" Batu suggested.

"No one said anything about eating," Hulagu said.

"*I* did," Batu replied.

"Let's go watch some of the archery contests," Hulagu said, and started walking that way before anyone could reply. The other two followed him.

Chapter 38

Karliss reluctantly followed his friends to the low bluffs south of the camp where the archery contests were held. Like so many of the activities boys his age spent their time on, archery really didn't interest him. Hopefully Hulagu would quickly lose interest and they could go find something else to do.

Fortunately, when they got there Karliss saw some of the other boys from Spotted Elk Clan standing in a group. Among them was Otgon, a boy a year older than Karliss. He was half a head taller than Karliss and twice as wide, thick-boned and meaty where Karliss was slim and fine-boned, almost birdlike. Karliss brightened up. Maybe this wouldn't be so boring after all. Karliss peeled off from his friends and went over to the boys. Otgon saw him coming and gave him a sullen look.

"What do you want, Karliss? You need someone to knock out one of your teeth?"

"No, my teeth are fine," he said brightly. "I came to cheer you on."

The bigger boy scowled. "No, you didn't."

"It's true. The honor of the Spotted Elk Clan, right? Don't you think that's more important than our little spats?"

Otgon's suspicious look eased slightly. "Maybe," he said cautiously.

"You have a good chance of winning this year, don't you?"

"Probably," Otgon conceded, still suspicious. It was true. Otgon was the best archer his age in their clan, better than boys several years older. He'd placed second at last year's Gathering.

"Well, I have a good feeling about this year," Karliss said. "That's why I came. I want to see your moment of glory."

Otgon grunted and glared at him. "Go away. I don't trust you."

"Don't be so grumpy," Karliss said cheerfully. "I only want to offer my support."

Otgon grabbed the front of Karliss' shirt suddenly and pulled him close. "You better not have some trick planned or..."

"Or what?" Karliss asked innocently.

"Or I'll pound you."

"Now, Otgon," Karliss said, patting his hand. "I know we've had our problems in the past, but none of that matters now. This is for the honor of our clan. That's what matters." And he gave him his most wide-eyed look.

Otgon's eyes narrowed and for a moment Karliss thought he was going to punch him anyway, but then the bigger boy let go of his shirt and shoved him. "Just get out of here."

"Yeah, go away," one of Otgon's friends said, a narrow, sharp-featured boy named Burilgi, "No one has time for your stupid games right now. This is serious."

"Got it," Karliss said. "Serious. I won't forget." He waved to the boys and walked away whistling.

"What was that all about?" Hulagu demanded when Karliss returned to his friends.

"Just having a little fun."

"You know, if you didn't taunt him all the time, I bet Otgon wouldn't punch you so often," Batu observed.

"You're probably right," Karliss agreed. "But I really can't help myself. It's so much fun."

"I don't feel like getting in a fight today," Hulagu said. Hulagu was a big kid, bigger than kids several years older than him, and when he fought it was with a sort of dogged intensity, a singlemindedness of purpose, that was somewhat frightening. In short, he always won. But at the same time, he intensely disliked fighting. "If you start something, you're in it alone."

"Why are you both assuming I'm going to start trouble?"

"Because you are," Batu said.

"It's what you do," Hulagu agreed.

"You two are starting to sound like my mother."

"Don't get me wrong," Batu said. "I hope you do make a fool of Otgon. He deserves it. I really hate him. I wish a horse would sit on him." Otgon was always making fun of Batu's weight and only the week before he pushed him so that he slipped in the mud from the snowmelt and fell on his face. "But I don't want to get slugged for it."

"It's a waste of time to hate Otgon," Karliss said. "It's like hating black flies. They can't help what they are and neither can Otgon. It's more fun to laugh at him."

"Listen to you," Hulagu said, "Karliss the wise, sharing his wisdom with us."

"I'd rather hate him," Batu said. "It's easier." He pulled a piece of flatbread from his pocket and bit off a piece. "What're you going to do?"

"I'm going to play with him a little," Karliss said mysteriously. "Come on, the contest is about to start and I want to be able to see." He led them over to a spot where they had a good view of the proceedings.

"If you make him lose this contest, he's going to beat you to a paste," Hulagu.

"And yet I'm going to do it anyway," Karliss said. "It kind of makes you wonder, doesn't it?"

"It makes me wonder if locusts didn't lay eggs in your brain," Batu said. "It's like you *want* him to beat you up."

"It's the wind," Hulagu observed. "It's made him crazy. Everyone knows it does that to you. Look at old Ihbarha."

"Let's enjoy the competition, shall we?" Karliss said. "This looks like a good spot." He sat down and his friends followed suit.

"It *is* a good spot," Batu said, motioning with his chin at the four girls who were sitting nearby. They were watching the boys surreptitiously.

"What are you talking about?" Karliss asked. He looked around and saw the girls then. One smiled at him and the others giggled. "Oh, I didn't see them."

"Of course you didn't," Batu complained. "You never do. But they always notice you, don't they? Never so much as a second look for poor Batu. Only eyes for Karliss and he doesn't even care."

"They're just little girls," Karliss said dismissively, his attention on Otgon, who was going to be shooting next.

"What?" Batu said incredulously. "Of course they're little girls. And we're little boys. That's how it's *supposed* to be!"

He was so genuinely indignant that Karliss had to laugh and Hulagu did too. Karliss looked over at the girls. He pointed at Batu. "My friend here thinks you're all as beautiful as the morning dew!" he called.

"What's *wrong* with you?" Batu exclaimed, shoving him. Karliss was laughing so hard he fell on his side. The girls were all laughing as well. "How could you *say* that?"

"Why not? It's true, isn't it?" Karliss said with mock innocence.

"But you didn't have to *tell* them!"

"Don't worry about it too much," Karliss said, patting him on the back. "Girls like it when you make them laugh. They also like it when they think you don't care."

Batu's eyes narrowed. "Is that why you always ignore them?"

"No, I ignore them because I really don't care."

"I hate you sometimes, too," Batu said. "You make it all look so easy."

"It *is* easy!"

"No, it's not. For most of us it's hard."

Karliss shrugged and turned back to watching Otgon. The boy was stepping up to the line. The target, a piece of hide stretched on a wooden frame and with a rabbit painted on it, was set up about fifty paces away. Otgon took a deep breath and raised his bow.

Right as he brought the arrow up to his eye, Karliss cupped his hands around his mouth and blew. A tiny gust of wind skittered across the ground, picking up dust and swirling it around Otgon's face so that he had to lower the bow. He glared at Karliss, who shrugged and gave him an innocent look.

"You simply can't leave him alone, can you?" Hulagu said.

"I didn't do anything."

"Sure you didn't."

"Let him shoot," Batu said. "Don't mess with him until he makes it to the finals. That will be better."

"You don't have to encourage him," Hulagu said.

"Otgon deserves to have sand ticks infest his armpits," Batu said sourly.

"When did you get so grumpy? Maybe we need to find you something to eat," Hulagu said.

"You're right, though," Karliss said. "I'll hold off and see if he makes it that far." Cupping his hands around his mouth again he called out, "Go get 'em, Otgon!"

Otgon glared at him again, then stepped back up to the line. He rolled his shoulders and drew back the bowstring again. He must have been expecting Karliss to do something because he flinched right before releasing the arrow, causing it to fly wide.

"Tough luck!" Karliss called. "We still believe in you!"

Otgon mouthed some words that Karliss was pretty sure his mother would have slapped him for saying, then took another arrow from his quiver and set it to the bow.

The next three arrows landed solid right where the rabbit's heart would be. It turned out to be enough so that he advanced through the first round. The target was switched out for one with a ground squirrel drawn on it. While Otgon was getting ready to shoot Karliss sent a tiny dust devil whirling across the range, then winked at Otgon when he whirled and glared at him.

"If you're trying to make him mad," Batu said. "I think it's working."

"There's not going to be enough of you left for your parents to bury," Hulagu observed. "I wonder how long they'll grieve for you."

Batu was right. Otgon looked like he could bite an arrow in half. But he mastered himself enough to land all four arrows in the target. When he was done shooting he stomped over to the boys, his friends following him.

"I'm going to thrash you when this is over," he said.

"Why?" Karliss asked innocently. "I'm here to cheer you on."

"I should put the next arrow in you."

"But then you'd lose the competition. I thought you wanted to win."

Otgon growled and raised one fist but right then the warrior running the contest called him for the last round. "If I don't win, you're dead," he said.

"Then I really hope you win," Karliss replied. "Because I'm not ready to be dead yet."

The final target was a mouse. Only Otgon and a boy from Sharp-Eyed Owl Clan were left. The other boy hit the target with three of his four arrows and then stepped back, his friends patting him on the back.

When Otgon stepped up to the line Karliss sent a little breeze to stir up some dust around him. Otgon turned and glared at him.

"Maybe you should just let him shoot," Hulagu said. "I don't want to bring the bad news to your mother."

"I intend to," Karliss said. "Go, Otgon!" he yelled.

Flustered now, Otgon missed the first arrow. He clenched his fists and muttered a curse. Then he rallied and landed the next two. If he hit the last one he'd force another round.

He raised the arrow to his cheek, then lowered it and looked at Karliss. Once more he raised the arrow and once more he lowered it.

"Quit stalling!" someone called out.

Otgon rushed his last arrow and missed the target.

As friends crowded around to congratulate the other boy for winning, Otgon threw his bow down and stalked toward Karliss.

"Here it comes," Hulagu said. "I warned you."

Karliss and his friends stood up. "I don't want to get in a fight," Batu said.

"You made me miss!" Otgon said. His face was red and his fists were clenched.

"What? How can you say that? I did nothing. You missed that last shot on your own."

"You made me miss," Otgon repeated.

"I think you're just confused. I think—"

But he didn't get to finish saying what he thought because right then Otgon punched him in the stomach. Karliss bent over, holding his stomach. Otgon stomped away with his friends.

"It could have been worse," Hulagu said.

"Why do you do that?" Batu asked. "Why do you always make him mad?"

Still holding his stomach, Karliss straightened up. "It was worth it." He gave his friends a triumphant smile. "Making him miss would have been fun, but making him mad so that he beat himself, that's ten times better, don't you think?"

"I think you're crazy," Batu said.

"Me too," Hulagu chimed in.

"So, what should we do next?" Karliss said, looking around. "I hear the Angry Bear Clan is making their famous mince pies today. Maybe they're not watching them so closely."

⚓   ⚓   ⚓

The three friends were walking back to camp at the end of the day when Hulagu looked up and said, "Uh oh. Bad for you, Karliss."

"What?" Karliss looked up and his heart fell. Ihbarha was standing by the big wagon where the food was served, his arms crossed, glaring at him. His first instinct was to run, and he came close to doing so, but it was no use. Ihbarha had already seen him. Running would only make it worse.

"Well, it's been fun," Hulagu said in a low voice.

"Nice knowing you," Batu added. Both boys darted away then, leaving Karliss to face Ihbarha's wrath alone.

Karliss made a split-second decision to bluff his way through. It probably wouldn't work, but he had precious few options.

"Hi, Ihbarha. Are you looking for me?"

"Come with me," Ihbarha snapped, grabbing his arm and dragging him away.

"Ow! Hey, that hurts," Karliss protested. Ihbarha ignored him. "I think I hear my mother calling," Karliss added. "I better go see—"

He broke off as Ihbarha rapped him hard on top of the head with his knuckles.

"That hurt too!" Karliss rubbed the top of his head. What was wrong with everyone? Why were they all hitting him today?

Ihbarha stopped when they were out of the camp. He spun Karliss to face him.

"You were listening in today."

"Who, me?" Karliss said, looking as innocent as he could.

Quicker than he would have thought possible, Ihbarha's hand flashed out and the old shaman rapped him on top of the head again.

"Why do you keep doing that?" Karliss cried.

"I've had enough of your lies!" Ihbarha barked. "I've had enough of *you*. It's not bad enough that you shirk your lessons and scoff at the wisdom of generations of *tlacti*—wisdom necessary to keep your clan alive—but you use your god-given abilities frivolously and dangerously. What am I to do with you? I've tried beating you, but it does no good." His voice had risen by then so that he was nearly yelling.

"It's not like that," Karliss said.

"Aaugghh!" Ihbarha suddenly shrieked. "Enough! No more! It is more than I can bear!" And for the next minute he went on in this vein, gnashing his teeth, wringing his hands, actually pulling at his hair, while Karliss stared wide-eyed. He'd seen his teacher get angry before, but never anything like this. The old man was practically weeping. It shocked him so much that for once he had nothing to say. Watching, he started to feel bad.

Finally, Ihbarha ran out of steam. He slumped, then sat heavily on the ground and put his head in his hands. Karliss sat down too.

"Maybe the failure is mine," the old man moaned. "The gods sent me this test and I failed it. I failed them and I failed my people."

"It's not your fault, Bagesh," Karliss said, using the formal word for master and teacher. "It's me. The wind seems to have blown something loose in my brain."

The old man was breathing hard. He looked at Karliss suspiciously. "Don't play me, boy. I've not the patience for it today."

"I'm not. I mean it. The fault is mine." Karliss lowered his head. "Maybe there is nothing more you could have done. Maybe the gods burdened you with me because they knew that you alone could handle it."

Ihbarha's eyes narrowed. "You're just saying that to placate me."

"No, I'm not. I swear."

"No other *tlacti* among the people has an apprentice like you, it is true," Ihbarha said slowly, almost grudgingly.

"I should not have listened in," Karliss said humbly. "I know better. *Tlacti* councils are not for apprentices."

"This is true," Ihbarha grunted.

And then Ihbarha surprised Karliss.

"For all your failings, there is no malice in you, Karliss. Underneath all your mischief and rebellion I believe you are a good boy with a good heart. You are selfish and thoughtless, but these are common afflictions of the young and with time you will probably outgrow them."

Karliss stared at him, stunned. This was not what he'd expected at all.

"I am harsh with you and often angry, it is true," he continued, "but it is because I worry. Not only about our clan and how it will fare in the future after I am dead and you are clan *tlacti*, but about you."

317

Now Karliss was glad he was sitting. He'd never imagined the old shaman would say anything like this.

"I worry about you. You are young. You think the world is all fun and games, but it's not. The gods have smiled on you, it is true. You have an affinity for the path of the *tlacti* that has not been seen among our people for hundreds of years, maybe forever. But that does not mean you cannot be hurt by the forces you treat so lightly.

"I know you chafe at the rituals and practices I force you to learn, but they are there for a reason. They are there to safeguard not only you, but our people. The world of the wind is a strange and powerful one, filled with forces and powers far beyond the ken of mortal man. The gods do not really care for us and the spirits only sometimes, at their whim." The old shaman looked up at the sky. "We spend a great deal of effort and time trying to appease the wind, but in my heart I wonder how much good it really does. Sometimes I wonder if it matters at all." He looked back at Karliss. "But what else are we to do? We have to do something. We cannot simply give up and let ourselves be thrown this way and that.

"What you did today, using the wind to listen in on us, it seems to you only a harmless prank. But it is much more than that.

"When you listen with the wind you are letting it blow freely through you. The human mind is not meant for that. If you let the wind's voices inside your mind too many times you will suffer for it. This is assured. Maybe it won't happen right away, but eventually, as sure as the sun rises in the east, you *will* go mad. I promise you this."

Ihbarha leaned forward and grabbed Karliss' arm, gripping it so tightly it hurt. "It happened to my predecessor. She was a powerful *tlacti*, one of the strongest ever. She thought it made her above the rules. She let the wind blow through her freely for years. And finally she paid the price. Even worse, the clan paid the price."

"What happened?" Karliss asked breathlessly.

"She went stark, raving mad. She began babbling about voices that only she could hear. She became paranoid, convinced that others were plotting against her. She claimed she could hear our plans." He saw Karliss' look and nodded. "Yes, she even thought I plotted against her, her own loyal student. Finally, she snapped.

She summoned a tornado and loosed it on the camp. Over a dozen people died that day."

"How did you stop her?"

"We didn't. None of us could even get close to her. Arrows shot at her, spears thrown at her, they were all deflected by the wind that raced and swirled around her. She stopped herself finally. She went too far. She let the wind in and it took her over completely. It scattered her mind. After the tornado dissipated we found her sitting in the dirt. She looked at us but there was nothing human in her eyes. There were only clouds. She opened her mouth to speak, but what came out made no sense. The sounds she made weren't even words at all. What came from her mouth sounded like the wind given voice."

Karliss felt himself grow cold at this last part. It sounded to him like she had spoken the language of the wind, the same language he spoke. Did that mean he was going to go mad too?

"On the terl's orders, her throat was cut," Ihbarha said.

"You killed her?" Karliss was shocked. "How could you do that to your own *tlacti*?"

"Understand something, boy," Ihbarha said. "He had no choice. He couldn't risk what else she might do, who else she might kill." He broke off and stared off into the distance. He was shaking slightly with some suppressed emotion. "I became *tlacti* for the clan that day. I was only fourteen, not much older than you. It was a heavy responsibility to bear."

"You became *tlacti* when you were fourteen? But weren't you too young?"

"Who else was there? It was the end of my childhood. I had to grow up very fast then. I had to take on a position vital to the welfare of my clan and there was no one to help me with it."

He turned his intense gaze on Karliss. "Do you understand now why I am so harsh on you?"

"I think so," Karliss said slowly.

"This is not a game. I could make a mistake and die any day and then it would be up to you to be shaman, to guide your people down safe paths and placate the hostile forces which surround us. It could happen tomorrow. Are you ready for that?"

Karliss swallowed. He suddenly felt very small and young. "You're going to live for many years, Bagesh. Surely."

"You don't *know* that!" the old man snapped. "You *can't* know that. That's why you have to stop acting like a child. You need to take your responsibilities and your powers seriously. Do you understand?"

Karliss seemed to be having trouble breathing. It took a moment for him to get the words out. "I understand," he said weakly. "I'll try to do better."

Ihbarha stood up then. "Sit here and think about what I have said," he commanded, and walked away.

Karliss looked up at the sky and wondered at what he had heard. He was confused. He found it hard to believe that the wind was as dangerous as the old man said it was. The *aranti* were his friends. Surely they meant him no harm. They were friendly, playful creatures, nothing like the malicious spirits that Ihbarha was always warning him about.

But at the same time Ihbarha's warning rocked him to his core. What if Karliss was wrong about the *aranti*? Maybe they weren't malicious, but that didn't mean they were safe either. Would he eventually go mad from spending too much time around them? He thought about how often he got in trouble, how difficult it was for him to take the world seriously. Might that not be a sign that he was already being changed by the wind?

How much worse would it get?

But the thought of closing himself off to the *aranti* filled him with great sadness. In many ways they were his closest friends, always there, always eager to play, to show him new and wondrous things.

When finally Karliss stood up and went back to camp he was no closer to resolving the problem. Conflicting thoughts and feelings battled within him. He wished there was someone he could talk to about this, but the truth was there was no one. No one could possibly understand what he faced. He felt very much alone.

Chapter 39

"What's wrong with you?" Munkhe asked Karliss the next morning. They'd already eaten and the rest of the family had left the yurt.

"Nothing's wrong."

"The sun is shining and you are still inside. Last night you hardly said a word and went straight to bed without arguing. Don't tell me nothing is wrong."

"You wouldn't understand. It's...*tlacti* stuff."

Munkhe pulled him close and hugged him. "I want you to remember something. You're not alone. You have your family. You have your clan. We're here to help you. Don't forget that."

Karliss pulled away. "Do you think I'm going crazy?" he asked her.

She gave him a questioning look. "No, I don't. What makes you say that?"

"But you'll tell me if you think I am, right? Please?"

"There's no chance—"

"Promise me."

"Okay, I promise, but it's not going to happen. You're not going to go crazy."

"You don't know that. Ihbarha's bagesh went crazy."

"So that's what this is about. You think what happened to Cheche is going to happen to you, is that it?"

"It could."

"But it won't. You are not Cheche. You're nothing like her. It all happened before my time, but I've heard the stories. What Ihbarha didn't tell you was that Cheche was always a little mad, even back to her childhood. She should never have been trained to be a shaman. Her bagesh should have seen the flaw in her from the beginning and sealed her away from the wind. What happened to her isn't going to happen to you. You should never forget that the wind is dangerous, but you should not cower before it either. The gods gave you this gift for a reason."

Karliss stared into her eyes for a minute, then nodded. "Okay."

"Feel better?"

"Some."

"Now go on and have some fun," she said, giving him a little push toward the door.

Karliss stepped outside into the sunlight and almost immediately Ihbarha swooped down on him. "There you are. I've been looking for you." He seemed angry at Karliss for some reason. Gone was the man who'd showed a flicker of concern for Karliss the night before.

He thrust a leather pouch at Karliss. "Fill this with moonglow seeds."

Moonglow seeds? "You're doing the seeing ritual after all?" Karliss asked.

"So you've paid attention to at least some of your lessons, I see," Ihbarha grunted. "The answer is maybe. But it's best to have the seeds." He pointed off to the south. "There's a patch of vines just past that bend in the stream. Other apprentices are already out there gathering seeds. Hurry up. You're making me look bad."

Karliss took the pouch and started to walk away but Ihbarha called after him.

"You do remember that the ritual of appeasement is tonight, don't you? I won't have to come looking for you?"

"I remember," Karliss said. How could he forget? It was only the biggest ritual of the year.

As he walked, he wondered how long it had been since a seeing ritual was performed. Certainly he'd never witnessed one. Why had Ihbarha changed his mind? Had he learned something new about the missing clan?

As he walked, a small wind sprang up and whirled around him. He heard an *aranti* within it, and knew the creature was trying to get him to play. Normally Karliss welcomed the *aranti*'s playfulness, but not this morning. He pushed back, deliberately rooting himself and not letting the *aranti* push him.

But the *aranti* didn't give up. It slapped at him with countless tiny hands and it whispered in his ears.

Play! Play!

"Go away," Karliss muttered, sticking his fingers in his ears. A couple of women were standing outside one of the yurts talking and they looked at him questioningly as he went by.

Even with his fingers in his ears he could still hear the *aranti*. Which wasn't surprising. He didn't actually hear the *aranti* with his ears. He heard them inside, somewhere deeper.

Frustrated, he took off running, as if he could run away and leave the wind behind. Naturally that didn't work and it actually seemed to make the *aranti* even more excited. It raced around him, tugging at his clothes, mussing his hair.

Karliss gave up running and resumed walking. He told himself the answer was simply to ignore the *aranti* until it grew bored and went away. But that didn't seem to work either. He thought about the lessons that Ihbarha had taught him about building an internal wall in his mind to keep the voices of the wind out. He wished now he'd actually practiced the lessons instead of pretending. But he'd never seen a reason to before. He liked having the *aranti* around. Only now did he realize how exhausting their endless chattering, their manic energy, really could be.

He tried working on it now, imagining himself building a stone wall in his mind, setting the stones into place one at a time. And it worked. Sort of. The voices receded somewhat. They didn't go away, but they weren't quite so loud. His own thoughts returned, now that they were no longer crowded out by the wind. It was a relief, but it was also difficult. His concentration kept wavering. So intent was he on this internal battle that he didn't realize he'd arrived at his destination until someone spoke to him.

"Hey, watch it! You almost stepped on my hand!"

Karliss blinked and looked around. The camp was in the distance behind him. He was in a small depression. Moonglow vines grew thickly everywhere. Down by his feet was one of the other apprentices, a girl a couple of years older than him. He'd met her before at previous Gatherings. He thought her name was Suren, but he wasn't sure.

"Sorry," Karliss mumbled.

"Are you drunk or something? Did you sneak some *achai*?"

"No. I'm…a little tired is all."

"Sure," she replied. She looked skeptical. "Well?" she asked after a moment.

"Well, what?"

"Why are you standing here? You came to help gather moonglow seeds, didn't you?"

"Oh, right." The truth was Karliss had kind of forgotten what he was supposed to be doing. He looked down stupidly at the pouch in his hand.

"Go gather somewhere else. I don't want to worry about you stepping on me."

Karliss looked around. There were three other apprentices gathering seeds. They were all looking at him. He felt very exposed. He walked to an area where no one else was working and dropped down to his knees. He began pulling the smooth, round seeds off the vines and putting them into the pouch.

The problem was that since he'd broken his concentration the wind had crept back in. He could hear its voices again, muttering about this and that. Sighing, he began to once again build the imaginary wall in his mind. It was a neverending task, he saw that now, like trying to dam a stream with handfuls of sand. As soon as he set stones in place, they were quickly blown away. The day suddenly seemed very long and bleak.

Chapter 40

"What's wrong with you today?"

Karliss was so lost in his inner battle with the wind that it took a moment to realize Hulagu was talking to him. Both of his friends had stopped walking and were looking at him. "What? Nothing. I'm fine."

"*Felk-naa*," Hulagu said, uttering a common imprecation comparing Karliss' statement to steaming yak dung.

"What he said," Batu agreed. "You've barely said a word all morning. And you haven't once suggested something guaranteed to get us into trouble. That *never* happens."

"So tell us what's wrong. Or do we have to beat it out of you?"

"I'm tired is all."

Hulagu shook his head. "Nope. Try again."

Karliss rubbed his eyes. His head hurt and he felt disoriented. The truth was that he couldn't stop worrying about what Ihbarha had said about going mad someday and hurting his family and his clan. The thought was unbearable. But he couldn't tell his friends. How would they react? They'd probably think he was already going crazy and stop being his friends. He settled for telling them part of the truth.

"Ihbarha chewed me out last night. He's really angry at me for listening in on the council yesterday. He said I'm the worst apprentice ever and if I didn't start taking my duties as *tlacti* seriously that someday I'd get my whole clan killed. I can't stop thinking about that."

"Wow," Batu said when he was done. "No wonder you look so bad."

"Don't say that," Hulagu admonished him. "You'll make him feel worse." To Karliss he said, "You don't look all *that* bad."

"Lying to him isn't going to help," Batu observed.

"It can't hurt," Hulagu retorted.

"Stop," Karliss said. "I don't care how bad I look. Do you...do you think he's right?"

"About being the worst apprentice ever?" Batu asked.

"No, about getting people killed because I don't take my duties seriously."

Hulagu shrugged. "It could happen."

Batu punched him in the arm. "Why did you do that? Why did you tell him the truth?"

"You just told me not to lie to him!"

"*Sometimes* you should."

"I'm not going to listen to you anymore. You're confusing me." Hulagu looked at Karliss. "If a saddlemaker doesn't make a saddle properly it could fail and the rider could fall and get killed. If a swordmaker doesn't make a sword properly it could shatter in battle and get a warrior killed."

"How does that help?" Batu said.

"What I'm saying is, yeah, it could happen."

"What Hulagu is trying to say is don't worry about it so much. Ihbarha is strong," Batu said. "He'll live for a long time still." He paused. "Even though he is really, really old. Older than everyone in the clan except for Yeke." He frowned. "I wonder what it's like being that old, knowing you're probably going to die any day now."

"*Now* who's not helping?" Hulagu said.

"Well, I don't know what to say," Batu protested. "I don't want to be killed if Karliss turns out to be a terrible shaman."

"You think I'll be a terrible shaman?" Karliss asked, his heart falling.

"I didn't mean it like that," Batu said quickly. "I mean, look at the things you can do with the wind. Truly you are blessed by the gods."

"Then what are you saying?"

"I...uh..." Batu looked to Hulagu for help.

"I think he's saying that maybe you could try a little harder. You do fool around a lot, you know."

"You never take anything seriously," Batu added.

Their words hit Karliss hard. He'd never dreamed that even his friends thought he was so unreliable.

"I'll try," he said glumly. "I'll work harder, be more serious."

"Hey, don't take it so hard," Hulagu said, giving him a friendly punch in the arm. "You look like your horse just died. You're not grown up yet. You don't have to turn into an old man today."

"Yeah, don't get boring," Batu said. "You're still a kid, you know."

⚜   ⚜   ⚜

The three friends wandered over to watch the trick-shooting contest, in which warriors vied with each other to see who could make the most difficult shots from horseback. The course consisted of four targets attached to the ends of poles stuck in the ground. The targets were about man-height and the size of a fist. One at a time the contestants galloped through the course, shooting one arrow at each target. A dozen older warriors acted as judges and points were awarded to the contestants based on the difficulty of the shots they attempted, the speed with which they completed the course and, of course, how many arrows actually hit the targets. It was one of the most popular of the contests.

Several dozen warriors had already completed the course and it was down to the last one. He was a short, slender man from the Striped Badger Clan. He'd won the contest the last two years and was heavily favored to win it again this year. He rode his horse, a beautiful palomino with ribbons tied in its mane and tail, up to the starting line. A number of last-minute bets changed hands and then the crowd grew quiet.

The warrior tapped his heels to his horse and the horse leapt forward. In one smooth motion he stood upright on the horse's back, nocking an arrow and drawing it back. Right before he loosed the arrow, his horse stumbled. He was falling to the side as he fired. A disappointed sound came from the watching Sertithians. It was a shame to lose before he even got started.

But just as quickly disappointment turned to sounds of awe as the horse righted itself and the warrior caught hold of his mount's mane and avoided falling to the ground. Even more unbelievable, his arrow flew true and struck the target. Clearly the stumble had been planned.

Hooking one leg over the horse's neck, the warrior fired under the horse's neck at the next target, striking it also. The crowd murmured in approval.

Swiftly he pulled himself back up on top of the horse. The warrior was wearing a wide headband and as he approached the next target he slid it down over his eyes. He plucked a fresh arrow from his quiver and fired all in one smooth motion. The arrow

327

struck the edge of the target and glanced away rather than sticking, but the difficulty of the shot more than made up for what he would lose for missing.

For the final target his horse began swerving side to side erratically. He switched his bow to his off hand, fired and struck the target. The crowd erupted in cheers.

"Imagine being able to shoot like that," Batu said when the cheering died down. He fired a few imaginary arrows in imitation.

"I think it's kind of hard to do that while you're eating," Hulagu said. Batu had a piece of flatbread in each hand.

"Hey!" Batu said angrily.

"Or maybe that would be your trick shot," Hulagu continued, laughing. "Everybody come see Batu shoot while eating a meat pie!" He elbowed Karliss. "What do you think?"

"Huh, what?" Karliss said. He'd been focusing on maintaining his inner barrier and had missed the exchange.

"We're going to hop on an eagle and fly east to meet Bai-ulgan, god of the east wind. She invited us for a feast. Want to come?" Hulagu said.

"That sounds good," Karliss said.

"You didn't hear a thing I just said, did you?" Hulagu asked.

Karliss winced. "Not really."

Hulagu grabbed Karliss by the front of his shirt and in mock anger said, "I see you in there skinwalker. Get out and give us our friend back!" He gave Karliss a shake.

"Yeah, we don't know you," Batu added. "Give us Karliss back!"

Karliss pulled free. "It's not that bad."

"Yes, it is."

"I think it's worse," Batu said. "I think we need to find a *tlacti* to perform a ritual and drive the skinwalker out."

"We could get Henta. She's no *tlacti*, but maybe she could beat it out of him."

"You two are hilarious," Karliss said sourly. "I'm trying to do something, okay?"

"Trying to be the most boring person in the world," Batu said.

Karliss looked at the sun and suddenly realized that it was almost sundown. "I have to go anyway. I have to get back to the camp."

"Now I know you're a skinwalker!" Batu crowed. "The real Karliss never goes back unless we drag him."

"Don't be dumb," Karliss said. "Tonight's the big ritual, remember? If I'm late Ihbarha…well, you're the ones who were just telling me I'm going to be a terrible shaman because I don't take anything seriously."

"Did I say that?" Batu asked.

"Someone did," Hulagu answered.

Karliss didn't wait to hear the rest. He took off running, ignoring the shouts of his friends, dodging through the crowd that was slowly breaking up. He arrived at the camp of Spotted Elk Clan a few minutes later and there was Ihbarha standing outside his yurt, tapping his foot.

"Even to this you're late?" he grumbled when Karliss skidded to a stop in front of him.

"I'm sorry, Bagesh. I was watching the trick-riding contest and I—"

"I don't care," the old shaman said. He was wearing his ceremonial robe. Feathers and brightly-dyed ribbons festooned it. Around his neck his *krysala* hung on its leather thong. "Grab up that bundle of wood and follow me. Everyone else will already be there."

Beside the shaman's yurt was a good-sized bundle of wood, lashed together with a leather string. The precious wood had been gathered during the winter specifically for the ritual of appeasement. The ritual was held every year during the Gathering, all of the clans' *tlacti* joining forces to beseech the gods of the winds for a favorable year. It was by far the most important ritual of the year.

Karliss followed Ihbarha out of the camp. To the west of the Gathering was a low, flat-topped hill where the ritual was held every year. Karliss could see that the other *tlacti* and their apprentices were already on top of the hill, preparing for the ritual. Additionally, a number of Sertithians were already gathering around the base of the hill, waiting for the ritual to begin. No wonder Ihbarha was angry. Too many people were getting to see him show up late.

Around the edge of the top of the hill, at the four cardinal directions, wood had been piled and apprentices and sacrificial animals were waiting. The *tlacti* were standing in a group in the center.

At the northern spot a goat was tethered. Tung-alk, the god of the north winds, was fickle and prone to sudden fits of anger. If Tung-alk was displeased the north winds, which blew down out of the massive mountains to the north, would blow strongly during the wintertime. When that happened, the snow piled up too deeply on the steppes and the horses and other livestock weren't able to dig through it to get the fodder they needed. Many would starve. People would freeze in their yurts.

But if Tung-alk was properly placated, the north winds came primarily in the summer, bringing respite from the blistering heat and helping the grasses stay green longer.

To the east a yak was tethered. Bai-ulgan was the god of the east winds. She was the friendliest of the wind gods and the one most revered. It was the east winds which brought most of the rains, the clouds floating in from the sea. If Bai-ulgan was happy the spring rains came on time, giving the steppes the water they needed to burst forth with life and new grasses, and the summer rains were not too fierce.

But if Bai-ulgan felt neglected the spring rains were poor or did not come at all. The summer rains came in torrents and the steppes flooded, the grasses mildewed and died. Game suffered and the Sertithians were not able to put aside enough food to make it through the winter.

To the south was a wild pheasant, snared for this purpose. The god of the south winds was Esegen, the least fearsome of the gods. The winds only rarely blew up from the south and so it was not as important to appease him. When he was appeased, the south winds came in the winter, bringing warmth to counteract the cold pouring down from the north.

But it was the god of the west winds who it was most vital to placate and that was why there was a horse waiting there as a sacrifice. Erlik Khan was the god of the west winds. She was the one they feared most of all, for when she was angered she sent the west winds in the spring and summer. The west winds blew the rain clouds away before they could come in from the east and the steppes suffered. Scorching heat and drought followed in the wake of the west winds. The grasses dried up. The clouds that blew in from the west brought no rain, but they did bring lightning which started fires that could burn for days, racing across the steppes like a ravening beast, consuming everything in its path. Entire clans had been wiped out in the past by those fires when they were unable to get away.

The west winds brought more than heat and drought. They also sometimes brought plagues of locusts, hordes of them that descended from the sky and blanketed the grasslands, devouring everything.

"You'll be helping at the south fire," Ihbarha said.

"Again?" Karliss asked. "I thought this year I was going to get to help with one of the other fires."

"That was if you proved yourself capable of it. The only thing you've proven over the last year is that you're still not ready for real responsibility."

Grudgingly, Karliss walked to the south and added his wood to the pile there. There was one other apprentice waiting there, a boy about seven who was watching everything with wide eyes. It was his first ritual.

Karliss had mixed feelings about the ritual of appeasement. He liked being up on top of the hill, the center of attention. It made him feel important. He scanned the gathering crowd, looking for people he knew. He saw his parents and his sister, but there was no sign of Hulagu or Batu.

He also liked the energy and excitement of the ritual. It was definitely a spectacle and it drew large numbers of *aranti*. The *aranti* always grew very excited which in turn got him excited.

But he didn't like the sacrifices. Killing things, even little things like bugs, had always been hard for him. Hard enough that he figured if he was in charge of hunting for the clan, the clan would have long ago starved.

Besides that, he also wondered how much good the ritual did or if it was just something they did for show—which he suspected was all that most of the rituals the *tlacti* conducted were good for. How much did the *tlacti* even know about what they were doing? For one thing, they thought the beings in the wind were spirits, while Karliss knew they were actually *aranti*. And the *aranti* were clearly not interested in the sacrifices at all, hardly even stooping to take a closer look at them.

Ihbarha had explained to him that the sacrifices were meant primarily to appease the gods, not their servants, the spirits. But how did he or anyone know the gods had any more interest in the sacrifices than the *aranti* did? Might they not be just as disinterested? Karliss often wondered about the gods. His whole life he'd heard people speak reverently, often fearfully, about them. But he'd never seen any sign of them, not like he saw the *aranti* anyway. Nor did the *aranti* ever say anything about any gods, and the *aranti* babbled endlessly about everything. If the gods were that frightening, if the *aranti* were their servants, then how come the *aranti* did not say anything about them?

Naturally, he'd told no one his thoughts on this. He'd learned at an early age that most people didn't want to hear his crazy ideas about the nature of things. Even worse, many of them got very upset when he shared his ideas with them. If he started questioning gods, there was no telling how people would react. They'd probably all turn against him. Whatever happened, it wouldn't be good.

The sun went down and the fires were lit. The *tlacti* stood in a large circle in the center of the hilltop and held up their *krysalas*. The *krysalas* were instruments used by the *tlacti* for a variety of purposes—among them summoning and controlling spirits—and featured prominently in most rituals. They were extremely difficult to create, taking years of effort by the most skilled and experienced *tlacti*. As a result, each clan possessed only the one *krysala* and the *tlacti* took great care of them. Some of the *krysalas* were hundreds of years old, passed down for generations.

Ihbarha's *krysala* was a flattened disc about a hand-width across, made of polished bone and with a number of small holes and grooves carved into it. The others were similar, though some were rings rather than discs and some were made of shell or wood rather than bone. All had distinct patterns of holes and grooves carved into them. The holes and grooves were not randomly placed. They were arranged so that when air passed over and through them different sounds would be created. Those sounds, if properly controlled by a *tlacti* who knew what they were doing, could summon the spirits and even control them.

The *tlacti* held their *krysalas* before their mouths and began to chant. The chant started softly and grew in volume. The *krysalas* amplified their voices, and after a few minutes they were as loud as thunder. Every Sertithian could easily hear the chants. The sound was so loud Karliss felt like his bones were vibrating from it.

The wind began to blow, gently at first, then increasingly harder as the volume of the chant increased. The wind blew through and around the *krysalas* and from the instruments a strange, eerie music began to play. Each *krysala* made a distinctly different sound, yet somehow they all fit together, rising and falling as one, becoming the musical accompaniment to the chanting.

And the spirits—or *aranti* as Karliss knew them—began to gather. On a day-to-day basis Karliss could only sometimes see *aranti*, but during the ritual it was easy. They appeared as formless wisps, glowing slightly blue. Their numbers increased rapidly until there were scores of them, racing wildly across the sky. Karliss stared at them, enraptured as always by their beauty and their freedom.

Dimly he was aware that the chanting had stopped and the *tlacti* were calling out to Esegen, beseeching him, but he was so wrapped up in watching the *aranti* frolic that it didn't really occur to him what was going on until the young apprentice waiting with him grabbed his sleeve and tugged.

"Hey," the boy said, "aren't we supposed to sacrifice the bird now?"

Karliss snapped out of his reverie and looked guiltily around. The boy was right. He saw Ihbarha glaring at him and he winced. One more time that he failed in his duties. Would he ever learn?

The boy held the pheasant secure under one arm, holding onto the bird's feet so it couldn't scratch him. Karliss steeled himself and drew out his belt knife, freshly sharpened for this very purpose. This was the first time he'd ever had to personally sacrifice one of the animals and even though Ihbarha had made him practice on chickens that were due for the dinner pot, still it made him feel sick to his stomach. The first time he tried to take hold of the pheasant's head he got pecked and jerked his hand back.

"Hurry up!" the boy whispered urgently. "Everyone's watching!"

Karliss resisted the urge to tell him to kill the pheasant himself if he was in such a hurry. This time he got a firm grip on the bird's head. Before he could really think about what he was doing he quickly slid the blade across the bird's neck and cut the head off. The boy held the flopping carcass upside down over the fire so its blood spattered on the flames. Karliss tossed the head in the flames, then took a handful of *rasich* powder from a pouch and threw it on the fire, which made the fire flare up with green and blue flames.

Next the *tlacti* moved on to Bai-ulgan, god of the east winds. The yak's throat was cut and the blood caught in a small bowl. Blood and *rasich* powder were thrown on the fire. After that the *tlacti* beseeched Tung-alk and the goat was sacrificed.

By then Karliss was so wound up that he felt he would burst. Between the energy of the racing *aranti*, the combined energy of the watching masses of Sertithians, and the power of the *krysalas*, he felt like he was ready to explode. It was all he could do to stand in one place and not start running in circles. He was fairly hopping from one foot to the other.

Last was Erlik Khan, god of the west winds. The oldest and most experienced apprentices were there. The horse was pulling at its halter, rearing in the air, its eyes rolling. It took three of them to keep it from bolting. Finally the apprentice with the knife was able to get close enough to cut its throat. The horse staggered, made one last attempt at freedom, then sagged to its knees. Its blood was caught in a bowl and thrown onto the fire.

As the flames of the last sacrificial fire subsided, the *tlacti* all threw their *krysalas* in the air at once. From the gathered Sertithians came a roar, their final appeal to the gods. There was a boom, as loud as if lightning had struck the hilltop. With the boom came a shockwave. The fires blew out and darkness descended.

Chapter 41

The next afternoon Karliss stood with a score of other boys, all around his own age, waiting for the distance race to start. His mother was there, come to cheer him on. For the third time she asked him, "Are you sure you're okay?" and felt his forehead to see if he was feverish.

He gave her a wan smile. "I'm okay. I'm tired is all."

"Maybe you should drop out of the race."

It was something Karliss had considered doing many times that day. But he'd decided not to. He needed to be more serious. He needed to carry through on things he'd said he was going to do. This was a good place to start.

"I'll be okay once it starts. You'll see."

Munkhe didn't look reassured, but she didn't say anything more except, "I'll be right here, Karliss. Remember that."

The warrior who was in charge of the race called for their attention and pointed into the distance. "On top of that rise is a rock cairn. Circle that and come back. Four times." The rise was far enough away that the cairn was only dimly visible.

"Ready? Go!"

The boys took off running. Karliss quickly fell behind and was running dead last. Normally Karliss enjoyed running. He liked the feeling of it, the ground falling away under his feet, the wind in his hair. He never seemed to get really tired.

But today was different. He felt heavy, leaden. Every step took so much effort. He didn't seem to have any energy at all.

He knew what the difference was. The wind. Normally he ran with the wind. He couldn't have said exactly how he did it. It wasn't something he consciously made an effort to do. It somehow just kind of happened. It was like the wind helped carry him forward. It made him lighter. It made running easy.

But he'd spent the last two days trying to build his inner wall to keep the *aranti* away and he was exhausted. It was a neverending struggle. He was also depressed. Despite his friends' best efforts to cheer him up, he'd spent most of today lost inside himself. Finally Batu said that he thought he heard his mother calling him and took off. Hulagu didn't last much longer. Karliss didn't really blame them. He knew he was miserable company. But still it hurt. And being alone left him with fewer distractions so it was more work keeping the wind away.

Somehow Karliss slogged through the first lap of the race. By then he was behind by a large margin. There were a few people from his clan watching the race and he could see the confusion on their faces. His mother had a worried look on her face. Everyone knew how much he loved to run, how tireless he was. What was happening?

Karliss wanted to lie down and quit. He'd never been so miserable in his life. His legs hurt. His lungs felt like they were full of sand. He kept stumbling. And always, always there was the unceasing pressure of the wind, pressing around him, whispering to him. He'd never realized how omnipresent the *aranti*'s voices were. They were always there. It was like being in a crowd of people, all of them talking. And there were so many. What had always before been a comforting background murmuring—something that made him feel like he was never alone—was now ominous and uncomfortable. He wanted to shout at them to stop. After his friends left him he'd actually done it a few times, surprising those people who were nearby. But it did no good. If anything the voices seemed to increase in volume.

Were these early signs of madness? he wondered. Was this how it started? Should he tell someone, warn his clan that he would soon be a danger to them?

He imagined the looks on their faces when he did that. His mother would be hurt. His father would probably disown him. But ultimately all of them would turn their backs on him. He'd be shut out, completely alone. Unless, of course, the terl ordered his throat cut.

Lost in thoughts like these Karliss completed the second lap of the race. He was stumbling out to begin the third—the race leaders were already running for the finish line, almost done with the final lap—when the wind suddenly buffeted him so hard that he lost his footing and fell down.

He struck his knee painfully on the ground and rolled over onto his back, holding onto his knee while he grimaced in pain. His guard slipped and he became aware of what the *aranti* were saying, had been saying for a while.

The only survivor! She's here, she's here!

The pain in his knee temporarily forgotten, Karliss stood up. The *aranti* babbled excitedly, such a welter of voices that he had trouble making out anything. Prodded by the wind, he looked to the southwest. He couldn't see her yet, the one the *aranti* were so excited about, but he knew she was there, coming steadily closer.

He became aware that his mother was standing over him. "What is it?" she asked. "What are you looking at?"

He looked up at her. "She's the last one."

His mother looked confused. "The last one of what? Who are you talking about?"

"The last survivor of Long-striding Antelope Clan. The others are all dead."

"Are you sure about this?" his mother asked, touching his forehead.

Karliss pushed her hand away. "I'm sure."

She didn't ask him how he knew. All his life Karliss had known things other people didn't. Long ago she'd accepted that the wind shared things with him. "Where?"

Karliss pointed to the southwest.

"Just one?"

He nodded. "She's only a child. She's tired. She can barely walk still."

A couple of the men from Spotted Elk Clan were standing nearby. Munkhe went to them. "There's a girl out there, a survivor from Long-striding Antelope Clan. Someone needs to bring her in." They looked at her, confused. "Hurry up!" she snapped. "You don't want her to die while you stand there, do you?"

The men mounted up and raced off in the direction she pointed. Meanwhile, people began to gather around Munkhe and Karliss, wanting to know what was happening. Munkhe told them and they in turn told others. News of the lone refugee's arrival swept through the Gathering like wildfire. By the time the men returned—one of them carrying a young girl before him on his horse—half the Gathering knew what was happening. Dozens of riders raced out to meet them and escort them back in.

The girl was probably only twelve or thirteen and she was terribly thin. Her black hair was tangled and dirty, her clothes torn. She had bruises on her face and her eyes were sunken. She stared at nothing, seemingly oblivious to the people swirling around her.

She was taken to an empty yurt. Healers and *tlacti* clustered around her and terls gathered outside. Most activities ground to a halt. Races were canceled, music stopped. Even the children were subdued. It was as if the entire Gathering was holding its breath, waiting to see what news would emerge from that one yurt.

It wasn't until sunset that healers and *tlacti* began to emerge from the yurt. But they bore precious little news. Yes, the girl was from the missing clan. But she had only spoken once and that was to say that she was the only survivor. The rest of them were dead. They had gotten her to drink a little water, but she would not eat, though she was so thin her bones stuck out. She had clearly been traveling for many days. It was surprising that she'd made it at all, considering the condition she was in.

Karliss wasn't surprised when Ihbarha came looking for him. "Did you gather the moonglow seeds like I told you to?" he asked gruffly.

Karliss had been anticipating this and he produced the pouch of seeds. Ihbarha took the seeds. "Come with me," he said.

They walked to the same low, flat-topped hill where the ritual of appeasement had been held and climbed it. Someone had built a small fire in the middle. A pot was sitting on the fire. Beside the fire was a large pile of a kind of dried grass known as *kamhut*. The grass was used in seeing rituals. Most of the other shamans and their apprentices were already there, the shamans sitting around the fire, their apprentices sitting beside and slightly behind them. One of the apprentices had a bowl and was grinding moonglow seeds in it. As he finished grinding each handful of seeds, he poured them into the pot on the fire. Ihbarha gave him the pouch of seeds Karliss had collected and then took a spot by the fire. Karliss sat behind him. Next to him was the apprentice from the day before, the one he thought was named Suren. She didn't look at him.

Across the fire was a *tlacti* who was even older than Ihbarha, her braids hanging down past her waist and thickly encrusted with shells and colored beads. That was Qara, leader of the council by virtue of her age. Next to Ihbarha was a middle-aged man that

Karliss thought was named Mek or Mak. Beyond him was the youngest of the *tlacti*, a woman barely out of her teens. Karliss remembered her from the year before when she was still an apprentice. He wondered if her teacher had died during the winter. Maybe he'd gone mad. She didn't have an apprentice yet. Sometimes it took years before a new one was born to a clan.

In a little while they were all there, eleven in all. All but two had apprentices with them, Qara and the youngest *tlacti*. All of them wore grim looks.

"I don't need to tell you how dangerous the seeing ritual is," Qara said. "The last time we tried it one of our number died." That was nearly thirty years ago, during what the Sertithians called the Time of Darkness. The rains were nearly nonexistent that year and when they did come there was something wrong with them. The drops burned bare skin. Most of the grass and other plants died.

"Yet I believe I speak for all of us when I say that we must attempt it, regardless of the cost. Out there somewhere is a foe with the power to kill an entire clan. We must know what it is we face." She looked around the circle. "Are there any who dispute me on this?"

To Karliss' surprise, Ihbarha spoke up. "I will be the point of contact," the old man said. "I volunteer."

Karliss' mouth went dry. The *tlacti* who took the point of contact, the one who actually linked his mind to one of the spirit's minds, was the one who bore the most danger. It suddenly occurred to him that Ihbarha could die. He had never particularly liked the old man, but he depended on his strength. The whole clan did. If something happened to him… It was too hard to think about.

"It should be me," Qara replied.

"Normally I would agree. But that was before your apprentice died. If you are killed your clan will be defenseless."

"Your apprentice is but a boy," she pointed out.

"True. But he is strong. He has an affinity for the wind I have never seen before."

"Perhaps Mek," Qara said, gesturing at the middle-aged *tlacti*.

"Respectfully, but I am stronger than Mek. I am stronger than any *tlacti* here but you."

Silence met his words. Karliss wanted badly to speak. He wanted someone else to take this role in the ritual. He had a sudden, irrational fear that Ihbarha would die. But when he started to open his mouth, Ihbarha clamped down on his arm and shook his head.

"Your words have wisdom," Qara conceded. "You shall take the point."

"Go," Ihbarha told Karliss. "Sit by Qara that she may draw on you."

Hesitantly, Karliss stood and made his way around the fire to sit beside the old woman. She never looked at him.

The pot was taken off the fire and the liquid inside poured into a cup. Cool water was added from a water skin and Ihbarha drank it. The tea made from the moonglow seeds would put Ihbarha into a heightened state. In that state his inner barriers would drop and his mind would open completely. A deep communion with the spirits was possible then. If it worked properly, Ihbarha would be able to share the memories of the chosen spirit.

When Ihbarha had drunk the tea, Qara said, "Let us implore the gods."

All of the shamans except for Ihbarha began to chant then, beseeching the gods of the four winds. Their words were not in the Sertithian tongue, but in one far older, from a time before the horse warriors came to the steppes. They asked permission of the gods because the seeing ritual involved luring in and ensnaring one of the spirits that dwelled in the wind. The spirits were the gods' servants and to use them without the gods' permission was to invite great peril.

They chanted for some time. Now and then one of the apprentices added more dung to the fire. Ihbarha's eyes rolled back in his head so that only the whites were showing. He was shaking slightly and he seemed to have stopped breathing.

At last the chant ended and the waiting began. They waited for a sign from the gods. What that sign would be, none knew. Karliss noticed that a line of spittle was running down from the corner of Ihbarha's mouth.

In the west came a sudden flash of lightning. A dozen heartbeats later the rumble of thunder followed.

"This is our sign," Qara said. "Let us begin."

From inside her coat she took out her *krysala*. The old woman held it in her hands and whispered to it, the words too soft for the others to hear. Then she blew on it.

The bone disc began to glow slightly, a soft blue color. She blew on it again and the glow grew stronger.

Qara threw it up into the air. It went up about twenty feet and hung there, dead in the center of the circle of *tlacti*. She pointed at the *krysala* and began to inscribe small circles with her finger. The *krysala* began to spin, slowly, then faster and faster. As it spun, an eerie wail, very deep and sonorous, began to emanate from it. The blue glow became even stronger.

Qara lowered her arm. The *krysala* stayed in place, still spinning. A soft wind began to blow.

The *tlacti* next to her took out his *krysala*. It was a little larger than hers, the bone yellow with age. Rather than a disc, it was a ring. There were grooves and holes in it. He blew on it and it began to glow blue. He threw it into the air. It rose about ten feet and stopped, directly below Qara's *krysala*. He pointed at it and twirled his finger. It began to spin in place. The sound it made was somewhat higher than Qara's. The two sounds merged, becoming indistinguishable from each other. Its blue glow joined with the glow from the first *krysala*. The wind blew harder.

One by one the other eight wind shamans did the same. Each *krysala* settled in a different place until the area they enclosed was a sphere about ten feet across. By that time the wind had become quite strong. Karliss had stopped trying to block out the voices of the *aranti*. There were too many in the area and they were too loud.

At a signal from Qara, one of the apprentices threw an armload of the dried *kamhut* grass on the fire. It caught instantly and thick smoke billowed upward. In the cloud of smoke shapes could be seen flitting this way and that.

"Behold," Qara said. "The spirits have arrived. The time is close. Begin feeding *shan* into the *krysalas*."

The *tlacti* all reached out and laid a hand on their apprentices. Karliss jerked when Qara touched him. It felt like the ground disappeared from beneath him and he was falling. An odd coldness began to tingle along his arms and legs and the back of his neck. This was his *shan*—the life essence from the gods that flows into the body with each breath—leaving him and being drawn into Qara, giving her the strength she needed for what was to come next. He wanted to pull away, but he steeled himself and forced himself to endure.

Qara stared up at the glowing blue sphere formed by the *krysalas*. The light that came from them was strong enough that the sphere was visible even through the smoke. She waited...waited...

"Now!" she cried. It was at that moment that only one *aranti* was inside the sphere.

The *tlacti* released the pent-up *shan* and the *krysalas* blazed with power, which leapt from one to the other, causing the sphere to suddenly glow intensely, like a small sun.

The *aranti* cried out then, its cry echoed by Karliss, who toppled over on his side. He could feel its pain as his own. The pain came, not from anything physical, but from being separated from the other *aranti*. The other *aranti*, outside the sphere, cried out as well, clustering around, trying to free their trapped brethren.

The wind was now shrieking, its turbulence filled with the animal cries of the *aranti*. The one inside the sphere raced back and forth, trying desperately to leave, but it was trapped.

"Stop!" Karliss yelled. "You're hurting it!" But his words were lost in the maelstrom. The only one who heard him was Qara and she could not spare the concentration to even look at him. Instead her grip on him tightened and she continued drawing *shan* from him.

"Show us what happened to the clan!" she shouted.

Ihbarha's white gaze was fixed on the glowing sphere. Tremors ran over his body steadily.

"Show us!" Qara yelled.

Kasai killed them! the trapped *aranti* cried. *The white-skinned one! It was Kasai!* Its cry was picked up and echoed by the others.

But only Karliss understood what the *aranti* were saying and when he tried to shout what he had heard to Qara her grip tightened more, so that her nails dug into his skin. He tried to break free but he felt too weak and her grip was like iron, strengthened as she was by his *shan*.

Ihbarha suddenly leapt to his feet and shouted through the chaos. "I see them! They're burning in gray fire! It's all around them! They can't escape!" His words were only barely audible through the din.

A second later one of the *tlacti*, the young woman who had only recently assumed her position, suddenly screamed. Her *krysala* wavered, then spun off to the side, leaving its spot in the sphere.

When that happened the sphere was broken and it abruptly collapsed. Power fed back down into the *tlacti*, who were knocked onto their backs as if struck by a giant, invisible fist. Ihbarha was blown backwards. The trapped *aranti* shrieked one last time, then bolted, the others following. In moments the wind had died down to nothing.

Karliss sat up gingerly. His ears were ringing and he felt sick to his stomach. Beside him Qara was flat on her back, blood leaking from her mouth. All of the *tlacti* and most of the apprentices were down as well. A few moved. Moans rose as several struggled to sit up.

Karliss' gaze fell on Ihbarha. The old shaman was lying outside the circle on his side, eyes open, staring at nothing. Karliss crawled over to him. He rolled him onto his back.

"Bagesh," he said urgently. "Wake up."

The old man shuddered, then began to thrash. Karliss helped him sit up. Ihbarha stared around wildly, animal noises coming from him. He looked at Karliss but there was no sign of recognition in his eyes.

"Bagesh, it's me, Karliss. Don't you know me?"

But there was nothing there. Ihbarha was gone.

The story continues in *Sky Touched*.

Loved the book?
Hated it?
Meh?
How about going and reviewing *Stone Bound* now that you've read it? Your comments are very much appreciated!

For advance news of new books as well as free books
and special deals:
ERICTKNIGHT.COM

About The Author

Born in 1965, I grew up on a working cattle ranch in the desert thirty miles from Wickenburg, Arizona, which at that time was exactly the middle of nowhere. Work, cactus and heat were plentiful, forms of recreation were not. The TV got two channels when it wanted to, and only in the evening after someone hand cranked the balky diesel generator to life. All of which meant that my primary form of escape was reading.

At 18 I escaped to Tucson where I attended the University of Arizona. A number of fruitless attempts at productive majors followed, none of which stuck. Discovering I liked writing, I tried journalism two separate times, but had to drop it when I realized that I had no intention of conducting interviews with actual people but preferred simply making them up.

After graduating with a degree in Creative Writing in 1989, I backpacked Europe with a friend and caught the travel bug. With no meaningful job prospects, I hitchhiked around the U.S. for a while then went back to school to learn to be a high school English teacher. I got a teaching job right out of school in the middle of the year. The job lasted exactly one semester, or until I received my summer pay and realized I actually had money to continue backpacking.

The next stop was Australia, where I hoped to spend six months, working wherever I could, then a few months in New Zealand and the South Pacific Islands. However, my plans changed irrevocably when I met a lovely Swiss woman, Claudia, in Alice Springs. Undoubtedly swept away by my lack of a job or real future, she agreed to allow me to follow her back to Switzerland where, a few months later, she gave up her job to continue traveling with me. Over the next couple years we backpacked the U.S., Eastern Europe and Australia/New Zealand, before marrying and settling in the mountains of Colorado, in a small town called Salida.

In Colorado we started our own electronics business (because, you know, my Creative Writing background totally prepared me for installing home theater systems), and had a couple of sons, Dylan and Daniel. In 2005 we shut the business down and moved back to Tucson where we currently live.

Made in the USA
San Bernardino, CA
10 February 2020